As if things weren't bad enough …

When I woke up, a voice was speaking. At first it seemed to come from deep within a long tunnel, but eventually it became more normal.

"Wakey, wakey, wakey children, it's time for the final preparations."

I opened my eyes. A vampire I hadn't seen before displayed his plastic fangs through a bright smile. I wanted to ask him something, but I couldn't open my mouth. I couldn't move anything but my eyes.

Stark terror.

I'd read those words a million times in a million adventure novels, but this was the first time I knew what they meant. I struggled to stay calm. If ever I needed a good writer to get me out of this one, it was now.

A naked brunette appeared above me. She held a sponge in one hand, and a wash basin in the other. The sound of chanting suddenly filled my ears and she began to give me a sponge bath. She began with my face, then my arms. She moved down my body and did a thorough job on my privates. Feelings of pleasure were at war with deadly fear. The fear won. She finished with my legs and disappeared.

She reappeared a short time later. She was holding what looked like a perfume atomizer. She forced the tube between my teeth and squeezed the bulb. At least my swallowing reflex was working, a liquid tasting slightly of apricots poured into my mouth and down my throat. I knew I should worry about what it was, but it hardly seemed to matter anymore.

I fell asleep again.

Cast loosely in the mold of such hard-boiled detectives as Sam Spade and Phillip Marlowe, Joe Gold is an old-fashioned kind of guy, adrift in a modern world he doesn't fully understand, full of characters he understands all too well. Times may change, but people don't. And being Jewish is just another hurdle.

Down on his luck and behind on his rent, he's approached by his old mistress, Maureen, now married to the corrupt mayor of Central City, with a serious problem. Their daughter, seventeen-year-old Julie who has no idea that Joe is her real father, has been abducted from her summer camp in a blackmail attempt of some sort. Before she can give him any important details, Maureen is murdered, and Joe is left on his own to put together all the pieces of the puzzle and rescue his daughter. Complicating matters, it appears that someone is out to kill him too.

Threading the dangerous needle that takes him through the seamy underbelly of Central City and Mayor Bill Wagner's corrupt administration proves to be a real challenge, and he's totally unprepared for what he finds at the end. The surprises don't end there, however, as he discovers in his next two cases: a man who believes he's a vampire, and another who purveys murder through the comments sections of a newspaper. Through all this, he's aided by Jenny Martin, his long suffering business partner and Girl Friday, who struggles to keep him on an even keel—and alive.

KUDOS for *Pure Gold*

In *Pure Gold* by Theodore Druch, Joe Gold is a private eye down on his luck. The author takes us through three of Joe's cases: the murder of the mayor's wife and the kidnapping of a seventeen-year-old girl; a murderous cult of vampires, or those who think they are; and a murderous blogger who selects his victims based on the comments section of a newspaper's blog—cases that take Joe to within an inch of his life. The book is well written, intense, and compelling, and the author uses humor to break the tension in just the right places. A really great read. ~ *Taylor Jones, The Review Team of Taylor Jones & Regan Murphy*

Pure Gold ~ Three Cases of Gold by Theodore P. Druch is the story of Joe Gold, a Jewish PI, down on his luck and struggling to pay the bills, who has a propensity to get cases that threaten his life. When the corrupt mayor's seventeen-year-old daughter, Julie, is kidnapped, her mother, Maureen, hires Joe to rescue her since she doesn't trust her husband to do anything about it. Since Julie is really Joe's daughter from an affair he had with Maureen before she married the mayor, he is highly motivated to find her. But before Maureen can give him any more details, she's murdered, and Joe is left to ferret out the clues on his own, with the help of his able assistant, Jenny. Joe and Jenny take on two more cases as well—one in which a man who thinks he is a vampire is accused of murder and his parents want Joe to clear his name, and the other in which Jenny's cousin is murdered by someone using a newspaper blog to select victims. I thoroughly enjoyed this book. Druch has a wry sense of humor that is both natural and subtle, giving extra depth and character to the story. With wonderful character development, intriguing mysteries, and plenty of surprises, *Pure Gold* is one you will want to read again and again, just for the "pure" enjoyment. ~ *Regan Murphy, The Review Team of Taylor Jones & Regan Murphy*

PURE GOLD

Three Cases of Gold

Theodore P. Druch

A Black Opal Books Publication

GENRE: MYSTERY/THRILLER/SUSPENSE

PURE GOLD ~ THREE CASES OF GOLD
Copyright © 2018 by Theodore P. Druch
Cover Design by Jackson Cover Designs
All cover art copyright © 2018
All Rights Reserved
Print ISBN: 978-1-644370-49-0

First Publication: DECEMBER 2018

Published by Black Opal Books http://www.blackopalbooks.com

DEDICATION

Being a great fan of flash fiction, I have always admired those who could cram a whole lot of information into a few words.

Few were better at it than writers like Dashiell Hammett, Raymond Chandler, and later, Mickey Spillane. Their solid, muscular prose created a new kind of character— the hard-boiled, unsentimental, and decidedly unromantic private eye.

Sam Spade, Phillip Marlowe, and Mike Hammer became icons of American detective fiction, names that are often better known than their creators and identified mainly by the actors who portrayed them on the silver screens of the mid-twentieth century.

It is their contributions and examples that lie at the heart of my own attempt to pay homage to the genre, and I can only dedicate these stories to their immortal memory and the ground they have broken in which to plant my own seeds and hope they germinate as successfully.

PART 1

The Case of the Mayor's Wife

CHAPTER 1

Sliced and spliced, I was crossing the street from the hospital when I saw Lieutenant Frank Gomez of the Twelfth Precinct walking toward me, looking, as usual, like he'd slept in his suit. Frank and I went back a long way, and I'd been surprised that I hadn't heard from him. He had a worried look on his face.

"Hey, Joe, I heard you got shanked. You okay?"

I smiled. "And the intrepid gumshoes of the ever-vigilant Twelfth have finally heard about it, huh?"

"Well, your name isn't high on the roster anymore, in case you hadn't noticed—somewhere between the cleaning-lady and the bottom. I only know because, out of idle curiosity, I glanced over the weekly notice of criminal injuries treated at General. You get yourself iced, and no-body'll know for days."

I laughed. "And few will mourn either, right, Frank?"

"I will."

"I know that. You—and Eddie."

Eddie was Ed Logan, captain of the Twelfth, who had never believed that I was dirty. After I was exonerated, but kicked off the force as an embarrassment for going off on my own, half-cocked, "for the last goddamn time," he and Frank were the only one's who'd have a drink with me. Maybe the rest would have liked me better if I'd been guilty. Cops can be funny that way. The fact that I'm a Jew didn't help either. Cops can be funny that way too.

I caught the flash just as I was turning to see his face better in the glare of the late afternoon sun.

"Down!"

I grabbed his shoulder and dragged him to the pavement even as the crack of the rifle sheared the air. I thought I heard the hiss of the round as it went by above, definitely high velocity.

Frank was a seasoned cop, and it took him no time at all to shimmy, with me, behind the nearest car that would block any further shots. The gash in my side erupted in fire, and I hoped that I wasn't bleeding through the stitches. The doctor had told me that any violent activity could do that.

There were no more shots.

Frank looked at me. He was breathing hard.

"What the hell have you gotten yourself into now?"

I shrugged my shoulders. "You know me. I can't resist a redhead."

"I should have figured. You just can't lay off the babes."

"Not this one. She's my daughter, and she's been kidnapped."

He gazed at me with an uncomprehending look all over his face. "When the fuck did you get married?"

"I never said I was married."

He thought for a while. I could see that he was going through a list of names in his mind. "Anybody I know?"

I shook my head. "It was a long time ago. Before I came to the precinct. She'd moved on up and didn't want to have anything more to do with me. But I've kept up with Julie's progress, and now she's been kidnapped."

"Why the fuck didn't you come to me?"

I gave him the fish-eye. "Give me a break. I've seen too many botched kidnappings by the cops, and so have you. I have to do this myself."

"Not anymore. A shot's been fired. It's a police matter now. I can't ignore this."

Frank was more right than he knew. I was about to plead with him when someone shouted.

"Help, somebody, please, there's a woman in a car. She's been shot. I think she's dead."

She was.

All bets were off.

I didn't know how off until I heard Frank, who'd raced to the sound of the shout, cursing, "Holy Mother of God and Jesus Christ our Savior, it's the mayor's wife."

I'd been trying to get back to my feet when I just sat down again, hard.

Maureen Wagner was Julie's mother.

I put my head in my hands. Now the shit was really gonna hit the fan.

❧❦❧

I didn't know how long I just sat there, on the sidewalk, behind a red Chevy, thinking about Maureen and all those years ago. It would've never worked out, of course. I was just a little guy, and she had bigger fish to fry. The mackerel she finally landed was Councilman William "Bill" Wagner, who she'd been hooking up with the nights she wasn't with me. She'd been diddling a few others on her booty-baited hook too, but he was first in the big fish-little fish race, so she told him it was his kid, and he married her. A beautiful wife would be an asset to him. He didn't even care who she slept with, as long as she was discreet.

She was discreet with me several times those first few years, but, as our paths diverged, mine to disgrace and hers to power, the fire just went out. I hadn't seen her in years. When she came to tell me of Julie's abduction, she'd been as beautiful as ever.

❦

"What are you still doing here?"

Frank's gravelly voice broke through my reverie, like a tractor plowing through a field of daisies.

"I thought you were long gone. Why the hell are you sitting there?"

It gratified me to see the real worry that painted his face.

"Are you okay? Do we need to get you back to the hospital or something?"

I just looked at him for a short while. Then I said, "Sit down."

He looked at me like I was crazy. "Like hell I will, you get your ass back up here," he barked, but he must have seen something in my face because his got even more worried. He reached down and hauled me up, all six feet, two inches, and 220 pounds of me. It was almost dark, and the colored lights on all the cruisers and emergency vehicles nearly blinded me. The strobe effect made me feel like a seizure was coming on.

"What the fuck's going on? Why is Maureen Wagner sitting there dead, and you're hiding behind a car?"

His question brought me back to grim reality and my head stopped vibrating.

"Maybe she was an innocent bystander?"

He gave me a sharp look. "Nah, not a chance. I can feel it in my bones that you know something about this, and maybe that bullet wasn't meant for you at all."

I actually hadn't even considered that possibility, but the sudden flash was lighting up some doors in my mind.

"Why would anyone want to kill her?" I thought I had a pretty good idea myself, but I wanted to see if Frank knew anything.

"Well, there's plenty of rumors around that she's not the nicest girl on the block, if you get my drift?"

"You mean she's a whore."

"Well, not to put too fine a point on it."

"She always was." I was just being factual but he gave me another hard look until sudden realization broke over his face. The mayor had a daughter named Julie, and Frank was a terrific cop.

"Oh, Holy Mother of God—No."

"Yes." I hoped my smile was rueful as I said it.

Frank dragged me back up the steps to Central City General and, flashing his badge, demanded that I be looked after immediately. The admitting nurse was a big, black woman who, for all his weight, could have taken him with one hand tied behind her back—if she could get it there. She just gave him a withering stare and pointed to the crowded waiting room.

"Siddown," she growled and the sound carried real menace.

The waiting room was buzzing with talk about the cops outside and a dead woman, who might or might not be the mayor's wife. I was happy to sit down and let the pain in my side return to the familiar dull ache as I listened to snippets of conversation.

Frank had asked me if I wanted to see her before they took her away, but when he told me that the slug had made a mess of her face, I declined. I wanted to remember her as she'd been.

The nurse must have been somewhat impressed by the badge, though—it couldn't have been Frank—and before too long, we were ushered into a cubicle. The doctor checked out the stitches, pronounced them sound, and rebandaged the gash in my side.

From there, Frank steered us to the cafeteria. The din was intense. Everyone was talking about the shooting. We sat down at an isolated table in a corner. Nobody would be likely to overhear our conversation. Frank ordered us coffees and cheeseburgers with fries, but I didn't have much of an appetite, so he finished off mine too. I smiled. You could almost see him getting fatter by the bite.

"One day you're gonna drop dead of a heart attack." I told him.

He looked up between bites. "My wife tells me that all the time. I should be so lucky. Her voice will likely be what finally knocks me off." He didn't even smile but attacked the last of my cheeseburger. "Now—" He looked at me straight. "—I want the whole goddamned story, from beginning to end, or I might be tempted to run you in as an accessory to murder."

I had to hold my side, but I laughed out loud.

"A material witness, anyway." He backtracked, but he wasn't smiling. "And who the hell knows what else? Also, if the mayor's kid's been kidnapped, how come nobody knows anything about it?"

I was as much at sea about it as he was. I couldn't really figure why anyone would be shooting at me, and why they wanted her dead was a complete mystery. It didn't make any sense, and the wheels were spinning around inside my head even as I tried to explain what I knew to Frank.

Julie had been away at camp when she was abducted. Apparently, someone claiming to be Maureen had called the camp saying that there was a family emergency and that someone would be coming to pick her up and bring her home. About a half-hour after Maureen got the call from the kidnappers, the camp director called her, wanting to know if Julie had gotten home safely.

"I was too stunned to think," Maureen had said, "but the guy on the line said that if any word of this got out, they'd kill her, so I just told the camp director that she was fine. I called you right after that."

"What about your husband?" I'd asked, wondering why she had come to me first. Her face went kind of blank then, and I knew from experience that meant a clam-up.

"God, Joe, he can't know anything about it. It's my problem. I have to solve it and keep it out of the papers."

I'd looked at her hard. Seventeen years and it all came flooding back, the tangled web of her life; the constant lies and excuses; the hot sex that kept me coming back for more, even though I knew she was bad for my health. What had she gotten into this time? I'd stopped giving a crap about her a long time ago, but Julie was in danger, and I couldn't say no.

Frank seemed puzzled. "Couldn't she give you anything to go on at all?"

I lied to him. "I figured that I'd question her at length after she'd calmed down, maybe get some idea of where to begin, but the next day I ate the shank, and I never heard from her again."

He still looked puzzled. "Didn't the kid create a fuss?"

"Apparently not. She must have known whoever came to get her. Otherwise, the director would've said something."

He thought for a bit. "Smells like an inside job to me. Anything else?"

"Not a whole lot. Maureen was really agitated. She begged me to check it out, said she'd get back to me with more information."

"Maybe she was coming to the hospital to see you with something, but why were either of you targets? It doesn't make sense. Why would kidnappers kill the only one who could pay them off, unless they really were aiming at you, and she was just an innocent bystander, after all? But why would they be shooting at you?"

I smiled. "My reputation for getting the job done precedes me, I guess. They must have been tailing her and knew when she came to me." I stopped and thought. "Right now, that's the only explanation I can come up with, other than that some pissed-off sore loser just tried to take me out. Somebody sure as shit knifed me when she wasn't there."

Frank looked skeptical. He always did. He was a cop. "Too damned much of a coincidence for me. Tell me about the knifing."

"Not much to tell. I came out of the can at Arturo's and a guy bumped into me. I felt the knife go in at the same time and, before I could do anything, I was on the floor bleeding like a stuck pig, and he was gone."

"Did you get a look at him?"

I shook my head. "It all happened too fast. All I can tell you is that he was big, bigger than me. It felt like I'd run into a bear."

Frank laughed. "Know any bears?"

"Several, but I can't think how any of them might be involved. I had a couple of days in the hospital to think about it, but nothing makes any sense."

"How far did you get in your investigation?"

I shrugged my shoulders. "Nowhere. I got shanked instead. Did I tell you that the knife just missed my liver?"

Frank said nothing for a minute. "When did this all go down?"

"A week ago."

"Was there a ransom demand?"

"Not that I know of. Maureen said that they would call in a few more days with instructions."

"A good reason why she might have been coming to see you. But why didn't she just call?"

I didn't say anything, and Frank shut up too. I could see the wheels turning around in his head like they were connected to his eyeballs. They were moving around this way and that, never focusing on anything. Finally, he heaved a great sigh. "I don't get it. Nothing makes any sense, but the mayor is going to have to know about this now, and since you're the only one who knows anything. You're going to have to be there."

I could almost smell the shit on the fan blades.

"He doesn't know about me. She never told him. Neither does Julie. She thinks that slug is her daddy."

He thought that one over. "How the hell can you be so certain the kid is yours? Maureen was doing the dirty with a lot of guys, according to the rumor mill."

"*My* name didn't come up?"

"Who the fuck are *you*?

"Point taken."

"So, how can you be so sure?"

"I followed Julie to the mall one day, parental curiosity, I guess. She and her friends left their soda cups on the table after lunch, and I got an idea. I took her cup to a guy I know in forensics, and he did a DNA analysis on both of us. She's mine, all right."

Frank pulled the silent bit again, then he busted out laughing.

"What's so funny?"

"You, a father? That poor kid."

I had to agree with him. Then I said, "Living with that bastard Wagner and her slut of a mother couldn't have been a bed of roses either."

❧❧❧

Frank drove me home, and I flopped into bed, fully clothed, without even a taste of my non-Haig Brothers swill. Imagine me, too distracted to drink. Well, that, and the massive doses of the Vicodin I was on. I may be stupid, but I'm not suicidal. Until now, anyway.

Too many thoughts were rolling around in my head, and they all ended with Julie.

I hadn't been totally honest with Frank for a good reason. Maureen had given me several possible angles to cover, but I wasn't quite feeling like sharing at the moment. I smelled some unsavory shenanigans going on in the mayor's mansion, and I couldn't trust the cops to do anything but sweep it all under the rug. I was certain that if Julie were to come out of this alive, it would have to be me to make it happen.

I didn't have anything but a feeling, but I always trusted my feelings.

I should have made an exception when it came to women.

Especially twisted ones, like Maureen, but it was the twisted ones I fell for the most.

CHAPTER 2

We had an eight a.m. meeting scheduled with the mayor, but I was wide awake by four-thirty. The Vicodin had worn off. Along with the pain in my side, Julie's face was invading my mind.

I distracted myself by shrugging off my clothes and heading for the bathroom. I was too dizzy to stand up and sat down hard on the toilet, sending streamers of agony up and down my side. Lucky for me, Maureen's training had taken, and the seat was down. I never knew when I'd have some female company.

Not enough, lately.

After a nice, long pee, I felt strong enough to brave the shower, being careful to keep the bandage dry. Ever tried that?

I'd decided to make an early stop.

I don't know why—though I can come up with a lot of unsatisfactory reasons to explain it—but whenever I'm in a pickle, I like to go sit in the *shul*. It gives me a chance to think.

I've been hanging out at Agudas Achim since I was a kid going to Hebrew School there. My parents forced me. I'd have rather been out in the street playing ball with the non-Jewish kids, who didn't have to suffer the indignity of going straight from school to school. My grandmother called them *schkutzim* in Yiddish, which I later learned meant "creepy, crawly things," like roaches.

Turns out that *I* was exactly the sort of kid my folks didn't want me hanging around with.

I like to get to the *shul* early, just after Shmuley, the *shammus*, unlocks the doors. It's an hour yet before the start of *Shachris*, the first prayer of the day, and I have plenty of time to just sit and think. The two Vicodin I popped were starting to kick in, and I waited for the lights to come on. Maybe my one really sentimental bone is the one that I used to feel as a child here. The brightly lit candelabras and chandeliers always made me think of heaven.

I stopped believing when I was about ten, but I could always count on a feeling of peace here. At least, for a few minutes. Funny, how your earliest experiences follow you around. Like ghosts, sometimes, and right now, the ghost of Maureen Wagner, nee Collins, had joined the ranks. Some weird part of my mind must have thought that maybe I could lose her, here, among the bright lights of heaven.

Not a chance. The lights she was going to be seeing were redder and hotter.

I was just getting up to leave, when Rabbi Schulson walked in and spotted me.

"Hoy, it's Joey Goldfarb. Nice to see you once in a while, *boychik*."

The man has got to be at least eighty-five, and he's got a memory like an elephant. He can't have seen me for a couple of years, at least, though I know that Shmuley tells him whenever I show up. He also moves pretty fast, for an old fart, and he was beside me in no time. I tensed for the slap on the back. It seemed weaker than before.

In spite of the fact that I thought his religious *shtick*

was for the birds, I'd always liked him. He never beat around the bush, and his wrinkled old face, surrounded by his bristly hair and beard, was always kind. He laughed a lot, and that was another point in his favor. Mainly though, whenever he stopped tossing the name of god around, he made perfect sense.

"It's Joseph Gold now, Rabbi, and you damn well know it."

He smiled. "I don't think that's what 'swearing before the Torah' is supposed to mean." He nodded his head toward the Holy Ark.

"The only time you ever come is when there's something bothering you, Mr. Joseph Gold. What is it this time?"

I told him the whole thing, leaving out most of the seamy stuff about Maureen. He wasn't fooled.

He looked at me without saying anything. Then he started to shake his head from side to side. "We always warned you about running with *shiksas*—" Female creepy, crawly things. "—but you wouldn't listen. Still, I am sorry for your loss, even Ahab would have mourned Jezebel, but it is better for you that she is out of your life."

"She hasn't been in my life for years, but now our daughter is, and anything I do might get her killed."

I was hoping for some wise advice from him, but all he said, after thinking about it for a while, was, "Hey, you're the big shot private eye. You figure it out. What do I know?" After I stopped laughing, he said, "You've always been a good boy, Joey, and a smart one too, for all your stupidity and *goyishe kopf*. You'll figure it out, I'm sure of it." He gave me a big smile. "Will you stay for *Shachris*?"

I laughed again. "You know better than that, Rabbi."

He shrugged. "It costs nothing to ask."

eɔeɔ

I met Frank in the corridor outside the mayor's office, and we coordinated our thinking, such as it was. He thought it was best that Wagner didn't know that I was Julie's father. That was fine with me. Bill Wagner and I had had "run-ins" before, and there was bad enough blood between us as it was. Maybe I could get through this thing with the secret intact. My next thought was, "in a pig's eye," but I just ignored the shit smell.

Some fat guy in a guard's uniform, who I'd never seen before, opened the door and beckoned us into the office. The mayor's desk was vacant, and there was a terrific view of the skyline through the large windows behind it.

There was also a terrific view of Wanda, the pool stenographer, sitting at her little portable stand, best positioned to arouse the beast. She was wearing her hiking skirt. As soon as we walked in, she jiggled around a bit, and it hiked a little higher. I gave her my most appreciative smile, and it hiked a bit more, making its way up the smooth, creamy curve of her thigh. I decided not to press my luck any further and sat down.

It was just in time, but the broad smile on her face told me that her sharp eyes hadn't failed to notice my growing "interest." We had a sort of arrangement, and this was exactly the kind of chance meeting that kicked it in. Maybe there was a chance for a nooner.

Blonde, blue eyes deep as the ocean, knockers just the right size, Goldilocks was fun to spend some time with, and she wasn't interested in a "relationship." She was perfect.

Then it occurred to me that she wasn't that much older than Julie, and I snapped back to reality and into a funk.

Besides us, the room was occupied by Eddie Logan, captain of the Twelfth Precinct who'd given me a brief smile when I walked in; Roger Capshaw, the chief of police, who hated my guts; and Police Commissioner George Wilson, who was new in town and didn't know me from Adam, but he owed Wagner for his job, so I figured that, as far as I was concerned, there were two for and two against yours truly. I didn't know if that meant anything, but I was in the habit of always figuring how any situation affected me first.

Maybe that's why I was still walking around, but how many times can you expect to see a flash off the rifle before the trigger's pulled, or count on an expert blade man to miss? The thought made me shiver. I was getting older. The odds were catching up with me.

Precisely at eight, Bill Wagner strode into his office from a side ante-room, accompanied by a couple of goons, his "security" officers.

His bearing indicated a man in charge, but he looked like he'd slept in his clothing, his top shirt collar was open and his tie was askew. Even Frank looked more put together.

Wagner's eyes were red and bloodshot, but his usually florid face seemed to have been drained of color. I thought of a pig going to slaughter and that I'd relish wielding the knife. A sharp pain in my side did nothing to change my mind. He stared at us for a minute before he finally sat down—more like a two-ton duck dropping from the sky. The goons remained standing, their eyes motionless.

He stared some more before he spoke and a haunted, or maybe hunted, look appeared in his glassy gaze.

"Okay." He sounded tired. "I've been bombarded by rumors. Now, what's the real skinny? I know that my wife is dead. I've identified her body, but what's this shit about my daughter? The last I knew, she was safe at camp. Now I'm told that she was kidnapped a week ago.

What the fuck is going on?" He pointed a fat finger at me, "And why the hell are you here?"

I stared at him, careful to keep my face blank. Well, blanker than usual.

"He's a material witness," Eddie answered for me.

"Material witness? How the hell is that?"

"Your wife hired him to find your daughter."

"Him? Why him?"

I couldn't help myself. Usually, I'm cool as a cucumber in situations like this, but the hot hatred in his face lit my fuse. "Because she didn't trust you, you steaming pile of shit—"

I'd come out of my chair and, while my eyes were focused on him, I was aware of the sudden tension in the goons, and my rage dissolved almost as quickly as it had come. Like I said, I'm not suicidal.

But I'd left an awkward silence in the room.

I looked at Wanda and the smile that was doing its best to break out on her otherwise rigid face.

"I hope you got that," I said, and she nearly broke up. I figured her panties might be a little damp.

She didn't dare answer, but a kind of choking sound, and an almost imperceptible nod, signified "Yes."

I sat back down, as though I hadn't farted, and just stared back at Wagner. The goons relaxed.

I could tell that everybody else was trying to figure what to say or do, but Wagner spared them.

"Once again, how did she get to you?" His voice was calm and the hatred in his face was back to its normal level.

"I'm not exactly unknown around town, you know. I imagine she made a few inquiries, and they led her to me."

"Bullshit!" He slammed his open palm on the top of his desk. I thought Frank twitched, and I actually started to feel better. "The parts of town where you're known aren't exactly the parts of town where Maureen is—" He sort of choked up. "—was known."

I could see that he really was struggling with his loss. Whether that was because of Maureen herself, or some jam he might be in, I couldn't say, but if Louie was making book on it, I'd bet on the latter. Still, I respected it enough to refrain from saying "That's what you think."

Besides, I knew perfectly well that he knew.

I just shrugged my shoulders and gave him my best blank look, the one I'd perfected as a kid whenever my sister accused me of peeking through her keyhole. She never stuck her key in it, though, and she was always dancing around in front of the door, undressing. Later, she became a stripper, and people said she was pretty good.

Eddie ended the drama. "It doesn't matter why she came to him. She did, that's that, and we'd better get the details from the horse's mouth. No offence, Joe."

"None taken."

"So why don't you just tell us what happened from the beginning?"

I went through my routine once again, and again, left out the parts I wasn't telling anybody just yet. "Now—" I turned back to Wagner. "—I'm going to need complete descriptions of everyone on your staff, and your wife's, with photographs."

"You need? You *need*?" The veins in his neck actually managed to push through all the flab. I began to hope he'd have a stroke or something. "Who the hell put you in charge of this operation?" He looked around.

The commissioner cleared his throat. "We decided that it would be best that the police remain officially unaware of this kidnapping. Any publicity could prove fatal. If what Mrs. Wagner told Mr. Gold is true, there should be no police profile to alert the vultures in the press. Let's keep them focused on the shooting."

"We? Who the hell's we, and for how long do we wait? Jesus Christ, it's my little girl you're talking about." Actual tears came to his eyes.

I wondered.

He stared at me again, but this time, there was more appeal than hatred in his look. "You have three days, and you'd better keep me and the cops up-to-date. Then we'll see."

The rest of the meeting was taken up by the details of my coordination with the police, most of which I forgot as quickly as the sight of an ugly broad. The only news was that they had traced the shooter to a particular rooftop, but there was nothing there but a spent cartridge. There were about a million guns that could have done the deed.

I was in a hurry to get out and get on with it. I left it for the others to pander to Wagner's need for pity and headed back to the street.

MAYOR'S WIFE MURDERED

The headlines screamed at me from every newsstand.

"Give me one of each," I said to Freddie and skimmed the stories. Not a word about any kidnapping. I tossed the papers back on the counter and walked away.

"Hey," Freddie called after me. "Don't you want your money back?"

I looked back. "Nah."

We'd been going through this ritual for five years. Ever since the first time I paid him for the papers, money has never changed hands. Freddie was a good guy. Too bad somebody blew off his legs during a mob war.

Oh, well. Bob Dylan once wrote a song about hearing

another hard-luck story every time you turn around.

It was then that I realized I'd forgotten all about Wanda. I hoped she wouldn't take it personally. Then I thought about her hiking skirt and wondered what the hell was wrong with me.

I knew, though.

Julie.

They say that cops should never investigate crimes involving their own families. Well, I wasn't a cop anymore.

CHAPTER 3

The pain in my side was getting worse as I climbed the steps to my office, being careful to avoid the one that was cracked. I'd fired her when she brought me a clean set of clothes to the hospital, but Jenny was at her desk when I walked in. She didn't say anything, just handed me a piece of paper. It was the third notice of back rent due. It said I had ten days to respond or face eviction. I crumpled it up and tossed it in the round file.

"That won't change anything, you know," she said.

"Fuck 'em where they breathe," I said. "Let them kick me out. They won't find anyone else to rent this dump." I retreated to my office, leaving her looking after me with that resigned, frustrated mother hen look on her face.

Jenny Martin was a gem—competent, efficient, and totally wasted on me. I hadn't paid her for months, but she never complained. I knew that she had a small annuity from her mother to keep her going, but it wasn't fair. She could have made good money in some corporate office. Why she stuck with me I could never really figure. I figured she was in love with me, but even love has its limits, especially the unrequited kind. And she wasn't some dopey-eyed kid out for thrills. She was plenty good-looking, her face framed by shoulder-length chestnut brown hair, and her figure was still dynamite for a woman in her late thirties, but I never mixed business with pleasure and had kept my hands off.

I went back out. "Get me a glass of water," I said, "and you're fired."

"Again?" was all she said.

I sat down at my desk and she brought the water, watching me with eagle-eyes as I gulped down a couple of Vicodin.

"Does it hurt a lot?"

"Only when I laugh, so don't try to be funny. And I meant it, you're fired. Go find a decent job."

"What, and leave all the fun behind?"

She was the only other person who knew about Julie, and I'd seen the *Times* open on her desk, so she knew what was probably going down.

"I told you not to make me laugh," I growled at her, "and bring me all the files on that asshole Wagner."

She looked at me with surprise. "Are you still on the job?"

I filled her in on everything that had happened at City Hall, leaving out the part about Wanda's hiking skirt. In addition to good secretarial skills, Jenny has a great eye for criminal details. She said it was because of all the detective novels she read. I told her they were all full of crap, but she devoured them anyway.

Writers can make anything come out any way they want. I could probably use a good one myself, but real life has a way of fucking things over that no writer could help. This was looking like one of those times.

While she was getting the files, I just sat there, staring at the crumbling plaster on the wall, wondering again what the hell I was doing in this crummy business. I was a damn good detective, but after everything that had happened, nobody but scuzz wanted to touch me with a ten-foot pole, and scuzz are usually just as broke as I am. That means that I've taken on a lot of shitty jobs for shitty pay, but even the scuzz are entitled to justice—whatever the hell that is.

The only really satisfying justice I know is revenge, but even that wears off with time, and still leaves you empty.

Jenny dumped the files on my desk. "Try not to spend the whole day in here, okay? Stop and get a bite to eat. You look like crap."

The usual. She reminds me of my mother sometimes. Maybe that's the real reason I've never popped her cork. Damn nice cork too, I thought as I watched her tight, round ass sashay out.

"Close the door," I called after her, "and keep going. You're fired."

"Yadda da, yadda da," she called back, and she made it sound sexy, like Lauren Bacall.

I pushed a bunch of crap off to the side and opened the first folder on the pile. It was full of newspaper clippings of my trial.

I couldn't see what that had to do with anything, but I had included them in the Wagner files because I thought they were full of little tidbits that might implicate him in bribery.

There might be something in there to put me onto a lead, even a slim one. As of now, I had *bupkis*.

The next folder was all about the landfill scandal that almost cost him the election, and maybe it had. There were plenty of allegations of electoral fraud, but nobody could prove a damned thing.

I knew the bastard was guilty, but there was just no proof. He may have been a bastard, but he was a fucking clever one, I'll give him that. I was also certain, as sure as

I was still breathing, that the acquittal was bought too, but none of the jurors ever broke ranks.

I thought for a while, wondering why I had such a powerful certainty that Julie's abduction had something to do with Wagner. I had even thought that he might be behind it himself, for some god-only-knows reason, but his obvious distress this morning made me rethink it. Still, it had something to do with something that he'd done. Of that I was certain, but where did Maureen fit in the picture?

What I'd been holding back was the names of five men she'd been screwing. It had taken me a lot of prodding, but I finally got them out of her. I couldn't understand her reluctance, but then, I never really could understand a lot of what she did. I figured that she'd get more talkative as time went on—and then she had to go and run out of it.

Most of them were prominent, and a public scandal would have devastating repercussions. She thought that any one of them could be blackmailing her, using Julie as the ace-in-the-hole. It was when I pushed her for details that she clammed up. She said she wanted to think it all through before giving me any more information, and now she was dead. I'd have to ferret it all out for myself, but where to start?

The third folder was all the details of Wagner's own sordid sex life I'd sniffed out over the years. There might be something in there that might help shed some light. Whatever this was about, I was sure that it had something to do with the past, a past that could blow the lid off Wagner and maybe even put him behind bars for good.

I sifted through each of the folders, but nothing jumped out at me. It wasn't usually easy. I'd go through them again maybe a dozen times, maybe more. Shit-hard work, but patience usually pays off if you can stick with it long enough.

I decided to take Jenny's advice. I closed the files and was getting up to go pay Arty a visit when everything started to get dark. It didn't feel like a seizure though, and the next thing I knew, I was on the floor and Jenny was on one knee next to me, holding up my head. I could see a lot of thigh up her dress, and that revived me more than anything.

"When was the last time you ate?"

Her tone was peremptory, and I thought that was no way to talk to a man who had just passed out. Still, I tried to remember. I'd only had a few bites of the cheeseburger and before that, probably breakfast at the hospital, if you could call it that. I bypassed lunch by sticking it under my mattress. "Breakfast, yesterday." It sounded like I was mumbling, but she must have been satisfied.

"Come on, let's get you up, and I'll treat you to lunch.

"Stop being nice to me," My voice had returned. "I fired you, remember."

She laughed. "No hard feelings. Now, get the hell up. You know I can't lift you."

The lights had come on again, and I managed to haul myself up without any more dizziness than the Vicodin provided, but my side was burning like fire. It took a few minutes for everything to calm down.

"Where do you want to eat?" she asked, now totally in charge.

"Your treat?"

"I said so."

"Okay, let's make it the Waldorf."

She laughed, "You should live so long."

"Actually, I was headed to Arturo's to see if they could shed any light on my knifing that they hadn't wanted to share with the cops."

"Okay then, Arturo's it is."

She took hold of my arm and led me down the stairs like I was an old geezer. She was fully in charge, like I said. God bless Jenny Martin. Somebody had better. I wasn't doing too good a job of it.

❧

Arturo's was crowded, as usual, easy enough for somebody to knife a guy and disappear in seconds. Even a bear, and a lot of the crowd bordered on obese.

The rest were.

Arturo's was the best cheapish Italian restaurant in town. Hell, for my money, it was the best, and Arty served food as though he'd never heard of heart disease.

"Heart disease?" he would scoff. "Don't you know that Italy has less heart disease than anywhere else in the world? What is it, if not the food?"

"Ever been to Italy?" I asked him once.

He laughed. "Hell no, what would I wanna go there for? My mama taught me everything I know. Any complaints?"

There weren't any, and since Arturo's was a big mob eatery, nobody ever fucked with him anyway. I'll give it to the big boys. They can afford to eat anywhere but they come here. Italian mobsters put good, above all else, when feeding their faces, and Arturo's is tops.

Marta had just finished talking to some guy when she turned and saw me. Her face turned into a mask of pure solicitude, and she came waddling over. She had her hands crossed on her ample bosom.

"Joe, Joe, is good to zee you valking. I nearly die ven zey carry you out, all zat blood dripping vrum za stretcher."

She threw her arms around me in a bear hug of the

kind that few men can manage. Then she grabbed my hand and dragged me toward the kitchen.

"Arty, Arty, see who's here. Is Joe Gold, is okay."

Arty came flying out of the kitchen with a huge smile on his face and pumped my arm like he was expecting to get water. He looked me up and down, and something in my face—probably because of the pumping and hugging—seemed to worry him, because he frowned. "You don't look so hot, *goombah,* but I'm happy to see you on two feet. I was fuckin' worried when they hauled your ass outta here. Cost me a bundle to get the mess cleaned up, there was so much blood. I honest to god thought you was dead."

I laughed. "Send me the bill."

It took him a while before he laughed too.

Arty and Marta are the most unlikely pair you could imagine. Marta will tell you that they met at the culinary academy, and it was love at first bite, but I got the real skinny from Arty. Seems like Marta was one of the unhappy hookers at Madam Flo's when he walked in one day.

He fell for her like a fat man spotting a buffet and eventually made an honest woman out of her. They'd been together for twenty-five years, and I never heard a cross word between them. You never know what'll work and what won't.

Arty hurried us over to a table. "Here, Joe. Siddown. Take a load off. What can I get you?"

"Actually, I'd really like some information, but if I don't get something down my gullet soon, I'll pass out again, and Jenny'll be pissed."

He looked at Jenny. "You still work for this bum, a nice girl like you?"

"Nope. He fired me."

"Ahh. Good." He laughed. "I have an opening for a

cocktail waitress, union wages and all the tips you can stick between your boobs."

Jenny laughed back. "I'll think about it."

"Well, don't take too long. Our son Jerry's crazy wife wants to have a 'career,' but she and Marta don't get along well, you know. I'm not looking forward to it."

"Goldeeger," Marta hissed.

Jenny opted to keep her girlish figure by ordering a light *antipasto*. I ordered the *scallopini* with mushrooms. Despite the pain in my side, I wolfed it down like some homeless guy who found half a pizza in a dumpster. I even ordered some chocolate soaked *cannoli* for dessert. I was feeling better—and Jenny was paying. Usually, I'm limited to some spaghetti dish or other, when I can afford to eat here at all.

After lunch, I beckoned them over. They pulled out the two extra chairs at the table and sat down.

"You eat real good, Joe, is verra good. Means you'se healthy."

I could never pronounce the name of the place she came from in Eastern Europe, but I never got tired of hearing her mangle the English language. Whatever she said, if Arty was around, he'd be beaming at his marvelous wife. I always hoped that they never did it with her on top—she'd have crushed him.

"Can either of you think of anything at all that might tip me off to who stuck the knife in my side? Just missed my liver, you know."

They both blanched.

"I can't help you at all." Arty sounded apologetic. "I was working in the kitchen when I hear screaming. You looked real bad, all crumpled up against the wall like that in a pool of blood. That's all I remember."

I looked at Marta with a hopeful look on my face, but she wasn't much help either.

"I thought it vunny ven zum beeg guy nearly bomp into me ven I come out of keetchen. He vas in beeg hurry get out. I forget about it ven somevone come get me about you, but I remember it later."

"Did you get any kind of look at him?"

"Naw, joost a beeg guy in a bleck coat, und maybe a vedora, but maybe I joost imagine zat. Ve tell all zis to za cops."

Still at square one.

I thanked them for their time.

When Jenny asked for the check, Arty wouldn't hear of it. "It's the least we can do for Joe. After all, he got shanked here. We owe him one."

Salt of the earth, Arty and Marta, real salt of the earth.

෴

Jenny managed to get me back to the office. I had planned to go over the files again, but all I really wanted to do was lie down on the beat-up old sofa in the "waiting room," and go unconscious.

I had nightmares about Julie instead.

The worst one was when I told her I was her father and she shot me.

That one woke me up.

I was sweating.

CHAPTER 4

I spent the afternoon poring over the files, but the pain in my side and the Vicodin high kept getting in the way of my concentration, and I was coming up dry. I opened the top drawer of my desk and pulled out the list of names I'd gotten from Maureen.

I really had to hand it to her. Married to the mayor and screwing some of the most influential men in town. Half the shit going down in the city might have passed between her legs, and it was my job to sort it all out. All I could think of was that she had one hell of a fucking nerve to get herself killed and leave me holding the shit bag—again.

I stared at the names: Connors, Stokes, Bellamy, Cooper, and Cohen. Maureen always said she liked kosher sausage the best, and Maury Cohen was rumored around the brothel circuit to have one hell of a salami on him.

Henry Stokes was the only black guy on the list, but since he wasn't an *aficionado* of the hooker culture, I'd heard no scuttlebutt regarding his attributes in the bratwurst department. Still, unless there was some other really important reason, I knew that Maureen was not a fan of the cocktail weenie.

The other three were known to me by name only. The only time I'd ever seen any of them was in newspaper photos and, occasionally, on TV. They were all rich and successful businessmen, way the hell out of my league. Cohen and Stokes were the only ones who seemed remotely human to me, being rich and successful hadn't turned them into corporate robots.

Were they all just unrelated pokers, or was there some thread that connected them, something besides what went through Maureen's needle threader?

My ruminations were cut short when the outer door opened and a messenger came in.

"Got a package here for a Joseph Gold." He got an eyeful of Jenny. "Do you work for him?"

"Nope, not anymore." I could see that he was confused, but Jenny kept her face straight. She pointed to my office. "In there."

"Joseph Gold?" he asked at my door.

"Who wants to know?"

Now he was really getting flustered, but then his training kicked in. "I have a package for Joseph Gold from the mayor's office. Is that you?"

"That depends," I said,

He was looking confused again. "On what?"

"On if I have to pay for it or not."

He must have finally decided that he was being played with because he broke out in a smile. "Naw, compliments of hizzoner, but a tip wouldn't hurt."

"Don't eat yellow snow."

It took him a couple of seconds, but then he burst out in guffaws. "Hey, that's funny."

"No. It's hygienic. Hey, Jenny," I called out, "do you have a tip for this kid?"

"Yeah, use deodorant," she yelled back.

"That sounds hygienic too." I said.

The smile kind of melted off his face, but he kept professional, handing me the envelope and a piece of paper to sign. Then he turned and left without another word. Jenny looked in at the door. She was smiling. "Do you think we were a little hard on him?"

"You started it." I said, and we both kind of broke up, but I was limited by the pain in my side. I popped a couple more Vicodin.

I opened the package. It was a complete roster of the staff of the mayor's mansion, with photos and background.

I stuck it in my briefcase along with the other files.

"I'm calling it a day." I said, "Carry me down the stairs and take off yourself."

"Don't tell me what to do. You fired me, remember?"

❧❧❧

Once on the street, I realized it was rush hour. The subways and busses would be packed with sardines, and I didn't have enough money to waste on a taxi. I looked around—nobody looked suspicious, or like they might be following me, but there was no way on earth that I was going to get into a crowd until I'd figured out who wanted me dead. The Vicodin was kicking in, and I felt well enough to walk the fourteen blocks to my place.

The whole time, my eyes were racing around, checking out the rooftops, the street, and watching for dog shit on the sidewalk. Anybody walking toward me might think I was nuts. All the while, I kept a lookout for a big man in a black coat and, maybe, a fedora. I didn't like being paranoid, but it was better than being dead.

Vicodin or no, my energy started to give out at the halfway point, so I ducked into the first burger joint I came to and nursed a cheeseburger and a coke for half-an-hour, until I felt ready to go on. I made it for another few blocks but the briefcase felt like it was full of bricks. I thought I might pass out and finally hailed a cab.

"Where to buddy?"

"One-Twenty-Three Gramercy."

He thought for a second. "That's two-and-a-half blocks from here."

"Yep. Got enough gas?"

He shrugged his shoulders, slammed down the meter, and eased into traffic.

Within a minute, he turned into Gramercy and pulled up to my building.

I handed him a fiver. "Keep the change," I said as I got out. The fare was four ninety-five. I could remember when it would have been a quarter. I must be getting old.

"Gee, thanks" he said and flipped me his version of the bird as he squealed his rear tires taking off.

I turned to go up my front steps. Someone was sitting on them.

Wanda.

Her face looked like anything but happy.

I put on my best sorry face. "Aw, jeez, sweetheart. Sorry for taking off like that, but I had a lot on my mind."

She seemed stumped for a second, then she laughed. "Oh, hey, it's nothing like that." She got serious again. "I have something you should know. Let's go upstairs, and I'll tell you about it."

The elevator was out of service again, and we had to climb up the five flights to my one-bedroom. It's a good thing she was there. I'm not sure I'd have made it alone. I only stay here because it's one of the most strictly rent-controlled buildings in town.

I'm paying hardly more than what I paid when I moved in fifteen years ago. The downside is that the owners spend as little as they can get away with on maintenance. It worked for me. I wasnt usually wracked up. Physically anyway.

As soon as I had a month's rent together, I'd stick it in a drawer and never touch it. This place was all I had between me and the street, and now that I was facing eviction from my office, I'd have nowhere else to flop.

There are two things I'm obsessive about, my work and my place, and it's always neat as a pin. If there's anything women hate, it's a messy house, and if I have any such thing as a "feminine side,"—like I heard some screwball broad talking about on TV one night—this was it. There was a practical reason for it too. Stumbling around drunk in the dead of night, I knew where everything was.

I hadn't made the bed and my dirty clothes from yesterday were still lying on the floor, but everything else was spic and span. I tossed the briefcase on top of my small corner desk and felt a hundred pounds lighter. I waved Wanda to the sofa and sat down next to her, losing another hundred pounds, or so. My head was spinning like one of those Turkish dancers, whirling dervishes, I guess they call them. She must have realized it, because she just sat there, waiting for me to come back down. I really didn't want to, but, like I said, I'm obsessive about my work, and I figured that whatever she had to tell me was related, so I forced my attention back to her.

That wasn't hard to do, her hiking skirt had been on the climb again, and she was exhibiting a lot of leg, what with them being crossed and all. The drag up to my place had been hot and stuffy, she had opened three or four of the buttons on her blouse, and the twins were trying desperately to escape. I wanted to watch her breathe deeply.

Instead, I said, "So what's so important that it brings you here now?" I was hoping she'd fess up that it was just a ruse to get me to bed.

It was a lot worse than that.

"After everyone left this morning, I really had to pee—" Her eyes get real wide when she's excited. "—so I popped into the mayor's john. I was just leaving when I heard the office door open. He was talking to somebody, I don't know who, but he said something like, 'Whatever you do, don't let that sonofabitch Jewboy get too close. He could be a real problem. He hates my guts and would love to see me swing. If it looks like he's on to something, steer him away—do whatever it takes.' Then he told him to get out, and I heard the door close. My heart was pounding, I tell you. I was hoping he didn't have to pee or something. There was no place to hide. Then I heard the sound of a lot of drawers opening and closing and he was muttering."

"Muttering? What about?"

"I don't know. I couldn't make anything out except 'sonofabitch' a couple of times. Then I finally heard him go out. I counted to twenty and got my sweet little ass out of there as fast as I could. Nobody saw me leave. I thought you should know."

"You thought right, sweetie."

"You don't know how ominous that last part sounded. He *meant* 'do anything,' didn't he? Oh, Joe, you know I'd feel terrible if anything ever happened to you. You know, like worse than just getting knifed." Her eyes were cast down.

"You mean like getting dead?" I laughed, but it wasn't real.

She looked up suddenly, and there were tears in her eyes. "Don't even joke about it. You know how I feel about you. I don't care what anyone says, you're really the sweetest guy I ever slept with." Her mouth did that little moue thing that it does so well, and I started to get hard.

I gave her my best horny smile, and I didn't even have to work at it.

She didn't miss it, and we had our nooner six hours late.

It hurt like hell, but it was worth it.

I smiled when I realized that she could have just called.

✐✐✐

Later, over a romantic dinner of bologna sandwiches and a small salad she managed to scrape together from the dregs of my kitchen, I decided to tell her everything. I needed a spy in Wagner's office, and the best way to get her to do it was to appeal to her romantic side.

Her mouth was hanging wide open for about ten seconds before she spoke, and damned if I didn't start to get hard again, until it occurred to me that she looked like one of those blow-up blow-job dolls, and I almost laughed.

"Julie's *your* daughter?"

I nodded. "That's what I said."

"*You* fucked Maureen *Wagner?*" Her eyes were about as wide open as eyes could get.

"We more or less lived together for five years—more or less."

Her look turned to something that looked to me like compassion.

"Jesus, you poor slob. I saw how men looked at her, like they'd give their right nuts to screw her. They were like fucking slaves. I always wondered how many of them she did sleep with."

"Maybe all of them." I said. "Maureen was a born slut, and she was good at spending her inheritance—very good."

Wanda looked at me with obvious speculation.

I laughed. "Don't ask. There's no way to compare Maureen to any other woman I ever knew. It wasn't like sex, it was like falling into a deep pit of oblivion. It was something else entirely, but her body was the perfect vehicle. Hippie friends we knew said she was a witch. They tried to warn me off her, but I was hooked. I couldn't get enough, and when she wasn't around, I felt real pain."

"Sounds like a junkie." Wanda had been listening to me very closely, and her eyes held mine.

"Exactly like a junkie. That's the effect she had on me."

Wanda was one in a million. Her eyes teared up and she said, "Oh, you poor, poor thing."

My appeal to her romantic side worked better than I'd expected, and we screwed again. No, I think we actually made love. There's a big difference. This time though, in order to spare my poor stitches, we used our hands and mouths. Anyone who says oral sex can't be making love doesn't know what the hell he's talking about.

Wanda was obviously scared, but she agreed to keep her eyes and ears open and keep me informed. She also agreed to stay the night so she could help me downstairs in the morning. Like I said, one in a million.

Then I thought about Jenny, and a few others, and thought that I was one lucky guy, for all the good that did any of *them*. That made me feel like a heel.

I'd managed to forget for a few hours, but more dreams about Julie troubled my sleep. At one point, my tossing and turning and moaning and groaning drove Wanda to the sofa where I found her in the morning, finally asleep.

CHAPTER 5

My first stop was back at General for a wound check. The doctor who'd sewn me up looked to me like he wasn't even old enough to shave. Shit, doctors are supposed to be older than you, aren't they? He told me once again to stay off my feet for a week or two. Yeah, right. I was still stuck firmly at square one, and time was flying by. It was more than a week since the kidnapping, there had yet to be any ransom demand, and the only one who was supposed to know anything about it was dead.

Whoever they were, the kidnappers had to be freaking out. What good was a hostage if nobody knew you had it? I was certain that they'd get in contact somehow, but how? Wagner was the obvious choice, but why had he been kept out of the loop to begin with? It was Maureen being blackmailed, but about what, and would it ruin some plan if her husband found out? And why had Maureen been killed? I still couldn't be sure that the bullet had, indeed, been meant for her and not me. How did that make a difference? Did it?

I still had to find Julie, and all I had were a lot of questions piling up.

I didn't have a clue, but what I did know, was the longer it took to get a ransom demand, the greater the likelihood that Julie was dead. I don't think that I ever felt more impotent in my life, and time was wasting.

All I really had was five suspects who Maureen thought might not be above blackmailing her. Thinking about how many there might be who *were* above it, made me laugh in spite of my funk. Just thinking about the complicated maze of her life was enough to make me dizzy, and the Vicodin didn't help.

The most obvious problem I had at the moment was empty pockets. Money buys information. Hell, it pays for the wheels to get you to where the information is. Without it you get nothing. If I'd been thinking straight yesterday morning, I'd have asked Wagner for some cash. She was his kid, after all. At least, he thought she was. There was nothing for it. I'd have to go to City Hall and beard the bastard in his lair. The sonofabitch should have thought of it on his own.

This Vicodin crap was screwing with my head, making me miss beats. Miss too many beats, and you wake up dead. What I needed was some good weed to mellow out, and that made me think to kill two birds with one stone. Maury Cohen usually had the best pot this side of California.

ↄ৴ↄ

Wagner was about as happy to see me as if somebody had told him that his dick fell off. He faced me across his big desk, his bulk framed by the much sleeker skyscrapers behind him but, by virtue of proximity, towering above them.

"You'd better have something for me."

"I need money." No point beating about the bush in idle chatter.

He thought for a while, his eyes screaming murder at me.

"How much?"

I was going to say five, but having been murdered by his eyes, I felt like he owed me. "Ten Grand."

The obvious relief in his face made me kick myself mentally. *Asshole.*

But it didn't stop him from being cagey.

"That's going to be tough to hide in the books. We do want this kept secret, right? I could manage two out of petty cash every once in a while." The sonofabitch actually smiled, like he was asking for my vote.

I smiled right back. "Why don't you pay for it out of your own damn funds—" I couldn't stop myself, "—you fucking piece of shit?" I didn't lose the smile.

I thought he was going to explode, but he knew I had him over a barrel, so he just sat there, killing me over and over again until he calmed down. I watched the color changes on his pig-face—scarlet, red, pink. When he was almost white again, he threw back his chair and stood up. For a second, I thought he might leap over his desk like a tiger and rip me apart. I tensed.

"Wait here," he said, and his voice was barely under control. I could tell by the high-pitched squeak of "wait."

He disappeared into his anteroom for a couple of minutes. When he came back out, he had a sheaf of loose bills in his hand. He thrust it at me. "Here, count it, you *sheeny* bloodsucker."

I just stared at him. "There's no need to get personal, you Nazi Kraut."

I counted the money, laying it all out on his desk. There were mostly twenties and tens. Few of them were new and fresh. I took my time about it, and I could see he was getting more pissed off with each bill I counted, but he finally just sat down and fumed.

It was all there.

"I'll send you a receipt," I said, and I thought that he actually almost laughed. Maybe it was just gas.

I stuffed it all in my briefcase, got up, and left without saying another word. I stood outside the door for a few seconds until I heard the bellow of rage behind it. I winked at his "old maid" secretary, who was rumored to have once been a madam. Hard to believe. She just sniffed her nose at me, like a Boston matron catching the whiff of a fart.

I looked around the mayor's floor, but Wanda was nowhere in sight, so I left.

☙❧☙

When I got to my office, Jenny was there, her feet up on her desk, filing her nails. She didn't have anything else to do. I hadn't had a paying client in three months. These fucking recessions screwed everybody over. People didn't have money to throw away on screwing *each other* over. I looked at her.

"Did you take the job at Arturo's yet?"

She looked at me and said. "I haven't decided."

"Guess what?"

"Let me think." Her eyes searched the ceiling. "I'm fired."

"No, you're hired." I stuck my hand into my briefcase and pulled out the wad of bills. I peeled some off. "Here's two month's back pay, and I'll give you the rest when I wrap up the case."

She looked at the money and didn't say anything for a while. Then she looked worried. "Are the cops after you?"

"I told you not to make me laugh. No, I shook down hizzoner the mayor. When push came to shove, he farted the money. Don't hold it too close to your nose."

"Dirty, huh?"

"Well, just look at it. It stinks of petty bribery. He took it from his safe."

"How much?" she asked.

"How is that any of your business? What are you, a union?"

She just stared at me.

"Ten grand."

She let the air out slowly between her teeth, almost a whistle. She knows how to whistle. "That's the biggest retainer you've ever gotten."

"Yeah, baby." I laughed. "And I had a lot of fun getting it out of him, though I thought for a minute he was going to pop me for sure."

She got serious. "Why don't you cough up the dough for the rent?"

"I've got ten days, right?"

"Nine, now."

"Hey, I could be dead in nine days. What's the rush?"

She just looked at me the way she does when she thinks I'm being particularly stupid, but she couldn't hide the fear behind her mask of motherly reproof.

"Hey, feel like taking the day off and getting whacked?" The minute I said it I realized that it was the wrong word at the wrong time, and her face kind of froze. I laughed. "I'm going to pay an unannounced visit to Maury Cohen on the pretext of scoring some of his dynamite grass. Wanna come along?"

"Maury Cohen?" She thought for a second. "Isn't he the one with the big…"

"That's him."

"What the hell," she said. "I've got nothing else to do anyway."

∽∾∽

I knew where Maury hung out most days, in his office at the Casino Club. Hell, it was his casino, and I'd always wondered if Maureen's pussy hadn't lubricated the deal. Wagner had had second thoughts about bucking popular sentiment and was refusing to okay the change. Then, in an about face, he rammed through the ordinance to allow a single casino within the city limits. Lo and behold, there was Maury with his city-block lot and enough millions to build.

Could that be it? I thought. Was there something shady in the deal? I slapped myself mentally. What could either of these guys do that wasn't? Anyway, it set me to a line of thinking that included what twisted games they might have been playing. Maybe Maureen had blackmail material and was being blackmailed herself to cough it up. There was no telling where the musky trail of her webs might lead.

∽∾∽

We had no trouble getting into Maury's office. He was beaming at me, exuding the good health of a tanned and toned athlete. Maury had two left feet, but he worked out in his private gym every day.

His shock of white hair framed the honey tan of his face like a lion's mane, and his deep, blue eyes were those of a con artist, inviting you to invest your life savings on a sure thing. How many Jews have blue eyes? He was wearing some body-fitting, collared polo shirt or something, with an animal logo embroidered on the pocket. Expensive. It showed off the muscles of his chest to perfection. It also betrayed the beginnings of a paunch, but you didn't notice that when he was seated behind his desk.

When all was said and done, Maury Cohen had no doubts that he was a special kind of person and that god had singled him out for success so that he could provide huge yearly donations to Israel and other Jewish organizations.

He didn't seem to wonder why god would want to take money from people who were cheated out of it.

But then, of course, his casino was a success. It brought in tons of tax money, and the pot-holes got fixed. People forgot that Maury had been a gangster. Well, they didn't forget, they just pushed it to the back of their minds as they drove along on the nice, smooth streets.

And Maury had given up being a gangster anyway. He didn't have to be anymore. He told me his marijuana operation was the only illegal thing he still dabbled in. "Gotta keep your hand in, you know, and it really ain't all that much. Mostly, I do it to keep me and my friends supplied with enough good weed. I'm sure I'm getting ripped off right and left down the line, but I really don't give a shit. 'Spread the wealth" is my motto. I can afford it."

He looked Jenny up and down, and he didn't seem disappointed. I noticed that she kept sneaking glances at his crotch. He turned his smile up to high beams, and I wondered if it was my imagination or were her nipples pushing through her sweater at the same time? My amusement was tempered by the thought that I might be jealous.

"And who is this delightful young lady?"

What a cornball.

I thought I heard a surreptitious cough from Jenny. I was willing to bet her nipples were deflating.

After I introduced them, he said, "Well, if you ever get tired of working for Joey, let me know. I'm sure I could find something well-suited to your talents."

The leer in his voice almost made me laugh. Among men, Maury was the boss. With women, he turned into a little boy. He never married, and that's probably why he was most comfortable in the whore houses, he didn't have to try to be romantic. How had Maureen beguiled him?

Jenny smiled at him. "I just might do that. He's always firing me anyway." She was still sneaking peeks at his crotch.

Maury and I went back to Hebrew School at Agudas Achim. His father owned a small hardware store, and he was several years older than I, but his sister was just the right age. Becky Cohen was the first girl I ever had sex with—all five seconds of it. But she was wise beyond her years, and she soon set me to rights with her mouth. We began an "affair" that played through the empty bathrooms of the *shul* for about a year. It was marvelous, and Maury never knew anything about it. At least I thought so. He never said anything, and I certainly wasn't going to bring it up. No pun intended.

Becky now lives in a villa outside of Tel-Aviv with her husband and three kids. He used to be one of Maury's bagmen. Now he's an independent contractor running guns for the Russian mob. I guess she's come up in the world. One time I thought about how she's still making a living from hardware though. It sort of cracked me up at the time, but there's really nothing funny about it.

I never thought for a moment that Maury was behind Maureen's killing. Whatever he was, he wasn't a killer. I knew him too well. His mother had been shot to death in a robbery at the hardware store.

"There's nothing lower on God's green earth than a

killer," he once told me. "Nobody has a right to take away anyone's life. Wasn't it Rabbi Hillel who said that to a kill a man was to kill a world—or something like that?"

"It was somewhere in the Talmud." Now how the hell had I remembered that? I haven't been a practicing Jew for years. Maury was taking classes in Jewish thought or something at the *shul*. He was the one supposed to be up on this stuff.

"Honest to god, Joey, you don't know how I itch to open up with a fuckin' machine gun on the scumbag killers I am sometimes forced to rub shoulders with."

"Then you wouldn't be any better than they are."

"That's what stops me but, one of these days…" He let the thought trail off.

I never carried a gun myself. Packing heat was likely to get you killed, but I knew what he was talking about.

Funny, wasn't it? Maury's mother's murder made me want to be a cop. Why did it send him in the other direction? Maybe it had nothing to do with it. Maybe he was just a born grifter.

Maury also knew all about me and Maureen. Like I said, we go back a long way, so there was no point in beating about her bush. He didn't know that I knew about *them* though, and I intended to enlighten him. Maybe he could come up with something.

He looked at me straight. "I'm sorry about Maureen. I know how you felt about her."

"'Felt' is the proper term." Then I looked at *him* straight. "I know about *you* and Maureen too."

I could tell that the color kind of drained from his face because his tan turned a shade darker. His eyes never moved. Then it was as though someone had let the air out of him, and he kind of shrank into his massive desk chair.

His face took on a furtive look, his eyes were moving around."

"How?" He almost whispered it.

"Maureen told me"

I could see him relax. Who else knew about it? About what? Would he tell me?

"When?"

"Two days before she died."

Maury caught on fast. His eyes got real big. "I swear, Joey, I had nothin' to do with it. You know me better than that."

"In my business—" I was still looking straight at him. "—it's never wise to bet on a sure thing. I'd like to believe you, I really would, but I have to know why she thought you might be blackmailing her."

"Blackmail!" He nearly jumped out of his chair. "About what?" Something had given him a sudden case of the heebie-jeebies. Again, no pun intended.

"Well, that's what I hope you can tell me." I hadn't taken my eyes off of his, and they suddenly had a hunted look. There was something big. I could smell it.

"Honest to god Joey, I don't know nothin' about any blackmail."

"But you do know something that could be used against her, right?"

He dropped his eyes like a kid caught stealing out of the cookie jar. He didn't say anything for a while. Then he raised them back up. "What I could tell you might make your head spin."

"I doubt that. I knew Maureen and all her shenanigans quite well, remember."

"I guess that's true. I'll tell you what I know, and I swear, Joey, whatever I can do to help, I will, but *you've* gotta swear to keep my name out of it."

"No oaths, but I'll try."

He looked at me hard. I guess he believed me because he started talking.

CHAPTER 6

Walking back through the casino was sheer hell. The blings, blangs, blongs of the games and those damned horns and bells, made a racket that was only mildly subdued by the plush carpeting. The whirr and click of the roulette wheels, the clink of ice, the clack of dice, the excited shouts of winners, the moans of losers, the slap of cards on felt, and the ever-winking, ever-changing lights on the slots were trying to give me a seizure of another sort—the kind that, if I hadn't left most of the money back in my office safe, could tear through ten grand in ten minutes.

Jenny knew all about my gambling. She'd been the one who got me into therapy, and she gripped my arm tight as she steered us out, blinking, into the bright light of the sun where normal people lived.

The therapy had sort of worked. Once I was *in* a casino, I had a problem, but I had conquered the urge to go in. Gambling and smoking were the only addictions I'd managed to bust, but there were still times when I just couldn't stop myself from lighting up. I wasn't sure that I wanted to give up any of the others just now, figuring that I'd be giving them all up sooner or later. What's the rush? The way my life was going, it looked like it would be sooner rather than later anyway. I wondered of I'd make it to fifty.

To tell the truth, I'd already been half distracted, mulling over the shit that Maury had laid on me, along with a baggie filled with some reddish gold weed that felt comfortable in my jacket pocket. We'd gotten high off two tokes up in his office, but it had mostly worn off, except for the flare-up in the casino. If there was ever proof that marijuana and gambling were not complementary, it was yours truly. I rarely ever won stoned, and one time that I did, the "buddies" who steered me to the game, whacked me on the head with a two-by-four and spent it on booze and broads.

I was hungry. So was Jenny. We were just two blocks from "Original" Henry's and I wondered if Stokes was in his office.

At one time, he'd been a gangbanger, but when he met Virginia, he decided to go straight. Actually, it had been she who threatened to cut off the nookie permanently if he didn't. Maybe something else too. Virginia was one hell of a cook, and he parlayed her talent into Central City's favorite Louisiana chicken and shrimp joint.

They started with a corner of a building. Now, they owned it. The restaurant occupied most of the ground floor, and there were fifteen franchises spread around the suburbs. They'd turned the original corner into a kind of fast-food take-away, and it probably grossed more than any of the outlying shops.

Location, location, location.

Only the downtown place was called "original," Virginia still cooked there every Sunday and, like Yogi Berra once said, nobody ate there anymore because it was too crowded. The rest of the week she stayed in their big house in the Heights, waited on by a staff of Hispanic servants.

"I couldn't find any suitable white folks for the job. They steal, y'know," Henry once told me, and he kind of laughed his ass off with that infectious guffaw of his. He was rumored to be a multi-millionaire, but since Henry's was a private corporation, there was no way for us *hoi polloi* to know just how multi for certain. One day, when I was feeling especially shitty about being such a loser, I looked up the value of his property in the Heights. It had been assessed at five million. His downtown building came out close to a hundred mil.

Multi enough, I supposed.

Rumor also had it that he never played around on Virginia, so I was curious why he'd been screwing Maureen. I didn't figure him for a killer either, though he did have that juvenile thing when he shot a kid dead. He always swore it was an accident. I thought I knew him well enough to believe him.

We went back a ways too. I don't think he ever set foot in Congregation Agudas Achim, but his family went to the Star of Bethlehem black Baptist Church across the street. We went to the same public school, and we hung out in the same crowd.

I got out before the shooting.

The big windows were full of people eating lunch, and there was Henry, beaming at us with his big, broad, white-toothed smile from the three-story sign above the restaurant. He had a tall chef's hat perched on his bald head, and his outstretched arms held a giant platter piled high with shrimp and pieces of chicken. Steam piped from the kitchen came out of vents in the sign and it smelled delicious. There was a movement on by some asshole do-gooders to have it stopped.

"Air pollution," they said.

Bullshit. It smelled a helluva lot better than the crap that all the buses farted.

Henry said it was just because he was black, but he used a stronger word. Only blacks could get away with using it nowadays. Lenny Bruce had been the only Jew who could say it and live.

We went in and managed to find an empty table in the back. The waitress, whose color was the natural shade of what Maury was trying to achieve in his tanning salon, didn't know if the boss was in, so we just ordered a couple of small platters of what was on the sign. At Henry's, small was medium and medium was large. Large could choke a horse. One of the main reasons for his success was that he gave great value. Every platter came with fries, though you could opt to order something else for a buck. We washed it down with Cokes.

While we were eating, the waitress came over to tell us that the boss was in. "Who should they say was asking?"

I told her.

A few minutes later, some big black guy came over, checked my name, and beckoned us to follow him. He led us through a narrow corridor in the back, lined with all the signed, glad-handing pictures of politicians, movie stars, and ball players there wasn't space for on the walls of the main room. It ended at an elevator.

"Fourth floor," was all he said.

For some reason, I thought of Charon, the Greek boatman who ferries the dead to hell.

The door reopened right into Henry's private office, and there he was, pushing back his desk chair so he could come around and greet us. I thought he was paunchier than the last time I'd seen him, but the smile was the same, just like on the sign.

He'd met Jenny before, so there was no need for introductions. We spent a few minutes in small talk before he got around to giving me his condolences. Henry knew about Maureen and me too.

"Well, Henry, that was all in the past. How is it that you poked her more recently?"

The question caught him way off guard, and he couldn't block the fear that came into his eyes, but he tried his damnedest. "What motha tole you dat," he tried to roar, but there was a catch in his throat.

Henry was so rich he didn't give a crap if people thought he sounded like the ghetto, and, when he was riled, his elocution lessons were left behind.

"Maureen did."

His eyes opened wide in an unintended parody of the black guy in all those old Charlie Chan movies, who was always terrified of something. But he could see that I was telling the truth, and it wasn't long before the smile reappeared, maybe a little sheepish.

"Well, hell, I'm sure I don't have to tell *you*."

"No, you don't."

"When did you find out?" Again, a hint of fear in those yellowish eyes.

"Two days before she died."

I almost laughed when his face went through the same motions as Maury's, and damn if he didn't say almost the exact same words.

"Hey, Joe. You can't be thinkin' it was me?"

"Naw. But I need to know what the hell's going on."

I gave him a bit of the story, but instead of Julie, I just hinted at doings in the mayor's mansion. What he told *me* just confirmed it.

He was awfully relieved when I told him the cops didn't know anything about it. When I said "yet," his mouth drooped again.

❧❧❧

We stopped at the cell phone place to recharge my phone for a month. It'd been empty for a couple of weeks.

"Why don't you just buy a year's subscription?" Jenny looked disapproving. She had that what-kind-of-asshole-are-you-anyway look. "It's cheaper."

I just looked at her and grinned. "I could be dead in nine days, remember?"

"You might also think about getting one of those that takes pictures, too."

Actually, I had thought about it. It would come in handy for surveillance, but I hadn't been willing to pay the price.

Being *unable* would be more to the point.

"Hey, what the hell," I said. "You're right, and who knows when I'll ever be this flush again."

They call them smart phones, or something, and I wasn't sure if I really wanted a piece of hardware that might be smarter than me resting in my pocket, but I walked out with one snuggled up against the half-dozen Cuban cigars Henry'd laid on me.

O' brave new world, I thought, but I couldn't remember who wrote that. I made a mental note to look it up, but I never did. I thought that it might have been Aldous Huxley, but then George Orwell and Timothy Leary kept popping into my head too.

I wondered what I could get for the cigars.

"I'm proud of you," Jenny said as she snuggled her arm into mine. "Taking a chance on the modern world. Maybe you'll even think about getting a computer too."

I laughed. "I love it when you talk dirty to me."

She pulled her arm away and slapped my shoulder. "Ooh, you, you're impossible. A computer could be a big help to you."

"Oh yeah?" I was skeptical, "How?"

"Well, for one thing, you could feed all those little bits of information in your files into it and let it come up with connections."

"It can do that?"

"Sure."

"Okay. How quick can we get one up and running, and how long will it take for me to learn how to use the damned thing?"

"A few hours, and I already know how to use them."

I was surprised. "You do?" I thought about it for a second. "Forget it. Next you'll be wanting a raise, and I can't afford it."

Jenny has the absolute greatest laugh of any woman I know.

ℰℛℰℛ

When I got back to the office, the first thing I did was pop two more Vicodin. Then I slumped in my chair and tried to digest all the information that had been fed to me. I hoped that it wouldn't lead to diarrhea or constipation. If I could just get it all out in one piece, maybe I'd get somewhere. The more I thought about it, though, the more it seemed that there were too many missing pieces. I wasn't even sure that any of it had to do with Julie, but I didn't have anything else. Tomorrow I was going to have to figure out how to see those other three guys.

Stumped, for now, I pulled the other files out of my briefcase.

Jenny looked in at the door. "I'm going out for a little while to do some shopping, maybe an hour. Maybe two. Anything I can get you?"

I was busy sorting through the files again. I waved at her. "Take all the time you want, sweetheart."

I thought I heard her grunt, but then she was gone. I heard the outer door close.

For the next couple hours, or so, I was engrossed in the files. I had a pad and pencil and tried to make notes about stuff, but it was all a big mess. Then there was that damned Vicodin, but it did keep the pain within tolerable limits, if tolerable limits meant getting a blow-job from some crazy Goth broad with sharpened teeth. I was about to give it up as a bad idea when Jenny walked in. She had a thin leather case in her hand. She pulled out some metal thing, flipped it open, and revealed a keyboard and a screen.

"Here," she said. "This is for you. I bought it with the money you gave me."

"What is it?"

"Jesus Christ, it's a laptop. Where have you been?"

I looked down at the front of the tight skirt she was wearing, right about where the wrinkles start. Then I looked back up at her.

"Doesn't look like any lap top I've ever seen, and I've seen a lot."

She made that exasperated sound. "Here, give me all this crap. I'll try to enter it all in some kind of order. You go do something constructive. I'll screw around with the machine."

"Can I watch?"

Like I said, Jenny has the best laugh in the world.

"No, you can't, and I still expect my back pay."

Then *I* laughed. "Like hell. That gadget is *your* boy-friend. Leave me the hell out of it."

She stared at me.

"Oh, all right, go take it out of the safe—and be sure to sign for it." She was walking out when I said, "What's that thing on the floor in front of you?"

"Where?" she said as she stooped over to look. She stood straight up again fast when the flash went off. She whirled around and I showed her the phone.

"You were right." I winked at her. "This is a helluva gadget."

⌘

I must have still been weaker than I thought, because I really needed Jenny's help to negotiate the steep staircase. I was getting fed up with this shit.

I was too tired to make any decisions, so I just popped into a pizza joint for an early dinner and grabbed a taxi home. I was sort of hoping that Wanda would show up, but I spent the night alone, grappling with all the shit about Julie and our non-relationship, and the terrible danger she was in, and how I couldn't do a goddamned thing about it, that I had been trying to push out of my mind.

The pot made it worse. I wanted a drink, but my head was still spinning from the Vicodin and I didn't relish getting my stomach pumped, supposing that anyone would know, then I thought about the phone, but I stayed away from the bar.

Shit.

My last thought before the nightmares was *Orgies in the mayor's mansion?*

CHAPTER 7

When I got to my office in the morning, Jenny was sitting hunched over her desk. A bluish light bathed her face in an eerie glow.

"Why don't you turn on the goddamn lights? We can afford to pay the electric bill now. You'll ruin your eyesight staring at that thing."

She waved a pretty hand at me with all the grace of a ballerina. "Shut up. I'm concentrating."

"On what?"

"On trying to make some sense out of this mess you call files." She looked up at me with that pissed-off-teacher look. "Can't you be orderly at all? Honestly, trying to figure out what's important in this mess is driving me nuts."

"You work for me, so you can't have too far to go anyway."

I loved that laugh.

"I don't work on orderly," I said, "I work on instinct. Sooner or later something clicks and then the pieces all fall into place."

"Yeah, yeah, I've heard it all before. This gadget here can get you closer to your instincts faster, but I have to know what's really important. Look, come around behind me."

"Should I bring my phone?"

"Shut up and get back here."

I shuffled over and had a moment's urge to aim the camera down her cleavage, but it was obvious that she really wasn't in the mood for joking around, so I didn't. Her elbow was too close to my nuts anyway.

"Look, I've set up categories. Like here, names of women known to have had sex with the mayor, and, over here, names of women known to have had sex with Lippincott, you know, the guy who owned the landfill. And I have other columns for other players."

"I'm impressed," I said with a straight face, "is this what they call computer porn?"

I got her to laugh again.

"Look, I need you to work with me on this. They're your instincts anyway."

I could see what she was driving at, but it would have to wait.

"Get on the horn and rent us a car for the day. A compact."

"Why, where are we going?"

"Up to Camp Fukamuk. Until now I've been concentrating on Maureen, but she's dead and hopefully Julie's alive. I want to look around up there, just to see if any—" I caught myself, "—anything jumps out of the wood pile."

My mother once washed my mouth out with soap for using that "n" word. Ironically, I suppose, I had said it to Henry. The fact that he'd called me a *kike* first I didn't bring up. It wouldn't have mattered. She belonged to the generation that was still supposed to shut up and take it. Still and all, whenever I felt myself about to use it, I could taste soap. Too bad she's dead. She'd need a whole cabinet full of bars to clean up my filthy mouth.

I left Jenny to make the arrangements, and sat down at my desk. I called Frank to see if there was anything new. There wasn't. I told him where I was going and hung up. Usually, no news is good news, but I had my doubts about now. It didn't fit with any kidnapping I'd ever heard about. There was still no ransom demand. I broke out in a cold sweat thinking about it.

Maury had sworn that he was only in it for his dick's sake. And I was inclined to believe him. He was really just interested in keeping his kosher salami shiny, even if it took a lot of *shiksas* to shine it up.

"I can't stand any of that political shit," he said, "but Wagner and Maureen knew the hottest babes in town, and it was free. I've got mine and I'm happy here. The only thing that would get me involved is if some assholes tried to run me out of town. Ain't nobody seems to be interested in that, though," he said with a laugh.

He did come up with something interesting when I pressed him.

He'd been walking by one of the bedrooms when he heard an argument between Wagner and Maureen. "Wagner seemed really pissed. He was yelling at her to stop leading some guy on because he wasn't interested in bucking the council on his petition. I don't remember it exactly, but I remember him yelling 'I don't give a flying fuck how much he's up to by now. The answer is no. Drop it.'"

"Got any idea who they were talking about?"

"Not a clue."

Henry was just in it for the fucking too. When I mentioned that I was surprised he was playing around on Virginia. He just laughed. "Hell, she was invited but she said, and I quote, 'I don't want nothin' to do with them disgustin' honkies, with or without clothes on.'"

"And she didn't mind you going on your own?"

Henry has the most infectious guffaw. "Hell, why should she mind? Whenever I go to an orgy, she's bangin' the gardener, big gorgeous hunk of Mexican cucumber. I hired him just for her. She bangs him when I'm not at orgies too."

"I thought you two had a pretty good sex life."

He just smiled. "We still do, but now, in addition to *our* sex life, I have my sex life and she has hers. It works for us."

When I asked him if he had any petitions in front of the City Council, he just looked blank. "Why do you ask?"

"Maury Cohen overheard a fight between Wagner and Maureen. About that, he said, she was cozying up to somebody and that she should stop."

He thought for a while. "Well, I dunno about that, but I remember that Maureen had been balling Dave Bellamy…oh, five out of seven, and then she just put him back into the regular rotation."

Not really much, but a possible avenue of investigation. "From grains of sand, mountains are built." I read that somewhere.

℘℘℘

The car arrived in about half an hour. The kid who brought it drove us back to their office to fill out the paperwork. I guess he was the talkative sort.

He smiled at me through the rear-view mirror, his face exuding good cheer. "Going on a trip?"

"Yup," Jenny said, "we're going to have a romantic picnic in the country."

"And then we're gonna fuck like bunnies on the grass," I said.

The smile flew from his face and landed on mine. He never said another word. Lucky for him, it was only a few minutes to the office on Tenth. I thought Jenny was going to choke.

"Are you all right, sweetie?"

I was very solicitous, but all she did was choke some more. She refused to laugh until we were settled alone in the car. You should have seen her in the office, bouncing from one foot to the other. She finally asked where the bathroom was.

God help the poor souls who had to bring us stuff. They'd be all right if they just kept their traps shut. We made a good comedy team. Unfortunately, insults went out with Don Rickles. Nowadays, we'd likely be sued.

Jenny had to drive. The way my head was spinning, I'd have had us up a tree in no time. Camp Wenatchee was about three hours from the city, up in the hill country. Once we left the hundreds of subdivisions filled with industrious ants, the drive was beautiful. Problem with all those ants, their hills all look alike. It's depressing as hell.

Camp Wenatchee was an all-girls camp, which set my sick mind to thinking of it as Camp "Weesnatchee." I'd have to be careful. Best not try to say it at all.

It was the kind of place where all the bigwigs sent their daughters. I wondered how many of the kid's fathers had done Maureen. The thought was disturbing. Poor Julie. I wondered if she knew. I wondered about their mothers too. Maureen was—had been—known as an accomplished muff diver, and after what I'd heard from Maury and Henry, hell, anything was possible. There was a whole shitload of blackmail material, and I hadn't even talked to the other guys yet. Problem was, I was sure that neither Henry nor Maury was the blackmailer, so I was still at square one. I couldn't figure out why Maureen might have suspected them either but, for some reason, I thought about *Murder on the Orient Express,* and I filed away the thought. That Christie dame could sure tell a twisted tale, and truth really could be even stranger than fiction. Or just as unlikely.

The place wasn't what I'd expected. My few miserable summers at camp were spent in ramshackle cabins meant to simulate the rustic hardships of backwoods life. They didn't need to simulate. The fact that we had religious services, and Hebrew lessons too, did not add to my enjoyment. Were any Jews ever really dumb enough to live like that?

This place looked like the set for *Gone with the Wind.* I almost expected to see Vivien Leigh come running down the considerable front stairs. Instead, we were greeted by a tough-looking guy in a suit.

We'd worked out the details in the car. Jenny went on about how we were looking at camps for our lovely and very friendly daughter, Winifred, who'd be fourteen next summer, and were wondering if Camp Wenatchee would be a good fit.

He didn't seem interested and just pointed up the stairs. "Office," he said.

I hate loquacious goons.

She went through it again when we were shown into the camp director's office.

Elizabeth Warden was one of those remarkable people who could be two things at once. In her office, she was prim and proper, her face tight, as though a good laugh would crack it into a million pieces. Later, when she showed us around the camp, she was the jolly director, smiling and laughing and joking with the girls. I was more interested in the few girls I saw, none of whom appeared to be as jolly.

Jenny did most of the talking, which freed me to do most of the looking around. Aside from the antebellum setting, the trophies and pennants and pictures were the same as could be found at any camp. There wasn't a single Hebrew letter to be seen, though.

I also noticed that Warden didn't wear a wedding ring, and she was going on sixty. I'd have given her one, but I'd given it to Jenny. I had one for me too. A good detective is always prepared—like a boy scout. You never know when you'll have to be married.

It never kept the broads in the bars away, though.

I remembered something that King Solomon was supposed to have written about finding loyalty in only one of ten thousand men, and none at all in women. I never pretended to be loyal, so I shouldn't complain about human nature. Still, I looked at Jenny and Wanda, and several more, and thought he was just plain full of shit. Generally, I trusted women more than most men any day.

Then I thought about Maureen. Maybe the exception proves the rule, but somebody once told me that was a logical fallacy. Probably my mother. She was educated. She'd actually managed two years at a women's college before I came along and ruined her life. She never blamed me for it, but *I* did. She should have done more with her brains. I always felt sorry for her.

Director Warden—what a hell of a title, it belongs in a prison—was nothing like my mother, which put me at ease immediately.

"What about security?" I broke into Jenny's babble. "I make a lot of money, you know, and we can't be too careful. Kidnappings, you know."

I was watching her face, and if the word caused any kind of flinch, I couldn't see it. She was obviously still in the dark—or one hell of an actress—an idea that recurred to me when I watched her outdoor performance.

Instead, her eyes lit up. "Oh, and what line of business are you in, Mr. Atkinson?"

"Software engineering. The name is well-known in the industry." My prompt was unnecessary. I knew that as soon as we were gone she'd be looking it up.

Jenny and I had done this before. I kept a list of names from the social and business registers, and we'd just appropriate one and play "Let's Pretend." I almost laughed, thinking about the strange call the Atkinsons were going to get. Their daughter is thirty-four and owns an art gallery in Venice. Italy. On the Grand Canal.

But I kept my face rigid with only the hint of concern that a successful business magnate would have.

"Oh, you needn't worry about that at all," she practically burbled, though her face remained rigid. "We have many wealthy families represented here and security is total. The cost is included in the price. We also have a razor wire fence around the perimeter and regular nightly patrols with jeeps and dogs."

This *was* a prison.

Jenny came to my rescue and drew her attention before I could smirk.

"And exactly what is the price?" she asked, "For a full summer with full services, of course."

Then I nearly choked, but I managed to look unimpressed anyway, and I even said "Hmpf," with a bit of a sneer.

That really got her attention and she rolled out the red carpet. She was already counting the money, but her face never changed all the time she was showing us the various priced rooms.

"Ms. Hyde" appeared the moment we stepped outside, and I wondered if I had actually detected a twitch in Warden, or if it was just my imagination. She became downright effusive as she showed us around "The Campus." There were tennis courts, volleyball courts, a gym, several different small workshops for arts and crafts, and an Olympic-sized swimming pool.

What was missing was a lot of girls.

I asked, and she said they were all mostly out on a field trip to the Natural History Museum with all the counselors. Why they went to camp to go to the city I didn't bother to ask. I'd have just sounded like a smart Alec, and successful businessmen aren't supposed to be smart Alecs, but I really wanted to.

The few girls who remained were playing on the courts and in the pool. There were none in the gym that was outfitted with all the best equipment and a basketball court.

"Why do the girls look so listless?" Jenny asked.

"Well, I suppose they miss all the other girls, but none of them wanted to go, so it's their own fault." Then she began her cheerleading routine, trying to whip up some enthusiasm, and I could see that she was tossing anxious glances our way.

"Time to turn some screws?" I looked at Jenny and she nodded. I appeared all innocent. "I understand the mayor's daughter is a camper here. Terrible thing about the mother."

Did she miss a beat?

"Yes, yes it was," and there was a definite hesitation in her voice. "Actually, Julie was called away on some family emergency just a few days before—"

Jenny was always quick. "Ooh, sounds like a mystery," and she turned herself into a little girl. "I love mysteries, don't you? So exciting. Do you think there could be some connection?"

There it was, a definite tic above Warden's right eye, but she was right on it. "Connection to what?"

"Oh, I mean the family emergency. I'm sorry."

"Oh, I doubt it."

"What was the emergency?" I asked.

"Well, I wouldn't be able to tell you that if I knew, but I don't have any idea."

Did that sound rehearsed?

"So, she went home?" I prompted, hoping she'd go on.

"Yes. Some nice young man from the mayor's office came to get her."

"I imagine she was pretty upset."

"I imagine she was. I didn't speak to her. I just watched her get into the car. She waved to me. I imagine she's going through hell, too, to have a mother killed like that." She shuddered.

For real? There was something about her that set my teeth on edge. Instinct or just plain dislike?

There was no way I could ask her about the nice young man without blowing the story, and there was nothing else to be gained, so she escorted us to our car. When she realized it was the compact, her mouth did some funny little things, but she remained polite.

Maybe we were eccentric.

Last thing I saw in the side-view, she was scurrying to look up the Atkinsons, and I laughed. Jenny wanted to know what was so funny so I told her. She didn't laugh.

"That woman's a vulture," she said.

"Anything else?"

"Hard to say. She was certainly uncomfortable when you mentioned Julie, but that could just be a natural reaction, considering the circumstances."

I thought about it. "You're right, but there's still something about her I don't trust."

She finally laughed that wonderful laugh. "Don't worry about it. We can't afford to send Winnie there anyway."

We both laughed for quite a bit of the way home, but I

was still stuck at square one and no closer to Julie.

By the time we got back, it was getting dark, and the pain in my side, which had abated most of the day, came back with a vengeance.

"I need to take some pills."

"Let's find a place to eat."

We did, and I never bothered her about the car that I thought might have been following us all day. Several cars, actually. I'd been inclined to be worried, at first, but then I remembered I'd told Frank where we were going. It was a pretty professional tail, and it smelled like cops.

Jenny dropped me off and went to return the car.

There was a note in my mailbox.

> *Tomorrow.*
> *City Hall.*
> *W.*

Getting to sleep was hell, and I wanted a drink. The whole night I tossed and turned and images of Maureen traded places with images of Julie. Warden showed up regularly too, like the nasty witch in *The Wizard of Oz,* and the flying monkeys looked like little girls. The lion looked more like Bre'er Bear, and he wore a fedora. In the background a voice kept saying, "Kill the Jewboy. Kill the Jewboy."

Again, the pot was no help. I must be getting old.

I had to get off the Vicodin. It was fucking up my head.

CHAPTER 8

I had a landline in my place. It was connected to an old-style phone that I found in some thrift shop. It cost two bucks, and I spent twenty getting it set up to take a regular jack. I loved it, especially the round dial that made that clicking sound as it went around. It reminded me of all those old fifties movies they showed on TV.

Close-up phone, finger dials, music crescendos, dialing stops, music stops, tinny, disembodied voice: "Hello? Hello? Is anyone there?" Cue bass drum.

Maybe I don't have it exactly right, but that's how I remember it. Sue me.

I loved that phone—except when it rings at five-thirty in the morning.

It was Frank. All he said was, "Gramercy Square. Nine o'clock." I guessed I was in hot water. Fuck 'em where they breathe.

After hanging up—that's another nice thing about it, you can slam the receiver down as hard as you want—the first thing I did was turn on the TV news. I didn't usually bother, but I thought there might be something new about Maureen's murder that Frank hadn't said.

The screen was full of pictures of people, all over the

world, killing each other over shit that no high school principle would accept as excuses for a playground fight. There were the usual politicians getting caught with their hands in the till or their dicks in some Jill. It reminded me of Bill Wagner, but there was nothing new about Maureen. They still had no information as to why she'd been at General Hospital, so I turned it off in the middle of the barrage of questions being tossed at the commissioner, and raided the kitchen. I managed to put together a breakfast of stale corn flakes and milk that was just this side of sour and called my doctor.

He agreed to write me scrip for something less head whacking than Vicodin. I gave him Louie's number, and he said he'd call it in right away. He also told me again about taking it easy and reminded me that I had another appointment tomorrow. I stuck my tongue out at him and hung up.

A loud, demanding *"yeeooowl"* alerted me that Roscoe had come to pay a visit, and I opened the window on the fire escape. I didn't know if he had a name, but he looked like a Roscoe to me, and he never complained when I called him that.

He was a big guy. He just sat there outside for a while, looking around my place before he decided to come in, like he'd never been here before and wasn't sure it was safe. It looked like he had a new scratch on his scabby neck, but there were so many it was hard to tell. I didn't know if he actually belonged to anyone, but he made the rounds of the building on a regular basis, cadging handouts from anybody who would bother. He'd lost part of an ear in a fight and his general appearance, from the hairless patches on his tabby coat to the kink at the end of his tail, was nothing at all cat-show-like. He didn't smell really good either, but who the hell would be crazy enough to try to give him a bath? Other than that, he reminded me of me.

He looked like I felt, but I was determined to never take one of those damned Vicodin ever again. I offered him what was left of the milk. He sniffed at it and then gave me that look that said "Are you shitting me?" I dug around in the cabinet and found a can of the cat food he liked. It was the last one. I'd have to remember to get more. I didn't want him thinking I was a cheapskate, or something. He gobbled it down, rubbed against me for a couple of seconds, and I watched his balls disappear out the window.

Fuck you too, I thought. At least, he didn't pretend to love me.

❧❧❧

Mrs. Greenspan was just leaving her flat when I came out. She gave me a big white-haired smile. "And how are you this morning, Mr. Gold?"

"I'm still alive, thank you."

She looked at me. "You'll excuse me for saying so, but you look like crap, you'll pardon my French."

I laughed. "You should never know how I *feel*, Mrs. Greenspan."

"That bad, huh?"

She reminded me of my Great Aunt Ida, the one who always told me I was too skinny. She was fat and jolly, and not too squeamish about words. She'd been a world traveler. I don't think Mrs. Greenspan had ever been out of Central City.

I knew she had a daughter living in Idaho, or someplace, but she never had anything good to say about her so I figured they weren't on visiting terms.

I wasn't important enough to make the news, so she could have no idea of my condition, and I decided not to enlighten her. We rode down in the elevator together. They'd gotten it fixed, but it made a nasty racket and jerked. It was one of those open cage jobs so claustrophobia wouldn't be a factor if it got stuck between floors. Starvation might, though, and I thought I remembered some movie about that.

"Isn't it just terrible about that poor Maureen Wagner?" she said. "Such a lovely woman. Too bad she had to be married to that awful man. I never voted for him, you know. She spoke at our Senior Citizens Club once. Very sweet."

I made some sort of noncommittal humph.

She was carrying her shopping bag and asked if there was anything she could get me. The only thing I could think of was cat food.

"Has that nasty old cat been around again? I was hoping he was dead. You really shouldn't encourage him, you know. God only knows what diseases that mangy thing is carrying around."

I couldn't blame her. A couple of years ago Roscoe got into her place and ate her canary, but she agreed to get me a couple of cans.

"The ones with 'gourmet' on the label," I reminded her. "He doesn't like the others."

She looked at me and laughed. "Screw the little bastard," she said, "you'll pardon my French."

We parted company on the sidewalk, but not before she told me for the thousandth time that I really needed to find myself a wife.

☙❧

I popped into Louie's drug store. There were no other

customers. The early morning crowd had split after lay-ing their bets on the modest book that he ran from the back room. He didn't have a license.

"Hey, Joe." He greeted me with his usual effusiveness, a big smile on his pudgy little face. His bald head reflect-ed the fluorescents on the ceiling and you could even make out the ice-cube tray pattern of the covers. "I've got a prescription for you. Whattsa matter? You sick? This is pretty strong stuff."

"It's for iron deficiency."

He looked puzzled. Then he looked down at the label on the bottle to make sure he had the right one.

"Somebody stuck a knife in me and now it isn't there anymore."

It took him a second, and then he didn't know whether to laugh or look worried, but he always thought I was a great comic, so my pathetic joke got to him first.

"That's a good one," he allowed after he'd collected himself. "Iron deficiency." And he giggled a bit.

You know how in comedy shows, after the laughter dies down, there's always still one guy laughing? That would be Louie—he was my greatest audience.

I filled him in on the details, leaving most of them out.

✤✦✤

I walked over to Gramercy Square. It was only a block from my place so I figured I was being staked-out, as though it would ever have occurred to me that I wouldn't be. Frank was sitting on a bench, feeding peanuts to some ratty-looking squirrel, and some ratty looking pigeons were trying to steal them. He was looking pretty ratty himself, as though maybe he hadn't slept well in his clothes. The pills were starting to take effect, but my head stayed on straight.

"You're in a shitload of hot water," he said as I sat down next to him.

This time, I articulated it. "Fuck 'em where they breathe. I don't work for them anymore, remember. And I told you where I was going."

"Yeah, and we had to scramble to get a tail on you. You're supposed to be coordinating. A half legible statement to me isn't coordinating."

"Yeah, and you nearly scared the crap out of me when I first spotted you."

"You made us?" He sounded surprised.

I just gave him the fish-eye. "Do you think I'm a fucking amateur? Why the hell did I need a tail anyway, for crissakes? I told you where I was going."

He heaved one of those big sighs of his. "Joe, you have no idea what's going on downtown. Everybody's nerves are on edge, and nobody trusts anybody else."

"Sounds like business as usual."

"It's worse, and the mayor's breathing down our necks. Not just through channels either, the sonofabitch calls me several times a day."

"Why you?"

"Because some asshole told him we were good friends. With friends like you, I don't need enemies."

I laughed. "I feel for you, Frankie, I really do. Had any knives stuck in *you* lately?"

He relaxed. "Look, Joe, I hate this as much as you do, but the mayor hates your guts and lets us know, all the time, that he doesn't trust your 'goddamn Jewish ass.' His words exactly."

"Tell me something I don't know." I filled him in about what Wanda had overheard.

He looked worried. "Are you sure about this? Can you trust her? She looks like an empty-headed skirt to me. Lots on the bottom and middle, but nothing up top."

I was offended for Wanda and said so, "She's smarter than that asshole Wagner."

"Then why isn't she mayor, and that's not saying a helluva lot anyway."

When I stopped laughing, I said, "While your boys are on my tail, make sure they look out for him, and a big guy in a black coat and maybe a fedora."

"Who'd wear a coat or a hat in this heat?"

"The guy who shanked me?"

"Jeez. Thanks for all the details. We'll pick 'em right up." He wasn't smiling. Then he got serious. "Have you found out anything useful? I know you've been to see Maury Cohen and Henry Stokes. Why them?"

Damn. I hadn't picked up on that one at all. Probably the Vicodin. Those days were over. I kept my face blank. "I went to see Maury to score some weed, and I had lunch at Henry's. So?"

"You went up to his private office."

"We're old friends. He gave me some Cuban cigars. Want one?"

"Are you trying to bribe me?"

"For what?"

"Then I'll take a couple." I saw dollar bills flying out of my pockets.

"What did you learn at Camp Whatever-the-fuck?"

"That you can't afford to send your kids there."

"Grandkids."

"Whatever. The dame who runs the place is a vulture. My guess is that she's at least a part owner. She seemed nervous when I mentioned kidnapping, but there's nothing I can really put my finger on. She said that Julie waved at her when she left, so it seems that she wasn't worried about anything."

Frank nearly leaped off the bench. "You told her about the kidnapping?"

I laughed. "Relax, for crissakes. We fed her a cock and bull story about wanting to find the proper camp for our daughter, and I just brought up the fact that Julie was a camper there and I wondered about security. I told you, I'm not an amateur."

He sat back down. "Even more it smells like an inside job."

"Correction," I said, "it stinks."

I promised to keep him better informed of my progress and got up.

"The cigars?" he said.

"When the job's done. That'll give you some real incentive to watch my back."

"In that case, I'll take three."

"Fuck you," I said.

❦

I stuck my head into the secretarial pool and got a lot of giggles.

Wanda was there. "Hi ladies," I said, "Just dropped by to give you a look at my handsome puss, y'know, a kind of mid-morning pick-me-up." I closed the door just before a steno pad hit it, thrown in good nature, I hoped, but when you've slept your way through a good part of a bunch like this, you never know.

I waited out in the marble-columned hall for about five minutes until Wanda found me.

"Take me out for coffee," she said, and her eyes were darting around. She was nervous.

"Won't they miss you?"

"It's my break." She smiled. "Your timing was perfect."

We fetched up in the coffee shop across the street.

"Sorry I missed you last night," I said.

She laughed. "It wouldn't have done you any good. I had a date for dinner."

"Anybody I know?"

"No." An impish smile played across her face, like the sun shining through scuddering clouds.

We ordered coffee and she filled me in. She'd gone well above the call of booty duty. She was placing herself in real danger. Yesterday morning, she'd decided to snoop.

"Whenever I got a chance, I ducked into Wagner's office and checked out whatever files he had on his desk and in the drawers. Most of it was unrelated stuff, but there were several files marked Maureen, and one with your name. Well, not your name exactly. Jewboy was scrawled on it. I looked inside and there were some notes. They were all handwritten, and they were all about your movements."

That reminded me that I'd been constipated. The Vicodin, I guessed. "Did you read them?"

"You went to the Casino Club, ate at Original Henry's, went into a cell phone store…Is that right?"

"Right on the money. Was there anything else? Anything with a name on it, like signed by the tail?"

"I looked. There was nothing."

"Well, at least I know he's there. I'll spot him sooner or later." Problem was, "later" was running out—fast. "Did you check the Maureen files?"

"Yeah, but there was nothing in the same handwriting. There was plenty about some pretty hinky goings on. If he's ever indicted for anything, these files are a material witness."

That gave me an idea. "Do you think you could copy them? I know it's a dangerous thing to ask—"

She pulled a file folder out of her bag. "Done."

"Wanda, I love you."

"Don't get carried away," she said, but there was a big smile on her face.

Her break was over. I gave her a big kiss, she gave me the tongue, and we went out. I remembered, just in time, and asked her to see if there was anything today about my visit to the camp. I'd put the folder in my briefcase with the rest of the dynamite. Any elation I might have felt was dampened by the fact that I was still no closer to Julie.

⌘

Jenny was hunched over the laptop. She waved that elegant hand at me as I walked in. "Hang on a minute, and then I'll show you what I've found so far."

"What?"

"Hang on, I said. Go in your office and jerk-off or something while I finish what I'm doing."

"Can I watch you through a crack in the door?"

"Whatever pops your cork."

Yeah, I got it from her. I never turned up my nose at a good expression. So what?

I did watch her through the door, but I had my hands locked behind my head. I was wondering again why I didn't just ask her to marry me. I knew, though. She'd say yes, and I just couldn't do that to her. I was no catch for a girl like her. She deserved a lot better. It doesn't matter to men so much, but women need a lot of dough to grow old gracefully, and I was about as useful as Al Capone's vault in that department.

I hadn't even served enough time for a decent pension, and what I had wouldn't kick in until I was sixty. I wondered if I could will it to somebody. Probably not. I never was much good at reading the fine print.

Crappy union anyway.

"Got it." she yelled, and the sound of triumph filled her voice.

I rushed over. "What? Have you busted the case?" I was feeling a rush of excitement.

She had a blank look, then she laughed. "Oh, no, sorry. I just figured out how to get this annoying little doohickey off the screen. It's been bugging me for the last five minutes."

Computers are the invention of the devil, and I was on much too close terms with him as it was.

She called me over again a few minutes later. What she showed me was all Greek, as far as I was concerned, but she walked me through it. One of her greatest virtues is endless patience. She could probably get a good job as an attendant in a home for the mentally challenged. She was getting plenty of practice with me.

Eventually, though, she just stopped trying to explain it and hit a button on the screen marked "collate." A bunch of letters started rolling over the screen so fast I couldn't read them except for really big ones like ethernet—what the hell is an ethernet? I remembered when I had my tonsils out. Didn't they put something like that over my face?

Jenny once called me a Neanderthal.

"My mother was Jewish," I said. "The Neanderthals lived down the block. Nice family. A bit on the brawny side. Even the kids. But boy, could they play football."

The letters all finally coalesced and the screen came to a stop. Much more of that could have triggered a seizure. I never knew what could do it, but I'd had the problem since my bike got hit by a bus when I was fifteen. The doctors said there was nothing they could give me for it and to avoid situations with stuff that moved around in patterns. Big help. The only good part was that they never lasted more than a few minutes. Jenny knew what to do, but if I was out on the street alone, anything could hap-pen. Maybe there was a bus out there just itching to have another whack at me.

There was a list of names.

"These would be all the women who slept with all of the men on the lists. Shared contacts, in computer talk." There was a hint of pride in her voice.

"Shared around, is more like it," I said. "So what good is it?"

"How the hell should I know? You're the one with the instincts, remember?"

"Is there any way to make a copy?"

"We'd need to buy a printer."

"What do they run?"

"About a hundred bucks for a decent one."

I digested that. "Okay."

From that day on, she never again swung the typewrit-er out and up onto her desk. I checked, but there was no market for used typewriters. Unless it was a really old one. Museums bought those.

I looked over the list, but nothing much jumped out at me. The names were familiar from all the crap I'd heard from Maury and Henry, but that was it. I'd really need to study it at length, but I was beginning to realize that I might be wasting my time.

There was just way too much material, and all of it was suitable for blackmail—against any one of them—and blackmail against any one of them threatened them all. It just didn't make any sense. I toyed with the idea of just forgetting about Connors, Bellamy, and Cooper, but then I figured that you never know what might turn up in the most unexpected places, and went back to figuring ruses to get in to see them. In the end, I decided I'd just let them have it between the eyes. Let's see them try to avoid me then.

"Keep working on this stuff." I told Jenny. "I'll go out and get some sandwiches, and we can eat here. What do you want?"

"Surprise me."

Shit. I'd stumbled into the worst trap imaginable. Chances of success were about on the order of not catching VD when you don't use condoms in whore houses.

I went out and I could feel the smirk digging into my back.

❦

I lucked out. The ham and turkey I brought her was a hit. I had a BLT, and I brought a cupful of fries and some Cokes too. We had a leisurely lunch and talked over the case.

"So, what have we got?" she asked.

"Nothing." I said.

It got quiet again.

"Are you kidding?" she said a bit later, after thinking it over between bites. "Sex parties and orgies going on in the mayor's mansion and we've got *nothing*?"

"What does any of it have to do with Julie's kidnapping?"

That made her think some more. "Maybe it all does."

"Smart girl. I was beginning to think that myself, but it still adds up to a big fat zero as far as finding her."

We both shut up while we were munching on the sandwiches.

"Get on the horn to Walter Connors in an hour," I finally said. "Don't let his secretary put you off. When you get him on the line, tell him my name and tell him I know about him and Maureen Wagner, and that I'm downstairs. Consolidated Steel is about a forty-five-minute cab ride from here." I looked at my watch. "What time do you have?"

"Twelve thirty-five."

I fiddled with my watch. "Twelve thirty-five it is."

She smiled. "Now it's twelve thirty-six."

☙❧

On the cab ride, I went over everything that I knew about Connors. For the next forty-two minutes, I just watched the city go by.

Walter Connors was something of a whiz kid. He started work at Consolidated as an office boy. Now he was the CEO, whatever that was, and he was only thirty-three. I figured he'd be attracted to Maureen. She had that effect on younger men, and their attraction turned *her* on.

His salary was somewhere around five mil, and he got more in bonuses. Probably even more in trades and shit that I understand nothing about. Money turned her on too. That's why she left me.

Consolidated Steel was located a prudent two miles outside the boundary that marked the end of the pollution free zone, and its smokestacks were free to foul the air over the suburbs. The suburbs couldn't vote for Mayor. Besides, a lot of their people worked there.

It was a sprawling complex, and the main office building was one of those ultra-modern jobs, all glass. The reflection off the noonday sun was intense and I had to shield my eyes until I reached the door. I checked my watch. Four minutes.

The lobby was immense, with a central atrium five stories high planted with the kind of shit I remembered from Tarzan movies. It wasn't big enough for an elephant, though, or I'd bet they'd have one.

I walked up to the main desk. The blonde sitting behind it wore a tight-fitting outfit that I later realized was the company uniform. On her it looked good. I almost saluted. In more ways than one. Terrible thing this male urge to procreate. It always reminded me of a Lenny Bruce routine. A guy is in a horrible accident, almost every bone in his body is broken, he might not make it, and he's figuring how to jump the nurse in the ambulance.

"Can I help you sir?"

I checked my watch, and gave her my name. "In three minutes, you're going to get a call from Walter Connors to send me up."

I could see she was a bit confused, but she smiled anyway. Company training, I supposed.

"Do you have an appointment with Mr. Connors, Mr. Gold?"

I checked my watch again. "I will in two minutes." Jeez, I hoped Jenny timed it right otherwise the weird look on her face would be on mine, probably as the two burly guards at the door were seeing me out. I was taking a chance, but I didn't want him to have any time to contact Wagner, if that's what he wanted to do. I just stood there, smiling at her, letting her know that what was inside her uniform wasn't lost on me.

I didn't have to worry. Like I said, Jenny's a gem, and the look on the desk sergeant's face got even weirder as Connors told her to send me up. A minute early. I love it when it works to plan.

It usually doesn't.

Connor's office was much the same as the other two I'd been in recently; big and impressive with a desk you could play tennis on. I wasn't impressed. Jealous as hell, maybe, but not impressed. There was only one picture on his desk, him and a woman and a little girl.

He tried to remain calm, but his eyes were doing a little dance to a tune that said "Oh-shit-oh-shit-oh-shit."

"Who are you, and what makes you think you know anything about me and Maureen?" he tried to be assertive, but since I didn't work for him, I didn't have to pay any attention.

"Maureen told me. She hired me to find out who was blackmailing her."

"Blackmailing?" His eyes went from hunted to confused. Then his face turned blank. "About what?"

"If I knew, somebody would be in a jail cell for killing her by now."

I stared at him until his eyes dropped. Then I let him have it with both barrels, and they flew back up. He didn't even try to hide the naked fear in them—they were watching his whole world tumbling down around his dick.

I'd definitely unnerved him, and he coughed up a lot of details of parties that Maury and Henry never knew about—or never mentioned. In my business, you can't trust anyone, and sometimes you just have to ignore the lies, or you might not have any friends at all. Apparently, though, there was a caste system ruling the orgy circuit and Connors belonged to a higher-class bunch of pokers—no blacks or Jews.

He was terrified that his wife would find out, so I could scratch her as a player. I tried to assure him that if he had nothing to do with anything, he had nothing to worry about. He didn't believe me. I said he was a whiz kid, but right about now he was close to whizzing in his pants.

I hadn't asked Maury or Henry because I knew the answer, but I looked him straight in the eye. "Do you own a rifle, Mr. Connors?"

There was no flinch that I could see, and he answered me immediately. "Yes, I do. Several, in fact. I'm an avid hunter." He got a puzzled look. "Why do you ask?"

Then he caught on and he looked shocked. "Surely, you can't suspect me?"

"Why not?"

I could see that he was struggling for an answer, but he finally just shrugged. I gave him my note pad and told him to describe every gun he owned. He didn't want to do it.

"Suit yourself. So far, I'm the only one in the world who knows anything about this, but I'm sure the police can get a warrant, and then it'll be in all the papers."

The whiz kid caught on right away and wrote everything down—I hoped. Would he be stupid enough to list a murder weapon, though?

"One more thing. Do you have any kind of petition before the City Council, or have you had?"

He looked blank. "What for? I want nothing to do with the city. I'm happy out here."

Scratch Connors.

I gave him my card and still left with a huge smile on my face. Catch them with their pants down, and the aristocracy looks pretty much like everybody else with dirty little secrets to hide.

I saluted "sergeant snatch" on the way out.

On the way back, it finally occurred to me that I'd given him a perfect motive to kill me.

"Goyishe kopf," Rabbi Shulson would say.

I preferred to blame it on the lingering effects of the Vicodin.

෨෨෨

When I got back to the office, Jenny greeted me with a puzzled look. "What on earth did you say to him? Both Dave Bellamy and Warren Cooper have called wanting to speak with you."

"Let 'em sweat. Connors spilled his guts. He mentioned them both. I'm not sure it's even worth talking to them. I've got enough to blow the lid off now, but no laws were broken, so what's the point? Sure, I'd love to take down Wagner, but the rest of them are just a bunch of horny *schmucks*. Big fuckin' deal, so am I. They could run around naked at City Hall too, screwing like monkeys, for all I really give a shit. I'd drop in and watch."

"What about all the deals made under the table using sex as a lure."

"Think of it like a fund-raising dinner with Maureen on the menu."

She laughed and made me feel a little better.

"Unless I can tie any of it to her killer, I've got shit, and I'm still no closer to Julie."

The new pills were starting to wear off, so I popped a couple more. At least my head had stopped spinning. Now if only all the wheels would.

The more I found out, the less I had. I just couldn't make any of it come out straight. I think it was in one of the *Sherlock Holmes* movies. Basil Rathbone says something like when you've eliminated all the rational explanations, you have to go with the irrational, no matter how weird it seems. Something like that. Jenny would know. She's got every book that Conan-Doyle ever wrote.

But what was the "irrational" I was looking for? I couldn't even see anything *rational* unless a bunch of old farts running around in togas or something and screwing everything that moves, is rational. There was even mention of a donkey during a Cinco de Mayo party.

Maureen had the most to lose of anyone but Wagner, I supposed, and there was certainly little chance of her spilling anything, so why did somebody want her dead?

Maybe I needed to turn Sherlock's dictum on its head.

Whoever it was, hated her and wanted her just on the other side of breathing. How rational can you get? But who?

Maybe there was something in the folder I got from Wanda. I decided to go home early and study it.

☙❧

When I got to my place, I found five cans of cat food stacked outside my door. There was a note with them.

This kind was five for a dollar. Screw the little bastard. Pardon my French.

I shrugged. I figured if he was hungry enough, he'd eat it.

If not, screw him. He wasn't exactly my favorite kind of pussy anyway.

I stopped dead.

I had a regular habit of leaving a piece of thread stuck between the edge of the door and the jamb. It was gone.

Somebody'd been here, and I had the only key.

CHAPTER 9

I grabbed a couple of cans in one hand and opened the door. Not much of a weapon but it was better than scraped knuckles. The place was empty. Whoever'd been here was long gone. I checked everything out. Nothing was missing.

I breathed a sigh of relief when I saw the rent money was still there. Problem was, whoever had been checking me out had gotten a good look at all the clippings and photos of Julie that filled a drawer. What would they make of that? Then it occurred to me that it could make me some kind of suspect. Why was I so interested in Julie? If it was the cops, I could be in deep shit. If it was one of Wagner's goons, it could be worse.

I called Frank. He swore that it wasn't the cops.

A few minutes later, I got a call from Wanda. There was a new note in the file about my visiting Camp "Weesnatchee." Wagner's boy had followed us too. After thinking that she could have come by, I called Frank back and told him.

"Your guys missed him," I said. "You're a bunch of amateur fucking assholes." I didn't wait for a reply. I just slammed the receiver down. Then I thought that I'd missed him, too. Or had I? There were so many cars following us, he could have been in any one of them. The tail would have given him cover. I bet he laughed his ass off.

Then I broke into a sweat, thinking that Wagner's info could have come straight from the cops anyway, no matter what Frank said. He might be out of the loop. Being my "good friend" had its downside. What a fucking mess this was turning into.

Whatever the case, I decided that it would be a cold day in hell before I told *them* anything. I was really on my own here. I'd have to keep watching my own back, and I'm a lousy contortionist. L-five, my neurologist said. I got it running after a guy who chased me back with a Harley. The human spine isn't meant to make certain kinds of twists.

The adrenaline rush had made me hungry, so I went back down for a quick bite at Ruby's Snack Shack across the street. Ruby was red-headed and hot, but I never shit where I eat. Her husband Wally, a big brute of a guy, was another consideration.

I asked, but neither of them had noticed any strangers going into my building. The buzzer system had been busted for months, and the front door was as easy to open as a down-on-her-luck hooker.

Back home, I took a good look at the pill bottle. It was one of those for the general illiterates who litter the world. There was a picture of a liquor bottle with a line through it. There was also one of a car, and one of what I assumed was supposed to represent a machine. They had lines through them too. My enforced abstinence would have to continue, but I didn't think that a can of light beer I found in the fridge would hurt. I nursed it through a couple of hours. It was easy. It tasted like piss. It must have been left over from some attempted seduction. I never drink that crap.

I checked over the surveillance notes first. It was all there, including the "hot fucking broad" who was with me. I put that one in my pocket to show Jenny. She'd get a kick out of it. I got up and went to the one window that looked out over the street. There was nobody around who looked suspicious, just a bunch of people on their way home. The alley below the fire escape was empty.

Even though nothing was missing, I still felt like I'd been raped. If I ever found out who it was, I promised myself that I'd shove the nightstick up his ass. I kept it as a memento of my days as a beat cop. It snuggled perfectly in the bottom of my briefcase. I once used it to knock a .38 out of some creep's hand. Then I whacked him on the head. He gave me no more trouble after that. I didn't bother to visit him in the hospital.

There wasn't much new in the Maureen files, but I did find a bill for a twelve-hour donkey rental from Pepe's Happy Animal Farm. That was really about the only actually illegal shit I could find. Maury did supply them with pot, and he said he knew that some of them were doing blow, but there was nothing in writing. I wondered how much I could get for this stuff from whoever'd be running against Wagner in the next election. Most of it wasn't illegal, but it sure was plenty "hinky," to use Wanda's expression. I'd call it as kinky as a cheap hose.

Shit. Right here was enough to blackmail the crap out of them, and it was only a tiny fraction of the rest. I had no difficulty at all seeing Maureen use her vivid imagination on the donkey. I'm sure Pepe got back one happy critter.

"Sweet woman?"

I toyed with the idea of showing the files to Mrs. Greenspan. Then I thought you never know what might turn an old lady on.

With a couple more pills in me, the pain was almost

not there. I'd finished looking through all the files, and I was feeling restless. It was just about the time that things started heating up at Carlene's. I might be able to hear something there, so I put a bunch of tens loose in my pocket, to help clear out my eardrums, and took off for the bar. I didn't bother to put another thread in the door.

ↂ

Carlene called it a "saloon." She thought it sounded higher class, and it did attract a higher class of people who came here to rub shoulders with the down-and-out regulars who, they thought, represented the "underworld."

The place was a dead end for these "underworlders," but Carlene had a heart of gold, and business was good enough for her to hand out a few freebies. I offered her a C-note to keep the liquor flowing, hoping that it might loosen some tongues.

Carlene and I had hit it off right away. The first time I'd been in, years ago, I'd noticed her name embroidered over the pocket on her bulging blouse.

"What do you call the other one?" I asked.

She cracked up.

She was aging well. Her honey blonde hair had turned snow white. It still framed her face with its bushy fullness, and her face looked like a smile had been sculpted on, complete with all those little lines you get from laughing a lot.

She was really surprised when all I ordered was a club soda, so I told her about my knifing. "Just missed my liver," I said. Then I asked her if she'd seen any big guys with black coats and maybe a fedora.

"In this heat?"

Actually, it was almost cold. Carlene had the A/C

turned up full. Heat brought more sales, but she was rich enough now to be able to indulge her comforts.

On the way over, I'd done my damnedest to pick up any shadows, and I thought I might have, but I wasn't sure. Neither of them was in the bar. I laughed to myself. I think this was the first time I was ever tailed by cops and goons at the same time. I hoped they'd bump into each other. Hell, it was even likely they'd know each other. They could even be related.

I wandered about the place for a while, glad-handing and joking with those I knew while some shitty country and western band stunk up my ears. At full volume. When I thought everyone was well-enough lubricated, I started asking innocuous-sounding questions.

I'd stopped at Freddie's and bought a pack of Pall Malls. Nothing like sharing your smokes to gain instant friendship. Sharing was the key word, and I told myself it was for work.

I hoped I wouldn't fall off the tobacco truck, but it's a tough drug to kick. They say that alcohol's worse, but I don't intend to find out. I hoped that I'd give away enough to get something.

I spotted Pruneface at the bar. His real name was Clyde McPherson and he'd been a fighter once, but he'd taken too many gloves in the face. He looked kind of like Pruneface in the Dick Tracy comics, and that's what everyone called him. He didn't mind, as long as you bought him a drink. To me he looked more like cauliflower face, but that's too hard to say. Even the underside of society has its poets.

He hung out at Carlene's most nights, but I knew that he made the rounds of seedy bars during the day. I'd gotten some good stuff from him on several occasions, so I ambled over. I almost had to yell above the noise of the band.

"Hey, Pruneface." I gave him my biggest, friendliest smile. "How's it hangin', buddy?"

He looked at me like he didn't know me. He always did. With everybody. It took a bit of time, but, eventually, the wheels started turning and a smile lit up his face, by which I mean that a wide slit appeared at the bottom of the cauliflower head. "Hey, Joe, whaddaya know?"

"Less than I'd like to." I stretched out the Pall Malls. "Here. Kill yourself."

"Y'know, Joe. I've been trying to do that for years," It didn't sound like a joke.

He reached out a hand. It was shaky. I finally just pulled one out and gave it to him. I lit it for him, and lit my own. For a second, it felt like the Vicodin had come back. Too bad it isn't like this every time—smoke a few a day and you're soon smoking a pack or more, and you still can't get that feeling back.

Pruneface wasn't one for chewing the fat. I think chewing anything was tough for him, so I got right down to business. "Heard anything about Maureen Wagner?"

He started to say something when the band hit a louder spot and I didn't hear it. Reading his lips was out of the question.

"What?" I yelled.

"I said, too bad. Such a gorgeous dame."

"Any scuttlebutt?"

"Jeez, I'm thirsty," he said.

I got Randy's eye and beckoned him over. "Give Pruneface whatever he wants. On me."

"Well, that's mighty nice of you, Joe. I won't take advantage." He turned to Randy. "Make it a Haig and Haig. Neat."

I couldn't even afford to drink that shit. For a second, as Randy was pouring the delicious honey-colored nectar, I thought I might join him. Hell, I wasn't driving or using any machines, and I could put it on an expense account. Then I thought about Julie. I needed to stay sober and healthy. I should have kept that in mind a little longer.

You know, that shit is meant to be savored. Like brandy. Pruneface just poured it down his throat—the glass almost disappeared in his mouth. Then he looked at me like he'd like another.

"What have you heard about Maureen Wagner?"

He looked around, then he beckoned me closer. "They say she was a slut."

Silence hung in the air between us. Except for the band.

"And?" I finally said.

He looked puzzled. Then he seemed to get it. "That's it. They say she was a slut."

I should've had the drink.

"Wasn't there anything else? Anybody have anything particular to say? Like, y'know, names? Places? Personal experiences?"

He thought about it for a while. Then he shook his head. "Nope. Just that she was a slut."

I looked at him for a while. I pulled out a sawbuck and laid it on the bar. "Knock yourself out," I said. I knew I shouldn't have.

"Y'know, I once did that once." His eyes kind of got a distant look in them.

"Nice seein' ya, Pruneface, stay healthy."

I got out of there before he could launch into the account of his third-round self-knockout against Floyd Mays. It's a pretty funny story, but I know it by heart. Everybody does. The bookies couldn't figure out who to pay off, so, for the only time in the long and illustrious history of wagering, they just gave everybody back their dough.

I spotted "Doc" spotting me. He beckoned me over to

the small table he was sitting at, nursing a glass. "Doc" had once been a regular doctor. He'd even had a practice on Central Boulevard, above some of the poshest places to throw your money away in town. He'd also had a wife and kids.

He'd also been nailed for performing illegal abortions on the daughters of some of the top society folks in town. The scandal didn't die down for months, but he managed to stay out of prison. Now he has no wife and no kids, no office on Central Boulevard, though the shops are still there, no medical license, and no money. He did have a two-day stubble.

"Hey, Joe, I heard from an old friend of mine at General that he saw your name on the OR list. What happened?"

I offered him a smoke. When he was a doctor, he'd advised his patients against smoking. Now, he grabbed one whenever he could. He should have advised them against fucking.

"Somebody slipped me the shiv at Arturo's." I saw him grimace. "Just missed my liver."

"Did he get an artery?"

"Just nicked it, I guess."

He studied me. "You're a lucky man to be walking the streets."

I had my opening. "Y'know, I was just leaving the hospital when Maureen Wagner got shot. At first, I thought it was meant for me."

"Why are people trying to kill you? You've always been a gentleman in my book."

I shrugged. "Somebody doesn't share your opinion, I guess, and I have no idea why."

Ha, ha.

"Did you see Maureen get it?"

"Nope. I was too busy ducking.

"Terrible thing, though," he said, "a woman that beautiful deserved to be sculpted in marble."

"Well," I said, hoping I wasn't being too crass, "she's stretched out on some anyway."

He laughed, but the empty look in his eyes didn't change.

"Can I get you a drink?" I said, knowing the answer. Does a Pope shit in the woods?

I looked around. Carlene was on table duty. I called her over.

True to his former station in life, "Doc" had the requisite tastes. He looked at me and the plea in his eyes was enough to make a grown man weep. It's a good thing I'm not a grown man.

"Do you know how long it's been since I've had a taste of Glenlivet? If you wouldn't mind, Joe, I'd surely appreciate it."

How the hell can you ignore such a gentlemanly plea to get hammered? What the hell, Wagner was paying for it, or the folks he shook down were. It didn't much matter to me. Most of them were no better than he was anyway.

"Two Glenlivets," I said to Carlene. I don't think I'd ever tasted Glenlivet before, and I threw caution to the winds. Fuck it, I thought, if I die, I die.

It was so worth it, as the kids say. I started to feel better than I had in days. I should have stopped at one.

"Doc" knew the proper way to drink fine whiskey. He took a sip, rolled it around in his mouth, and finally swallowed. For a second there, I thought he'd spit it out, like those wine drinking kind-of-sewers. I don't have a very sophisticated palate. I can tell the difference between Mogen David and Pussy-filet, or whatever the hell it's called, but that's about it. Champagne always gave me a headache, tough, two-fisted lush that I am.

I steered the conversation back to Maureen.

He asked me if *I* had any idea why she was at the hospital. Then he said, "I'll tell you, Joe, I hear so many stories. Some say she was going to get an abortion. Others say she had cancer and was getting regular treatments. Then there are those who say she was having an affair with someone in the hospital."

He was about a dozen years late, but he had the last one right.

I shrugged. "Damned if I know. Hey, Doc, you get around." He didn't but I thought I'd stroke his ego a little. God knows he needed it. "Heard anything interesting about her?"

"Interesting? Salacious would be more like it. Word is she was a slut."

Jeez, tell me something I don't know. In fact, that's all I was able to glean from everyone I talked to who'd heard anything at all. After a few more drinks and exhausting the Pall Malls, what I found out was she was a slut. Sometimes they used the word "whore" but the inflection was the same. Everybody would have liked to have balled her themselves, though. Even Carlene, who also knew nothing.

Doc used the Yiddish word *schtup*, which was, by far, the most expressive of all the epithets I heard.

I'd had it. I said goodnight to Carlene and walked out into the hot, humid air of the real world.

The lights went out, and I could feel myself falling.

⌘

The shitty doctor kid didn't even try to hide the disapproval in his eyes.

How I made it to the appointment on time was only because I spent the night on a bed in the ER.

He smelled the alcohol on my breath. I know. I'd seen

that look before on people who'd gotten too close to me. "Fucking Wino," it said.

I always wanted to tell them that I never touched the stuff, but it was never really worth the bother. Wine, Whisky, Beer, it was all the same shit when you came right down to it, and I had. Many times.

He took the bandage off the gash in my forehead and looked at it. Then he looked at me. Disapproval had turned to disgust.

"How did this happen?" he almost barked. I remembered my mother, aunts, teachers, and cops who'd had the same look and about the same inflection. I was too tired and hungover to lie.

"I passed out leaving Carlene's Saloon."

"Terrible."

"No," I said, "it's really a pretty good place. You should try it sometime."

"It's terrible that you ignore sound medical advice to go off bingeing. You're supposed to be getting plenty of bed rest. I told you that any activity could open the internal stitches. You could bleed out and be dead before you know it."

I gave him my most sardonic look. "Sounds like a good way to go."

I know he wanted to laugh, but he didn't. Tight-ass.

"You're lucky this only needed a couple of stitches. They say that God looks out for fools and drunks."

"Nope. It was Fat Eddie who saw me falling and got in the way."

Damn. I know he wanted to laugh. Backup was called for. Where was Louie when I needed him? This medico was one tough nut.

I wondered if they had special classes for it in med school. Along with how to pad the bills so the administration took the heat when the shit hit the fan.

"And drinking while taking this medication could give you a heart attack."

"*Now* you tell me?" I gave him the look that said he was the lowest of the low, and he didn't deserve to reproduce.

He laughed. Finally.

"Look. I'm serious. You've suffered a dangerous injury. You've got to take it easy."

I shook my head. "I can't. I have a job to do."

"Well, it can't be a matter of life or death now, can it?"

He shut up when he looked into my eyes. He didn't ask. He just dressed my forehead and all he said was, "Try."

෴

Jenny was hunched over the laptop again when I finally dragged myself up the last steps. I felt like I'd gone a couple of rounds with Pruneface. I wasn't sure who'd won.

She whistled. "What in god's name happened to you?"

"I was having wild sex, and I fell off the bed."

She just looked at me. "Next time, tape your other hand to the headboard."

I was feeling too crummy to laugh.

"I was doing research at Carlene's and I guess I got drunk. Passed out. They told me that Fat Eddie broke my fall, or it could have been a lot worse."

"Research?" She had that who-do-you-think-you're-kidding look.

"Yeah, research. I thought I might find something out from the local rumor mill. I did. I didn't plan to get drunk, though. It just sorta happened."

"What the hell were you drinking?"

"Four—no, five shots of Glenlivet."

"Glenlivet?"

"That's a scotch."

"How much of the ten grand did you go through?"

"Don't be funny, only a few hundred. What the hell's that?"

I was pointing at the black box on her desk that I'd just now noticed. Some detective.

"That's our new printer."

"Printer? Isn't it supposed to have gears or wheels or something?"

She searched my face for any sign of a laugh, but I played it straight. She didn't buy it.

"I know you're backward, but you aren't that backward."

"Wanna bet? How does it work?"

"Well, this end of this wire plugs into the printer, here, and the other end plugs into the computer, there."

I was fascinated. "Is that legal in this state?"

She ignored me and opened the top of the printer. She put in several sheets of paper and hit a key on the computer. Nothing happened, at first. Then there was a whirring noise, and then it sounded like something was flying around loose inside, but Jenny didn't look worried, so I figured it was all part of the show. Suddenly, one of the sheets of paper looked like it was being sucked down into quicksand, or something, but it was fighting all the way. Then it came out the bottom with writing on it.

"Yeah," I said, "I've seen 'em before. Marty at the butcher shop has one like it. He puts in a hunk of meat and it comes out all sliced. But his doesn't write anything."

She gave me that fake resigned look, but I could see her lower lip was starting to tremble.

"What did you find out?"

"Where?"

Any moment now.

"At Carlene's, for crissakes."

Almost there.

"Maureen was a slut."

Did I mention that Jenny has the best laugh in the world?

CHAPTER 10

I tried to get some work done, but I was still restless. There were two guys I hadn't interviewed yet. I was skeptical that I'd find out anything new…well, substantive anyway, but like I said, I'm obsessive about my work and I like to dot the "Is" and cross the "Ts." I'd hate to miss something because I was lazy. And there was Dave Bellamy who'd been put on hold by Maureen. Today was also the last day that Wagner had given me, and if I didn't come up with something, there might not be a tomorrow—for me or Julie.

Why the hell hadn't there been a ransom demand? Nothing made any sense.

I told Jenny to keep working with my notes. I decided to pay a visit to Dave Bellamy. *Slumber Well*'s main store was only a few blocks away and I figured he'd be there.

His grandfather had been a rag peddler who sold old, but usable mattresses from his horse-drawn wagon. His father developed the business, and now Dave Bellamy was the undisputed bed and mattress king of Central City. My guess was that all the orgy mattresses came from his warehouse—at a discount, of course. No one could say that Bill Wagner wasn't careful with the taxpayer's dough, as he reminded us at each election.

Mrs. Greenspan still wouldn't vote for him. She had his number. She called him a *gonnif,* which is an old Yiddish expression meaning "Don't take your eyes off him, and hang on to your wallet."

Slumber Well's main store occupied half a city block and the first three floors of an older, forty-five story office building. A lot of the offices it held were of the same kind as the shops below Doc's old practice, which was only a couple of blocks away. They were places where people went to throw their money away only not on clothes and jewelry, but on stocks, businesses, and shit I've never even heard of. The financial headlines are mostly gibberish to me. The only words that stand out clearly all mean *gonnif.*

Or *drerd,* which, loosely translated, means your money's dead and it's burning in Hell.

The first thing you saw when you walked in was acres of mattresses. Literally. His ads all said so. He used to say how many mattresses, but he was badly outpaced by McDonald's, and the numbers got too big for the sign, so he just switched it to "acres." I had no reason to doubt him.

The entire main floor was almost all beds, nearly touching each other, with just enough room for the customers to walk between them. It was surreal. The place was fairly crowded, and there were people wandering around, some lying down to test them out. For some reason, it reminded me of when we had to go and pick out my mother's casket.

Hanging above, and ringing three sides of this enormous space, mercifully leaving the two-story windows clear, were a warren of horizontal bins, each of which held a stack of mattresses. There was a catwalk behind them from which they could pull out whatever mattress was needed.

The place seemed so gigantic, that you'd almost expect to see a high wire act. They could do it without nets. Terrific test for the mattresses. They could fall on purpose. I wondered if he'd pay me for the idea. Then I wondered if Maureen ever tried to talk him into holding an orgy here. So far, no one had mentioned it.

The offices were on the third floor, and there was a private elevator, so I didn't have to ride up and down with the mattresses. The elevator opened out into a plush carpeted suite. The sudden change in volume felt like I had just taken off in a plane, or like I'd just shoved ear plugs in. Weird.

Dave's wife Melanie was also the receptionist and his private secretary too. She was that when he married her. The story heated up the wires for weeks. It was a particularly vicious divorce but, in the end, they were free to wed. It cost him a bundle, but he managed to hang onto the business and had more than made his money back. It was rumored in the gossip columns that he was negotiating to buy the building.

The gossip columns. You'd be surprised at how much actual dirt gets dished, well-camouflaged behind the banter. That's how I know everything I know about Dave Bellamy. What surprised me was that his name was on Maureen's list at all. There was never a hint of scandal or problems between Melanie and him, and they did make the rounds of the clubs.

They had three teenage kids and were beginning to look it, which was what endeared them most to people, I suppose. Their lurid past had been buried in the good old American tradition of sin and redemption. Once in a while, I'd catch one of their commercials on TV. They always featured the whole family and were kind of funny, in a way.

The Bellany family: good old down-home folks, just like you, even though you aren't rumored to be buying a forty-five-story office tower. And, they are seriously concerned about you getting a good night's sleep too. Presumably so that you can work hard and make enough dough to graduate to the Super DeLuxe Swedish Miracle Bed. You used to be able to buy a car for what those babies cost.

I gave Melanie my card. She didn't stiffen.

"Do you have an appointment, Mr. Gold? I don't recall the name."

"I do now. Just give him a call."

She looked at me kind of funny. "Perhaps if you tell me what this is in regards to…"

I gave her a big smile. "It regards some private business that I am not at liberty to divulge. Now please give Mr. Bellamy a ring, would you. He's expecting me."

She looked doubtful, but she didn't seem particularly worried about anything. She hadn't recognized my name so he hadn't told her about me. Scratch another player?

She finally picked up the phone and buzzed his office.

"There's a Mr. Gold, a private investigator, here to see you?" There was a pause. "Hello, did you hear me?" She looked puzzled for a few seconds, then she nodded and put the phone down. "You may go right in, Mr. Gold."

I guess I was wrong about his expecting me. He nearly pounced on me the second I got the door closed.

"Are you out of your mind coming here? My wife doesn't know anything about this. How the hell am I going to explain this to her? She thinks we have no secrets."

I looked at him and shrugged. "That's your problem. I'm investigating the murder of Maureen Wagner. If your wife kills *you*, I'll investigate *your* murder too. Fair enough?"

He wasn't in a laughing mood, but he got out of my face and retreated behind his desk. I wondered if he kept a gun there.

He was jowly and paunchy with a noticeable middle-age spread. He was also thinning on top, but he had the good sense not to do a comb-over. He was short and looked nothing like a king, unless you remember that comic strip, *The Lil King*. Did *he* smoke cigars?

Bellamy did and the smell of Havana filled the room. I was finding it hard to breathe. He had one in his mouth now, but it had gone out. He made a big show of lighting it, probably trying to psych me out and show that he wasn't nervous. I wasn't buying. His hands didn't shake, though. I'll give him that.

He took a few puffs to get it going good, and then he pointed it at me. "So, what do you want to know? From what Connors told me you already know everything. There was no need to come here and fuck up my life. I run a respectable family business."

I didn't laugh, but I wanted to, real bad. I just said, "Give me a break. It wasn't my dick doing the cha cha with Maureen and the rest."

He didn't have any comeback for that one. Instead, he reached into his top drawer. Oh crap. When do I hit the deck?

The shot never came. He handed me a sheaf of papers. "Here's a list of all my weapons. I collect hand-guns."

There were at least five or six pages. "Any rifles here?"

"No, I hate rifles. I was a sniper for six months during Desert Storm. I never want to fire a rifle again. Never even want to see one."

For a few seconds, the fear in his eyes was replaced by

something else, a hurt that nothing could eclipse but death. I know. I'd seen it before, sometimes in my bathroom mirror. But he was a marksman. Could Maureen have been in his sights? Was it he on that rooftop?

I decided not. He wasn't a killer anymore. The aversion therapy that had been his job had cured him.

Still, I have been known to be wrong at times.

I asked him to tell me everything he could about the shenanigans in the mansion. There was nothing new. His accounts jibed with Connors' but they'd been in contact.

I took a chance. "How about the petition you wanted to put to the Council?"

He didn't flinch, but he was curious. "How the hell did you find out about that?"

"I'm a detective. It's my job to find out about things." I heard that in a Humphrey Bogart movie once, and I use it every chance I get.

"No big deal. I wanted to expand, and I hired a consultant who told me the best location would be the northwest corner of One Hundred Forty-Third and Jackson, on the South Side. I had convinced all the other property owners to sell, but there's a fuckin' church that takes up most of the block, and they were adamant. Maureen was on my side, and she'd sweet-fucked me up to half a mil, but Wagner didn't want to fight the church. Then this latest crappy recession hit, and I couldn't afford it anyway, so I just dropped it."

Nothing here but a grain of sand. I gave him my card. "Call me if you think of anything else."

He hesitated before taking it. "What are the chances of none of this ever getting out?"

I thought for a bit. "Probably about the same as a down-and-out drunk's chances of getting a shot of Glenlivet."

I flashed Melanie a big smile as I left. I'd have given anything to be a fly on the wall.

∽∾∽

It was a twenty-minute ride on the subway to Warren Cooper's offices at BO James. The name seemed especially apt for a brokerage firm caught up in the latest financial scandal. Cooper was not under indictment, but the buck stopped at him anyway. He was probably finished as chairman of the board, and it would probably be a while before anyone else would hire him. The shit-smell would have to go away first. In today's highly moral business culture, that would probably be about two months.

Why any of these guys actually gave a crap about working at all escaped me. They were all richer than god. It was probably the power. It's as big an addiction as heroin—or Maureen. You had to really enjoy the assholes' groveling.

I'd asked Bellamy to call him, so I breezed right in. Cooper was sitting behind his desk. He didn't get up to shake my hand. That was okay with me, I knew where it had been.

About fifty, he looked every inch the successful stockbroker, square-jawed, hair closely trimmed and mostly still black, perfectly manicured fingernails, a dark-blue suit that cost two grand at least, and a red silk tie.

Hard blue eyes.

"Why are you here? I can't tell you anything you haven't already heard."

"Curiosity. I wanted to look into your eyes and ask why a guy like you, with the world by the balls, would be so fucking stupid as to get involved with Maureen Wagner and go traipsing around in fuck parties with her and that fat slob husband of hers."

He dropped his eyes for a second, but only for a second. When he raised them, they were full of pain. "I don't even know anymore. I don't know anything anymore. First, I'm knifed in the back by my employees, then my fucking wife takes off with the kids, and now this."

I almost felt sorry for him. "I can't speak for your employees or your wife, but you aren't the first asshole who got led down the garden path by his dick."

He was silent for a while, realizing he wasn't going to get too much sympathy from me. When he spoke again, he was subdued. "I don't suppose there's any chance of keeping this out of the papers, is there?"

"That depends on whether or not there's any connection to Maureen's killing. If there isn't, you may all be home free. Tell me what you know. Don't leave anything out. Oh. Do you own a rifle?"

"I never fired a gun in my life."

He told me everything he knew and, as he went on, it seemed like a load lifted off of him.

"Is there anything at all besides this that you can tell me?" I asked when he was finished with his pathetic recital of booze, babes, and soaked mattresses. "Anything at all?"

He thought about it for a bit. "There is something. I don't know if it's important, but I was on the can off one of the bedrooms when a couple of guys came in. One of them was saying something about having the girls lined up for a big party. I don't remember much beyond that I was pissed not to have been invited. He said something about everybody taking their own cars but don't make a caravan out of it, so I figured it was someplace out of town. That's all I remember."

I should have spoken to him first. *Why is it that you never find what you're looking for until the last place you look?*

⌀⌀⌀

Jenny greeted me when I got back to the office. "I can't make any heads or tails of all this crap. You should just toss it out."

"Go ahead," I said, "we've been barking up the wrong tree."

She gave me a hard look. "What did you find out?"

"It's just a hunch, but see what you can dig up about that Warden broad."

"Why?"

"Never mind for now, just do it. I've got an itch and it needs to be scratched."

Did I say Jenny was a gem—she's a fifteen-carat diamond. Within an hour, she'd been on the phone with a friend of hers in criminal records—I couldn't trust the cops on this one. What she found put a whole new slant on things.

Elizabeth Warden, aka Georgina Spelvin, had done time for procurement and running a brothel in San Francisco.

Bingo.

How does an ex-con get to be the director of a camp for the aristocracy? For girls, yet? Really sloppy vetting—or something worse? There were still a lot of missing pieces, but I was sure that when they all came together, they'd show that the Warden had graduated to kidnapping.

I filled Jenny in on what I suspected.

"I have to figure a way to get back up there without the cops, or anyone else, knowing it."

She thought about it for a while. Then she went to the shelf where she kept all the detective novels. She checked titles and finally pulled one out. She flipped the pages.

"Here, I thought I remembered this. Dick Danger has the same problem."

"Dick Danger? Are you shitting me? That's a name?"

She gave me that what-a-cretin look. "Didn't you ever hear of Colin Hamilton? He wrote ten Dick Danger mysteries, and they were all best-sellers."

Dick Danger? Jeez, you never know what the public will swallow. Sounded like the Hardy Boys to me.

"He got a million bucks a book, and that's not counting royalties."

Maybe I should quit the business and write detective novels. I'm sure I could come up with something better than Dick fucking Danger.

Maybe not.

"So, how does this dick solve the problem?"

"He puts on women's clothes and walks out of his building in the middle of the night."

"I'm not putting on a dress."

"Got any other ideas?"

I didn't. But where was I going to get women's clothes? Then I remembered that Big Donna kept a set of hers in my closet. I'd first met her on a flight to Seattle. I was going to help a buddy on a case. The airlines had relaxed their standards or she would never have gotten a job as a flight attendant. She was as tall as I am but curvier. On her, it looked spectacular.

She worked the West Coast routes mainly, on the rare occasions that she flew into Central City, she'd drop by for a romp. She kept some clothes in my closet so that she didn't have to pack extra in the piddling hand luggage they were allowed.

Sometimes I think I'm really sick. The thought of putting on her underwear was starting to give me a hard-on, but that could have been mostly because I visualized where she wore it.

"Got it." I said. "If you don't hear from me by two o'clock tomorrow, call Frank and fill him in."

She had that frightened look on her face, but she didn't say anything.

❧❦❧

Putting on Big Donna's clothes wasn't as easy as I'd thought it would be—all those hooks, buttons, and miscellaneous fasteners. I left off the underwear, but I stuffed the bra with paper towels. I had no intention of remaining in her clothes any longer than necessary, and I packed my own in a shopping bag.

I felt like a total asshole trying to put on lipstick. There was always some in the bathroom cabinet. How the hell did they do it without looking like clowns? It was nighttime and it was dark, so I figured I could get by.

There was no way I was going to try to get into her high heels, but there was a pair of flats that actually fit me. They'd have to do. I wrapped my head in a scarf that somebody else had left.

It was close to midnight when I went out, trying to look as nonchalant as a hooker coming from a house call, not that anyone but a guy with advanced cataracts could see me as a hooker—more like the cleaning lady. I walked a few blocks just to make sure that I wasn't followed. I got a really funny look from the cabbie I hailed down.

"Where to, buddy?" He was trying to keep from laughing.

"Budget car rental on Sixteenth, and take your time while I change clothes. There's a ten-buck tip if you don't watch." At least I seemed to have fooled my tails.

"Costume party?"

"Something like that."

The guy at the car rental place looked at me real funny too, but I had no trouble renting a car. I stopped in the bathroom to pee. The lipstick was still on. How the hell do they get this crap off, I wondered. I nearly rubbed my lips raw with paper towels.

I didn't relax until I hit the suburbs and was certain I wasn't being followed. More than once, I told myself I must be out of my mind. Then I thought about Julie.

CHAPTER 11

All during the drive, my head was spinning with a lot of thoughts I really didn't want to think. One was that Julie was dead, another was that she had been used in a pedophile fuck ring, and I didn't know which was the more disturbing. Even worse, that dickhead Wagner may have known all about it. I could have been way off base, of course, was he really capable of pimping his own daughter? Would Maureen have allowed it? Is that why she was killed? All I had to go on was an overheard conversation during an orgy but, like I said, I worked on instinct, and what it was telling me stank.

I also couldn't figure the kidnap angle. Why had Julie been kidnapped and why had only Maureen been told? Then I remembered the looks on the girls at the camp and remembered what they'd reminded me of, bored hookers, sitting around the whore house between tricks. I considered myself to be a pretty worldly guy—there was little that shocked me—but these thoughts were really hard to take. Particularly when it concerned my own daughter.

Not that she'd ever really been my daughter. She didn't even know I existed, but there must be something really powerful in us when it concerns our offspring, even though they might be strangers. Then I thought about friends of mine with teenage kids. They all said the same thing. They're fucking strangers. Maybe this wasn't so different.

Then I thought that maybe she'd found out about it, and was going to spill the beans, and they'd killed her to shut her up and concocted this kidnapping story to cover it up. But then, why hush it up? Sooner or later, she was going to turn up missing.

The main thought that kept drumming in my head was that she was dead, dead, dead, dead, dead.

I was starting to get drowsy, so I turned off the main road onto a rural trunk, pulled over to the side, and tried to get some sleep. Fat chance, but maybe I dozed for an hour or so.

In the morning, I stopped at a roadhouse to get some breakfast and take a couple more pills. I was pretty certain that I hadn't been followed, but I checked the other customers out. No one was suspicious looking.

I'd been trying to think what I'd do when I got there, and decided that I'd just tell her who I really was, and that Julie'd been kidnapped. *Let's see her reaction.* I knew that I'd be blowing the case wide open, but I couldn't think of anything else. If my suspicions were right, I'd be putting myself in a lot of danger, but I figured I could finesse it. I always figured I could finesse it. At what age do people start learning?

The main gate was locked and there was a guard outside. I told him to call the office and tell the Warden that Mr. Atkinson was here. I figured she'd want to see me, whether she had contacted the Atkinsons or not.

She did.

I drove up to the main house and climbed the stairs to the office. Warden was sitting at her desk, straight as a ramrod. There was a goon standing at attention behind her. He reminded me of that guy with the Frisbee hat in some James Bond movie. She didn't waste any time.

"Who are you? I know you are not Dwayne Atkinson."

I reached into my pocket. The goon tensed but relaxed when I pulled out my card. I handed it to her. She studied it for a minute, and I could almost hear the wheels going around.

"What can I do for you, Mr. Gold, and why did you come here under false pretenses the other day? I don't like being lied to." She looked at the goon, "Do I Jimmy?"

He grunted.

She turned back to me. "I'm waiting."

"Julie Wagner has been kidnapped. She never reached home."

The sudden shock on her face seemed real enough, but now that I knew she was a class-A felon, I wasn't too impressed.

She didn't say anything for a while. "What can I do to help?"

I opened my briefcase and handed her the pictures of the male members of the Wagners' staff. "Do you recognize any of these men? Is one of them the guy who picked up Julie?"

She took some time looking them over. Then she handed them back. "None of them."

"Are you certain? Why don't you look again? Take your time." I was still hoping I was wrong about the camp, but Camp "Weesnatchee" was beginning to look more apt all the time.

She shook her head. "I don't have to. He's not there."

She seemed to have recovered from the shock.

I looked at her for a while. It was a kind of staring contest that wasn't going anywhere, so I asked her if she'd ever been to San Francisco. There was that same tic over her right eye. She was good, but not good enough.

"Ever heard of a woman named Georgina Spelvin?"

She didn't move, but her face filled with fear. "What do you want?"

"I want to find Julie."

"What makes you think I know where she is?"

"Do you?"

She seemed to make up her mind about something. She picked up the phone on her desk and punched in a number. I could hear it ringing on the other end. Then the ringing stopped, and she said, "There's a Joseph Gold here. A detective." She listened for a while without saying anything, but her head was nodding. Something told me I was in deep shit.

She put down the receiver and looked at me. She stood up and came out from behind her desk. "Okay, Mr. Gold, follow me."

Too late, I realized that I shouldn't have turned my back on the goon.

The lights went out and were replaced by a lot of whirling stars and stuff, along with a pain in the back of my head. It didn't last long.

When I woke up, I was sitting in a chair in what looked like a plush bedroom. Standing across from me were three teen-age girls in nightgowns. The one in the middle was Julie. She was pointing a snub-nose .38 at me and her hand was rock steady.

All the lights in the stadium came on at once.

ⲉⲁⲉⲁ

It wasn't that I was woozy from the blow. She looked exactly as Maureen had the first time I saw her when she joined the senior class at Grover Cleveland. There was the same lustrous golden-red hair. She was even wearing it the same, high on top and curls tumbling down to her shoulders. The same ice-blue eyes you could drown in, the same peach complexion. The same boobs.

May god, if he truly does exist, forgive me. I wanted to see her naked. I wanted to know if her bush was the same perfect red triangle. Probably not, she was likely shaved. I could never get that. The thought made me see her as a little girl again, and the twitch in my dick disappeared.

She looked like a high-class hooker and the gun never wavered. She was barely seventeen. Hard to believe.

The two girls with her were almost carbon copies, but one was blonde and the other was dark. All their faces were hard, like concrete.

"Who are you?" Her voice was as rigid as her face.

I was tempted to tell her, but I remembered the nightmare I'd had in my office. I'd never forgotten it. It's not that I'm superstitious, the time just wasn't right, but there was a coldness in my feet and hands that I'd never felt before.

"My name is Joseph Gold. I'm a private investigator. Maur—your mother hired me to find you."

"You were going to say Maureen."

"Yes."

The hardness in her face turned to something like disgust. "You were fucking her too, weren't you?"

So much for wondering what she knew. I looked straight into her eyes. "A long time ago in a galaxy far, far away."

Now was the time.

"I have something important to tell you, but we need to be alone."

She was doubtful. "In a fucking pig's eye," she said.

Now I knew for sure she was my daughter, the same foul mouth. Her grandma would have attacked her with glee.

"It's something you want to hear. Look, tie me to the chair, if you like. You've got the gun. Do you know how to use it?"

"Try me." Her eyes were ice. "I don't need to tie you up, believe me."

I did.

She thought for a while. Then she motioned the other girls out. They were reluctant, but they left.

She Who Must be Obeyed?

Whatever else was going on, the way she held herself kind of filled me with something like pride.

"Okay. Mr. private dick," she said when they'd gone. She put a lot of emphasis on dick. "What is it you have to tell me?"

This was it. Now or never.

"You asked if I'd screwed Maureen. Maureen and I lived together for five years. We split up a little less than sixteen years—" I paused. "—and nine months ago."

It took a while, but her eyes started to widen, like a curtain rising, and, for the first time, I saw a waver in her hand. It wasn't a heavy gun.

"Bullshit." she finally said, but the hand was still trembling. "Are you trying to tell me that you're my father?"

Smart girl.

I never took my eyes from hers. "It's the truth. That's why she came to me. I have a drawer full of photos and news clippings about you."

I could see she was digesting this.

"Why did you never say anything?"

"I was Maureen's slave."

She knew the effect Maureen had on men. She was trying it on herself. Her eyes finally softened, but just a little, she was still wary. "That I can believe."

"You can put the gun down," I said.

She just looked at me. "You're shitting me, right." The same look Roscoe had. Women and cats.

"No, I'm not. What I really want to do is go lie down on that delicious-looking bed and let the ringing in my head die down. Believe me."

There must have been something in my voice, because she lowered the gun, but I could see she'd have it up again in a second if I moved.

"I'm sorry Jimmy hit you so hard. He was really just supposed to disable you." She thought for a bit. "All right, go lie down, but no funny stuff?"

"I'm not Bill Wagner."

I could see that I'd hit a nerve. Was he diddling her? I'd kill him with my bare hands, but was it fatherly anger or jealousy?

I kind of hobbled over to the bed and collapsed, being careful to avoid hitting the lump on the back of my head. I could feel it growing—like Pinocchio's nose. I'd better not tell any lies.

She sat down in the chair and crossed her legs, just like her mother did, offering nothing but a flash of imagination. The real deal was in her eyes. I just lay back and tried to think while everything was whirling around me. At the same time, I could see that she was doing a lot of thinking herself. Whatever else she was, she was younger than seventeen and in some kind of a jam. I figured to find out all about it.

"I know you're in trouble here. Maybe I can help you out."

"Like you never did before?" She didn't deny she was in trouble.

It was strange, but I thought I'd feel more of a sense of relief by telling her, but there was nothing. It seemed like an ordinary conversation. Maybe because she'd caught on so fast.

She made it even stranger. "What the hell should I call you? Daddy?"

I could see she was highly amused.

I laughed. "That would really be nice, but why don't you just call me Joe. I think that would be better all around." I hadn't forgotten my dream, and she still had the gun. I had to be careful. Despite her seeming aplomb, she had to be a seething cauldron inside. With that red thatch, she was a volcano ready to erupt.

Come to think of it, that's one of the things that made Maureen so irresistible.

She finally came to some kind of decision, and she started talking.

CHAPTER 12

I knew all about the orgies years ago." She smiled. "They always thought I was asleep in the little cottage in the garden. They let me sleep there as a 'special treat' whenever they had a party. I hated being left out, so one time I snuck back to the house and peeked in the window," she said with a cold laugh. "God, it was disgusting. I couldn't take my eyes off them." She looked directly at me. "And it turned me on like crazy."

"I should think so, if you're my daughter," I said.

She laughed a knowing hooker's laugh. Just like Maureen.

There was little hope of my ever talking to her like a daddy to his little girl. I'd have to talk to her like the world-wise hooker she was. I wasn't sure whether that bothered me or not. She didn't know me from Adam. To her, I was just another guy with the weirdest story she'd heard yet. I'd have to return the compliment, and her story was even weirder. That suited me fine. I knew how to talk to hookers.

She never took her eyes off mine. "I masturbated right there at the window."

Was she testing me?

I looked right back. "I would've."

Her laugh was now less like a hooker's and more like a little girl's. It occurred to me that this could get confusing, and my head still wasn't on straight.

I smiled at her. "How many times?"

More peals of a thoroughly delightful girlish laugh. "Hey, you're okay. If I had to tell this to some old fogey, I'd just as soon shoot him."

"Speaking of which…" I nodded toward the gun.

She just laughed. "Not on your life. The gun stays with me."

Christ almighty, she wasn't even nervous.

I was.

Somehow though, I didn't think this was the kind of nervousness fathers usually had when talking about the birds and the bees.

Most little girls didn't have snub-nose .38s either.

Most little girls masturbated under the covers like they were supposed to. Then I wondered if she masturbated with the gun.

"Suit yourself. You're in charge," I said and waited for her to go on.

"I *am* in charge, you know." She looked almost wistful. Maybe she didn't like it. How "in charge" was she? She had the gun, and neither Warden nor Jimmy were anywhere to be seen. Against my better judgment, I was again kind of proud of her, but I couldn't let her know that. Not yet. Then I wondered how sick I must really be. Was this how mobsters felt when a favorite son gunned down a rival? I thought of *The Godfather*.

"What happened to your forehead?" The change of topic caught me off guard.

"I got drunk and passed out."

I guess that satisfied her because she went on. "I began to think that I could do that too. Y'know, the screwing. The first time I went to camp, I knew what I had to do."

"What was that?" I thought I knew.

"Recruit girls."

Bingo. "How did you do that? Sounds kind of dangerous to me."

The hooker laugh. "You haven't known many little girls, have you?"

I had to admit it.

"We talk about sex all the time, and I could tell which ones would go along."

"Little boys talk about sex all the time too." I smiled. "The only ones who wouldn't go along would be dead."

She didn't laugh and she had a look that I could only describe as dry. "So do big boys—and big boys have the money."

God. This was my daughter? She was Maureen all over again. The very last of my fatherly fantasies went out the window to die a violent death on the rocks of grim reality. I thought about all the hours I'd spent poring over all the clippings and pictures, and I couldn't help myself. I laughed out loud.

She looked puzzled. "What's so funny?"

I laughed again. "You're the exact opposite of what I expected. Please excuse the sound of a father's fantasies being dashed to the ground in a million pieces."

She laughed, and for the first time, it was a normal adult laugh. "I never suspected that *you* even existed." She stopped to think. "Although I always wished that Bill wasn't my father."

"Who'd you have wanted for a father?"

She looked at me with no expression. "I dunno. Maybe George Clooney. Maybe you." The fact that she didn't mention some young heartthrob spoke volumes. Julie was seventeen, going on seventy. She knew stuff that no kid should. Then, I thought, maybe she had a father fixation. Hard to believe.

Maybe not.

"How'd you get started?"

"Warden. Maureen checked her out very carefully. She was perfect. She knew how to run a whore house."

That set me back hard. "Maureen set this up?"

"Yeah." She actually looked a little apologetic. "I guess I forgot to say."

"Say *what?*" My inflection made her laugh.

"One day I walked in on Maureen. She had a vibrator stuck up her snatch. I guess that made me nervous, and I just blurted out, 'What do you need that thing for? Aren't all the men you're fucking enough?' Or something like that." She broke into more peals of girlish laughter. This wasn't good for my head. "I'll never forget the look on her face. I thought maybe she'd drop dead of a heart attack or something. I told her that I knew all about the orgies and straight out told her my plans for the camp."

"Camp 'Weesnatchee,' right?"

More peals.

"Say, you really are an all right dude. Some people might be puking by now."

I smiled. "I've heard it all before, believe me." I hoped she did, because I didn't. I was exploring new territory without a guide. "What about Bill?" I wasn't expecting another shock, but I got about a million volts.

"Oh, Bill never knew anything about it. It was our secret, and we kept the money for ourselves."

"He still doesn't know?"

She shook her head in that mock rueful way that Maureen had.

So that was why he had to be kept out of the loop. And I'd been accusing him of banging his own daughter. *It just goes to show how wrong we can be about people.* Not that he stopped being a bastard, of course. With Wagner out of the picture, the pieces were all starting to fit into place, but I was still puzzled. "Why were you blackmailing Maureen? I assume that it was Jimmy or some other goon who made the call?"

"I wanted out. I was bored. I knew that the last thing she wanted was for Bill to know she was pimping me. I wanted the money so I could take off and start a new life far away from them. I hated them both. Neither of them ever gave a flying fuck about me." Her eyes were flashing fire, and this was the first time I'd ever seen any real emotion in her. "But I didn't want her to know it was me until after I was gone. I used to fantasize what Bill would do to her when he found out. I hoped they'd kill each other. Then she had to go and get *herself* killed. She was never supposed to tell anybody." She was pouting.

"You're lucky she did."

I felt a profound sense of relief that Julie hadn't been behind it. Then it occurred to me that the bullet must have been meant for me, after all. My ducking got Maureen killed and ruined Julie's chances. Now she was stuck here between a rock and a hard place.

Without even knowing it, I had replayed the classic father-daughter scenario. What were the odds? I thought about my dream again. She still had the gun, and she was, most likely, nuts.

I also thought that all my fishing up to now had caught nothing but red herrings. That's how it goes sometimes. But the net was filling up with tuna now, and the jackpot lights were flashing in my head.

I took a chance and tried to sound fatherly. "So, Little Miss Madam, what are you going to do now?" What father ever said that?

To my absolute surprise, she just fell on her knees and started bawling. *This* was how I thought about teenage girls. Jeez, I was getting confused, and I was still scared.

She finally shut off the waterworks. "I don't know

what to do. There's not anywhere near enough money in the safe, and I still have to pay off Warden." Her eyes hardened in an instant, "Or kill her." She paused for a second. "And there still wouldn't be enough."

"You don't like her, do you?"

"She's a fucking vulture."

I laughed, "That's what a friend of mine said."

She looked puzzled, but I let it go.

She started to laugh, the girlish one. "I'll bet you think I'm crazy."

I remembered the lump on my head. "The thought has crossed my mind."

"Well, I'm not. Really." She looked at me, and for the first time, there was a sincere plea in her eyes. "So, what do I do?"

"That depends." I was keeping my fingers crossed. "You could kill me and Warden, and the goons too, and maybe any girls who happen to show up, take whatever money there is, get in a car, and take off. Of course, every cop in the state would be looking for you."

"Or?"

That one word made my blood run cold. She really needed an "or?"

"You could give yourself up. You'd be out in four years and your record sealed, if you actually went to prison at all. A smart lawyer might get you off completely." I gave her my absolutely most sincere face, the one I gave my mother when she asked if I was peeking through Karen's keyhole.

"Not that you actually have much of a choice anymore," I added.

She answered instantly. "I've never killed anyone. I doubt if I could, and I don't know how to drive. Daddy— Bill—thought it was too dangerous for me to be driving alone." She was beginning to sound normal, like a seventeen-year-old with a problem.

I didn't bother to point out that there was really no reason that she couldn't just blackmail Wagner now. How had she missed that one? He'd have forked over the dough in no time. Did she have some deep-seated loyalty to him, or was she really just behaving like a dumb seventeen-year-old? She certainly showed no loyalty to Maureen.

It was almost like she read my mind. "I suppose you're wondering why I don't blackmail Bill, huh?"

"The question had occurred to me."

She laughed. "I noticed that you didn't include that particular option."

Sharp as a razor blade this one was. "I didn't want to encourage you. Your best option is still just to give yourself up."

She actually sighed. "I'd pretty much decided that, but I didn't know how. This might be my operation, but I was a prisoner of it too." She looked at me with a real question in her eyes. "Does that make any sense?"

"Perfect," I said.

"There were the other girls to consider too. I'd just be abandoning them."

"They're in the same boat as you, y'know, and the solution is the same."

"I suppose." She was more subdued than I'd seen her.

"How many girls?"

"Twenty-two."

Jeez! That was pushing almost a quarter of the camp.

"How'd you keep it secret from the other girls?"

She laughed. "Most of them are real dweebs. They don't know their pussies from a hole in the ground." She thought for a while, and a kind of wicked smile covered her face. "There were a few who caught on, but they didn't have the balls. I charged them to peep." She laughed. "I called them the 'Finger Fuckers.'"

Girls needed balls? Who knew?

"What were their ages?" I was anxious to keep this confessional moving.

"Most are between thirteen and seventeen, but Lily's only nine. She never wanted to fuck, but she gave BJs that kept 'em coming back for more. She was one of my biggest money-makers." Her eyes had turned wistful again, and distant, like she was in an old folks' home and telling her memoirs to a reporter. "We made a ton of money, you know, but Maureen kept it all in a special account outside the country. I can't touch it. I'm fucking underage. Can you believe that shit?" She was laughing hard, but it was just this side of hysterical. I still couldn't be sure if I was dealing with a normal person or an A-1 nut job, though.

"How'd you keep it from the counselors? Surely they were smarter than the dweebs."

She laughed. "That's what you think. A few did catch on, and I just paid them off to shut up about it. A couple even tried it themselves a few times. I let them keep the whole price. Warden said to think of it as insurance."

I didn't say anything. I sat up on the bed and held out my hand. She looked at me for a second then she came over, handed me the gun, and sat down. I put my arm around her, and she rested her head on my shoulder. After a few minutes, she said, "You're the first guy I was ever in bed with who didn't paw at me."

"We aren't really in bed." I was trying to lighten the atmosphere. Instead, I felt her stiffen. "Relax." I gave her my best smile. "I'm a detective. I just state the facts, ma'am." I'm sure the reference escaped her, but she understood, and she relaxed back into me again.

I wasn't sure if this was really happening or if I was

still under the influence of Jimmy's blackjack, or whatever the hell he'd hit me with. Maybe it was his fist. The thought made me shudder.

But, here I was, with my daughter in my arms, and it was my job to deliver her to the cops, maybe to prison. Exactly how I was going to do that was escaping me. Then I remembered. The lump on my head must have been pressing on some nerve centers. I looked at my watch. It was two o'clock. If Jenny followed orders, the cops would be here soon. Frank would have sense enough to alert the locals.

"Are there any more guns around?"

She thought for a bit and counted on her fingers. "Warden has one, so do Jimmy and Gunther." She stood up and lifted her nightgown. I could see her panties— transparent, white lace doohickeys with not a smudge of red to be seen—but what really got my attention was the fucking .45 strapped to her upper thigh. I must have reacted, because she dropped the gown and laughed. It sounded normal.

Was she a girl or a chameleon?

"Actually—" She looked at me and the smile was genuine. "You're like a gift from heaven, y'know? I really was at my wits' end, and Warden was threatening to take off." She looked me straight in the eye. "Were you telling me the truth? About maybe getting off?"

I didn't say anything, I just crossed my heart, like I'd seen Frank do a lot.

"So, what do we do?

"Nothing," I had a vision of crossed fingers in my mind. "Just sit tight and wait for the cops to show up. They should be here any minute."

Her eyes got wide.

"I never leave anything to chance," I lied. "You'd better give me the forty-five."

Now her eyes got mischievous, just like Maureen's. "Supposing I tell you to take it yourself?"

Her cheek really got to me. "You know you're not too old for me to take across my knee and spank." I knew that was a mistake the moment it left my mouth, but she just laughed.

"That'll cost you extra—Daddy."

She was very much Maureen's daughter, but she was my kid too.

The telephone on her nightstand rang. We both jumped. She picked up the receiver and listened. She mouthed War-den at me. Then she spoke. "So what if he's been here a long time? Don't worry about it. He's doing an all-nighter. Five grand." Pause. "Looks can be deceiving, and who cares about his suit?" Another pause. "I said, don't worry. Who the hell's the boss here anyway?"

I could hear a shout and the click of the receiver on the other end. It sounded loud. Julie looked at me, her eyes filled with fear. "I think maybe we're in trouble. She's been bugging me for a payoff, and she's on the rag, too."

Did people still say that? Teenage girls? Then I remembered she was going on seventy, but she looked like a frightened little kid right now.

"Lock the door."

"It is."

It was silent for a minute or so, except for the sound of girls playing outside, muffled by the heavy drapes on the windows. Where were we? It didn't take long to figure we were in the main house, because I heard footsteps running outside the room. A rattled door knob told us she was here.

"Open up! Now!" Unless she was really a man, that would've been Jimmy.

"Gunther," Julie hissed.

I doubted that Jimmy was far behind.

"Go away," she said, and she sounded as imperious as any social worker I'd ever met. I suppose she was, in a way. "I'm busy."

Gunther wasn't buying. I heard his shoulder as it slammed into the door.

"Get under the bed, quick!" I told her, and she dropped and slithered. I guess Daddy was really in charge now.

On the third thud, the jamb splintered and the door flew open. Then everything went into slow motion. Gunther stood there for about an hour, staring at me. He had a gun in his hand. He floated toward me. I fired.

A red dot appeared on his forehead, and he floated to the floor. I barely heard the shot, but I felt the bullet go into my shoulder. Jimmy was floating along right behind him, and he hadn't waited to shoot. He started toward me when his face got all red and bloody, and he floated down on top of Gunther.

At first, I couldn't figure what happened, but when I looked down, there was Julie on the floor, half out from under the bed. At the end of her outstretched arm, the .45 was still pointed at the spot where Jimmy's face had been. I guess she *could* shoot. I hadn't heard that shot at all.

There was real shock in her eyes, though. I grabbed the gun out of her hand. The pain in my shoulder felt like what ice must feel when it's being picked. We just sat there for a minute. I was certain that they were both dead or vegetables. They didn't move. Neither did vegetables, but they were beyond being a threat.

The play outside had turned to screaming.

"Warden," Julie said, and she seemed to come alive again.

She leaped up and ran out the door. I dragged myself

along behind her. When I finally got to the office, she was just standing there, staring at the open safe.

It was then we heard the sirens. Then the shots. We ran to the front windows. "Keep down," I said, but there was no need. Looking up the road, I could see a lot of police cars around a civilian vehicle. Lying on the ground was what I figured must be Warden. She wasn't moving either. She'd tried to shoot her way out. I guess she succeeded.

The sound of girls shrieking was what my shoulder felt like.

❧❧❧

By the time Frank had gotten to Goobersville, or whatever the hell the place was called, I was out of the ER, my arm in a sling and with a headache that was worse than any hangover I'd ever had, sitting in the police station, waiting.

Julie was in a cell by herself. She'd changed into a shirt and blue jeans, and she looked like any normal seventeen-year-old girl in a jail cell. She looked vacant, too.

I'd refused to answer any questions until Frank showed up. He'd brought Jenny with him. It was obvious that she wanted to run and embrace me, but she wisely figured that I might break.

I filled everybody in on everything.

Jenny drove the rental car back. The rest of the girls were piled into two police vans. Julie and I rode with Frank. None of us said much of anything the whole way, but Frank had one piece of news.

"We got the guys trying to kill you. Remember Jerry Miles?"

Miles was a two-bit grifter I'd put away. He'd sworn to kill me, but I thought he was such a pathetic *schmuck* that he didn't have the balls. "When did he get out?"

"A week before he shot Maureen instead of you."

"What about the guy who knifed me?"

He laughed. "You're gonna love this. His name is Bennie 'the Bear' Hogan.

I hurt too much to laugh, but I wanted to. "How'd you find them?"

"My tail on you spotted him on the fire escape outside your place. He tried to run, but my guy caught up with him. He spilled the beans in about five minutes. Miles was going to pay him two grand to put you on ice.

Julie'd been taking it all in from the back seat. "You mean the bullet was meant for you?"

"It looks that way, doesn't it?"

She was silent for a while before speaking again. "I'm glad you ducked."

I was trying to figure how we could keep this all quiet, but when we pulled up to police headquarters, there were about a million reporters standing around.

Remember those old cowboy movies and the cattle stampedes?

CHAPTER 13

Pretty much the same headline appeared on all the papers. I picked up the *Tribune* because it had the biggest picture of me on the front page. Even then, it was pretty small, but I'd made it. I tossed it back on the pile.

"Don't you want one for a souvenir?" Freddy was looking at me with something like hero worship.

"Nah, I already know what I look like."

He picked it back up anyway and handed it to me. "On the house."

❧❧❧

When the shitty doctor kid saw me next, he about had a stroke. I told him to read the papers.

"No time," he said.

"Then watch TV."

"No time."

I just shrugged.

Bet he went out and got a paper or turned on the TV.

☙❧

They finally got around to burying Maureen. There were few mourners, but thousands of gawkers lined the road into the cemetery. Peanut and popcorn vendors circulated among them, and a couple of hot dog stands and food trucks had even been set up outside the gates. It reminded me of the Fourth of July, or maybe the public hangings that used to be an American spectacle.

Wagner had resigned. He still looked at me with death in his eyes, but the fire was gone. He was busted, and he knew it.

He stood next to the grave, and it looked to me like he was thinking about jumping in. Julie had been let out of her cell to attend, and she was accompanied by a couple of tough looking matrons. There was no expression at all on her face. She smiled at *me*, though.

☙❧

All the johns at Camp Weesnatchee had used aliases, so most of them were home free, except for the ones who'd been diddling their friend's daughters and could be identified.

Henry's business actually increased. Nothing like notoriety to spark curiosity, and Maury never had to worry about people stopping gambling anyway.

Sales at Slumber Well went up too, and the Bellamy family TV commercials went on as usual. America's a funny place. It occurred to me that the wife and kiddies seem to have taken it all in stride, and that made me wonder about what went on behind their closed doors.

Cooper was finally eased out, but was working again within the month. I guess I'd overestimated the morality of the business community.

Connor's wife divorced him, but that was about all he suffered.

It's a damned good thing for them that none of them was accused of littering. People really get pissed off about that.

The DA also refused to make a case about Pepe's donkey. Kids listen to the news, you know, and they didn't want to rile up the animal people either. I should say, the new DA. The old DA had been one of the johns, and I wondered about the new guy. Maybe he'd had a turn with the donkey himself.

I didn't really mind about any of it. Wagner was out, but I did have a twinge when I realized that all my files were now worthless to his political opponents.

There was also no chance in hell that he'd cough up any more dough, but it didn't matter. My phone was jumping off the hook. I wasn't scuzz anymore, I was a fucking hero. I paid Jenny all her back pay and gave her a raise, and I could also afford to buy Roscoe all the gourmet cat food he could eat. Best of all, I could afford Haig & Haig now.

❧❦❧

Not even the best lawyer in town could get Julie off, but she would be out in four years. She just shrugged. She was getting regular counseling. So were the rest of the girls, but I really wondered if Lily wasn't giving them BJs on the sly.

I visited her every Sunday, and we made plans about all the great stuff we'd do together when she got out. She'd never been to Disneyland. Neither had I. Maybe I could be a mule for Maury and pay for the trip that way. I'd only rip him off for a little.

I did have to talk her out of trying to recruit some of the girls in "Juvie" to provide services to the guards. "They don't make enough money anyway," I told her.

I could see that she was going to be a handful. I actually started reading books on parenting. Better late than never, but none of them was quite up to advice about this kind of shit.

✁✁

I asked Jenny to marry me. She just laughed. Then she looked at me with that whatever-gave-you-that-idea look.

"All I really want is a partnership," she said.

To tell the truth, I was relieved, and I hired guys to come and paint *Martin & Gold, Private Investigations* on the door window. I know that G comes before M, but it just sounded better that way. I figured that it wouldn't be too long before we could actually move out of the joint, so I continued to pay the rent by the month.

I also bought my own personal laptop. I couldn't resist when Jenny told me you could get free pornography on something called the internet.

PART 2

The Case of the Reluctant Vampire

CHAPTER 14

Sliced cabbage covered about every square inch of my kitchen.

"Here. This is for you." Jenny had smiled when she handed me the gift-wrapped box for the one month anniversary of our partnership. I hadn't gotten her anything. What the hell was a one month anniversary called? Toilet paper?

I gave it the fish-eye. "What is it?" I'd once gotten a bomb wrapped just like it. Just about the same size too.

"It's an electric vegetable slicer. You know how much you love coleslaw. Now, you can make your own."

There was nothing in the instructions about getting it off the ceiling.

I finally got the mess cleaned up and was heading out to KFC. I'd gotten a taste for coleslaw in my head, and it needed satisfying. Sometimes I'd just order three sides of it. I like to make a meal of appetizers in Chinese restaurants too. Better than KFC.

The phone rang. I was going to ignore it, but I'm obsessive about my work, so I answered.

There was a bunch of babble, and I thought for a second about those ridiculous party-porn lines they used to have, but I'd cancelled my subscription years ago.

There was a lot of shrieking or screaming going on in the background. Maybe both.

"Joseph Gold?" The man's voice was hesitant. It sounded scared.

"This is Gold. Who's calling?"

There was more yelling.

"We need help."

The taste of coleslaw was driving me nuts.

"Call my office in the morning. How did you get this number?"

More noise. It sounded like a pretty violent argument.

I was tempted to just put the phone down, but my curiosity had been piqued. I waited to hear if the voice spoke again.

"Please help. Twelve Fifty-Three Adams Circle, apartment eight-seventeen."

I heard the click as he hung up, and everything went silent, except for the noise going on in my head. Hands down, that was the strangest phone call I'd ever gotten. I thought that it might have been a prank by some of my asshole friends, but most of them were smart enough to have come up with something better. And there hadn't been a punch line.

There was always a punch line.

Problem was, once my curiosity starts to itch, it won't be satisfied until it's scratched.

First though, I needed that coleslaw.

⁕⁕⁕

The building at 1253 Adams Circle was located in a prosperous, middle class apartment block that showed no imagination whatsoever. It was mostly a façade of phony brick punctuated by a million windows, and it rose fifteen floors into the night sky. Pretty much like all the other apartment blocks that surrounded it. Even prosperity could be depressing.

For a minute, I thought of telling the cabbie to turn around but, in the end, curiosity got the better of me so I paid him off and told him not to wait.

I pushed the button for 817 and felt a twinge of jealousy for the busted buzzer system at my place.

There was no response. My instincts kicked in.

I pushed the buzzer again.

No response. They went from low to high gear in an instant

Again.

Nada.

I pushed a bunch of buttons until I heard the buzz and click of the door opener. You can always count on some asshole to do it. I pushed through the door with all the staticky "Hellos?" from the smarter folks pouring out of the bank of speakers at the entrance.

I took the elevator up to eight.

The cold steel smell of fresh blood was coming from 817. It was wafting out from under the door like a summer breeze playing over a battlefield.

My first thought was *Jeez, there's got to be a lot.*

My second thought was to put my shoulder to it, but it was still sore from the slug I'd taken about a month ago, and the other side, where I'd gotten knifed, still hurt too.

That led me to my third thought, which was to call 911, which led me to my fourth thought.

I called Frank.

Frank Gomez and I go back a long way. He took me under his wing when I'd started as a rookie beat cop at the Twelfth Precinct. He knew I wanted to be a detective, and he mentored me. It wasn't his fault that I'd been such an asshole, but most of the cops in the precinct were even bigger assholes. Or so I thought. I was pretty much right, though, as it turned out. I was, shall we say, loose with the regs too. That was always a recipe for disaster, and I'd had my share. I'd put away my share of bad guys too, but that paled into insignificance against the embarrassment I caused the Department.

They canned my ass.

"Yeah?" Frank's gravel voice cut through my reverie. I filled him in. "I don't want to go in there until the cops get here. Thought I'd give you a heads up."

He told me not to call 911, that he'd take care of it and to sit tight.

I did. As far away from the blood smell as I could. Problem is, I've got a good nose. A big Jewish one, with a slight twist. "Deviated septum," Dr. Epstein, my pediatrician said.

I was a big hit on the muff-diving circuit. It'd been worth all the taunts.

The cops finally showed up, and Frank wasn't far behind. The boys from the Twenty-Third wanted to know why a looie from the Twelfth was there, and it took a while to get everything straightened out, particularly, who the fuck *I* was.

I'd been right about the blood. The floor was soaked with it. The ceiling was painted with it too. Like a Jackson Pollack.

ღჯღ

I'd gone over the story of the phone call at least a dozen times until Frank put an end to it, and dragged me out of the Twenty-Third and into the all-night coffee shop at the Belmont Hotel. I had a crazy aunt who used to take me there when I was a kid. It seemed seedy then, and it was definitely seedy now. The neighborhood was full of old, once-elegant hostelries, many of which had been turned into subsidized housing for old geezers.

The Belmont's all-nighter was usually full of the insomniac social security crowd, taking advantage of the coffee-for-a-buck deal from ten to seven. I remember when it was a dime. I must be getting old.

Sasha was still sitting at the register. He'd been there when my aunt would bring me, but he looked a lot different now, and he hadn't been young then. He'd been part of the European aristocratic tradition of the old Belmont, probably because he spoke with a Russian accent. His family had been peasants who'd run away from the revolution. The czar's should have too, but they weren't smart enough.

He had to be pushing ninety. He was still sharp, but his eyes had a look that said "Enough already." He remembered me, though I hadn't been here in years. He flashed me a smile, and I went over to say hello.

"When are you going to retire, you old war horse," I said.

"Ven dey lay me in my grave."

There was something missing in his laugh, though, and I heard a few months later that he died at the cash register. For only the second time in history, the coffee shop was closed. In his honor. The first time was for Franklin Roosevelt.

We grabbed an empty table.

Millie spotted us and came over to take our order. She'd just started working here when I was a kid. Her hair was pure white, and her skin looked like tissue paper. It even crinkled when she smiled. Her eyes were still a clear blue, though. "

Hey, Joe. I seen your pic'ure in the papers. Guess you're a hero or sump'n, huh?"

"Hi, Millie. Still pulling the night shift, I see."

"You bet. All the interestin' people come here at night. Movie stars and actors too, sometimes. Hey, that reminds me."

She pulled out a small booklet from her apron pocket. "How's about your autergraph? I don't ask everybody, y'know?"

Fancy that, somebody wanted my autograph—besides banks, loan companies, lawyers, and other such blood-suckers. I signed with a flourish and added *with all my love*. She gave me a big smile when she read it, and I thought she might faint. I guess I have that effect on women, even the older ones. It's my curse.

"Jeez, Joe. Nobody never wrote nothin' purty like that. Thanks."

I laughed. "You hang on to that now. Someday it might be worth a lot of money."

She finally got around to slapping me on the back. She was laughing.

"Lordy, Joe, yer a card. I ain't got a whole lotta some-days aheada me, y'know?"

"Then I'd better get on with the heroics, huh?"

We ordered coffee and Danish, but Frank didn't seem too interested. He was looking a little pale to me.

"What's wrong, Frank, stomach bothering you again?" I was concerned.

He didn't say anything for a while, looking kind of absently at the Danish. Finally, he heaved one of his patent-ed sighs, his eyes found mine. "How long have I been a cop, Joe? I make it going on forty-five years. I'm getting close to being put out to pasture." He stopped.

I figured I knew what was eating him, but I kept my trap shut.

"Jesus, Mary, and Joseph, I work in one of the most crime-ridden cities in the world, and I've never seen any-thing like *this*."

I gave him my most compassionate look, and I really meant it. "Nobody has, but maybe guys who were in Vietnam or Iraq."

To tell the truth, I'd almost puked, and I was at least as hardened as Frank.

"I don't know what the fuck to make of it." He went on. "Five people with their throats cut from ear to ear and all the rest of it. I know we'll have to wait for forensics, but it looked they never fought back. And what was that goddamned star on the floor, with all the candles burning inside."

I knew what that was. "It's a pentagram. Witches use it in their rituals."

Frank's eyes opened wide. "Witches? What the fuck are you talking about?" He gave me a questioning look. "You been dating Snow White or something?"

"Jeez, Frank, don't you ever watch horror movies?"

"You're shitting me right? Horror movies? I've got enough with my wife—" He thought for a bit. "—and this fucking job."

I couldn't argue with him about the job, but I'd never met his wife. For all the crap he said about her, I'd bet she was a lovely woman. She'd put up with *him* all these years. Maybe she had a martyr complex.

"The Pentagram is also used in Satanic rites," I added.

"You mean like summoning the devil, or something?"

"Yep. Or something."

"Come on. You can't be serious. The devil?"

"Nope. Whoever killed them is as human as you or me. Me anyway. I'm not too sure about you."

He didn't bother to laugh, or he really was more disturbed than I think I'd ever seen him.

"Human? If you say so, but you might have trouble making that stand up in court."

We didn't say anything for a while. I was having trouble getting the image out of my head. Do you have any idea how much blood five people have? While we were there, the couple from downstairs came up to bitch about the wine, or whatever it was, dripping from their ceiling. When they realized what it was, the wife puked.

A cursory investigation of the neighbors elicited nothing but that the Bochinkys' son had brought them over from Romania a few years back, and that they were a quiet couple. A few had heard a lot of noise coming from their apartment, but it hadn't lasted long, so they forgot about it.

My name and number were scrawled on a piece of paper next to the telephone. I had no idea how they'd gotten it. Even less of why they'd called *me*. I'd never heard of them before.

Problem was, all the bodies were young, and they were all naked, two guys and three girls, none much above twenty. In addition to the cut throats, they were sliced up the middle, from groin to head, and sliced down the middle of the face, making a kind of macabre cross.

Where were the Bochinskys?

Descriptions were soon out on the wires and waves, and a full city manhunt was on. There wasn't much to go on. Few of their neighbors ever saw them for more than quick hello in the corridors. Do you have any idea of how many nice, older couples there are in this town?

Then I thought that they could be sitting at the next table over.

They say that cops who work together for a long time have a kind of telepathy. I laughed when I saw Frank eyeing the customers, just like I had.

I got real quiet, thinking that if I hadn't stopped for coleslaw, I could have been there when it went down.

I got drunk when I got home, and I still didn't sleep well.

CHAPTER 15

I got to my office early, only a little hung over. The horror in my head was cutting right through it. Peggy, the receptionist, wasn't there yet, but Jenny was. Her office door was open, and I could see that she had the Tribune in front of her. She looked up and saw me.

"Jesus Christ." She held up the paper. "Have you seen this?"

I just looked at her for a while. "I was there. The papers don't say much."

For a while she just looked back at me. Then her lower jaw sort of dropped. "Huh?"

I filled her in on the phone call from the Bochinskys, or whoever it was, and what I found when we got the door open.

Her eyes just kept getting bigger and bigger.

"I could've been there, you know, if your *farshtunkiner* machine had worked right."

She stared at me. "What kind of an asshole forgets to put the cover on?"

I had no answer for that one.

"It's a damn good thing you weren't."

I had to agree with her on that one too.

I went into my office and closed the door. Not for the

first time, I wished I had a bottle stashed here, but I knew that if I started drinking on the job, I might as well just shoot myself and spare me the misery.

I popped a couple of Alkies in the half-full water glass from yesterday and gulped it down. A lovely belch helped, but even I winced at the odor of rancid whisky.

I tried to look over the recent case requests, but the image of five grisly crosses wouldn't go away.

I just pretty much thought about that I might have been there.

I really wanted a drink.

My phone rang.

I jumped.

For a moment, I toyed with the idea of ignoring it, but when it rang a third time, the old Pavlovian response kicked in.

Peggy had gotten in.

I let Jenny talk me into hiring her niece as receptionist and secretary, though I had misgivings. Aside from the problem of relatives working together, there was the problem that she was really hot, and I wasn't sure that I could stick to my business and pleasure oath, what with a gorgeous twenty-one-year-old with a preference for mini-skirts sashaying around the way she did.

She didn't do it on purpose. She was really a good kid, but she seemed oblivious of the effect she had on the men in the waiting room. The women weren't quite as smiley, but since it was usually the men who paid best, I chalked it up to advertising.

Besides, if I ever looked like I was making a move on her, Jenny would have resuscitated the old typewriter and whacked me with it.

It was a narrow line, but the eye-candy was worth it.

The worst part was she was a redhead. I consoled my-self by figuring her bush had been Braziled out of exist-

ence. I don't get that at all. It's too much like child pornography for my taste. But I'm getting to be an old fart, I
guess. A bare bush doesn't stop me from plowing the
ground beneath, though. The works are still there.

I laughed when I thought of the time I picked up a
broad who'd neglected to get her works changed over. I
nearly did it for her, but the only damage was a black eye.
I really don't give a shit what anyone wants to do with
their works, but I feel that people should be duty-bound
to reveal the way they swing. I hate dirty tricks. No puns
intended.

I guess I *am* getting old.

"Good morning, boss." Peggy's voice was as perky as
her boobs.

Jenny was a detective fiction fan. Peggy was sci-fi all
the way. She even went to those dopey conventions. I
was sure that whatever costume she wore—or didn't—
would be terrific. Her favorite writer was Robert
Heinlein, one of the oldies, whose hero was always surrounded by beautiful women who called him "boss." I
didn't mind, but I think Jenny was a little exasperated.
After all, she was the boss, too, and I know she really
didn't hold with the whole women idolizing men deal.

Maybe this experiment wouldn't work out after all,
and it wouldn't be my fault. I'd miss her.

"Good morning, Peggy." I tried to be cheery.

"There are some people here to see you?" That was
the only thing wrong with Peggy, that annoying uptick at
the end of sentences. It made everything sound like a
question.

Shit. Oh well, maybe they'd take my mind off things.
Probably another runaway kid.

"An older couple?"

I knew the answer before I asked.

"Who are they?"

"A Mr. and Mrs. Bochinsky?"

Bingo.

Just because I'd guessed didn't mean that that I wasn't shocked. I thought of those crosses again and had a momentary notion to call Frank, but I thought I could do that later. Then I wondered if there would be a later.

"Are they real old?"

"I'd say so, yes."

That meant nothing since she thought I was old too, but I took a chance.

"Send them in."

I dialed Jenny. "You'd better get in here."

Jenny had studied Jiu-Jitsu.

"Why."

"The people whose apartment I visited last night are here."

Just as I hung up, Peggy showed the Bochinskys into my office. Jenny was on their heels.

They *could* have been sitting next to us last night. They looked like any elderly couple. He was paunchy, but held himself erect, like a man with pride in his appearance, though his suit looked like he'd slept in it. He was bald except for a band of white hair that encircled the back of his head just above his ears.

That reminded me of David ben Gurion, but there was nothing Jewish about his face. Its younger manifestation could have stricken the heart of a Jew cold from behind its brandished sword.

It was still trying to stay square, but his dentures wouldn't totally cooperate. He looked like an aristocrat gone to seed, and he was unshaven.

The missus also stood erect. She was unshaven, too. There was a hint of moustache above her lip. She was wearing a pink dress that showed off what once were probably quite acceptable curves. Now they were badly in need of a repair crew. She had a ratty looking piece of fur over her shoulder, but she wore it as if it might have been mink. Her hair, like his, was snow white, but it covered her whole head except for a bare spot just above her forehead.

His eyes were furtive, hers were made of steel. They were definitely in their eighties, though they looked anything but decrepit.

I introduced them to Jenny. I didn't want to give them a chance to open.

"Where were you last night? Every cop in town was looking for you."

Bochinsky looked directly at me for the first time, and his eyes were no longer furtive, as though he'd come to a decision about something.

"Ve haff long experience eluding polize. You should haff liffed in Romania, zen you'd know." He sat back in his chair and made a dismissive sound. "American polize? Amateurs."

I had to agree with him there, for too big a part of the force that I knew.

Why'd they been eluding the police in Romania?

"Ve slept on park benches ven ve could." Her voice was strong, like the steel in her eyes."

"How did you get to me? Was it you who called?"

"Our son, Dmitri," he said.

"Ve named him vor ze great Shostakovich," she said, and there was a hint of pride in her voice. She leaned toward me. "Do you like maybe music, Mr. Gold?"

"Only when I'm sleeping."

She sat back. She seemed offended. I was glad black-belt Jenny was there.

They reminded me of some of my relatives from my mother's side, the "aristocratic" ones. They even sounded the same, an almost elegant English punctuated by Low

German Vs and Zs. They also reminded me of an old vaudeville comedy act I once saw on TV.

I didn't say anything for a while. Then I asked why he'd called me. "And why are you here?"

She looked at him, and he spoke.

"Vell, as it turns out, now ve vant you to vind Dmitri."

"Every cop in town will be looking too. At least they will when I tell them."

"No!" she practically screamed. "Dmitri didn't do zis. A vew minutes after he called you, he made us leave. He vass viz us until two o'clock. He said zat someting terrible vas going to happen, and zat ze police vere sure to blame him. He told us zat he vuz going to disappear, and zat he vould let us know vere he vass ven it vas safe."

Bochinsky got more animated than I'd seen him yet. He sort of waved his arms around. "Ze goddamn varies. Zey're to blame."

I had to think about that one for a while. "Fairies? Is Dmitri gay?"

Mrs. was shooting daggers at him from those cold steel eyes. She turned to me. "Dmitri, no, but zere vere a view in hiss crowd, along vid zum udder strange pipple."

"How strange?"

Bochinsky decided he wasn't going to be intimidated by his wife. He tossed back a few of the knives. I don't really know why, but I was proud of him.

"You alvays make excuses for zem. Now see vut it makes." He turned back to me. "You vant to know strange? Wampires, Verevolves, and god knows vut else."

Mrs. seemed like she'd better get on board. She shrugged. "Vitches. Men and vimmen."

I looked at Jenny who was seated next to me behind the desk. She was rapt.

So was Peggy. I could just see the edge of her silhouette behind the frosted glass of the door. Part of it was clearly an ear. She had a lot to learn about the detective business. I tried not to think about how much fun it would be to tutor her.

I turned my attention back to the Bochinskys. "Why did you call me last night, and why did you have my number? Where did you get it?"

Mrs. spoke, and it seemed like some air had been let out of her curves. They sagged even more. "Ve let Dmitri use our plaze for his parties. Last night somebody started a vight."

"About va—about what?"

"I don't know. All of sudden, zere vass pipple shouting and arguing about a sacrifice."

"A sacrifice? What kind of a sacrifice?"

"I don't know. Sometimes zey vould draw a star on ze floor and slaughter a chicken in a big pot. Zey vould all be chanting."

Bochinsky had been sitting quietly. He erupted. "And you let zem do it," he shouted at her. He looked at me. "I vanted to call ze polize, it vas disgusting." He looked back at her. "I told you zat nutting good vould come of it, but 'no,' you said, 'Zey're just having fun,' you said."

The steel never left her eyes.

The air seemed to go out of him suddenly. He shut up and sank back into the chair.

"Who were the five kids who were killed?"

Mrs. took up the story. "Ve don't know, but zere vas alvays some nize young pipple who came and vent. It vas nize to see zer yute."

I was doing some calculating in my head.

"How old is Dmitri?"

Mrs. counted on her fingers. "Fifty, next year."

"Why did they have parties at your place?"

"Dmitri lives in small apartment, and most his friends

don't haff big enough plaze eider. Sometimes zere vas as many as tirty pipple. Ve haff lots of room." Again that hint of pride.

I changed tack. "If Dmitri wants to disappear, why do you want to find him?"

Bochinsky looked at me and, for the first time, tears ran down his cheeks. "He's our son. Do you haff children, Mr. Gold?"

I thought of Julie, presently doing four years in Juvie for running a child hooker ring at her summer camp. I smiled. "Yes, I do." Now why did that make me feel so damned good? Like some matron bragging on her son, the popular porn-flick director, to another biddy whose son, the banker, has just been given thirty years for investment fraud.

"Zen you know vat I mean. Dmitri iss in bad trouble, but he did not do zis ting. Ve vant him to give himself up."

I was still puzzled. "Vy—why did you call me last night? What did you think I could do?"

"It vass Dmitri's idea. He tought zat you might be able to help, but…how you say?…tings got out of hand. Zat's ven he dragged us out."

"Got out of hand" as a descriptor of five grisly murders?

"How did you get my number?"

"From ze book for ze telephone. Ve saw your name in ze paper. About how you rescued zat poor girl, ze mayor's daughter, from zat awful plaze. Such parents shouldn't be allowed to live."

I couldn't have agreed with him more.

It was not yet public knowledge that Julie was my daughter, not Mayor Wagner's. One of the stipulations concerning his resignation was that it be kept under wraps. He felt that he'd been humiliated enough, and I actually took pity on him.

No good deed goes unpunished, but that's a different story.

Jenny finally spoke up. "Do you swear that he was with you until two?"

They both bobbed their heads up and down.

"Did anyone see him with you, anyone at all?"

They were silent, I could see they were trying to recall.

"I suppose so," she said, "ve saw many pipple, but zey vere all strangers."

"Did you go in to any stores or shops, restaurants, cafes?"

"No. Dmitri said ve should not be seen anyvere. He vas very afraid."

"Did he give you any hint what he was afraid of."

"No. He only said ve vould vind out soon enough. Ven ve saw ze papers, ve knew ve had to come to you."

I thought for a while. "You realize that I am professionally bound to call the police. Dmitri is a material witness, at least."

Both their faces registered shock.

Mrs. recovered first. "But he did not do zis ting."

"I have only your word on that." I gave them my best double whammy look. "And, for all I know, *you* did."

Now they looked like they'd been hit with a million volts, but they weren't completely stupid, and they said nothing.

I knew I was sticking my neck out. Jenny was tossing me daggers of her own, but I was a hero now. Fuck 'em where they breathe.

"I won't say anything for the time being, but I can't promise more time than a day or two. Then, no matter what happens, you are going to have to turn yourselves in. I won't help you unless you agree to that. In writing."

They looked at each other, and there was nothing left of the haughtiness with which they'd come in. They both nodded their heads.

The rest of the meeting was dedicated to us dragging information out of them.

Verevolves, wampires, and vitches indeed. It sounded like the script for a horror flick.

Jenny kindly offered her services on this case.

What she said was, "If you try to cut me out of this one, I'll cut off your balls and hang them like mistletoe at a Christmas party."

She was only trying to be funny, but it reminded me of five bloody crosses.

Jenny was still throwing eye-daggers at me, but I took them to a cheap hotel and booked them a room as Mr. and Mrs. Gold, my parents. They promised to stay put and only leave the room for meals downstairs in the hotel dining room.

Why I trusted them, I didn't know.

❦❦❦

I still toyed with the idea of calling Frank, but all that would accomplish would be to get the Bochinskys locked up and start an even bigger city-wide manhunt for the wrong guy.

If they were telling the truth.

They were screwy as hell, but I did believe them. At least, I went about the investigation as though I believed them, but in my line of work, it becomes second nature to believe no one. Hard to get too surprised that way. It helps you to keep a straight face when the shit hits the fan.

I tried to make some sense of their story, to try to put it into some kind of perspective that would explain the Pollack on the ceiling. Something that was human. Frank had been right.

Killing chickens is a long way from slicing up five people, though.

We were in my office. I'd told Peggy to close up shop and go home. I could see that she wanted to stay. I questioned Jenny with my eyes. She shook her head. So much for me being "boss."

"You can't. Go home."

"Okay," she chirped, and left. She wasn't the type to hang on and whine. If she wanted to be a detective, I'd have to break her of that.

For a long time we didn't say anything.

Jenny broke the silence. "Where do we start?"

"I was hoping *you* knew. All I can think of is to follow the trail the Bochinskys laid out. His studio first, I think."

"You can't think he'd be there?"

"Not likely, but you never know with nuts."

"What makes you think he's nuts?"

I just gave her a long look.

"I see what you mean."

"He won't be there, but we might find something to help."

It was about three. We'd be able to get to Dmitri's place in about a half-hour.

What we didn't know at the time was a good thing. We'd have gone to a good horror movie instead. You always know it's make-believe.

CHAPTER 16

Apartment 15-A had a pigeon's eye view of the city. That was all it had to recommend it. It was a small studio for which Dmitri was, no doubt, paying big bucks. It was on the lower slopes of The Heights in an "artist colony" of sorts, peopled by some artists and a lot of ancient hippies. People said it reminded them of Haight-Ashbury in San Francisco in the good old days. That was what it said in the big newspaper article a few years back in the *Sunday Times*. I wouldn't know.

My first impression of Dmitri, from what the Bochinskys said, was borne out. The place was filthy, and it was a mess. The dirty clothes smell was the first thing that hit us when I finally got the door open. Dirty dishes were piled up in the sink. I checked the dishwasher. The same.

Dmitri was a spoiled mother's boy. He'd never grown up.

We piddled around for a bit, poking through the mess, but there was nothing that might give us a clue. There were a lot of books about vampires, mostly scholarly looking works, but there were a few titles with lurid covers mixed in. I riffled through some, there were a lot of sentences and paragraphs highlighted in pink, but I couldn't see anything that might offer a clue to where he might be.

The note pad next to the phone was pristine. I pulled out my handy pencil and shaded it in. Nothing.

"I wonder what this guy likes to eat," Jenny said. She was rummaging among the canned foods in the overhead cupboard. She grabbed the handle to the fridge.

"Yucko!"

I came over.

"Is that blood?"

One shelf of the refrigerator was covered with plastic bags filled with what was either red Kool-Aid or blood. I'd never seen any Kool-Aid that red. Maybe it was cherry syrup. I opened one and sniffed. It was blood. "Yucko," I said.

"Wampires?" Jenny was laughing in that way that people did when they were really bothered but didn't want to admit it.

"Or long-distance bicycle racers." I didn't really buy that one, though. The photo of Dmitri that Mrs. Bochinky laid on me showed a middle-aged man with a puffy face going to pot.

Too bad. I'd have loved bike racers.

We stared at the open fridge for a while until I finally just slammed the door shut. Jenny laughed that great laugh of hers, and this time it was real.

"What's so funny?"

"Did you ever see that old movie *Abbott and Costello Meet Frankenstein?*

I hadn't, but I got the picture.

There was another horror show behind the screen that separated his sleeping area from the rest of the studio. Every inch of the walls above the bed was covered with paintings.

Jenny's mouth flew open. "Oh, my God."

In lurid colors, the canvases portrayed naked, young bodies, mostly female, with a crimson cross drawn from forehead to groin and across the neck. The figures occupied the foreground and were large. Behind, and surrounding them, were a collection of strange-looking creatures, obviously meant to depict "wampires, verevolves, and vitches." They were drawn like wraiths, their bodies stretched out and distorted as they wandered across the canvas, often intertwining like pretzels. Each painting was different, but the overall effect was the same. The artist had a disturbed mind. At the bottom right of each was written D. Bochinsky.

The Bochinskys hadn't mentioned that Dmitri was an artist. Maybe they didn't know. They said they'd never been here.

"Is this stuff any good?" I asked after I'd looked them over.

"Not as far as I'm concerned," Jenny said. "They just give me the creeps. The bodies aren't even anatomically correct. The proportions are all wrong. They just don't look like real people to me, and I think they're supposed to. That's why they're removed from the background full of obviously not human things." Jenny studied art once but gave it up after admitting that she couldn't draw a straight line. "I couldn't keep the crayons inside the coloring book lines either," she once confessed.

I didn't remember what brought it up.

The most disturbing thing to me was that it looked like the works had been pulled out of the girls and hung between their legs. Like deformed penises, their clitorises were exaggerated.

This guy was sick all right.

I pulled down a couple. They were attached to the wall with thumbtacks. They weren't real big, maybe eleven by fourteen inches or something. I rolled them up and stuck them in my inside coat pocket. I knew a guy in the psych department at the U. I thought I'd get his take.

There was nothing else interesting beyond the yellowing cum stains that covered the sheet.

"Doesn't this asshole ever do the laundry?" Jenny's nose was turned up, like a terrier who'd come upon something that even she didn't want to roll around in.

I opened the closet door. It was filled with a rack of expensive looking suits, mostly black, and some expensive looking shoes lay on the floor beneath. His dresser was filled with expensive looking shirts, obviously Chinese laundered, so he was careful about his professional appearance, at least. His ties were silk.

I wondered how this guy made his money. He obviously had plenty. The Bochinskys didn't have a clue. The mother said he told them he worked in the financial field, but was pretty mysterious about it. When I asked them if they weren't curious, she said "It's his life. Ve don't vant to mix in."

Bochinsky got a disgusted look when she said it, but he kept his mouth shut. I had a feeling that I wouldn't find his name in any of the financial registers and wondered what he did that required an immaculate appearance.

I checked through the drawers of his small desk. Not a checkbook or bankbook in sight. There was a small desk calendar from some funeral home. That might be promising. It was a place to start anyway.

Tucked away in a corner were an easel and a small table that held all his painting materials. It was the only part of the place that was orderly.

There was a small bulletin board on the wall of the dinette. The only thing it held was a business card. It was for a café-bar called Grab-a-Bite. The Bochinskys had mentioned that he hung out there a lot. Word was that it was one of the weirdest hangouts in town. It catered to the werewolf and vampire crowd. Witches too, I had no doubt.

I looked at Jenny. "Ready for a night on the town?"

She looked at the paintings. "No, but I'll go."

One of the things I liked best about Jenny was that she was adventurous.

We were about half a block away when the cop cars came screaming up the street and half-a-dozen SWAT guys went running into the building.

"Took 'em a while. Lucky for us," I said.

It was well past lunchtime, so we stopped at a Red Lobster and got the all-you-can-eat seafood platter times two. I thought it was strange that we had any appetite at all, but we wolfed it down—no pun intended. Horror and hungry both started with H, but maybe it was just the adrenaline rush.

Afterward, I told her I'd pick her up in a taxi about seven-thirty, and we parted company. She went home. I had another destination in mind.

ↄ⊙ↄ

I didn't really know why I thought that Rabbi Shulson would know anything about vampires, but I thought he might. He knew a lot of stuff about a lot of stuff that had nothing to do with God or the Jews. I figured it was worth a shot.

I couldn't remember a time when my family didn't have a membership at Congregation Agudas Achim, and I can't remember any Rabbi but Shulson. He was approaching middle age then and was probably something close to eighty-five by now. He was one of first teachers in that Hebrew school my parents made me attend every day after public school. When I got older, I appreciated him more. I realized that he was a fountain of information about a lot of things, not just religion. He had a PhD and a rabbinical degree both from Yeshiva University, but he always said that his *smicha* was worth more to him than the doctorate.

When I was a teenager and thought I was troubled—until I realized that I was pretty sure that almost anything anyone told me wasn't worth shit—I used to come to him for advice.

He'd never hide behind a religious argument. Oh, he'd trot one out for good measure, for sure. I supposed that was one of the things he was hired for, but he never stopped there. Usually, he'd just stop talking, look at me, and say something like, "You're not buying it, are you, *boychik?*"

I never did, probably since I was ten and Maury Cohen's mother was killed in a robbery at their hardware store. I think I loved her as much as Maury did. I certainly loved her more than my own mother—or maybe it was just easier to get around her.

Once he dropped the religious stuff, he always had some bit of information to impart touching on whatever it was I had come to ask him, and it usually helped. At least, it always gave me something to think about beside what I was thinking about.

When I got older, he got tougher, and made me recognize my own bullshit when I spouted it.

I still came to sit in the *shul* whenever something was on my mind. I found the atmosphere soothing and conducive to thought. I didn't really know why.

I figured I'd find him puttering around before *mincha*, the afternoon prayer. I also figured he'd be damned surprised to see me, since I usually try to get there early in the morning to avoid him. Problem is, in his later years he's become a *nudge*. He just won't give up trying to entice me back into the fold.

I figured right, but he recovered pretty quickly. I think he was genuinely happy to see me. He did once say that I was his brightest pupil, but he always knew that I'd never fit in, and I think he took it as a personal failure.

He smiled at me in the way he had. His hair and beard were now almost completely white, but his gray eyes seemed as sharp and piercing as ever through the small wire-rimmed spectacles he'd worn for as long as I'd known him. He always reminded me of an eagle I once saw in the zoo.

"So, Joey, I've been reading about you in the papers. Didn't I tell you you'd figure it out?"

I laughed. "I suppose that makes you a genius?"

Actually, it had been a couple of months since I'd uncovered the sex ring at Julie's camp and the orgies at the mayor's mansion, and the uproar had been replaced by at least three others by now. If you mentioned it to most people, you'd probably draw a blank. That's the modern memory span for you.

He looked up at me, and the face above his bristly beard was inquisitive. "Tell me about your daughter."

I was tempted, but there was still too much going on in my head about that subject, and I wasn't sure that I wanted to deal with it now. I'd come for another reason.

"She's a very troubled young woman," I said. "What do you know about vampires?" The look on his face was worth about a million bucks. I roared with laughter. "No," I finally managed to say, "*she's* not a vampire. I guess I put that wrong. It's somebody else."

I certainly got his mind off Julie, though.

He stared at me. "What do you mean vampires? You mean like Bela Lugosi?"

"No, I mean real vampires."

Now his face registered alarm. "Are you okay, Joey?"

I laughed again. "I mean people who think they're vampires."

He finally got it. "*Meshugginers*, crazy people, you mean?"

"Yeah, *meshugginers* who kill people.

The man had lost no quickness of mind with age. He looked at me with real comprehension. "You're talking about those murders last night?"

"Yes."

Now he looked at me with real fear. "How are you involved?"

"Someone called me from there for help, but I got there too late. I'm looking for the guy who called me, and I have reason to believe he thinks he's a vampire. But he's a vampire in trouble."

"He killed those people?"

"No, but he knows who did."

He stared at me for a while. "I don't know how you get yourself into these things, but how do you think I can help you?"

"What do you know about vampires?"

He looked up toward the ceiling, then he looked at me. "Nothing much. There's no such thing in Jewish folk beliefs, *per se*. There is the figure of Lillith, of course."

"Lillith?"

"According to Midrashic legend, she was actually the first woman that the Creator of All, Blessed Be He, made for Adam, but she was rebellious and, according to other legends, she was banished to the underworld. In some legends, she can appear to men and drink their blood. It's all *bubba myses*, nonsense, of course."

"Is that it?"

"There's nothing else that I can think of. I'm sure I could find more if I researched the subject, but I doubt that any of it can help you. You are obviously dealing with a crazy person. You'd probably get more information from Freud and other psychologists. How much time do you have?"

I laughed. "None."

"Then, once again, you'll have to figure it out on your own. You've picked my brains clean." He cocked an eye at me. "Maybe you'll stay for *mincha?*"

"You know the answer to that, Rabbi."

"Well, it can't hurt to ask." He cast a long glance at me. "You be careful now," he said, "*meshugginers* are not to be trifled with."

ഩഩ

It was about eight when we got to the Grab-a-Bite. A garish neon sign greeted us, the name of the place surrounded by vicious looking fangs that changed from open to closed. It looked like they were snapping shut. Red lights blinked on and off in sequence as they dribbled down like drops of blood. The crowd was spilling out onto the sidewalk, and most looked like vampires and werewolves.

"Shouldn't we be in some kind of costumes?" Jenny said.

I had a vision of her in a slinky vampira dress, most of her boobs hanging out. "Nah. I hear that this place attracts a lot of straights gawking at the freaks."

The smell of alcohol was almost erased by the heavy incense smoke that rose from every corner. Dozens of lit sticks were stuck into colorful, sand-filled urns that looked expensive.

It was a big place. The long, curved bar area was separated from the café by an arched entrance. A sign above it said *Crypt Room. Abandon all hope ye who enter here.* I wondered if that was a warning about the coffee.

There were three steps down. It was noisy, even at this early hour, and cigarette smoke mixed freely with the incense. Wagner had fought the anti-smoking crowd tooth and nail, but I figured that the next guy would cave. There was just too much public opinion. Sometimes I think there's too damned much public opinion about everything.

The center of the café was filled with tables made of pine coffins. Each had a glass top beneath which lay either a vampire or a skeleton. They were illuminated by a string of LED lights strung around the top edge.

Smaller tables were large brass funerary urns, and a grinning skull, set upon a bed of dried and withered flower petals, looked up at you from below.

We'd fallen into the land of perpetual Halloween.

Lighting was provided by fake torches set in sconces along the walls made to look like the inside of a cave. They looked kind of crappy, but the fire department would have closed the place down in a minute if they'd gone for the real thing. Too bad. Bureaucrats never have any imagination.

There were enough straights to provide us with cover, but most of the customers looked like refugees from the People's Republic of Freaks. I wondered if they carried passports.

The bar was filled mainly by the freaks, apparently those close quarters weren't too appealing to the straights, who mostly just gawked from the safety of their coffins.

Our waitress was wearing the outfit I'd thought about for Jenny. Her boobs were pretty much hanging out too. I could just make out the hint of pink aureoles at the edges. Her face was make-up white, with lips as black as charcoal. Her eyes were outlined with black, smeared to look like shiners. Did they think people really wanted to order food from a ghoul? Apparently, plenty did.

Jenny ordered a latte. I hate that fancy crap and stuck with plain old Colombian. Whatever the warning was about, it wasn't the coffee. It was delicious and at five bucks a cup, it had better be. It was served in white mugs that looked like skulls.

The walls were covered with posters and stills from a bunch of old-time horror flicks, Karloff, Chaney, and Lugosi menaced us from within. I thought that sounded like a legal firm and I laughed.

"What's so funny?"

I told her but she didn't think it was funny.

"I'll stick with Dewey, Cheatham, and Howe," she said.

I'd heard that one too many times to laugh.

When the waitress brought our coffee, I asked her if she'd seen Dmitri Bochinsky around lately. She just looked at me for a while.

"You a cop?"

"Why would you think so?"

"I can read the papers, y'know."

It was then that I realized she was chewing gum.

I gave her my wide-eyed open look. "No, we're just old friends."

"I can't help you. I'm new here. Check with Lyle. He's the head bartender. He's been here forever and knows everybody."

She was turning to leave when Jenny said, "What's a nice girl like you doing in a place like this?"

She laughed. "Hey, I have to pay tuition and buy textbooks. This place pays real good, and the tips are great."

"A college girl, huh. What are you studying?"

"Psychology." She laughed, "I figure I'm killing two birds with one stone. Ever seen so many weirdoes in your life?"

She had us there.

"Lyle's the one with all the hair," she said and moved on.

I searched behind the bar and there was no mistaking Lyle. He was a dead ringer for Lon Chaney Jr. in *The Wolfman*. I remembered a show I'd seen on TV about some screwballs who wanted to look like animals. There was a whole bunch of plastic surgeons catering to them. I wondered if he'd had facial hair transplants.

"Guess I'll go get us a couple of drinks. Wanna come along?"

"Hell no," she said, "I'll just watch from here as he bites into you."

"Suit yourself, but it's bound to be entertaining."

"I'll restrain myself."

The gang at the bar looked like a bunch of extras in a fright film. There were vampires, werewolves, a couple of aliens, and assorted other type creepies. There were also a couple of dynamite broads in long, see-through dresses. I figured them for witches. They looked like they came right out of that witch movie where Jack Nicholson played the devil. They could cast a spell on me anytime. You could just make out their nipples through the fabric.

More of the extras were crowding around, waiting either for drinks or a stool. A lot of them were obviously wearing costumes, but there were plenty, I was willing to bet, who were keeping the plastic surgeons in their Ferraris and the gas to run them. How could they afford it? What kind of fucking job could any of them possibly get? Besides here? I had a vision of them all taking each other's orders.

I managed to insinuate myself between the witches. I

smiled at them in turn. "Hi, ladies. Mind if I squeeze in?"

"Suit yourself," they said in unison. A sister act.

For a while, I was comfortable just standing between them. Their perfume was heady. It was White Shoulders. I knew because an old girlfriend used to wear it. It was the scent of gardenias, a funereal flower if ever there was one.

"You girls come here often?"

The blonde looked at the brunette and the brunette said, "Get lost."

I put on my most hurt look. "That wasn't very nice. I just wanted to ask you if you know where I might find a friend."

"Try Facebook," the blonde said.

Jenny had told me all about Facebook the other day. She wasn't interested, but a lot of her friends were on it, so I didn't have to feign the laugh.

"Say, that was pretty good. Dmitri Bochinsky. Know the guy?"

That shocked them into silence.

The brunette's eyes looked scared. "Who are you?"

"I'm an old friend. I saw where he's in trouble and thought I might be able to help him out."

She didn't look like she believed me, but she relaxed a little. "I have no idea where he is. We don't usually travel in the same circles."

There are "circles? And here I'd thought it was all the same circus. "Did you ever attend any parties at his folks' place?"

"Say, who the hell are you?" The blonde had come alive, "You sound like a cop."

I laughed. "Used to be, now I'm just trying to help out Dmitri."

"Yeah? Where do you know him from?"

I had a sudden inspiration. "We took art classes together."

The brunette spoke up. "I don't know much about art, but those paintings of his were sure terrific. They gave me goose bumps. You paint stuff like that?"

"No. My style is more non-representational." I'd read that in an article. I didn't know what the fuck it meant, but I was sure neither of these babes did either. I was right, their faces got kind of respectful.

"Have you been up to his place?" I asked.

"His place? Oh, no. He had an exhibition here a few months back."

"Did he sell many?"

"Oh, Dmitri always said that he didn't paint for the money, but for his soul. He wouldn't give them away either."

"What's he up to, nowadays? We lost touch a few years ago."

They both shrugged. Then the blonde brightened up. She was looking past me.

"Sheena might know. She knew Dmitri better than us."

"Did someone mention Dmitri?"

The voice came from behind me and had a distinct purr. I turned around to face a tawny black woman painted, maybe tattooed, with spots like a leopard. She was naked. Her bush had been dyed a golden color to match her skin, but she hadn't shaved it. Three sets of nipples marched up her tawny torso, the second two topped small but nicely shaped hills, and the top two ended at the tips of some beautifully sculpted boobs. The leopard spots covered her face and she sported cat whiskers. I'd never seen multiple nipples before, and I looked hard to make sure they were real. They were.

"See something you like?" she purred at me.

I rarely get flustered, but I was speechless now. I'd seen a whole lot that I liked. I was wondering about my sanity, but my dick didn't care about that at all, it was clamoring to bust out. She was frighteningly gorgeous, auburn hair in a million cornrows tumbling down to her ass.

She didn't have a tail, but I was willing to bet that there was a plastic surgeon who could give her one. Weird as it was, the overall effect was stunning. I'd never balled a leopard.

I really couldn't trust myself so I just blurted out Dmitri's name. "Y'know him?"

Her eyes turned from playful to hard. "You a cop?"

Blondie saved me. "He's an artist, an old friend of Dmitri's, and he wants to help him."

Thank god for alcohol. It makes people even dumber than they already are. Sheena's eyes softened again, now that she had a personal endorsement from my old friend Blondie.

"Look," she said, and her tone was earnest. "Dmitri couldn't have done this. He's nuts, but he's not a killer."

"I know that, but he really needs help. Do you know where he is?"

She shrugged. "Don't have a clue. Hey, Lyle," she had to shout to be heard above the background noise, which included ghostly music coming from speakers in the walls. It sounded like right out of some old horror film.

Lyle came over. He looked at me like I was some kind of exhibit in a zoo.

"This guy's an old artist friend of Dmitri's. Says he can help him."

"Yeah? Whaddaya wanna know?"

I was willing to bet that Chaney Jr. was turning over in his grave. His diction had always been impeccable. Except when he was growling.

Lyle was definitely the product of the nip and tuck boys. That hair coming out of his face was real, not just his normal beard, but a whole lot of extra. It wasn't even the same color, so you could tell. Hair was even growing out of his forehead. He was wearing a short-sleeved shirt and his arms were also full of transplants, unless he was naturally hairy, but I didn't think so. I wondered about his chest.

I tried to ignore it, but he was laughing. "I get that look a lot."

"Do you know where I can find him?"

"I don't, but I'll ask around. Maybe somebody does. Where are you sitting?"

I pointed to Jenny.

"Hey, nice," he said.

"You with her?" Sheena sounded disappointed.

"For now," I said.

"Well," she purred, "you know where to find me."

I ordered a couple of Haigs, nodded to the witches, and wound my way back to the table. My erection had gone down after the playful little tug Sheena gave it before she moved off.

"Was that woman naked?" Jenny asked before I even sat down.

"As a jaybird, but more like a leopard. She has six nipples. Can you believe that?"

"Real nipples?"

"Near as I could tell. I didn't know her well enough to feel them."

"That never stopped you before."

She had a point.

I filled her in about everything I hadn't learned. "The bartender's asking around. Maybe he'll come up with something."

"He's asking? What are you, old buddies or something?"

"As soon as my old buddies Blondie and Sheena vouched for me, I was in."

We nursed our drinks until Lyle came over. I wanted a lot more, but I never drank to excess on the job. That was a sure way to find yourself in some dark alley, dead.

He looked Jenny up and down. "Say, didn't you used to be a pole dancer at Cherries? You look familiar."

She smiled. "That was years ago. I'm over at Vinegar Lil's nowadays."

I could see he was confused. He hadn't really expected *that* answer. Jenny was an old hand with the come-on boys. He gave up.

"Here. This is all I could come up with. The guy said he hangs out there sometimes." He handed me a business card.

"You ever cater any of his parties?" I said it kind of offhand.

He surprised me. "Nah, but he hired me as a bartender a few times. Under the table, y'know. Damn good thing he didn't ask me last night."

"Any idea who the dead kids might be?" They hadn't been officially identified yet.

"Not a clue, but I'll bet I'll know them. Dmitri liked the younger crowd. He painted them."

"You like his paintings?" I asked.

"Yecchh. Too creepy for me, and what's with that cross he draws on them?'

I shrugged my shoulders. I figured he'd find out soon enough. "Do a lot of people from here go to those parties?"

"Not really. I know we look like a bunch of rejects from a sideshow, but this is a good crowd. Everyone's here for fun."

"Who owns this place?"

He shrugged. "Dunno. Never met 'em. I take my orders from Archie, the manager."

"Is he here now?"

"Naw, he usually hangs out at some Irish joint he manages too. Duffy's Tavern, it's called. Over on Tenth and Vine. He hates this place." He laughed. "I think he's actually scared to come in."

"Who gave you this card?"

"Can't say. I promised."

I shrugged.

I gave him *my* card. His eyes got kind of wide and he looked like some bizarre Teddy Bear.

"If you hear anything, give me a call. His parent's hired me. They were with him most of the night, but he's got to turn himself in. He knows who killed those kids, and he's in danger himself."

I must have convinced him, because he got all serious.

"I will," he said. "This is just terrible. Those poor kids."

He gave Jenny another big smile before he went back to the bar.

I looked at the card in my hand.

The Wolf's Lair.

CHAPTER 17

If the Grab-a-Bite was a circus, The Wolf's Lair was more like a London Club. There was no hint of a restaurant from the outside. The simple sign stood above a double doorway of wood at the top of a short staircase. That was it. There were no windows behind which diners could be seen, they were all covered by heavy white draperies.

"Is this place actually open?" Jenny said. She was giving the building the once over.

"Only one way to find out." I grabbed one of the fancy brass door handle that was shaped, at the top, like a wolf's head. The door opened onto a long, low, marbled corridor with an elegant oriental runner down the middle. My head barely missed scraping the ceiling.

There were three fluted half-columns lining the corridor on either side. They were topped by Grecian busts with a votive candle burning in front of each. The lighting was low and the candles threw their features into high relief. I couldn't figure what this had to do with werewolves, but it felt like the entrance to a tomb.

An arched opening covered by a red curtain stood at the end.

"Well, this is weird," Jenny said.

"Yup." I reached out and pulled back the curtain.

The corridor continued for a bit. On one side was a black leather banquette. The other side held a very ordinary looking restaurant desk. It was manned by a tuxedoed maitre de'. At first, he looked at us as though he wasn't expecting strangers. It was half a double-take, but he recovered in the middle, and flashed us a phony maitre de' smile. He held out a couple of large leatherette menus. I didn't know about Jenny, but I felt disoriented.

"Is this your first visit with us, sir?" I'll bet he got an A for saccharine obsequiousness at Maitre de' U.

"Yes it is," Jenny said, "and we're very excited."

His smile never changed. It was like it was frozen on. "Good, good. I am certain that you will be pleased." He turned around, "This way, please."

His mincing walk made me wonder if he was part of Dmitri's party circuit.

A few steps, and around a corner, brought us to a wide opening. We were at the top of a staircase and looking down into a dimly lit grotto. As my eyes adjusted, I could see that it was filled with tables, and curtained booths lined the fake rock walls. Votive candles burned at each table casting the same kind of shadows on the diners as on the busts in the corridor. Two huge crystal chandeliers hung from the rocky ceiling, but the lights were dimmed low. They looked more like stars than bulbs.

I counted ten steps down, and the stairs were lighted with two rows of votive candles. Again I got the feeling of entering a tomb. Jenny had her arm in mine and I felt her shudder.

As we were led to a table, I noticed another curtained entrance. A sign above it said Members Only. Members of what? I figured *they* probably knew. I wanted to too. I've always hated being left out.

We passed tables filled mostly with straights, but I

caught sight of more than a few highlighted faces that reminded me of my Aunt Lily's chows. I hated those little buggers, they always snapped at me.

Lily said that was because they didn't like ruffians. They had me nailed.

I wondered who all the straights were. The atmosphere was nothing like at the Grab-a-Bite, there was no circus to be seen. Maybe they were closet werewolves. They were all expensively dressed. Even in the dim light I could smell wealth.

Classical music was playing in the background, at a reasonable volume.

"It's Baroque," Jenny said when I mentioned it.

"Who broke it? Sounds okay to me."

She flashed me that lame-joke look, her cute little mouth turned up on one side of her scrunched up face.

When we finally sat down, I asked about the *Members Only* sign.

"That is the Black Forest Society, sir."

"The Black Forest Society? I don't believe I've ever heard of it?"

The smile gave way to a look as though he'd smelled something bad. "Of course you haven't. It is a very exclusive private club." He said it with a sniff.

I ignored being made to feel like a bug. "What kind of club is it?" I smiled at him, one of my more personable ones.

He just sniffed again. "It's an exclusive private club. If that will be all, I'll send over your waiter, Hans."

"Jeez," Jenny said after he'd given us a cursory bow and left, "I think you offended him."

I laughed. "Anything to wipe that smile off his face."

She giggled. "You succeeded."

I opened the menu and could see why this place smelled of wealth. Jenny's eyes got kind of big too.

"We can't afford this," she hissed at me, "there aren't any prices."

"Yeah, I noticed. You want to walk out?"

"Hell no. I've always wanted to eat at one of these places. They say the food is always worth it."

The menu was heavy on German food with special delicacies like Boar's Head soup, and freshly-killed venison. I wondered what went on in the kitchen. There was no Wienerschnitzel. No sausage either.

We ordered the house red.

"So, now what?" Jenny said.

"We start pumping for oil."

When the wine waiter brought our wine I asked him his name.

"Sergei, sir."

"Tell me, Sergei, I'm looking for an old friend of mine. Someone told me he's a regular customer here. Dmitri Bochinsky."

Sergei didn't miss a beat. "Are you a cop?"

The smile left his face. It really is a shame that people are so suspicious nowadays.

It worked before, so I tried it again. "No, we were in art school together. I just got into town, and I thought I'd look him up, but nobody answers at his place. I'm only in town for a few days, and I'd hate to miss him. Why do you ask if I'm with the police?" I gave him my most honest look."

He must have bought it, sort of, because the smile sort of returned. "I guess you haven't read the papers." I kept my face blank, "There was a murder at his parents' place last night, and he disappeared."

"How terrible," Jenny gasped. "Did he kill his parents?"

"No. They're missing too."

I put on my most puzzled face. "So who was murdered?"

"Five people. They haven't given out any names yet."

"Five people!" Jenny almost shouted, "Oh, my God in heaven." She put her hand up to her mouth and her eyes held a wild and frightened look.

The waiter was no help. He hadn't seen him for a while, but he said he'd ask around. Bartenders and waiters are some of the best sources of information. Not too expensive, either.

After he left, I looked at Jenny. "I could have sworn I told you about the killings."

She laughed. "You liked that, huh?" Jenny did a stint at acting school for a while, but she got sick of the artificiality. "Hell," she said, "I do just as much acting in real life, and that's for real."

She could be as cynical as I, at times. That's another reason I liked her, no phony cornball emotional crap. "Tell it like it is," was her motto.

I didn't always like to hear it, though.

Hans, our waiter, like all the staff, wore a black tuxedo, but only the maitre de's had tails. It occurred to me they were forked. I'd have to be careful not to let my imagination run wild. This case was doing funny things to my head, but I wasn't laughing. The image of five crosses wouldn't go away.

"What do you recommend?" Jenny looked all bright-eyed and bushy-tailed.

"Ah, for starters you will not find anything better than succulent *Kaninchen,* served in a delicious leek and onion soup."

"Sounds delicious," I said.

"What's *Kaninchen.*" Jenny always did have an inquiring mind.

"Spring rabbit, killed at six months and marinated for a year. Absolutely delicious."

Even in the dim light I could see that her face lost some color.

"I think not," she said.

He turned to me. "For you sir?"

"I think not too. We aren't very hungry. I think we'll just stick with an entrée." I looked at Jenny. "Is that all right with you, dear?"

She smiled. "That will be fine."

The waiter seemed disappointed, but he was a professional. "In that case, may I suggest the roast pork, simmered in a sauce of mushrooms and truffles, served with baked-to-perfection *kartoffel* imported from Bavaria, and fresh spring peas. It is our most popular item and is always delicious. The pork will melt in your mouth."

"What's *kartoffel*?" Jenny looked worried.

"Potatoes."

"That sounds good." I looked at Jenny. She nodded. "Roast pork, it is."

As he was writing the order I asked him if he knew Dmitri. He stiffened. I gave him my *schtick*, coming up with a few new embellishments here and there. I guess he bought it too, because he relaxed. He said he'd ask around.

He was right about the pork. It was about the best I'd ever had. Jenny agreed. I wondered if I'd find this place in *Michelin*. I doubted it. I'd never seen an ad for it, and I'd never heard of it. It was off the beaten track. How did all these people find out about it? Was it only the food that kept them coming back? After finishing the last delectable morsel, I could believe it.

"People are looking at us." Jenny's eyes were parked somewhere over my shoulder.

"Who?"

"Waiters."

"I guess asking around got us noticed."

Hans came over. He carried a brass tray upon which two brandy glasses held a ruby liquid. "Compliments of the house," he said, "in the hope that you will become regular customers. It has been a pleasure to serve you." He set the tray down, bowed, and left after placing the check on the table, snuggled in a plush leather binder. I wasn't sure that I wanted to open it. I did though.

"Well." Jenny was prodding, "how much?"

I passed it over to her. She whistled. "Holy shit. For two roast porks?"

"We *could've* walked out, for all the information we've gotten."

"Oh well, down the hatch." She picked up her snifter and tasted. Then she smiled. Then she gulped it down. "Like cherries," she said.

She was right. It did taste like cherries. Something else too, but I couldn't place it just then.

We got as far as the Banquette when I started to feel faint. I sat down hard. I thought Jenny did too. I also thought she was hanging on to *me* pretty hard. As the lights went out, I remembered that slightly bitter after-taste…

ຂຈຂ

Rohypnol. *Roofies*, I thought, but I wasn't sitting on the banquette any more. I was sitting in a straight backed chair. I was also tied to it. I looked to my left. Jenny was too, but she wasn't awake yet, her head was hanging on her chest. I knew what I saw, but I was having trouble making sense of it. My head was spinning and it took a while to slow down.

I looked around. We were in some kind of an office.

There was a big desk. It was unoccupied except for the contents of my pockets and Jenny's purse, all spread out on it.

"What the hell happened?" Jenny was awake but her voice was slurred.

"I think there were *roofies* in the brandy."

"*Roofies?*"

That's the date-rape drug."

"I know what *roofies* are, for chrissakes." She sounded exasperated so I figured she'd be all right. Then I wondered if either of us would. Stupid, stupid, stupid. Never drink anything that anyone you don't know gives you for free. Five bloody crosses danced in my head.

"I think we're in trouble," she said.

"Tell me something I don't know."

❧❦❧

We sat there long enough for most of the wooziness to go away. When the door behind the desk opened, I was fully expecting a werewolf, or something, but the man who came through it looked more like he could have been the fat man in a sideshow. To say he was portly would be stating it at least one port too short. He was big too, taller than I. He was bald, and his head shone like it'd been polished. It was a little too small for his size, but his steel blue eyes reminded me of a Siamese cat I'd once had. She was a good hunter and I'd usually wake up every morning to my mother's screams.

I wondered what *he* hunted, then I thought about the Boar's Head soup and venison. Then I figured he'd probably kill *himself* before anything else. He needed something more defenseless, like human beings tied to chairs.

He was followed into the room by a pair of goons. He directed them toward us. I tensed, but all they did was untie us and leave. The big guy sat down at his desk. He had a gun in his hand—a .45.

"I sincerely trust that you will do nothing foolish. I am an excellent shot." His voice was surprisingly tenor for a bass fiddle. There was also a slight hiss about it, as though his bulk was making it hard for him to breathe."

"You're holding the cannon," I said.

"So I am."

He assumed an apologetic look. At least, I thought he did. The folds of fat on his face and jowls were hard to read.

"I am sorry for the ropes, but they were for your own protection. We wouldn't want you to fall and hurt yourselves now, would we?"

"I don't know. Who's 'we'?"

He sat back in his chair and didn't say anything for a while. "There is no need for you to know. It is enough that I know who *you* are."

"Where are we?" Jenny was pissed.

"In the Wolf's Lair. My lair." He laughed, and it was surprisingly good-natured under the circumstances. It changed real quick. "Why are you looking for Dmitri Bochinsky?"

"His parents hired me to find him. They want him to turn himself in."

There was a hint of surprise on his face. What kind of answer had he been expecting?

Then he boomed a laugh, and the full power of the bass fiddle became apparent. He went on laughing for some time and tears began to pour down his cheeks. "Excuse me," he hissed, and pulled the handkerchief out of his pocket and dabbed at his eyes. The gun never wavered.

"Occam's razor it is, by God. The simplest explanation is the most likely." He was still laughing. Then his eyes turned cold again. "Can you prove it?"

"The receipt should be in my purse or somewhere in that mess on your desk." Jenny still sounded pissed.

"You will please come and find it. Do not try any funny stuff."

He kept the gun on her and one eye on me as she rifled through the small pile. I'm always amazed at the amount of crap women lug around with them and constantly bitch about.

"Here it is." She picked it up and handed it to him.

"Go sit back down."

When she had, he looked over the receipt. He grunted.

"Why else would you think I'd be looking for him?" I said.

He gave me a hard look. "Please do not take me for a fool, Mr. Gold. Dmitri's life is in danger, and you could have been hired by someone who wants him dead."

"That's why he needs to turn himself in."

He studied my eyes for a bit longer. "I agree."

"Do you know where he is?"

He shook his head. "Alas, no. Dmitri can be very hot-headed at times. Like a bull in a china shop. He refuses to submit to direction."

My curiosity was in high gear. "What's your relationship with Dmitri?"

"Why is that any of your business?"

"I'm a detective. Everything is my business when it concerns a client."

He gave me another hard look. "Let us just say that we are something like master and pupil."

"Which one are you?" Sometimes Jenny doesn't know when to keep her trap shut, but he just laughed.

"It is a poor master who cannot learn from his pupil, but I note your impertinence. I like it. Too many of your sex have had the fire inside stamped out."

I knew that Jenny didn't know what to make of that. I didn't. Her mouth was still just a little bit hanging open.

"Was that a come on?" she finally said.

He laughed again. "Hardly, my dear, I was just stating an unhappy fact."

"I'm not your dear." There was fire in her eyes and I was glad she had a black belt, but going up against this guy would be like hitting a brick wall. "And I don't take kindly to being slipped a Mickey. If you didn't have that gun, I'd come over there and slap your face."

He laughed again. "I might enjoy that, but don't get any ideas." He could go from amused to menacing in a heartbeat. *Who the hell was this guy?* I figured I should change the subject.

"What's the Black Forest Society?"

He actually smiled—I think.

"It is an exclusive private club."

"What kind of club?"

His eyes turned menacing again. So did his voice. "You are trying my patience, Mr. Gold. There is no need for you to know."

I decided to let it drop. "Do you know what he does for a living. His parents didn't have a clue"

He shrugged, it was like a mountain during an earthquake. "Nor do I. We are not interested in such matters here."

"Just so long as he's wealthy, right?"

He laughed again and I thought about Santa in *The Night Before Christmas*. Then I thought about the venison on the roof.

"You are a very cynical man, Mr. Gold."

"I've been around for a while."

He said no more but reached into his jacket and pulled out the rolled up paintings. "Where did you get these?"

"From his studio."

"Ghastly, are they not?"

I had to agree.

"Dmitri has several unsolved problems, as I'm sure you can see. We are working them out, but he still has some way to go."

"To go where?"

"To know that, you would have to be a member of the Black Forest Society. And you are not." He was silent for a moment. Then he tossed the drawings onto the desk with the rest. "One thing." It almost sounded like he was pleading. "If you find him, I would appreciate it if you would bring him here first."

"Why?"

"So that I can see with my own eyes that he is all right. He is very dear to me. For all his stubbornness, he is an apt pupil. That is a rare gift indeed. Any master would treasure it."

"I'll see what I can do," I said. *In a pig's eye*, I thought.

"We are finished here," He pushed a buzzer on his desk. The goons came in. "Please escort Mr. Gold and Miss Martin—"

"Ms." Jenny hissed at him.

"—Ms. Martin to the front."

"One thing," I said, holding my palm up to the goons, "why the hell did you have to slip us the roofies? Couldn't you just have asked us nicely?"

"I had no way of knowing if you were armed. Incapacitating you was the safest option. We wouldn't want a scene now, would we?"

"I wouldn't have minded."

"I'm sure not, but, to tell the full truth, it was also an experiment."

"An experiment?" Jenny was really pissed now.

"Yes. What you were given was not normal roofies, as they are called in the vulgar vernacular so prevalent in your culture nowadays. We have been experimenting with mixtures and dosages. What we gave you lasts for little more than fifteen minutes, and has few after effects."

"Don't expect us to thank you," I said.

He boomed another deep laugh. "No thanks necessary," he finally said. "On the house."

"Who's this 'we' mixing up drugs?"

"Another thing you have no need to know." He'd stopped laughing.

It took a while before we could collect all the crap on the desk, but he didn't rush us. The goons led us through a maze of corridors until we emerged at the main desk. The maitre de smiled at us. "I hope you enjoyed your dinner. Please return again soon."

If the sonofabitch thought I was going to tip him, he had another think coming.

Before we could leave, one of the tuxedoed waiters came out of the john next to the banquette. He wasn't looking, and he bumped right into Jenny, knocking her purse to the floor.

His face turned scarlet. "Oh, I am so terribly sorry." He bent down and picked it up. Jenny grabbed it and didn't say anything. It was not like her to be impolite, but she was more pissed than I'd seen her in a while.

I did the honors. "Thanks. Next time, watch where you're going."

He said nothing more but turned to go back to the dining room.

We made our way back through the mausoleum entrance and out into the fresh air.

Jenny looked at me. "What just happened?"

"Damned if I know," I said.

❦

It was a little past ten. I called Frank. I knew he was pulling the late shift. I'd told him earlier that I was following a promising lead in the case, but I couldn't be specific. He hadn't been happy about it.

"Yeah?"

"Is that how you always answer the phone?"

"Only when it's you."

"You're psychic now?"

"Ever hear of caller ID?"

He had me there. I'd forgotten all about it.

"Have you ever heard of something called the Black Forest Society?"

Silence for a minute. "You mean like in Germany?"

"Bavaria."

"Whatever. What about it?"

"That's what I'm asking you. It's located in a restaurant called the Wolf's Lair on Gregory and Fourteenth in Stanford Court."

More silence. "If I remember rightly, Stanford Court isn't zoned for restaurants. You sure about that?"

"I'm standing in Stanford Square right now, and Ulysses S. Grant's horse is about to shit on my head."

He laughed. "Stay right where you are, don't move."

"How soon can you get me something?"

"Dunno. It's busy right now. Could take a couple of hours. Is it a rush job?"

"Naw, I guess it can wait, but my curiosity's been pricked. Also, check if anything comes up about a big, fat, bald guy. Looks something like Orson Welles before he died."

"Orson Welles?"

"Yeah, you remember. *War of the Worlds, Citizen Kane*, porked Rita Hayworth."

"I know who he was, f'crissakes. It's just that some-thing's poking at my memory button, but it ain't coming up. I'll have to think about it." He paused for a bit. "Y'know I'm putting my ass in a sling for you here. You've got one day left. That's all the slack I'm cutting you. Bochinsky's in my office by six, or we'll all be looking for him." He paused again. "Don't get in trou-ble."

"Too late," I said, and hit the little red, old-time re-ceiver icon on my cell phone. I still hadn't gotten tired of doing that. It always made me feel like I was in a science fiction movie. My head was still in the Dick Tracy com-ics, but all he had was some stupid wristwatch radio. It probably didn't even come in designer colors.

Take that, Tracy.

❧❦❧

It was late, but I figured I'd give Gordon Harrison a ring. Gordon was an old friend. He was on the psychiatric faculty at the med school, and I wondered what he'd have to say about the paintings.

He answered on the second ring. "Dr. Harrison."

"Gordon, its Joe Gold. Listen, if you have some time tonight, I'd like to run a couple of paintings by you. Get your professional opinion."

"Nice to hear from you, Joe. What kind of paintings?"

"That's what I need you to tell me."

"Well, I'm in my office right now. If you can get here in half-an-hour, I'll hang around."

The U was just about a half-hour cab ride from here.

"Can do, thanks."

❧❦❧

Gordon met us in his shirtsleeves. His jacket and medical whites were hanging on hooks. I hadn't seen him for a couple of years, ever since we worked together to put a homicidal maniac behind bars. He hadn't changed much. Maybe his hair was a shade grayer. He had the rugged good looks of an adventurer, but he once told me that he couldn't wait to get home from a surprise camping trip his kids had sprung on him.

I introduced him to Jenny and, after the usual social preliminaries, unrolled the paintings.

His expression didn't change. These kinds of things were probably part of his regular fare. He looked from one to the other, and back again. Then he looked at me. "Why did you need me? I'm sure that you can see he's nuts. That's not an accepted medical term, but it's a fact."

"Nuts how?" I felt honored to be included in the professional fraternity of those who could tell a nut when they saw one, but he was giving me more credit than I had coming.

He thought for a bit. "Well, there are some obvious signs of at least a mild pedophilia, his obsession with youth. The background figures are pretty phantasmagorical. I assume they're supposed to be vampires and werewolves, but without knowing something about the artist, it's hard to say what they represent in his psyche. I've never come across this kind of thing in cases of pedophilia, so I really don't know what to say. And the crosses. That kind of throws me for a loop, but it's such an obvious religious symbol, that I'd have to say that the artist is a deeply religious person. Perhaps he paints the crosses as a talisman against his pedophilia."

"Huh?"

"He has sexual feelings for the children he paints, and he superimposes the cross to make them sacred objects, thus removing them from his basest desires. Elevating them, even. It's a catharsis, of sorts. He's able to relieve his sexual tension without committing the actual sin."

I thought about it. "That really doesn't make a lot of sense, does it?"

He just looked at me. "He's nuts. Remember?"

Jenny burst out laughing. "I was in therapy once, and I'd have given anything for my therapist to be as honest as you."

"A psychotherapist?

"Yes."

"Quacks." He looked closely at her. "You aren't still seeing him, are you?"

She laughed again. "I thought he was a quack by my third visit, but I kept coming back, feeding him a line of total bullshit, just to see what he'd make of it."

Now, Gordon laughed. "What was his final diagnosis?"

"That I needed to be committed to a mental institution as soon as possible. He assured me it was for my own safety and for those around me."

She started laughing again and he joined her. I thought it was pretty funny, too.

"What about the distorted genitals on the girls?" I asked.

"Well, again without knowing the artist, the enlarged clitorises on top of the vaginas, making them look a lot like testicles, lead me to suspect that he has homosexual tendencies. Can you tell me who the artist is?" He was definitely curious.

"Keep it under your hat, but I assume you've heard of the Bochinsky murders."

His eyebrows rose.

"The papers have only reported that the victims had their throats cut. What they don't say is that they were also slit open from groin to neck and from forehead to chin."

"The cross."

I could see he was startled.

"Yep. The artist is the son of the old couple who hired me to find him. It was their apartment, but they swear he hustled them out of there before anything happened and was with them until two."

He was speechless for a moment. "What do you want from me?"

"Is there anything you can see that might give us a clue as to where he might be?"

He looked over the paintings for a few more minutes. Then he looked up at me. "Nope. There's just nothing here. I'm sorry that I can't be of more help."

"Well," I said, "it was worth a shot."

As we were leaving, he stopped me for a moment and looked at me hard. "Be careful," he said.

CHAPTER 18

There didn't seem like a whole lot more for us to do, so I took Jenny home in a taxi and then crashed myself.

I was just starting on my second Haig and water, neat, when the phone rang. It was Jenny. She sounded disturbed.

"When I got home, I found a strange piece of paper in my purse."

"How strange?"

"The only thing on it was an address. I have no idea where it came from."

I remembered the clumsy waiter. "I do. That waiter must have slipped it in when he picked up your purse. What's the address?"

"One, One, Two, Seven, Three, Five Sleepy Hollow Road. Where the hell is that?"

"*Y'chupitz*," I said.

"Did you just sneeze?"

"*Y'chupitz*. It's a Yiddish expression meaning 'Drive to the end of the road. Then drive some more. It's in Brentwood Hills."

"Brentwood Hills? That's way to hell and gone."

"*Y'chupitz.*"

"What d'you suppose it means?"

"It means that somebody wants us to go there. What else? Rent a car in the morning. Right now, get some sleep."

"I'm not sleepy. There's a National just down the block. I'll pick you up in an hour." She didn't give me a chance to object. I heard the click of the receiver.

I looked at the Haig Bros.

"Catch you later," I said. "'Boss,' my Jewish ass," I said to the walls.

❧❦❧

Brentwood Hills was one of the poshest suburbs of Central City. It was nestled in among a range of low hills, a glacial moraine, I'd once read. Whatever that was. The smallest lots were three-quarters of an acre, and only millionaires could afford it. It was an hour's drive, when the Freeway was clear, and no public transportation was available. The closest place to catch the commuter train was Walnut Grove, and you might as well drive for all the time that saved.

The house at 112735 Sleepy Hollow was set well back from the street at the end of a winding road, up a rise, and surrounded by suitably gnarly oaks.

Suitable for a horror movie.

I'd turned off the headlights when we turned off the street and stopped just out of sight of a house, visible through the trees. The place was dark.

"I see it, but I don't believe it," Jenny said, there was the hint of a laugh in her voice. Maybe she was just pretending. "Werewolves, vampires, witches—and now this?"

A nearly full moon shone on a house that also looked like a prime location for a fright flick. It was basically square and squat in spite of having three floors, at least. Several chimneys lined the perimeter, and a few more protruded up through the mansard roof. Numerous windows looked out like blind eyes. A couple of circular towers were topped with pointed "witches' hat" conical roofs. There were a few lighted windows in one, but the rest of the place was dark. They also reminded me of dunce caps and that made me wonder what the hell we were doing here in the dead of night.

"What the hell are we doing here in the dead of night?" I said.

"Looking for Dmitri Bochinsky, of course."

"Why now?"

"Why not?"

I had no good answer that didn't mean I wasn't remembering those stupid old horror movies that still played in a few art houses around town, and how I once wet my pants at a Friday midnight show my mother had forbidden me to attend. The thing was, I was certain I could outrun any of those lumbering creeps, so why the hell did I mistake my seat for a toilet? Only Dracula was any real threat. Who the hell could outrun a bat?

"Let's come back in the morning," I said.

Jenny peered at my face in the moonlight. "You're scared, aren't you?"

"Aren't you?"

"Yeah. So what?"

I told you she was adventurous.

There was a trace of hysteria in it, but she laughed, "This is all wrong."

"What's all wrong?"

"It should be pouring rain, with lightning and thunder."

"It was a dark and stormy night?" I said. "Like that?"

Her laugh was still tinged with fear. "Like that."

"Well, I, for one, am happy that it's not."

"Me too."

I looked at her for a while. "Okay, Sherlock, this was your idea. What do we do next?"

"I don't suppose we could knock on their door and say that we're having car trouble?" She was half-serious.

I laughed in spite of the knot in my throat. It actually loosened a bit. They say that laughter is the best defense against fear, but when push comes to shove, a Smith and Wesson is better.

Someday I might start carrying one. Then I thought that would probably be a good time to retire. A detective who counts on brawn over brain is as good as dead. Somebody always has a bigger piece.

We just sat there for a while, neither of us saying anything, trying to hatch plans in our minds.

"I'm hungry," she said.

At least one of us was hatching plans.

"Ignore it."

"Okay, but if my stomach rumbles just when some bad guy thinks he's lost us, it'll be your fault."

"I'll take the chance. You can always say 'I told you so.'"

"Yeah, just before he sinks his fangs into my neck."

The knot in my throat loosened a little bit more, but the laugh was weak.

While we were sitting around, the last lights in the tower went out.

"Let's wait a few minutes and then start snooping around," I said. "Maybe there'll be an open door or window."

"I guess we really do have to go in, huh?" She wasn't exactly displaying the height of enthusiasm.

"Yep. Wanna come back in the morning?"

"Nope. If you can do it, so can I."

"No you can't."

"Yes I can."

"No, you can't."

"Yes, I can," She was sounding frustrated.

"No, you can't, no, you can't, no, you caaaan't," I sang. I remembered that tune from *Annie Get your Gun*. I watched it a lot on tape when I was a kid. Guns fascinated me then. They just scared me now.

Her laugh was still frightened, though.

We waited about a half-hour. I hoped the last guy who'd turned out his light wasn't an insomniac. I could send him to the Belmont Coffee Shop. Right now I thought I'd rather be joking with Millie there too.

We didn't do much laughing anymore, though. Just sitting. I was hungry too, but I didn't say anything.

We reconnoitered the front. There was a curved driveway that went under a portico. Off to the left was a large parking area. There were at least a dozen very expensive looking jalopies parked there. *They must have a full house*, I thought. Nobody was around, but there was no cover for at least fifty yards, too dangerous to go in that way. We aimed for a side approach.

It was cold. Autumn wasn't far off, and the nights were already nippy. I was also painfully aware of the bright moonlight, the sky looked like clouds hadn't been invented yet.

We left the car out of sight of the house. A grove of oaks afforded us cover until it ended before a wide expanse of lawn. The mansion loomed beyond, like a gray phantom. Anyone crossing the gap could be picked off with ease from the tower that rose to our right. Maybe a dark and stormy night would have been better, after all.

There was nobody around.

I grabbed Jenny's hand and sprinted across, mostly dragging her along. It's a good thing she was wearing flats, smart girl. I didn't stop until we reached the house. The windows were high enough so that we only had to duck our heads a little to avoid being seen by anyone inside.

It had been hard to tell from a distance, but the walls were solid rock. Along the wall and just below the windows, the uneven stone was mortared with pitch, or tar, or something, turning it into a mosaic.

We inched along, testing the windows. They were as tight as an old maid's works. I was hoping I wouldn't have to jimmy one. I hadn't seen any security company signs, but that was scant comfort. They could have rigged up their own and didn't like signs messing up the lawns.

Then I thought of a mouse trap.

I still hadn't seen anyone. Maybe we were in luck.

We came to the rear door. I figured it was the rear door from all the garbage bins outside. It was unlikely to have been left unlocked, but it was worth a shot.

We tip-toed up to it. I grabbed the doorknob.

"Looking for something?"

When people say they jumped out of their skin, I know what they mean.

We whirled around and what I saw first were the twin barrels of the shotgun. Next I saw the guy holding it. He was tall. His face was pale in the moonlight, but I got the impression that it would be pale in the sunlight too. His head was big and square.

He reminded me of Lurch in the Addams Family, and the raggedy clothes he wore only heightened the impression. My heart was pounding too hard to allow for a laugh.

Where the fuck had he materialized from?

Later, Jenny told me she nearly peed her pants.

She did later, though, but she wasn't wearing any then.

Lurch never let the shotgun waver while he pulled a

cell phone out of his pocket. I couldn't make out what he was saying. He put the phone back.

"We wait," he said. He spoke in a deep baritone.

Jenny started to say something. He waved the gun at her. "We wait," he said.

She shut up.

We waited long enough for my heart to stop pounding, but the sick feeling in my gut wouldn't go away.

The sound of a lock being opened came from behind us.

"Turn around," said Lurch.

It's a good thing I was scared too shitless to laugh. The door opened and there was a guy who reminded me of Uncle Fester.

Except for the gun.

He patted us down and he didn't seem embarrassed doing it to Jenny. He took his time, too.

He relieved me of the small jimmy bar in my pocket. I figured I wouldn't have to do any jimmying after all.

His voice was even kind of squeaky. "Who are you and what are you doing here?"

The desperation in Jenny's voice was quite real. "You probably won't believe it, but our car broke down. Can we call a garage?" She could have done it without any acting lessons at all.

He didn't believe it. "Perhaps you will be more forthcoming inside. Follow me."

We followed him, and Lurch was right behind. He'd cocked both barrels before we went in.

We walked through a huge kitchen. The lighting was low, but the pots and pans hanging from ceiling racks were a dead giveaway. We followed a long corridor past it and I could hear a soft murmuring. There were arched openings in the wall, and I could see a roomful of black-hooded figures, they looked like monks, all down on their knees, chanting. It sounded like Latin, but I hadn't done well in that at Grover Cleveland High. The large room was lighted by big fat candles in tall sconces that surrounded it.

Things got decidedly less Catholic as we approached the end of the hallway. Now I could see two naked figures, male and female, in their early twenties, I thought. They were glowing golden in the candlelight. They were facing each other.

He had an incredible erection that reached up past his navel, almost to his bulging pecs. She was blonde all over and spectacular.

She didn't look real, but who cared? She was massaging his erection, and her mouth was open.

Then I couldn't see any more, but I was pretty certain what was going to be happening.

We stopped in front of a door. Uncle Fester fiddled with some keys, picked one, and unlocked it.

"The accommodations aren't much, but you'll only be needing them for a short while." He laughed a disturbing, high-pitched cackle.

Lurch's shotgun nudged us into the room.

"Now," Fester said to Jenny, "you will please hand over your purse." He turned to me. "Your wallet, cell phone, car keys, and wristwatch, please."

Did we have a choice?

The door closed behind, and I heard the key turn in the lock. It sounded louder from inside.

There were five army cots in the room. A middle-aged puffy-faced man was sitting on one. It took him a while before he seemed to notice us. His expression never changed.

I had no doubt at all who he was.

"Dmitri Bochinsky, I presume."

At first, he said nothing. Then he nodded. "Who are you?"

"Joseph Gold. Your parents hired me to find you."

Another pause. "You found me? How? This place is known to very few." His speech was long and drawn out,

"Somebody at The Wolf's Lair gave me the address."

"Who?"

"I didn't get the name. One of the waiters."

"I knew I was right to call you."

"A lot of good that does us now," I said.

He pointed at Jenny. "Who's she."

I introduced her. Most men found it hard to take their eyes off Jenny. She was filled in in all the right places. He barely acknowledged her existence. Judging by his paintings, I figured she was probably way too old for his tastes. According to Harrison, she was probably the wrong sex too.

I'd been keeping my curiosity in check, but everyone has an endurance limit, and mine was overflowing. I gave him my best tell-the-truth-or-I'll-break-your-fucking-arm look.

"Okay. What the hell is going on here? Why are we being held prisoner? By who?"

"They're planning to sacrifice me,"

The words shocked me cold, but he said it without much emotion. Now that I looked more closely, his eyes were vacant, almost as if he were in a trance. Drugs? "Who is?"

"The Black Forest Society."

At first, I couldn't process the information. It didn't make any sense.

Why did fatso tell me he didn't know where Dmitri was? The lights came on. I looked at Jenny. "I was wrong. It wasn't the waiter. He was just a clumsy oaf.

Fatso gave you the address mixed in with all the crap from your purse. But why?"

"Fatso?" Dmitri came out of his trance.

"Yeah. Big fat guy, looks like that blob of jelly thing in the *Star Wars* movie." I gave him an expectant look. "Know him?"

He was silent for a while, as though he was trying to connect back with reality but didn't know how. Then his eyes cleared. "That would be the grand magus."

"The grand magus? What the hell is that?"

"He's the head of the order."

"What order?"

He tried to focus on me, but I could see he was having trouble. "I can't tell you. You're not a member."

I was about to laugh when Jenny came up off the cot. She leaped over to his and grabbed him by the shirt collars. She actually pulled him up. "You listen to me, you fat fuck—" Her face was right up against his. "—we were hired to find you and suddenly we're in deep shit, so if you don't want me to rip your heart out with my teeth, you'd better start coming clean. Don't jerk us around."

She let go his collar and took a couple of steps back. There was still no emotion on his face, nothing but a few drops of Jenny's spittle that he didn't seem to notice. He sat back down. Then, to my utter surprise, he laughed. It was short, but it carried a note of irony.

"You or them," he said. "I hardly matters who tears my heart out."

I'd had it. "Who's *them*, you motherfucker." The total menace I put into my voice usually loosens the tightest tongues. He just looked at me without the slightest fear. This guy was whacked on something all right.

Suddenly, a dim light seemed to turn on in his eyes. Was there an appeal there too? "The Order of Vlad," he said. "They're going to sacrifice me."

"When?" I was having trouble believing any of this. Then I remembered the five bloody crosses. Suddenly, it didn't seem so unreal anymore.

"Midnight tomorrow. It's the full moon." His eyes began to fill with fear. Maybe the drugs were wearing off. "Oh, shit." Now they turned wild and he leaped up and began to pace. "We've got to get out of here," he almost shrieked.

That did my nerves no good at all.

"Sit. Down," I shouted at him.

That seemed to work. He stopped pacing and almost fell onto his cot.

I stared at him for a while. "Your Grand Mr. Magoo told us he didn't know where you were. Then he slipped us this address. Got any idea why?"

It was his turn to stare at *me* for a while. Then his eyes got big. "The law of five." He said it like it was some kind of great revelation.

"What the hell is that?" I couldn't tell if Jenny sounded more scared or pissed.

"The ritual requires a body at each point of the Great Pentagram."

"What ritual?" I don't know why I bothered to ask.

I think he'd finally come out of the trance though, because he sounded exasperated. "The sacrifice, of course." He looked at me like I was stupid.

"Is that what happened at your folks' place?"

He got real contrite, and now there was a hollow look in his eyes. "It wasn't supposed to happen. It was just supposed to be a rehearsal, but the magus had given the order to do it for real."

"What was all the yelling I heard over the phone?"

"I didn't want to do it. Neither did a few others. That's when I called you. I had some idea you might be able to help, but I couldn't wait around. Everybody was arguing, so I took advantage of the confusion to slip out. I took my parents to the park and told them to get lost."

"Let me get this straight." Disbelief must have been written all over my face. "You were going to kill five people with your parents there?"

"No. I told you I wouldn't do it. It wouldn't have been right. It has to be done on the full moon."

This guy was stark-raving mad, I thought, a perfect candidate for some nice, quiet hazel-hatchery. With padded cells.

"How were the kids killed? Were they drugged?"

He nodded his head. "They were out cold."

"Fatso's chemistry set?"

He nodded again.

"Oh, my God." Jenny's sudden ejaculation was loaded with fear. "The law of five includes us, doesn't it?"

"I'm afraid so. That's the only reason I can think of for you being here."

"How did you get caught?" I was trying to put off dealing with the awful truth, interrogation procedure was numbingly rote.

"They were waiting for me at the funeral parlor. I'd gone there to pick up some things."

"Funeral parlor?"

"Where I work."

"You work at a funeral parlor?" This was getting stranger by the question. Then I remembered the desk calendar.

"Actually, I own it. That's one reason I got into the Society."

"Maybe you'd better start from the beginning."

He didn't get a chance.

I heard the sound of the door lock opening. The blonde beauty I'd seen earlier was still naked and still spectacular. She was carrying a tray with three glasses of a yellow liquid. She glided into the room followed by Uncle Fester.

Where was Lurch?

"For your refreshment," he said.

"We're not thirsty," Jenny and I said it at almost the same time.

"Sure you are," he said, and he raised the .38 in his hand.

I stared at the .38. Then I stared at Jenny and all I felt was desperation. "Remember *Road to Rio?*" I said.

She looked blank for just a second, then the lights came on in her eyes. She began the rhythmic patting that began on her knees and ended with clapping her hands together. I did the same, and we chanted, "Patty cake, patty cake, baker's man…" When we reached the end, we clapped our open hands together and both made a lunge for the tray. Whatever was in the glasses flew all over the girl and Fester, and I managed to plant a solid right on his jaw. Lucky for me it was glass. He was out cold. I grabbed for the gun just before Lurch came through the door. He didn't have time to pull the trigger. My shot sounded like a cannon.

Jenny and I had laughed about it when we watched the DVD. Who would ever expect that it would actually work?

We were out in a flash. I had an iron grip on Dmitri's wrist. We raced down the hallway, through the kitchen, out the door, across the lawn, and into the temporary safety of the oaks.

They weren't far behind us.

Vampires.

A lot of them.

Crosby and Hope never had to deal with anything like *this.*

We were running ever farther away from Sleepy Hollow Road and any chance of flagging down a passing car was gone, even supposing that anyone would be out at this time of night. There were still no clouds and it was even colder.

The oaks had given way to real woods. The environmentalists had been adamant that as much virgin forest as possible should be saved, and the millionaires who inhabited the place agreed. I'd seen aerial photos, and it looked like a huge tract of rolling forestland dotted with small cleared areas containing houses. Swimming pools, too, and a few private lakes.

Y'chupitz.

Right now it was looking like the end of the world.

A coyote howled.

Coyotes used to be prevalent here, in the old days, before the march of civilization and its motor homes drove them ever farther west. The environmentalists convinced the millionaires to reintroduce them, and they'd never been sorry. The critters did so well that they began marauding in adjoining subdivisions so, each year, the millionaires got the added bonus of a coyote hunt to cull the packs. It's a week-long party. There was an article about it in the *Sunday Tribune* not too long ago. The animal people got them to stop using dogs, though.

There were more howls, but these were distinctly human. Far more terrifying.

I had no idea in which direction we were moving. Enough light filtered down through the trees to outline the narrow trail we were following, probably a deer path. Problem was, our pursuers were following the same one.

Jenny spotted it first. "Look. Here's a cross trail."

I moved us to the one on the right. The vampires would have to split up. That would even the odds somewhat, but there were an awful lot of them. I'd gotten a glimpse of them pouring out of the house, capes flying behind, and I thought about the flying monkeys in *The Wizard of Oz.* They scared the crap out of me the first time I watched it.

This was worse.

Bochinsky had said not a word the whole time since we left the room. I'd let go of his wrist, but he followed along like a puppy dog. He did say "ouch" a lot, just like me and Jenny. The narrow path was overgrown, and a lot of skinny branches stung us as we went along, but I don't consider "ouch" to be a word. Otherwise, we'd have been carrying on a lively conversation.

"I hope none of this is poison oak or ivy," Jenny said, giving me one more thing to worry about.

Like I said, I had no idea where we were, but we were winded and had to stop. At least for a minute or two, to catch our breaths. I also had no idea how close our pursuers were, but some of the howls seemed too close for comfort. They were coming from all around now. They must have followed us. It didn't seem like our ruse had worked very well. I wondered why they didn't just shut up. That would have been even more terrifying, if that was their intent.

Jenny shrieked. I whirled around. A guy in a cape had his arm around her throat. He was bringing a gun up to her head, but I was faster, I'd never let go of the .38. He shrieked louder than Jenny had, and he let go of her before he crumpled to the ground.

We were out of there in a flash, running like a pack of vampires was on our tail.

The howls were getting louder, and I could hear the sound of breaking twigs coming from behind us.

Sudden bright lights illuminated us, but were gone as the car rounded a curve of the road I could see outlined in a wide break between the trees. We raced for it, hoping to get to where we were heading before the car did.

We did.

We ran out into the road waving our arms like monkeys. The car slowed down but never stopped. The driver kept his window rolled up. It looked like he was alone.

"Please, you've gotta help us." Jenny didn't have to feign being frantic. "There are bunch of people trying to kill us."

The driver thought about it for a minute. "Get in," he said, and motioned to the rear. I heard the sound of doors unlocking. It took us no time at all to scramble in.

It also took no time at all to figure it out when I heard the doors lock again, and a window rose up between us and the driver. When he turned and smiled, his plastic fangs nailed it.

They'd been howling to drive us to the road, just like in every goddamned documentary I'd ever seen about tiger hunting.

The .38 was useless. The bullets would probably bounce off the glass and hit *us*.

A vapor began to fill the back seat. It wasn't long before I smelled the gas. It was nitrous oxide. We had a good laugh before the lights went out.

CHAPTER 19

I came out of the darkness with lights flashing in my head, and I thought I might puke, but the feeling passed after nothing more than a strangled retching. It took a while for all the disjointed bits of information that were flashing on and off in my head to get their act together, but they finally did, and I remembered everything.

I wished I hadn't, but if "wishes were horses, beggars would ride," as my mother never tired of saying. I could never ask for anything without a guilt trip being laid on me, so I just started stealing stuff. It was easier on my conscience. No starving children were involved.

I was lying on a comfortable bed, not an army cot. I opened my eyes and saw a lacy canopy above. I turned my head from left to right. I was alone in a big four-poster. I sat up, and that set my head to spinning for a few seconds and again I thought I might puke. Again the feeling passed.

I was naked except for a thin gown of some sort of gauzy material. Then I saw the bed next to me. Jenny was lying on it, still out. She was dressed like I was, and the thin fabric of *her* gown left no reason at all to imagine what lay beneath. I'd always wondered. I wasn't disappointed.

A groan from behind startled me, and I whirled around. There was another bed. Bochinsky was just coming to, and what lay beneath *his* gown was better left to the imagination.

There were two more beds on the other side of the room. Unoccupied. All were expensively draped with gauzy white silk, heavy draperies, all white, covered the windows and others could be drawn between the beds.

Above each bed a shell-shaped sconce provided the lighting. A cord hung from each. It looked like a posh hospital ward, and we were the patients.

Jenny began to stir and I turned my attention back to her. It took her a while to realize what was up, and when she did, her eyes got kind of wide, and she tried to hide her nipples with her arms. She looked around like a startled deer and made a sudden leap for the drape next to her bed. She wrapped herself in it as best she could.

"What's going on?" she said, but I noticed she was staring at my package. I'm not a bashful guy, but there was something about her frank stare that kind of shamed me, and I wrapped myself in my own drape. It wasn't long before Dmitri followed suit.

So, there we were, the three of us, standing next to our beds, wrapped in our drapes, pretty much stuck to the wall, unable to move, and looking like total assholes.

Jenny was the first to break. "Fuck it," she said, and removed the drape. I thought of Cleopatra delivering herself to Caesar wrapped in a rug. She gave me a look that said, "Leer at me and I'll cut off your balls."

"Keep your eyes to yourself," she said.

"You too. I saw you staring."

"Never you mind that,"

"That's hardly fair."

I dared her by shedding my drape with a flourish. Her eyes never left my face, but I thought I could see the struggle in them. I laughed. "Aw, go ahead," I said. "*I will, no matter what you say.*"

She did.

So did I.

We both cracked up. Maybe it was the lingering effects of the gas.

"If you two don't mind." Dmitri got into the act. "I'll stay like this."

"We don't mind," we said in unison and cracked up again.

It wasn't long, though, before the laughter stopped. This was no laughing matter. We were trapped like rats.

It was already light, but beyond the lawn and the oaks, there was nothing to be seen. I figured we'd been out for about three or four hours. We must have been given something beside the gas. I didn't bother to try the door.

A partially open door in the opposite wall led to the bathroom. I had to pee. So did Jenny. Dmitri refused to move, I hoped he wouldn't soil the lovely white drape.

I went back to my bed and looked at him, stuck to the wall, but no longer naked, thank god.

"I want you to start from the beginning. If I'm going to be a sacrifice, I want to know why and for what."

He kept his gaze directed at me, like he was embarrassed to look over at Jenny, though his eyes did keep creeping over to her side of his face. Not totally gay, after all?

"It all began when I started to research my family's history. It turned out that I was descended, on both sides, from Count Vlad, of Transylvania."

"Vlad the impaler?" Jenny said, "the original Dracula?"

"The very one. That got me interested in vampires, and I began to study the literature. I'd heard about places where people who were vampires would gather."

"Like the Grab-a-Bite?" I said.

He looked surprised. "You know it?"

"I have old friends there. Sheena says hello."

He looked even more surprised. "You know Sheena?"

"We've met. She says you're nuts."

He actually looked hurt. "Talk about nuts," he said, "that tattoo job of hers cost more than a car."

I was curious. "How did she pay for it?" I wondered what kind of job she could get? Stand-in for a leopard in a jungle movie?

"Are you kidding?" he said, "guys pay big bucks for a night with her."

I could believe it.

Crazy guys.

Like me.

"Anyway, I hung out there for a while, but most of the people weren't serious. To them, it was just a lark, but I'm a real vampire. I needed something more."

"A real vampire?" Jenny laughed, but the tinge of hysteria was back. "Give me a break, will you? There is no such thing. It's all play-acting."

He got kind of heated, at least he was showing some normal human reactions. "It's not like in the horror movies," he said that with more than a trace of disgust, "We don't really bite people's necks. It's hard to get enough blood that way"

"The blood in your fridge?" I said.

His eyebrows shot up. "You've been in my *place?*"

He sounded really put out about it. I remembered some goon who'd invaded mine when I wasn't there so I knew what he was feeling. It didn't make me feel any more sympathetic toward him, though. He was stark-raving mad.

I just gave him a level look. "I'm a detective. What about the blood?" I was bracing for the answer.

"We have a deal with Trostle's slaughter house and tannery."

I remembered Fatso's laugh about Occam's Razor.

"Why on earth do you drink blood anyway? Yecch." Jenny was disgusted.

"To ordinary mortals, like you—" Dmitri started to sound like a lecturer. "—blood has no great value, but to those of the line of Vlad, it is a necessity to maintain our full power as vampires. Somebody told me about the Black Forest Society, and he took me there. You have to be brought by a member. When the grand magus realized that I was descended on both sides from Vlad, he took a special interest in me and tutored me in all the secret ways of vampires. It was quite an education. I became a priest."

"So the Black Forest Society is a vampire den, or whatever you call it?"

"No. Not at all. We're only one of the orders of the society. There's the Order of Talbot for the werewolves, and there's a witches' coven as well. There's a group of aliens from Arcturus who want to open a new order, but I doubt they'll succeed. They're really weird."

They're weird? I wanted to laugh, but there was nothing funny about it. There was nothing funny about our situation either. In about twelve hours, we'd be having our throats cut and our guts sliced open. Whenever I caught myself not believing it, I remembered those five corpses lying beneath a Jackson Pollack, and any laughter was dissolved in the boiling pit that my stomach was starting to become.

"What's with all the slicing?" I asked him.

"That was the magus's idea, but I'm afraid he got the inspiration from me."

I thought about it for a second. "Your paintings?" I said.

"Yes. It sent him on a whole new line of thinking."

"What was the old line?"

"They'd just been putting scrounged body parts at the ends of the pentagram, but the ecstasy was limited. When the magus found out I owned a funeral home, he got the high council to give me a free membership in exchange for whatever good parts I could get him. Penises and vaginas were always hard to come by and of the highest value. Hearts and brains too. I think he saw me as a goldmine. Little by little, his vision grew, and he decided it was time for living human vessels."

The boiling pit was about to boil over. I had to swallow hard. "What's the high council?"

"It's a governing body made up of two members from each order. They decide on matters pertaining to the society as a whole, but their approval is necessary for all who wish to join."

"If you're vampires, how come werewolves and witches attend your parties?"

He got kind of huffy. "They aren't parties. They're religious ceremonies, and we have a strict anti-discrimination clause in our charter. Anyone can attend any ceremonies they wish."

Political correctness?

Multiculturalism?

Total insanity?

"How many members does this society have?"

"Last I heard, it was getting close to five hundred."

I shook my head. *There are that many screwballs around?* Then I thought that in a metro area of almost ten million people, that wasn't so much. It was plenty enough, though.

"What's the actual point of all your rituals?" Jenny was always one to cut right to the heart of the matter.

"I really can't tell you. You aren't initiates." He

thought for a while. "It's a deeply spiritual experience. That's all I can say."

I really wanted to know more, but I could see that he wouldn't be pushed, and it really wasn't important anyway. "So why has he turned on you?"

"Because I didn't like the idea of making the sacrifice on an inauspicious day. I thought it was frivolous. The rules are very clear on which days it can be done."

I just stared at this nut. "Rules? It didn't bother you that you were killing people? On any fucking day?"

He stared back with disapproval. "It isn't necessary to resort to profanity."

Profanity bothered him?

"To answer your question, they are merely vessels for the power of Vlad to use to descend upon us and make us one. I told you it was a deeply spiritual experience, and that's all I will say."

"You're insane," Jenny shouted. "People as vessels. You should be locked up."

He still wouldn't look at her. "You don't understand," he said, "mortals never do."

"If you're so fucking immortal," I said, "why are you so worried about being a sacrifice?"

He looked at me with no hint at all of irony. "A sacrificed vampire loses his immortal nature."

I'd read as much about vampires, here and there, as anyone, but this garbage was all new to me. I was sure that they were just making it up as they went along. They were as mad as hatters. No question about it.

Mad or not, as Jenny had said earlier, we were in deep shit.

I really couldn't see a way out of this one. Nobody besides the vampires knew where we were. The boiling pit in my belly threatened to boil over again. What the hell had I gotten us into this time? Curiosity kills more than cats, and I'd used up close to nine lives already.

"Have you done these sacrifices before?" I was trying to think if there were any similarly gruesome murders in my memory.

"No, tonight will be the first."

"Tonight? What do you call the butchery the other night?"

"I told you, that was not valid."

I looked at him, wrapped in his drape, jammed up tight against the wall, telling me that five murders didn't count because they weren't done on the full moon. I felt like Alice in Wonderland.

"Who killed them, if you wouldn't?"

"The only other authorized priest there was Randy Mueller, so I figure he must have done it. Nobody else would have dared, and please stop using that vulgar term."

"What term?"

"'Killed.' Sacrifices are not 'killed.' Their souls are liberated to a higher plane."

I was about ready to send *him* to a higher plane, but I figured he didn't deserve it.

I hadn't heard the key turn in the lock, but the door was thrown wide open. Two vampires holding pistols came in. It was hard to tell them apart. They both looked like Bela Lugosi, but I thought one was slightly taller than the other. They wore black capes.

Who are these characters? I wondered. *Where the hell do they come from?* I remembered the diners at The Wolf's Lair. Normal people probably rubbed elbows with them on a regular basis. You never really know who the hell anyone is.

Jenny wasted no time with formalities. "Why are we dressed like this? What have you done with our clothes?"

Tall Bela answered. "You are wearing purification

gowns. Ordinary clothing blocks your aura from its full melding with the universe. You have no further need of them."

I could tell she was stuck for a comeback line.

He even spoke with a Transylvanian accent. This really was too nutty for words but that was little comfort. The matter-of-fact way he said it was freezing my blood.

"I am certain that you must be hungry," he continued. "Your breakfast will be arriving shortly. I advise you to take full advantage, since you will be fasting for the rest of the day."

"And if we refuse?" I said.

He pointed to short Bela. "Karl here, will force it down your throats. He has much experience at it and enjoys his work immensely."

Karl flashed a plastic fanged smile. We'd fallen into a loony bin, and the inmates were running the joint.

I figured the food was drugged, but I didn't see any way out. Besides, I was hungry in spite of the horror roiling in my gut. Maybe food would help. I figured the drugs would anyway.

He snapped his fingers. The blonde from last night and her twin sister glided in. They were wearing purification gowns too. They really did seem to glide. They walked in a kind of slow motion. Each carried a large silver tray of food and drink, the silver food platters were covered with silver lids. There was no expression on their faces and their eyes were blank.

There was a table in the center of the room, and they set the trays down on it.

"You may eat now," he said, and each girl picked up a covered platter, and walked to each of the unoccupied beds. I was beginning to figure out who would be the other two in the sacrifice.

Tall Bela waved the gun, motioning us to pick up our platters too.

"You too, Dmitri. Please remove yourself from that foolish drapery. Are you a clown in the circus?"

Couldn't be more right, I thought.

Dmitri had no choice, but he kept trying to hide his body with his hands and arms. I appreciated the gesture.

Breakfast was green eggs and ham. No kidding, they'd colored the eggs. Tall Bela laughed when he saw my face. "Our cook is an incorrigible practical joker, wouldn't you agree? She's a great admirer of Dr. Seuss. She used to be a nursery school teacher."

I wasn't sure, what with my stomach churning, that I could manage green eggs, but the gun waved in my face overcame my squeamishness. I wondered what the green was. The only thing I could come up with was cyanide, but that was blue. I didn't think they wanted to kill us just yet either, so I figured that I'd find out what it was—at least what it did—before too long.

The drink in the glasses was orange. It tasted like orange juice. It even had pulp.

"I am sorry that we cannot offer you coffee, but caffeine is inimical to the freeing of the spirit."

"Fuck you," I said.

He just laughed.

They waited around until we'd finished eating. They left the two girls behind. Both were now lying motionless in their beds, staring up at the canopies. Neither had said a word.

I looked at Jenny and shrugged. "I'm sorry, sweetheart. I really am."

"It was my idea, remember?" she almost snapped at me. "Don't go getting all chivalrous toward me now. It doesn't fit you. Better you figure a way out."

We shut up after that, and I lay down on my bed waiting for what was coming next. I'd even lost my desire to look at almost-naked Jenny.

∽∾∽

Nothing happened, at first, but I began to get drowsy after a while. Soon, the horror that was staring me in the face began to recede into the background, and I must have fallen asleep.

I awoke to Indian *Raga* music. I used to listen to that stuff a lot when I was doing my hippie thing, along with others who felt cheated to have been born a few decades too late and were trying to relive the 'sixties. For some reason, it was the only music I liked and, for a while, I just kept my eyes closed listening to Ravi's riffs on the *sitar*. I was sure it was Ravi Shankar. I must have worn out that very recording.

Way in the back of my mind there was something troubling me, but I couldn't put my finger on it, so I ignored it and immersed myself in the music. What was happening in my head was a lot like what I used to feel on LSD. The music was exploding in my mind in gorgeous Technicolor images of nothing in particular.

I opened my eyes.

Jenny was dancing in the middle of the room. She was moving around like a snake, writhing her body around this way and that. I watched her for a while, aware that I was getting harder by the second. I got up and joined her, and we writhed together for what seemed like eternity. Every time my dick rubbed against her, flames would shoot in my head. My head was the universe and the Lord Shiva was dancing amid the flames.

Loud groans were coming from Dmitri's bed, but it took a while before I became aware of it. I looked over.

The twins were working on him, one sat on his face, and the other was sliding her pussy up and down on his penis. Neither of them made a sound.

I felt Jenny's mouth surrounding my erection, and the flames became a conflagration. At some point, she stood back up and somehow, managed to lower herself onto me while we were still writhing.

I exploded into her.

A riot of colors chased themselves around in my head, and then everything went black.

❧

I awoke with a start. Something had happened. What?

I thought there had been music, but it was dead silent now.

I looked over at all the beds. Everyone was just lying there, eyes closed.

I had no idea about how much time had passed. I managed to finally drag myself out of my bed and lumber over to the window. It was still light outside, but I could see the sun hanging low in the sky. I made it to be about six o'clock. There was something about that number that was tickling my memory, but I couldn't dredge it up. I forgot about it.

I looked around. Everyone was still asleep. That sounded like a good idea—lying down. My legs felt like rubber. I managed to get back to the bed before things went dark again.

❧

When I woke up, a voice was speaking. At first it seemed to come from deep within a long tunnel, but eventually it became more normal.

"Wakey, wakey, wakey children, it's time for the final preparations."

I opened my eyes. A vampire I hadn't seen before displayed his plastic fangs through a bright smile. I wanted to ask him something, but I couldn't open my mouth. I couldn't move anything but my eyes.

Stark terror.

I'd read those words a million times in a million adventure novels, but this was the first time I knew what they meant. I struggled to stay calm. If ever I needed a good writer to get me out of this one, it was now.

A naked brunette appeared above me. She held a sponge in one hand, and a wash basin in the other. The sound of chanting suddenly filled my ears and she began to give me a sponge bath. She began with my face, then my arms. She moved down my body and did a thorough job on my privates. Feelings of pleasure were at war with deadly fear. The fear won. She finished with my legs and disappeared.

She reappeared a short time later. She was holding what looked like a perfume atomizer. She forced the tube between my teeth and squeezed the bulb. At least my swallowing reflex was working, a liquid tasting slightly of apricots poured into my mouth and down my throat. I knew I should worry about what it was, but it hardly seemed to matter anymore.

I fell asleep again.

☙❧

The next time I awoke I felt normal. I sat up. Facing me, seated on what looked like a throne, was fatso himself, Mr. Magoo, the grand magus, or whatever the fuck. He still held a gun in his hand. Maybe it was glued on. I looked around. Everyone else was waking up too. Except the twins.

He noticed me noticing the gun. He smiled. It was ghastly.

"I have learned, through bitter experience, to never give a sucker an even break." His voice was level. "Or a cop."

"I'm not a cop, I'm a private investigator." I was surprised that my voice came out normal.

He waved his hand in a dismissive gesture. "Same thing."

I didn't feel like arguing with him. This was no time for Talmudic sophistries.

He gave me a hard look and the smile disappeared. "I really would like to commend you on your professional abilities, but two of our members are dead, and one requires extensive jaw rebuilding surgery. You were a very bad boy, Mr. Gold."

I stared right back at him. "Sue me."

He laughed. "Oh, I shall do more than that. Rest assured I shall."

I thought about Santa Claus again, but he wasn't dressed in red, he wore a long, white gown that camouflaged most of his bulk.

"What are you going to do with us, you fat fuck?" I guess Jenny figured she had nothing to gain by being diplomatic.

"Please, my dear, don't pretend to be stupid. You know perfectly well what will happen at midnight, about two hours from now. I should, however, inform you of a slight difference. In order for us to receive the greatest blessing from your sacrifice, you will not be drugged. You will face Vlad fully conscious. It is your terror that will complete the unholy circle."

"You do realize that you are as nutty as a fucking fruitcake, don't you?" I said to him.

He just looked at me. "You do realize that you are as a good as dead, don't you?"

He had me trumped.

"I don't suppose we could buy our way out of this, could we?' Hell, it was worth a shot

He laughed at first, then he got serious. "I don't suppose you could scrape together ten million dollars, could you?" I thought he really was serious, for all the good that did us.

I shrugged.

He laughed again, "I didn't think so." Then *he* shrugged. "It appears that there is nothing for it." He motioned to several of his goons who busied themselves tying us up in supine positions. There was no point in resisting, no way to resist. I couldn't move anything but my eyes and my head. I could wriggle like a worm, but that would accomplish nothing. I didn't want to face death like a sniveling coward. Then I thought that I really was facing death, and I had to resist the urge to wriggle.

"I shall leave you to your thoughts, now," Fatso said, "the ceremony will commence anon."

"Wait a minute," I shouted as he was leaving. "Why didn't you just give us this address? Why all the subterfuge."

He laughed. "Oh, but you will have to admit that this was more amusing. No?"

There was no point in answering.

We were alone for a few minutes. We must have been left to our own thoughts, because none of us said a word. The two girls across the room had not been tied up, but they were still in some sort of trance. I figured it was going to be up to the three of us to satisfy Vlad's lust for terror.

I could feel it already.

Time had stopped having any meaning.

Eventually, a bunch of vampires came into the room. Groups of five carried large silver trays, long enough to hold a human body. One group placed their tray next to me on the bed, and in no time, I was lying atop it. I thought of a turkey at Thanksgiving. I swore that if I ever got out of this, I'd actually accept my sister Miriam's invitation this year and even put up with her dimwit husband and spoiled brats. I was almost relieved that I probably wouldn't have to. Your mind does funny things in situations like this. I was a long way from laughing though, I thought I might puke.

They lifted us up over their heads and walked out of the room. They were chanting.

We were carried through several hallways and into a large room. The tall sconces I'd seen when we first came, or similar, were now spaced around this one. In the center of the floor was a huge metallic basin. To catch the blood, I figured. They'd obviously learned something from the debacle at the Bochinskys'. In the center, on a slightly raised platform, a large pentagram had been described with votive candles. Our five trays were laid on long tables set at the points of the star, but outside of the basin.

My heart was pounding and my thoughts were jumbled. The only thing that registered clearly was that this was it for sure.

The chanting stopped.

The grand Magoo was unfazed and began to intone something in what sounded like Latin, but it was all Greek to me. Then there was a period of what seemed like the responsive readings at *Congregation Agudas Achim,* but it wasn't Rabbi Shulson leading this *schul* in prayer.

At last, he began to speak English. He motioned to my honor guard, "Place him at the point of the pentagram."

They lifted me off the tray and set me into the basin. It was cold. The candle at the point was inches from my midsection. I wondered if I could do something to start a fire. Then I figured I'd probably just burn to death.

One by one, we were each laid into the basin. I thought it took a long time, until we were all in.

Then it seemed way too fast.

Jenny started screaming at the top of her lungs until, I guess, somebody stuffed something in her mouth.

There was some more Latin gobbledygook and the chanting started up again. Fatso waddled into my field of vision. He was holding a long, curved blade. It gleamed in the candlelight. It looked sharp.

"I believe I shall start with you, Mr. Gold. You should have no fear. There will be little pain, and you will soon discover you have attained a higher plane of consciousness. I wish you a speedy journey."

He raised the knife and the chanting grew louder. I was sure I was going to crap myself.

The chanting got even louder as he readied to slit my throat. They say that people who are about to die have their whole lives flash before their eyes, but all thoughts flew out of my head. All I was aware of was the knife descending to my neck.

Jenny must have spit out whatever they'd put in her mouth, and her scream cut through the chanting. So did a shot.

The knife dropped from his hand. It clattered on the porcelain. He followed it down, just missing me and extinguishing a whole arm of the star.

I think I passed out for a second. When I came to, the place was swarming with cops, and there was a lot of shooting.

Then it got real quiet.

I heard Bochinsky blubbering like a baby.

e⌇e⌇

Frank was staring down at me. He looked like a Macy's balloon. He was still holding his pistol and he wasn't smiling. "You okay?"

It took me a while to locate my talking apparatus. "I think so." It sounded like a croak, but I guess he understood.

"Good. Now tell me why I shouldn't put my last slug in you."

"Why?"

"Why? Because you obviously have a suicide wish, so why don't I just help you out and get you out of my hair for good."

Maybe he was right.

"And for withholding evidence that might have cracked this case hours ago without you having to get trussed up like a chicken."

"Turkey," I said.

"You got that right," he said, and for the first time, his smile busted through.

"Even if it had to be you, Frank, I've never been so fucking happy to see anyone in my life." To my utter surprise, tears sprang to my eyes, and I could hear myself bawling, kind of like Bochinsky. I put an end to it real quick. "How about untying me and getting me the hell up." I could feel that whatever drug had paralyzed me was wearing off fast.

He smiled again. "I dunno. I oughtta let the forensics boys get some pictures first. They'll be here in an hour. Can you hang on?"

"*I* can't, you miserable flatfoot." If there was any relief in Jenny's voice, it was drowned out by fury. "Get us the hell up, for crissakes."

"Nice to see you again too, Ms. Martin." He never averted his eyes from her supine gorgeousness. "*Very* nice, I must say." He and Jenny were old wisecracking buddies so he wasn't really taking liberties. It didn't calm her anger, though.

"Just get me up. Okay? You can ogle later."

"Promise?" He was laughing but, after looking up, he motioned to someone who came over and covered us with blankets. "We'll get you up in a jiffy. We do need to take some pictures, though. Evidence."

Trussed up as I was, I couldn't see anything much beyond the ceiling, now that Frank had left my side.

"Are you okay, sweetheart?" I said.

"You talking to me?" Jenny said.

For the first time in hours, I really laughed.

I figured she'd be fine.

I wasn't so sure about me.

CHAPTER 20

The drugs finally wore off, and they got us up and untied. A search of the kitchen found our clothes and stuff in a closet. I wondered if they'd been planning to sell them at a membership fundraiser, or an auction. All our money was gone, but everything else was there. Even the jimmy.

These were apparently all rich folks, no?

Maybe that's how they got rich. Stealing. One way or another.

Decently covered by our everyday aura blockers, we were finally informed as to how we were saved.

But not before getting another stern lecture from Frank. He'd convinced the cops from the twenty-third to let him handle me and Jenny.

Only one of their guys, a Lieutenant Sprague, was sitting in officially. Presumably so Frank couldn't pull a fast one.

A few of the others were sitting around in an "unofficial" capacity. They never said a word. I'll say this for our esteemed cops, they're suspicious of everybody, even their own. That's the legacy of years of corruption. With Wagner out of the picture, maybe things would improve.

I wouldn't bet on it, though.

After a whole litany of the laws I'd probably broken, and a few questionable references to my ancestry, he got to the end.

"Once again, I want to remind you that, if nothing else, I could arrest you for withholding evidence."

"What evidence?"

"How did you know to come here?"

I looked down at Fatso, decently covered with a sheet, still lying sprawled prone on the remains of the pentagram. The rest of the candles had been extinguished too. In the bright working lights the cops had set up, the place looked like a charnel house, sheet-covered bodies lay scattered around a blood soaked floor. I counted five. Several others of the vampires had been hustled off in ambulances. The cops only suffered a couple of skin grazers and a busted shoulder.

Surprise rules the day. Except when it doesn't.

"Fatso here slipped Jenny this address. I had no idea what I'd find other than a clue to Bochinsky."

"Fatso there, is—was—Leonard Holloway. When you mentioned Orson Welles, I thought I remembered something, but it wasn't until I was going through the list of owners of The Wolf's Lair that I saw his name and everything clicked."

"Everything?"

"Well, enough to get suspicious. Holloway was an actor who'd played Dracula in some really lousy B movies, and his personal reviews were shitty too. I looked him up to refresh my memory. His career ended on a sour note after he was arrested for beating the crap out of his manager. I remembered thinking, at the time, when I saw his picture in the paper, that he looked like Orson Welles. I tried Googling him, but there was nothing at all after the arrest. We didn't have anything either. It was like he dropped off the face of the earth. Then I noticed another familiar name on the list, George MacKenzie. He was another failed movie star, only he played werewolves. I remembered what you said about the pentagram and witches and such, so I decided to take a closer look. There was nothing at all anywhere about anything called the Black Forest Society, but I had enough to set my big copper's nose to sniffing.

"When you didn't show up by six-thirty, and you never answered my calls, I decided to go there and stake out the place for a while. About nine o'clock, a whole shit-load of limousines pulled up in front, and a bunch of people, all wearing black capes, came out a side door and got in. I spotted Holloway right away, big sonofabitch. I followed them out here. I didn't know what I was looking for, but the number of cars parked in the lot said there was a big party going down. A really big party. That's when I called Sprague here and told him something was up and that it might have to do with the Bochinsky case. 'No sirens,' I said, and I sat tight until they got here.

"The place was dark, it didn't look like any party I'd ever seen. It kinda scared me. I couldn't figure what the hell was up. A few minutes after the twenty-third cavalry rode up and secured the perimeter, we heard a really horrible scream. Jesus, Mary, and Joseph, I thought, it didn't even sound completely human."

"Thanks a lot," Jenny said.

He gave her a hard look. "Lucky you did. I think I even crossed myself. Nobody hesitated. We shot out the lock with a silencer and rushed in. We caught the guards by surprise, and they didn't resist. There was a loud chanting coming from upstairs. When we got here, I was just in time to take out Holloway. It was only afterward that I realized he'd been standing over *you*. Imagine my surprise." His voice was dripping sarcasm. "How the fuck did you get onto him?" He pointed to Bochinsky, who was just sitting quietly. He hadn't said a word since he'd stopped blubbering.

"His parents hired me to find him."

Frank looked startled. "When was this?"

"They showed up at my office the morning after the murders. They swore he was with them until two a.m. They wanted me to get him to give himself up."

"And you didn't think to call me? That kind of evidence?"

"Oh, I thought about it, but a job's a job. Gotta eat, y'know. I made them sign a paper saying they'd turn themselves in if I couldn't find him in two days. Since he wasn't guilty, I figured I could give them a break. Now you give *me* a break. I did tell you I was onto something, and if I hadn't, my dead mother would be washing my mouth out with soap again right about now, and you'd all be scratching your heads about another set of corpses—if you ever found us."

His eyes didn't change. He wasn't buying my self-serving rhetoric. "Where are the Bochinskys?"

"I signed them into the Taylor Hotel as my parents."

Sprague had been wiggling around in his chair. He finally opened his mouth. "I see where you come by your reputation. If it was up to me, I'd lock you up and throw away the key. You're a fucking menace." He kept his voice level, though.

I looked at him, "Thanks, I do my best."

He didn't laugh.

Frank went on. "Well, if Bochinsky here didn't kill those kids, who did?"

"A guy named Randy Mueller. At least Bochinsky thinks so. Mueller was the only other authorized priest able to do it."

He just stared at me for a while, his mouth partially open. "Authorized? Priest? Maybe you'd better fill us in.

Right now, I'm having trouble wrapping my head around any of this." Then he pointed to the twins. "Who are they, and why are they like that?"

I shrugged. "All-purpose dishrags, I suppose. They're probably drugged. Fatso had an active chemical lab, I gather. Which reminds me. Have all our blood tested. I want to know what kind of shit we had poured into us."

"How come you weren't out like them?"

"That's the best part. Our terror was supposed to feed their ecstasy."

"Huh?"

"They get off on their victim's fear of death. The rest of it's just bullshit. See what drugs they're on too. It's gotta be something powerful."

Frank looked puzzled. "The rest of what?"

So I told him.

I could see he was really struggling to believe me. I couldn't blame him. I was having trouble believing it myself.

"So," he said when I'd finished, "they're a pack of nuts."

"That's what a psychiatrist friend of mine said too. He actually said 'nuts.'"

✧✦✧

It was about four in the morning before we could leave, but neither of us was tired. I guessed we'd gotten all the sleep we needed during the long day. We drove for a while, not saying anything. Then I remembered the *ragas*, and all the rest.

"Umm, Jen…" I wasn't sure how to broach the subject. "…did anything strange happen to you while we were out?"

"Strange?"

"Like, did you hear any music?"

She thought for a bit. "Come to think of it, I remember hearing Chopin sonatas. I played one for my first recital, and I'd listened to a lot to get the hang of what they sounded like."

She could play the piano?

She thought a bit more. "I remember a lot of colors flashing around in my head, too."

I was beginning to relax. "Have you ever dropped acid?"

"You mean LSD? No."

"Well, it was a lot like that."

"Did you hear the music too?"

"Not Chopin. Ravi Shankar. *Sitar* music."

"Yuck, I hate that stuff."

I didn't say anything for a while. "I think we were just hallucinating."

I could see her turn to look at me, puzzled by the relief in my voice.

✿✿✿

When I finally got home, I just got drunk.

Maybe it was only that I'd gone through so much crap that I didn't want to think about it anymore.

I thought about Sheena instead.

I stayed drunk all day.

That night, for the first and only time in my life, I had sex with a leopard.

On the house.

Think about it, six boobs.

CHAPTER 21

The newspapers went wild and they printed a big picture of me this time. Freddy, the newsboy, gave me a free copy of each.

Millie's "autergraph" had definitely increased in value.

People even recognized me on the street.

My phone was never silent. Peggy had her work cut out for her.

And I was bored.

None of the cases we interviewed seemed remotely interesting, just the usual husband and wife or business partner crap. Jenny confessed to feeling the same, but, as I'd said to Frank, you gotta eat.

We were both kept pretty busy and, bit by bit, the horror bits that I kept finding in hidden places in my brain disappeared into the back rooms of my memory, locked up, except for the occasional prison break, usually in nightmares from which I'd thrash myself awake in order to escape the fangs. I'd be soaking wet.

It turned out that Randolph Mueller III had been killed in the shootout, so nobody could be tried for first-degree murder, but several people went to jail on lesser offenses. Bochinsky was declared mentally incompetent and a danger to the community. He was committed to an indefinite stay at the state mental institution.

Jenny and I were witnesses at his hearing. His last meeting with his parents was pathetic. They were hanging on to him and crying. All I heard of their conversation as I passed by was Dmitri's plaintive, "Aw, Ma."

The Wolf's Lair was shut down for good. There was a chemistry lab in the basement that could have leveled the whole block.

Where the werewolves, vampires, and witches who were left went, I neither knew nor cared.

$$\sim\!\sim\!\sim$$

I was having lunch one day with Frank, shooting the shit.

"Y'know, I've often wondered how they picked the name for the Black Forest Society. It certainly brought forth images of the mysterious and dangerous Bavarian woods. Scary fairy tale stuff, like *Little Red Riding Hood.*"

He started to laugh. "I guess I forgot to tell you. I interviewed MacKenzie, you know, the werewolf guy. I asked him the very same thing, but he only laughed. It was an inside joke. He said the Black Forest Society was named for the hams.

PART 3

The Case of the Bigoted Blogger

CHAPTER 22

Sliced fruits of various kinds filled a large platter in the center of the table, but I didn't think I could eat another bite. My sister, Miriam—I called her Mimi—was a great cook, and she had a secret recipe for Thanksgiving turkey. I must have had fourths, along with all the trimmings. I had to loosen my belt, and I was afraid I might fart.

I hadn't seen Mimi in months. She was several years younger than I, and I always thought of her as my little sister. It was hard to do now. She had two kids of her own, bloody little monsters, is more like it.

The other turkey at the table was Ralph Wasserman, her husband. I rarely accepted her invitations because I really couldn't stomach him, and the kids drove me nuts. Whenever I was there, I had to restrain myself from tearing off my belt and whacking them with it. Their parents let them get away with murder, and they were only eight and ten, two boys. I shuddered when I thought what they'd be like as adults. I pitied their wives, if any woman would be stupid enough to hook up with them. Their mother was doing *her* suffering now.

Ralph was pretty much the same. He was a demanding sonofabitch, and he had her cowed too. I really hated to see it. Mimi had always been a popular girl, the life of the party. Not like our older sister Karen, who was the party. She broke our mother's heart when she moved to Las Vegas to become a stripper. I used to watch her develop her routines through her keyhole. She complained, but she never blocked it up. She needed an audience.

I supposed I wasn't the only one who couldn't stand Ralph. After our mother died, it was usually only them for Thanksgiving, except when I showed up. The upside was that there was plenty of turkey for everybody.

Nowadays, Miriam was pretty much subdued. From time to time, I'd invite her to lunch in the city. I should really do it more often. She came alive then, like the old Mimi, who was the first Jewish cheerleader at Grover Cleveland High.

The trick was getting her out of the house. It had become more like her prison and, like many prisoners, she'd grown comfortable with it.

I was only there now because of a vow I'd made when I was inches from death a few months back. I was wondering at what stroke of the clock my vow could be considered fulfilled. I was saved by my cell phone. It was Jenny.

"Sorry to bother you, but something has come up. There's a cousin here at Martha's with a very interesting story to tell. He has to drive home out of town tonight, and I think you should hear it. Can you tear yourself away from the bosom of your family?"

She knew perfectly well how I felt about my family.

"Well, I'm pretty busy here." I paused for a bit. Jenny said nothing. "Okay," I continued, "if you think it's that important, I'll head out there right away." I put on my most apologetic face, but I didn't think either of them was buying it. "Something important has come up. That was Jenny with a line on a new client, but the guy's leaving town tonight, and we have to see him now. I'm really sorry to have to cut and run so soon, but putting bread on the table is still my number-one priority."

Mimi looked hurt. "But it's Thanksgiving."

I hoped that my really deep feelings for her came through on my face. My insincere tone sounded hollow, even to me. "I know, sis, but justice takes no holidays. Great turkey, as always. You're the best." I gave her a big hug. I could hear the kids shouting upstairs. "Say good-bye to the kids for me, okay?" I reached my hand out to Ralph. "Good to see you again. We should get together more often."

I'd forgotten I'd loosened my belt, and my pants almost fell down before I got to the car.

But I was out of there.

∽∾∽

I'd rented a car for the holiday weekend. You can get surprisingly good deals. Jenny's aunt's house was about an hour's drive from Mimi's, and I figured I'd need the whole time to wind down from the strain of being in the bosom of my family, but the snow was coming down hard, and I soon forgot about it in the strain of trying to stay on the icy roads. At this rate, it would take me all night.

It wasn't only Mimi's misery that had me depressed. That afternoon, I'd paid a visit to Julie. Juvie was holding a special Thanksgiving visitor's day so that the inmates could spend time with their families. I was one of the few people there. I figured that if these kids had had loving families to begin with, they'd be at home right now, not languishing behind locked doors.

Julie had only recently realized that ex-mayor Wagner was not her father. She found out that I was just before she got arrested for running a whore house at her summer camp. I'm the one who got her arrested, but she didn't hold that against me. She'd been relieved.

She'd been happy to see me, and she certainly seemed to be doing okay with the therapy, but it was depressing to see an intelligent, free-spirited seventeen-year-old girl stuck in a prison. Juvenile facility or not, there were bars on the windows.

The only real satisfaction was that she refused to accept visits from Wagner.

By the time I hit the freeway, the snow had stopped, and the snowplows were out in force. It only took an hour-and-a-half. The snow had turned the city into a fairyland. I knew it wouldn't last long. The sparkling white stuff pushed off to the side by the plows was already a dirty, slushy brown, but I had managed to shed most of the tension. I was wondering what story this mysterious visitor had to tell. Jenny had a nose for interesting cases.

♥♥♥

Aunt Martha greeted me with her usual open arms, and her husband, Max, was pumping my hand like an old friend. I barely knew them, but they were happy that I'd made Jenny a partner and given their youngest daughter, Peggy, a job as our receptionist.

I could hear a lot of noise coming from the dining room, the sound of happy people enjoying each other's company. What a contrast to Mimi's. I'm not usually sentimental, but I felt a pang of regret that things had worked out as they had.

Oh, well, that's life, as they say. Things rarely work out the way you want. It helps to be filthy rich, but even that's no guarantee.

I looked in on the merriment. I knew Peggy, of course,

and a couple of Jenny's other relatives, and we exchanged greetings.

"This is Joe Gold, Jenny's detective partner." Uncle Willie introduced me to the others, but they all knew who I was, what with my name and photo being splashed all over the papers for weeks during the various hearings and investigations into the "Vampire Murders," as the press dubbed them. It went nationwide. My picture even made it to the front page of the *New York Times.* I refused to be interviewed by the TV networks, though. Like I told one guy, "The day you put on some decent fucking programs is the day you can interview me."

Really. I did, but all they said was I refused to be interviewed.

Jenny flipped them the bird too, but she did it nicer.

She got up and came over. She brought along a guy. "This is George Mason." She introduced us. "He's a distant cousin on my father's side, but we've always been close. Lucky he was in town on business. You should hear his story. Let's go into the den, it's quieter." She looked around, her hands on her hips. She raised her voice. "Aren't people supposed to get quiet and fall asleep after the turkey anymore? What did you put in them this year, Aunt Martha?"

We were followed by good-natured hoots and jeers as we made our way to the den.

Max's den was a male retreat. Nowadays they'd call it a man cave. When Martha refurnished the house, the most comfortable of the old furniture had been moved into it, and there was a fully stocked bar at one end. In his younger days, Max had been a hunter, and there were more heads of dead animals on the walls than I felt comfortable with. It's not that I object to killing animals for food, or even for sport, but bragging about it later, when all you really had to do was pull a trigger from a safe distance, seems chickenshit to me. I was sure that Max had never faced a lion with a spear in his hand, like a Masai warrior. The huge, maned head that was the centerpiece of his collection had been bagged at a wildlife hunting club in Texas.

If you looked closely, you could tell that it had been pretty old. Maybe it had been glad to go.

Advancing age had put an end to Max's hunting, too. Arthritis made it difficult for him to move without pain. I liked Max, in spite of his murderous proclivities, but I couldn't help but feel that there was, at least, a modicum of justice in the world.

Mason looked to be in his late thirties, though he was already showing the signs of male pattern baldness. He was thin, brown eyed, clean shaven, about five-eight, and nervous.

He was wriggling around in his chair like someone had poured itching powder down his back.

"George thinks somebody might be trying to kill him," Jenny said.

"Who?" I asked him.

"I don't know." He hesitated. "At least I don't know his real name, but I think it's a guy who calls himself 'Avenger Two.'"

"Huh? Some comic-book hero is out to get you?"

I threw a hard look at Jenny. She just smiled. Maybe this was just a ruse to get me out of Mimi's. I was more than happy to play along.

He could read the disbelief in my eyes. "Maybe I should start at the beginning."

"That's usually a good place to start," I said, "that puts everyone on the same page."

He thought for a while, as though maybe he wasn't sure what the first page was himself. "I'm a lecturer in physics at the state U in Pleasanton. Sometimes it's a tiring job. I like to relax on the comments sections of various newspapers."

That made no sense to me at all. I had a picture of him lolling around on a pile of newspapers. I must have looked blanker than usual.

"On the internet," Jenny said. "Every on-line paper has a comments section where readers can post their thoughts about the various stories."

Live and learn, I guess. I was still a neophyte in this new world of the web. I'd gotten pretty good at Googling for information, but the first time Jenny'd told me about it, I thought she was pulling my leg.

"Google?" I'd said, "Are you talking baby talk to me now?"

I caught on to the porn sites quickly enough, though.

"I started about five years ago," he continued. "There was a story about global warming deniers, and when I went to the comments section, I was amazed. The article was all about how ignorant the deniers were of simple scientific concepts, and damn if everything the article said about them wasn't laid out there for the whole world to see. Most of them were convinced that climate change was just a conspiracy on the part of the socialists and communists to destroy the corporations and the American way of life. Then there were those on the other side who accused the corporations of destroying the planet for profit."

"Sounds pretty balanced to me."

"I guess it does, if being balanced means they're mostly nuts. There was almost nothing rational in most of the arguments. They all sounded crazy. Few ever addressed the topic of the article directly. They just fulminated about their own viewpoints and usually ended up calling each other names. I did too, I guess."

"What kind of names?" It sounded to me like bar arguments after everyone had downed a few.

"'Asshole' is one of the favorites. 'Idiot' and 'moron' are also well-represented, and the occasional 'motherfucker' gets thrown in for good measure."

Yep. Bar fights.

"You can use words like that in the papers?"

"Actually, some of them are tightening up on the language and deleting posts like that. I lost interest in them, though. They tend to be really boring. As I said, I go there mostly for amusement, and I'm no slouch with the 'assholes' and 'motherfuckers' either, though I usually limit myself to 'idiot' and 'moron,' and I find I use 'ignoramus' a lot too. You can't believe the level of abysmal stupidity these people exhibit."

"Sure I can. They elected the congress, didn't they?"

He laughed. "You've got it."

"Where does Avenger Two fit into the picture?"

"Most of us bloggers use anonymous names. I came upon Avenger Two almost from the beginning."

"What's yours?"

"Philosopher Phil. I hated it after a while, but they won't let you change it for some reason, so I guess I'm stuck with it. It sounds kind of pompous, but it was a spur of the moment thing."

"Tell me about the avenger?"

"This guy's incredible. He's all over the place. It doesn't matter what the topic is. He's there ranting about it. He once let on that he's a history professor, but his knowledge of history makes that a lie, or the state of our education is even worse than I thought. Being in the sciences, I'm pretty much out of the speculation business. It's hard to fudge demonstrable facts. But what goes on in the academic departments sometimes seems like a free-for-all. Facts are secondary to opinions. It looks that way in the faculty lounges, and that's what it looks like on the blogs. It's really pretty scary."

"Why do you think this Avenger guy is trying to kill you?"

"Well, when I get pissed, I can get pretty heated, and this guy's pissed me off for five years. I'm afraid I may have been a bit even more intemperate in my language with him. Not that it would matter much. He hates my guts. He's a fully formed bigot, sprung full-blown from the forehead of Adolph Hitler. He hates blacks, Hispanics, Jews, Republicans, Democrats, liberals, and anybody else who disagrees with him about anything."

"Sounds like a former mayor I used to know."

He laughed. "I read all about it. You ought to get a medal."

"Well, I got publicity, and that's even better. I got so famous, I almost got myself killed. Nearly took Jenny along, too."

"There you go again—" Jenny was laughing. "—hogging the spotlight. It was my idea to go out there in the dead of night, you'll remember, so share the gory."

"You mean glory?" George said.

"No, I mean gory."

We all broke up. I guess it was funny, but I still had nightmares, so maybe not so much.

"Back to the Avenger." I said, "What specifically leads you to suspect him?"

"Not much really, beyond occasional veiled threats couched in circumspect language."

"You're right. It's not much. Got any examples?"

"I do. They're on my computer at home. I can email them to you."

Something was puzzling me. "If you're all anonymous, how could he know who you are?"

"I've thought about that a lot, and I used it to console myself that I was just imagining it all, getting paranoid. But something happened last week that shattered my last reserves of skepticism. Now, I'm just downright scared."

"What happened?"

"I was coming home late, one night. The highway was nearly deserted. Then a car behind me put on its brights. I had to shield my eyes from the glare in the rear-view. When I got it adjusted, I could see that he was gaining on me. He was coming up fast and his passing signal wasn't on. Just before climbing up my trunk, he veered left. I was about to heave a sigh of relief when I realized he was way too close. I just reacted when I saw his front end turn toward me. I spun the wheel to the right as hard as I could and went flying off onto the shoulder. It was icy, and the car spun around. I just missed hitting the divider fence. The other car continued speeding away, but I think he flashed his lights at me. It was hard to tell."

"Did you get a good look at the car?"

"It was big and black, maybe dark blue. That's all I can say. I was scared out of my skin."

"I suppose you didn't get a look at the driver"

"I never even tried."

"Anything on the license number?"

He shook his head. "The whole thing took a matter of seconds. I was concentrating on keeping control of the car."

"Did you file a police report?"

"Let me ask you. What would you do with the information?"

"Honestly, I'd probably toss it in the wastebasket the minute you walked out the door."

"That's probably what they did. They told me that drunk drivers were a dime a dozen but they'd see if they could run him down. I never heard back. I don't think he was drunk."

"Of course, you don't, but you have no way to prove anything else. I've had enough run-ins with drunken nitwits myself. Why does this make you suspect the Avenger—or anybody, for that matter?"

"Because it was just the worst of several incidents over the past few months."

"More car shenanigans?"

"Sort of. The nearest I can figure the beginning of this, someone had keyed my car pretty badly—doors, fenders, and roof. I put it down to ordinary vandalism, but mine was the only car on the block that was touched."

"Do you have any enemies besides the Avenger guy?"

"Nothing more than some minor academic squabbles with colleagues, but I can't imagine that any of them could have done it."

"You'd be surprised what people can do. Maybe one of them didn't think it was so minor."

He didn't even hesitate. "Not to the point of keying my car. Most of them are over fifty. It doesn't fit."

I looked at him hard. "So, that makes you the new, young guy, right?"

"You mean they're jealous of my youth? Maybe you don't understand academia, but they all have tenure. They don't have to worry about me. I'm the one trying to get in."

"Maybe somebody doesn't want you to get in."

He thought for a while this time, but he still shook his head. "Very unlikely. Scholarly disputes can get pretty ugly but not to the point of driving somebody off the road. Besides that, my relationship with everyone on the faculty is totally collegial. No matter how angry we might get, we usually settle down with a few beers afterward.

Once we've left the hallowed halls for the nearest bar, the disputes are forgotten. We're all pretty friendly. Wives too."

"Are you married?" He wasn't wearing a ring, but you never knew.

"No, so far I've managed to avoid it." He looked a little wistful. "Not always of my own choosing, I should add."

"I have to ask this. Are you messing around with any of the wives?"

His raucous laughter convinced me he wasn't.

"Got any girlfriends?"

"Not at the moment. I don't have any time for it, anyway. Right now I'm very busy on a research project. It takes up most of my free time. That's why I'm in town. I was consulting with other members of the team at the university. Do you know anything about physics, Mr. Gold?"

"Call me Joe, please. Nothing much beyond the ones my mother used to give me when I got sick."

That kind of threw him for a second, but his eyes lit up finally, and he laughed. "Physics. That's a good one."

I looked at Jenny. "He thinks I'm kidding."

She looked at him. "He isn't. He's remarkably poorly educated. We only put up with him for his razor sharp mind. He's what they call an *idiot savant*."

I thought he'd bust a gut. Jenny and I make a great comedy team when we put our minds to it. Her straight face is as good as mine, but ours both just dissolved, probably all that holiday punch.

When the merriment died down, I asked him what other incidents he could recount.

"Well, there was the time I was working late. I think I was the last person in the building. It was close to midnight when I heard a noise in the outer office, and then all the lights went off. I figured it was a blown breaker. I had been on the way out but I wasn't too keen on walking around in the dark. I remembered I had one of those small flashlights in my drawer, but the batteries were almost gone. I figured I'd still have enough light to keep from bumping into things, and I was halfway through the outer office when I saw a large shadow move out of the corner of my eye. I was so startled, I whirled the flashlight around, but there was nothing there. Then I had the distinct impression he was behind me. At the same time somebody yelled out in the corridor. Turns out it was the night cleaning crew. They'd just arrived and wondered why the lights were out. One of them had shouted to check the breakers. By the time the lights came back on, I was alone."

"Assuming there was somebody there, how could he get out without being seen? Did you check any of the offices to see if someone was hiding there?"

"Hell no. I was shaking like a leaf. I told the foreman of the cleaning crew about it, and he said they'd take a look around and let me know if they found anyone or anything suspicious. I never heard anything more."

"So now we're chasing shadows?" I said.

"I'd swear on a stack of bibles there was somebody in that office with me. I'm a scientist. I'm not trained to ignore the evidence before my eyes. I saw that guy."

"Anything else?"

"A few weeks ago, I thought I heard a noise outside my house. I think it was also close to midnight again."

"The witching hour," I said.

He ignored me and went on. "I turned off all the lights and looked out between the drawn drapes. Another shadow just moved off to the edge of my vision. I wasted no time turning on all the outside lights. I shouted as loud as I could too. When I looked out again, I couldn't see anything, but I called nine-one-one to report a possible prowler. They were there in about a minute. They couldn't find anything, but I figured he was long gone. I didn't get any sleep at all for the rest of the night."

"Any chance your house might be haunted?" I said it with a straight face, "Anybody ever murdered there?"

He laughed. "I know you have to explore every possibility, but I can assure you, I know what I saw."

"That's what people who've seen Bigfoot say."

"Look, you have to believe me." He really looked desperate.

"I do."

You could cut the relief on his face with a knife. "You do?"

"Sure. You don't come off as a flake, and when people have this many encounters, you can't just ignore them. That doesn't mean that we might not eventually find that it was all coincidence and an overactive imagination, but it deserves a shot."

"You'll take the case?"

"I will. But I'm still puzzled about how he could know who you are?"

"I really don't know. I wrote to all the papers, but they assured me that their encryption codes made it impossible for anyone to know my identity. I'm not sure I fully believe them. There's nothing impossible in the world of encryption technology. Why do you suppose they have to come up with new algorithms all the time?"

I didn't know what algorithms were. To me, they sounded like they could be a seventies dance band, but I was pretty certain what he was driving at. "Let me guess, the old ones get hacked."

"Exactly. It's a poorly kept secret. Only the badly educated don't know it."

"That would be most of us, I take it."

"Me too, actually. Beyond the laws of electronics, I have no more real idea what goes into computer innards than most people. It's all a mystery to us macrophysicists."

I didn't bother to ask. I figured I could Google it if I really needed to know.

There was nothing more I needed to ask right now. I'd have to go through the stuff he sent me in order to get my "sea legs" as it were. I figured I'd have plenty of questions later.

The only advice I could give him was to avoid lonely roads and other places. I also told him to get a vicious German shepherd to guard his house. To be thoroughly safe, I said he should turn himself in to the nearest cop shop, act nuts, and confess to several grisly murders. While they investigated, he'd be kept in a nice, safe cell.

His laughter was muted.

We spent the rest of the night with me and Jenny going through our tale of the Vampire Murders yet again.

We were very entertaining. The old farts knew exactly what we meant about the Hope and Crosby patty cake routine, and I brought the house down when, during a particularly pregnant pause, just before the end, I leaped up and yelled "Boo!"

I suppose I should mention that Aunt Mildred called from the hospital later to say that, just as she'd thought, Uncle Henry hadn't had a heart attack, after all. It was a just a bit of panic. Henry had suffered from PTSD since Vietnam. I guess he hadn't heard the story before.

Mildred was determined to ride with him in the ambulance, so Uncle Willie went to pick them up. They missed the end.

CHAPTER 23

I slept until noon on Friday, and lolled around in bed until most of the headache was gone. I'd just gotten out of the bathroom when I heard Roscoe yowling and scratching on the fire escape window.

I called him Roscoe and he never complained, so I figured Roscoe it was. He was thoroughly disreputable, the very image of alley-cat, from his torn ear to his scabby coat to his crooked tail. He was big too, so I figured he was probably top cat in the alley. He came around, from time to time, to scrounge whatever he could. I was a soft touch. I fed him gourmet cat food. What was gourmet about it I couldn't figure. It looked like all the other disgusting mush, but some of the cans had little pieces of something or other floating around in a gravy.

Whatever it was, he gulped it down.

He gulped the other crap down too, but I didn't want him to think I was a cheapskate.

"You're in luck today, Roscoe," I said.

He actually cocked his head. Maybe Alley and English have words in common. I went to the fridge and took out the foil wrapped hunks of turkey Aunt Martha sent me home with. Her house was the traditional gathering place for the clan on Thanksgiving, so she always roasted two turkeys, and there was plenty left over. I was planning to have most of it for lunch, but I was still a bit hung over, and I opened it on the table so I could tear off a few pieces for Roscoe.

I never got a chance.

Roscoe, being of sound mind, and not knowing how long his luck would hold, leaped on the package, grabbed the biggest hunk in his mouth, and took off out the window, dragging his prey along.

No good deed ever goes unpunished.

He'd be back again in a few days, looking all innocent—and I'd feed him gourmet meatballs and gravy.

Roscoe obviously subscribed to the dictum to never give a sucker an even break.

Most of my lunch gone, I stuck the few remaining pieces in my mouth, added some stuffing from another package, and washed it all down with a beer. I'd been thinking a lot about what George Mason had said, and I was curious. My stuffed-in-mouth lunch over, I sat down at the laptop and checked my email. Nothing. My next thought was to check out some papers on-line. I started with the *Tribune.*

It was a pretty slow news day. Congress was in recess and the president was on vacation with his family. Most people were spending a quiet weekend, but there were still a couple of murders being reported. I wondered if murders went up during Thanksgiving.

The Middle East was in its usual turmoil, people killing people for god-knows-what. It was such a regular occurrence, that I often just found myself feeling sorry for the cars that got blown up. I'd remembered what Mason had said about anti-Semites, so I brought up a story about Americans in Israel celebrating Thanksgiving. It was pretty much a nothing story, filler for a slow day. I wasn't fully awake yet, and it almost put me back to sleep.

I jerked awake pretty quick. The very first entry in the comments section was all about how the Jews were no better than the Nazis, persecuting the Palestinians like Hitler had persecuted them, and how the Israeli Prime Minister was a warmonger who paid the Jewish Lobby to bribe the US Government to support Israel in its Zionist, colonialist, expansionist enterprise to take over the entire Middle East, and, eventually, the world. No kidding. It was liberally spotted with all caps lines too. A very noisy fellow.

I wondered if, as a sort-of-famous Jew, I could get in on the profits.

Now, while I totally disagreed with the commenter, I allowed that he had a point of view, but what it had to do with Thanksgiving in Israel I couldn't figure out.

There were several more such posts, followed by a measured and reasoned rebuttal from someone who supported Israel. The post after that called him a fascist son-ofabitch, among other things. The name on top was Avenger 2. I scrolled down the column. Avenger 2 was a regular contributor. I was starting to read one of his other posts, when my screen was invaded by a video about some car.

"What the fuck?" I said it aloud.

I was so surprised. I searched for the little X in the upper right hand corner that would make it go away, but it wasn't there. I was beginning to feel a little frantic as my mouse searched the window for an X. There it was, in the lower left. Even after it disappeared, I just sat there looking at the place it had been.

Now, I understand that newspapers survive on their advertising revenue, but in the ones I get from Freddy, the newsboy, the fucking ads stay where they belong. They don't suddenly materialize before your eyes. There were plenty of stationary ads on the side bar too, but I could ignore those. Usually. Sometimes they feature almost naked broads selling everything from bathing suits to potato chips. It's just a come-on, though, when you open the ads there's rarely a babe to be seen. I don't do it much anymore, but the Pavlovian response is hard to beat back.

But how the hell can you ignore an ad that materializes before your eyes? *Dirty pool*, I thought. My reading was interrupted several more times, and I wondered why anyone would put up with it.

Most of the posts were just plain looney, when they weren't downright racist and nasty. I figured that only dedicated souls would waste their time. Maybe it was addictive. For the hell of it, I downloaded a story about the president's Thanksgiving. The first comment was from Avenger 2. It was filled with nothing but virulent hatred and how he'd been a failed president about this that and the other, without a single actual fact to back him up. It was long on talking points, though. Mostly, he was pissed that he'd celebrated Thanksgiving with his family instead of slaving away, chained to his desk. That's what we were paying him for, wasn't it?

He didn't much care for his playing golf either.

I didn't see anything from Philosopher Phil, but I figured he was still recovering from last night's feast and hadn't gone online yet. I was going to try another story, but when the ad for Tampax popped up, I just shut the damned machine off.

I'd seen enough to set me thinking. Mason had been right. I almost couldn't believe it. When he'd told me about it, I was certain he'd been exaggerating. But there it was, really, in black and white. There were those who hated the Republicans and wanted to see a burning Bush. Cheney and Rumsfeld were also names that took the limelight—or the torchlight. There were those who hated the Democrats, and wanted to see a black man burning on the White House lawn. They hadn't been able to get rid of him in the old-fashioned American way, but I read more than a few calls for impeachment. I just had to shake my head.

I sincerely hoped that I was wrong about what I'd said about the people who elected the congress. I just didn't want to believe that any of these morons were of voting age. The best of them sounded like they were writing their graduation speeches from kindergarten. What was that song popular in the 'sixties, Kumbaya? If we all just sat down together, held hands, and let the love flow from all of our hearts, we could solve all our problems and usher in the real Age of Aquarius.

I couldn't wait for them to get to the first grade. That's where you learn that all human hearts are not full of love. It usually takes until the fifth to finally get that *most* aren't. Problem is, the truth is so awful for gentle souls, that, by the time they graduate from college, they've forgotten it again.

I'd never gone to college, so I never had that problem.

Cop college just reinforced it.

What really got me steamed was the naked hatred of Jews. That kind of shit was on the way out when I was a kid, but I suffered my share of head-smashed-against-wall incidents. I was under the impression that the old way of thinking was gone. Ex-mayor Wagner was a virulent anti-Semite, but he was a rarity nowadays, I thought. There were more than a few cops who shared his opinion, but they mostly kept it to themselves.

Not that I suddenly thought that America was on the verge of a pogrom, but these assholes were really dangerous. I figured as long as they contained their disgusting fantasies within the confines of the comments section, they were harmless. But suppose one guy was really nuts, and decided to undertake a personal vendetta?

But how could he? Clicking on the name Avenger 2 brought up a bunch of his recent posts, but there was nothing in his profile at all. Anonymous he was. I figured that the *Trib* must be able to retrieve that information, but Mason said he'd been down that road, nothing doing. I wondered if you could get it with a court order. Usually, you have to show criminal behavior, that a crime's been committed.

My phone rang. It was Jenny.

"Cousin George is dead."

 confront

Jenny and I spoke little on the drive up to Pleasanton. She was probably reminiscing back on her childhood when she and Mason had been close. *I* couldn't stop kicking myself. Why the hell had I let him go home?

His frozen body had been found by a guy walking his dog past his house in the morning. Mason was lying against the snow bank next to his parked car. The plows had blocked the driveway to his garage, and he'd had to get out at whatever passed for a curb. Someone had emptied five slugs into his belly and one to his forehead. The *coup de grace*? According to the cops, it must have happened during a late Thanksgiving fireworks show, so nobody noticed the shots.

"Or maybe he used a silencer," Captain Carson of the Pleasanton Police told me when I called. At first, he didn't want to give me anything, but when I mentioned the Vampire Murders, he started to fall all over himself to provide information.

Even though the car heater was up on high, I felt chilled. Gut wounds are about the most painful. I wondered how long he'd suffered until the bullet in the head. Whoever had killed him, hated him. He'd said that the Avenger hated him, but I was never one to jump to conclusions. There were a few others whose comments seemed only tenuously connected to reality. Any of them could be the killer too. At least, I'd have to start with that assumption. I was hoping I could get access to his computer. I wanted to see what veiled threats he'd spoken about. Maybe I could eliminate a lot of the others at once.

Mostly though, I felt like I wanted to die too. Mason wasn't the first client to buy the farm on my watch, but I always consoled myself with the thought that 20/20 hindsight is worthless. It didn't make me feel any better now, though. Especially not with Jenny sitting next to me, sighing and sniffling.

The only things she said, from time to time, were, "I can't believe it," or "I just can't believe it."

❧❦❧

Pleasanton was really nothing but a college town. Most of its residents had some connection or other to the U, even if it was only selling groceries. It looked like it too, or at least it looked like the popular image of a Midwestern college town. I was sure that beneath the snow lay well-manicured lawns. A lot of white picket fences surrounded them. There was little difference between the architectures of the town and the U. Red brick and stone houses gave way to the larger red brick buildings of the campus. There were a few glass and steel monstrosities, but not too many.

The state university extension here had been a sop to some long dead local politician who didn't want his daughter to have to leave home to go to college. He hadn't been too overjoyed that she wanted to go to college in the first place. The administration building was named for him. The Campus itself was named for his daughter, a fiery suffragist.

Hetty Cooper's story was famous in the state. She supposedly worked closely with Susan B. Anthony as her confidante and secretary. I once read an article about her, and the rumor was that they didn't get much work done.

The school was small and they tried to keep it that way. Hetty U., as the locals called it, had a reputation for snobbishness that was almost as high as its academic standards.

It was already starting to get dark when I pulled up in the parking lot of the small red brick cottage that was the Pleasanton Police Department. There were some nasty looking blackish clouds tearing across the sky with ominous speed. It looked like a storm was coming. I hadn't bothered to check the weather report.

Captain Carson figured who we were the minute we walked in. Good cop.

"Big storm coming. Lucky you got here now." He offered us coffee, and it was surprisingly good. He rendered his condolences to Jenny. He turned to me. "This is only our third homicide in five years. We aren't used to this, and on Thanksgiving too. You said on the phone that you had some information that might be helpful?" He looked hopeful.

"I do, but first I'd like to know if you have any suspects."

He shook his head. "Not a one. Whoever did this cleaned up after himself. He picked up all the spent shells, and it looks like he swept the area with a broom. He probably walked backward, sweeping out his footprints in the snow. The trail ends at the curb. That's it. There are too many overlapping tire tracks to get a clear tread. I've got a drawer full of notes from our interviews with the neighbors and those on the faculty who knew him, but there's nothing there that I can see. You can look them over if you want."

I stopped him from opening the drawer. "That won't be necessary. Nobody from here killed him."

His eyebrows rose, and I filled him in.

CHAPTER 24

Jenny didn't say anything for a while. Then she took a deep breath. "Yes. That's him."

As his nearest relative, Jenny had to do the honors. It was George Mason, all right. He looked just like he had last night, except for the round hole in his forehead. It was turning black, and his skin had turned a sort of gray-green. Other than that—

Jenny tightened her grip on my arm, interrupting my morbid reverie. She was probably thinking the same thing. It was never easy looking at a corpse, even when it was a stranger. You couldn't help thinking that it was a living breathing person, and then it wasn't—I snapped my fingers mentally—just like that.

Some day that would be me.

You could only evade taxes.

What was really boiling my gut was the way his killer made him suffer. I'd been thinking of ways to make the killer do the same, but I wouldn't kill him. Not for a while, anyway.

Mason had been shot with a .22, slugs small enough to cause a shitload of pain without killing him outright. The hole in his head had been point blank. He'd have been in too much pain to fight back. The blood pouring out of his mouth would have choked off any screams.

I was relieved when we finally left the morgue.

☙❧

The coming storm seemed too dangerous to drive through, but Carson wouldn't hear of us taking motel rooms.

"Mom runs the best boarding house in town, and the place is almost empty now. She gets lonesome. She'd love to have some company, and it's on us."

I really didn't want to have to face some officious desk clerk, and Jenny was agreeable, so we followed him to Mom's Place. That's what the big sign over the front porch said. Besides that, it looked like any of the other houses on the block, with fraternity and sorority houses scattered among them. Like most in the prosperous neighborhood, it was three stories high, built of red brick, and a large wooden porch, painted white, extended along the entire front. The street was lined on both sides with a procession of stately elms. Skeletal branches intertwined high above, creating a natural cathedral arch. Smoke arose from chimneys, and I could see dozens of little black birds huddled along the ledges surrounding the vents. It was cold, as cold as death, I thought, and the wind was picking up. It felt like my pants were frozen to my legs. I was glad to get inside.

Mom reminded me a lot of Carlene. Carlene runs a sa-loon for the worn-out dregs of the underworld. To her everlasting surprise, it became popular with the straight world. People came for the thrill of rubbing shoulders with gangsters and grifters, and even a few of the real mobsters showed up from time to time. Probably to rub shoulders with the straights. The other side of the fence, you know—or the freeway. The tracks disappeared a long time ago.

Mom had the same shock of white hair, and the same laugh lines were etched into her face. I liked her immediately. Jenny did too. Turns out that she wasn't Carson's mother at all. Everybody called her Mom, and she was everybody's mom in return. Any problem you had, you brought it to her, and she'd either help you solve it, or commiserate with you about the unfairness of it all.

Maybe bartenders and boarding house operators are cut from the same cloth. You've got to like people. I'd probably go broke in a month. I'd been trying to work on my empathy, but I was having a rough time of it. Too many people just didn't deserve it, and it was sometimes hard to tell them apart from those who did. Age five was a good cutoff point, and even then, you could be fooled. I thought of my monster nephews. I hadn't liked them any more when they'd been five.

I try not to judge, though. In my line of work, I've come upon straight, decent, upright folks who were rotters at heart, and I've met rotters who had hearts of gold. That seems strange, but there it is. Still, not judging doesn't change anything, and I've always tried to keep that in mind, always tried to keep the truth foremost in my thinking. Doing anything else can buy you a shallow grave.

Mom was all apologies, but she'd rented one of the available rooms that morning and only had one left, with a double bed.

"That's okay," Jenny said, "even if I had any hanky for him, my panky's out to lunch. I just lost my dearest cousin."

I was interpreting that in so many ways.

I remembered overhearing Rabbi Shulson once counsel a distraught couple. Her mother had just died, and the night before the funeral, she and her husband had wild sex. "Not just sex." She wanted to be clear on that.

He told them that it was a natural impulse—in the face of death, we celebrate life.

I figured that maybe the old lady had been a bitch on wheels. Maybe she always complained about the noise. I didn't think they'd feel guilty for long.

Mom was suitably round, but not to the point of obesity. You'd almost expect her to have been created on some Hollywood back lot, or found in central casting, but she was perfectly real. She was everybody's ideal mom.

When she heard my name, she lit all up.

"Well p'shaw."

She really did say that. It reminded me of the Old Ma and Pa Kettle movies. They'd play them on TV when I was a kid, and I'd roll around on the floor laughing. I caught one at a revival, a few years back. I laughed twice.

"I've been followin' your exploits ever since the Wagner business, and those Vampire Murders. You're both quite the heroes, you know. It's an honor to have you in my house. Now you just make yourselves comfortable in the sittin' room while I get your room ready. She bounced around a bit, and I wondered if she was going to ask me for my autograph. She didn't.

Millie, a waitress at the Belmont coffee shop told me that she'd been offered a thousand dollars for the autograph I once gave her. Good old Millie turned him down cold.

"That autergraph is the pride of my collection," she said, "I couldn't let it go for less than two."

I told her I'd give her a few more autographs and her eyes lit up like a slot machine.

I knew that she had a comfortable bundle socked away, but greed is not tempered by age or wealth.

There was a roaring fire burning in the huge hearth, but it did little to heat the large room. That job was being done by the central heating. I could feel the warm air blowing on me from a vent. The main beneficiaries of the dancing flames were the poor little birds huddled together above. Good enough, I thought. Then I wondered what would happen if the fires went out. I had a vision of dozens of little frozen-solid bird carcasses littering the snow-covered lawns. People going on vacation could create a wildlife disaster.

That's what all the conservationist nuts say, but I don't think that's exactly what they had in mind.

The sittin' room was full of comfortable looking over-stuffed sofas and chairs. A bunch of old fashioned floor lamps were scattered around the room. They had frilly lampshades with lots of fringes. We had a few like them when I was a kid. My mother sold them to the junk peddler for peanuts when we bought all those modern things. They cost a fortune now.

I've never really forgiven her for throwing away all my old comic books too. But then, who knew? Comic books?

"I'm leaving you in good hands," Carson said. "I've got to go check on all our storm facilities, keep everybody on their toes. It looks like this is going to be a big one."

Jenny and I sank into the furniture. We didn't say anything. We just sat there, staring at the fire, thinking whatever morbid, wintry thoughts came up. At least, I did, and Jenny had a pained look in her eyes, so I figured we were probably on the same wave length. The dancing flames reflecting from them were of another kind, but they were only reflections in a mirror. Still, they made her look beautiful, as though maybe it wasn't reflection at all, but the inside shining through.

You can tell that I have a high regard for Jenny. In my own way, I'm even in love with her. I once asked her to marry me, but all she wanted was a partnership, strictly business. It was better this way.

Don't ask me why. You'll get different answers on different days.

Our room was large. It made the double bed look tiny. There was a small, uncomfortable looking sofa in the room. "Look," I said, "you can have the bed. I'll sleep over there."

She laughed for the first time today. "You'll do no such thing. We've already seen each other naked. What's left but to sleep together?"

"Define 'sleep.'"

She mimicked a snore.

By the time we were called down to dinner, the storm had already begun. Gusts of snow played the windows like snare drums, but their powdery blasts were impotent against the strong glass. In the background, you could hear the wind, whining to break through any cracks and get into the house. Maybe it just wanted to get warm. Who could blame it?

There were only four of us for dinner. The fourth was a pinched-looking little man named Thaddeus Gray, and his name fit him perfectly. I figured he was pushing fifty, at least. He'd arrived by plane in the morning for a week-long meeting with the engineering department. He was some kind of systems analyst, but I couldn't make heads or tails of it. He didn't say much. He seemed like a quiet, introverted type. Something about him reminded me of someone, but who it was escaped me.

With all the students home for Thanksgiving, the turkey looked like it had been barely attacked yesterday, and we did our best to make up for the callous insult. Such a fine bird deserved better.

Mom kept pumping me for details of my most interesting cases, but she was so good-natured about it, that I was happy to oblige. Jenny loosened up too and interjected a lot. I guess it was a kind of therapy for both of us.

Gray said little, but I could tell he was taking it all in. He rarely took his eyes off me, and when the conversation got around to the present case, he was all ears too. That's when he finally came alive for a while. He had lots of questions.

"I may not look it," he said, "but I'm a big fan of detective fiction." He looked a little ashamed, like he was admitting a secret tendency to masturbate outside the windows of women's dorms. "Such cases as this are fascinating. There's not a suspect in sight."

He had Jenny's full attention. She probably has every detective book ever written. The two of them babbled on, and I got the dope on Mom. She and her husband had been unable to have children, so they opened their home to students who were otherwise too poor to afford either dorm fees or the high rents of a university town. When he died suddenly, about twenty years ago, she kept the operation going. The insurance gave her the house free and clear, and he had left her well off anyway. She could have sold the house and taken off for sunny climes, but the students she housed had become like her children. She was happy here.

Jenny and I were both tired and excused ourselves. As we got up from the table, Gray stood too and extended his hand.

"It was very nice meeting you, Mr. Gold. I envy your ability. I may be a fan of detectives in books, but I'm afraid that I would never have the courage to do the things you've done. I'm a timid soul at heart. I wish you a great deal of luck on your present quest. It sounds like you may have a very clever killer on your hands. I do hope you'll be careful." He turned to Jenny. "You too, Miss Martin. You're a very lovely woman and an expert on detectives. I would hate to see anything bad happen to you."

"I'm always careful," I lied.

"I keep him that way," Jenny said.

She tried, anyway.

❧❧

It was a long time before I got to sleep. I could tell Jenny was awake too. The storm was really howling up a storm, and that didn't help my nerves any. The bare branches of a tree kept scratching at the windows and made it even worse. I had a vampire dream, but it wasn't too bad.

I woke up to find myself pressed right up against Jenny. My arm was slung around her. I looked at her still-closed eyes, but what I was most aware of was my morning wood pressed up against her thigh. It was getting stiffer by the second. I knew I ought to move away. Instead, I started to rub.

It's a Pavlovian reaction. Give me a break.

Her eyes popped open. Then they looked down. Then they looked back at me.

"When did you buy a gun?"

"Wanna see it shoot?"

"Wanna see it lying on the floor?"

I moved away. I hated to, but I did.

I got up and went to the window. I didn't even bother to hide the errant limb bulging out the front of my pajamas. I was hoping she'd feel bad for it, but she didn't say anything. The storm had stopped, but the white monster had buried all the cars up to their windows. It didn't look like we were going anywhere any too soon.

"What's it like out there?" she said.

"You should go back to sleep."

"That bad, huh?"

"That bad. We appear to be stranded.

She looked at me. "I'll go back to sleep after you put that thing away."

I leered at her and wiggled my eyebrows like Groucho Marx. "Where would you like me to put it?"

"How far around can it stretch?"

She always won.

❦

We slept back to back until about eleven, when Mom knocked on the door to call us to breakfast. I looked out the window again. Nothing had changed. It was really quite beautiful—if you like that sort of thing. Mostly, it was a pain in the ass.

Carson had called to say that the snow plows would be getting to us in about an hour, and to sit tight. As though there was any choice. All I could think of was the plow burying my car until the spring thaw.

We heard the plow scraping along down the street. I was getting ready to go out and flag it down, when it stopped. Six guys got out of a car that was following behind. They each had a shovel and, in no time, my car was freed from its snowy prison, after which the plow continued on, burying it yet again. The crew set to work to free it once more. I hadn't even had to work up a sweat. I wondered why they didn't just ask me to back it up into a cleared section. *Then again*, I thought, *they had jobs*.

We said our goodbyes to Mom. She hugged and kissed us both, as though we were members of the family. Gray was nowhere to be seen.

We stopped at the cop shop to say goodbye to Carson. I promised we'd keep him informed. He gave me the CD onto which he'd copied the contents of Mason's computer.

By the time we got to the main highway, it was open, and traffic was flowing. I asked Jenny what she and Gray had been talking about at dinner.

"We were trying to remember if there was anything like this in any of the novels, but we drew a blank. He did scare me with one idea."

"What?"

"If the killer hated George, why wouldn't he go after the other posters he might hate?"

"Jesus. A serial killer?"

"Scary, huh?"

"Terrifying."

Carson had agreed to get a warrant to force the *Trib* to disclose the identity of Avenger 2, but how we'd have cause to force any other disclosures escaped me.

It was dark by the time I got home. I stuck a frozen pizza in the oven and had a stiff one.

I remembered that's how I woke up, too.

CHAPTER 25

I woke up in a foul mood that wasn't helped by the headache. After manhandling a few innocent pots and pans, I decided that I didn't want breakfast after all and sat down at my laptop with a cup of coffee. I skipped my email and went straight to the *Trib*.

Mason's murder was big news. Apparently, he'd been too modest to tell us how important the project he'd been working on was. The project chairman said that he didn't know how they could replace him, but they always say shit like that. I didn't really understand any of it, other than it had ramifications for the Big Bang Theory. I had a vague idea about that stuff, but when I tried to think about it, I'd get lost. It was all very confusing. People were a lot simpler to understand. Fewer moving parts.

According to the story, the cops were refusing to speculate. No details of the crime were released either. Just that he'd been shot at close range. I sped down to the comments. There was nothing from the Avenger, but I recognized the monikers of a couple of religious nuts. They claimed that God had avenged himself for Mason's heresy in denying Divine creation in favor of an atheistic, communist cult. There was nothing in any of their posts that led me to think they could be violent, but I couldn't dismiss them out of hand.

The first post I came across from the Avenger was in another story about Israel. I don't know what I expected to find, but if it was something like a veiled reference to justice being served, there was nothing. Just his usual Jew-hating diatribe. There was nothing in any of his other posts, either. I kept going back to the Mason story to see if he'd show up, but he never did. I thought that if it was him, he might want to gloat. Then I thought that he was probably too clever to take a chance on being connected to it. There's nothing worse than a smart criminal. Give me the dummies any time.

The only thing that raised my eyebrows at all was a remark by someone named Dave36. He was another bitter enemy of Philosopher Phil. He wondered why he hadn't heard from him regarding his latest rant. *I hope somebody put a couple of bullets in your brain, and you're dead*, he wrote.

I wondered if that was enough to get a warrant for his identity.

While I was wondering, I got a call from Carson. He'd gotten an emergency warrant for the Avenger, but nobody was going to do anything about it until Monday anyway.

I spent the rest of the day searching almost every story, but beyond the remark from Dave36, I came up dry.

That shit *can* be addictive. I was shocked when I realized that it had gotten dark again. My stomach finally drove me to the other half of the pizza from last night. I ate it cold.

Sunday came and went and I still had nothing beyond Dave's fervent hope. I called Jenny several times to see how she was holding up and to tell her about Dave.

"I'm doing okay," she said, "coming to terms with reality." She'd spotted Dave's post too. We kicked it around for a bit, but there really was nothing particularly substantial or surprising about it.

I was never so happy to see Monday come. The world shook off the last of its holiday lethargy and went back to work. Peggy and Jenny were already there when I got to the office. I scanned the day's papers but there was nothing new beyond the same old insanity.

I checked out the CD of Mason's files, mostly just copies of the correspondence between him and the Avenger. He included a few comments from some others but, on the whole, nothing really jumped out at me. I figured I'd have to go over it all with a fine-tooth comb. There was nothing in any of the other's posts of any interest to the case either, beyond that they hated Philosopher Phil's guts too.

My phone rang at noon.

"There's a Captain Carson on the line for you?" Peggy asked.

That was the only thing that set me on edge about Peggy, who otherwise was eye-candy personified. She ended too many of her sentences like a question. They used to call it Valley Girl-speak. I don't know what they call it now besides annoying.

"Good news," he said, "the *Tribune* coughed up the name Orville Watkins. Problem is, his email address is in Los Angeles. I've called the LAPD and they're checking him for priors. Of course, we have no way of knowing if that's his real name or not, but it's a start. I'll get back to you when I hear something. I asked them to rush it. Maybe they will."

I thanked him and hung up. That was one of the main problems. These clowns could live anywhere. The miracle of the World Wide Web. But if Orville was in LA, he couldn't have been in Pleasanton. I was hoping they'd find he flew out before the weekend. Then I thought that he could have hired a hit-man too, but I was still stumped as to how he got Mason's name and address in the first place.

I went back to the computer. I hadn't paid any attention before, but above the start of the posts, there was a time notification. All of the Avenger's posting times were in Pacific time. Like I said, though, that, in itself, didn't prove anything. It didn't *disprove* anything either. I was still at square one. It was familiar territory.

Jenny had put all her other clients on hold. She wanted to concentrate on Mason's case. I told her that there just wasn't enough here yet for two people and to take her mind off it by working on something else, but she wasn't buying.

"I wouldn't be able to do it justice," she said, "I can't stop thinking about poor George. I need to see this one through."

I thought about offering her the case solo, but I wasn't interested in anything else on my blotter either. Contrary to most people's idea, private detectiving is mostly pretty boring. Once you've exposed your first few philandering husbands and wives, the thrill is gone. Even the best photos of the hottest broads look the same after a while. The ones that really stand out are the ones where you wonder why anyone would even bother. Usually there would have to be a lot of money involved. Enough money can be like a paper bag over the head. Some of the bodies wouldn't fit in one.

Then again, love can be a funny thing. Until you stop laughing.

"Besides." I hit her with the old stand-by. "You're too close to the case. It warps your judgment."

She flipped me the bird.

I guess I lost again.

"But I'm taking the lead on this one. What I say goes."

She flipped me the bird with her other hand.

"I'll take that as a yes?"

She saluted me with both well-formed middle fingers.

"Yes, it is then," I said.

With nothing more to go on, we went to Arturo's for lunch. I hadn't been there for a couple of months, and Marta's eyes lit up when she saw me. She came waddling over.

"Allo, Joe. Long dime no zee."

"Hi, Marta. How was the Thanksgiving business?"

"Terrific. Ve cook tventy birds and only have dwo left for ze charity."

"Great. Anybody order spaghetti?"

She laughed. She reminded me of a bowl of Jell-O. "Nod zinze you, Joe. Arty's ztill home recuperating. He vill be zorry he mizzed you."

Neither of us was hungry, so we just shared a large *antipasto* and had a good-natured laugh about Marta's accent. Jenny couldn't pronounce where she was from either, someplace in Eastern Europe. I never got tired of listening to her. She'd been hooking for Madame Flo when Artie fell in love with her and saved her from any further life of sin.

Carson called just as we got back to the office. "Orville Watkins spent Thursday night in jail on a D and D. He and a bunch of his punk friends were harassing a Jewish grocer."

I felt my chin hit my toes. "Are they sure it's the right guy?"

"You bet. Get this, when the interviewer asked him if he was Avenger Two, he went wild, flew into a rage, and threatened to sue the ass off the fucking Jew *Tribune*. It took five guys to subdue him. We can scratch him, but I'm sending you his mug shot anyway."

As soon as I hung up, I checked my email. I downloaded the mug shot and nearly laughed my ass off. His head was shaved, but he had a beard that disappeared below the bottom of the photo. He had numerous little silver balls marching up and down the edges of his ears, and outlining his lips and eyes. I was sure he had some in his tongue as well. They made a silver line down his nose, and the profile showed several on the side, just before the nostrils. Small swastikas were tattooed all over his face. The look in his eyes was defiant. *Insane too*, I thought.

I doubted he could hire a hit man, all his dough was tied up in silver, but maybe he had friends who'd do it for nothing. I wasn't as ready to scratch him as Carson, but I stuck him away in the back of my mind. Then I thought that no hit man would do that to Mason. A shot to the back of the head would be more likely. Of course, he could be an amateur. I still thought that whoever had pumped those slugs into his gut had to be motivated by personal hatred, though, so I was pretty certain Watkins was just an innocent asshole. He had the hatred, but he'd been in the can. In LA.

I wondered what the weather was like there. We were a still a month away from winter and I'd already had enough.

I thought it was kind of ironic that the guy who was after Mason wasn't the one he'd been certain of. Not that it mattered. He was still dead.

I showed the mug shot to Jenny when she came out of the john. "He's not our guy. He was in jail when your cousin was killed."

She was disappointed. So was I. We'd hit a dead end.

"Got any bright ideas?" I said.

She didn't say anything for a while. That usually meant she was thinking.

"I've been thinking," she said. "If this guy won't reveal himself of his own will, maybe we can trap him."

"Huh?"

"We can go on-line ourselves, pretend to be other people. Maybe we could get him to make a mistake."

I thought about it for a while. "Exactly how do you propose to go about doing that?"

"I don't know yet, but I'm willing to wing it. You in?"

"Why not? Two bloggers are better than one."

I looked at the CD. My first thought was to toss it, but then I thought that it might be a historical document. Someday, in the future, maybe archaeologists would come upon it and get a good look at why our civilization fell apart. Rational science could make no inroads whatsoever against the forces of hatred and superstition. Maybe it would be an object lesson to them.

I tossed it.

☙❧

We had a few laughs picking aliases.

"How about Charlie Chan?" I said.

"For you or me?"

"You couldn't pull it off. Your Chinese accent is lousy."

It took a second, but she finally laughed that wonderful laugh. It was the first time I'd heard it since Thanksgiving night.

"It's no good anyway. If this guy is clever enough to go undetected himself but find his victim, a detective's name might make him suspicious."

I couldn't argue with her logic.

"How about 'Dragon Lady?' she said.

"For you or me?"

She laughed again. "You couldn't pull it off. Your tits are too small."

"Now I'm offended," I said. "You shouldn't make fun of people's bodies. I can't help it if my tits are small. It's genetic."

She was determined to be Dragon Lady, and we finally settled on The Voice of Reason for me. I wanted to take over for Philosopher Phil. Maybe I could get our killer pissed off enough to make some threats. Credible threats, but threats that didn't give away too much. He was too smart for that. I wondered if I was smart enough to catch him.

"How about you?" I said, "What kind of blogger do you want to be?"

"I think I'll just let instinct be my guide. You start."

There was a problem, though, and Jenny spotted it.

"If this guy can find out the identity of his victims, he can find out ours too. As soon as he sees your name, he'll figure it out and just clam-up."

I could see she was thinking again. I could always tell because she'd stop talking and just stand there, kind of expectant, like a bird about to take a dump. That was fine with me. She was the one who really understood this computer crap, and I didn't have any ideas.

"Red Barnes," she said.

"Come again?" I had a vision of old barns on the side of the road.

"Harry Barnes. He was a friend of my mother's when she worked at the *Trib*. He's still there."

"What about him?"

"He's pretty high up on the chain of command in the editorial department."

"Is that something like a food chain?"

She laughed. "Pretty much, when you come to think

about it. Maybe we could convince him to provide us with false identities."

"Could he do that?"

"I'm sure he could, but whether he will is another question."

"Supposing we could get some kind of court order. Would that help?"

"It would be like a battering ram, I think, but on what basis could we get one?"

I thought about it for a while. "How about to prevent another murder?"

It was her turn to think. "On what evidence?"

She had me there. All we had was a dead body who, when it was still breathing, was sure that some guy was coming after it, but the guy it suspected was in the can at the time. Anything beyond that was pure speculation. And Mason was still dead. He'd have a tough time swearing out an affidavit.

We'd have to do it for him, but it wouldn't be much easier.

❧❦❧

Barnes's eyes lit up when he saw Jenny. He gave her a big hug. I'd say he was in his late sixties from the skin on his neck, but the rest of him looked younger. They exchanged pleasantries for a bit. He was really happy to meet me. He'd been following my career ever since the Wagner affair, he said.

Maybe this would be easier than I'd thought.

His office was at the end of a long line of desks with people sitting at them writing on computers. In the old days, city rooms were noisy places, with the sound of dozens of typewriters clickety-clacking away. The silence now was eerie. I almost felt like I was walking through the set for a silent movie. Even the clanging phones had been replaced with ones that just sort of hummed or beeped.

Harry was in his shirtsleeves, though, and they were rolled up. Maybe some things never changed. He gave Jenny what I could only describe as an "avuncular" look. He had been like an uncle to her after her father died, she told me.

"You were very mysterious on the phone," he said. "Supposing you explain what you want."

We did. We filled him in on everything. I hoped that it didn't sound too outlandish, but he never once looked like he might laugh.

"I was wondering, after Jenny started talking about encryption, if it had anything to do with the Mason business. Little did I know you were right in the middle of it. We complied with the court order because of the murder, but what you're asking is a bit of a different kettle of fish."

His major problem was ethical, but that dissolved as soon as Frank walked in with a smile on his face.

Frank Gomez was one of the best cops in Central City. He'd mentored me when I first joined the force. All you need to know about what kind of guy he was, is that he continued to turn down promotions to captain, preferring to stay in the harness with his detectives, as their all-wise looie. He didn't trust the higher brass much anyway, but that's for another time.

I'd called and filled him in on the case. He'd agreed to get in touch with Carson and said he'd do his damnedest to get a court order. I was relieved when he walked in. He'd had to call in a chit he was owed by a friend in the DA's office, but he had it. Turns out that he and Barnes had worked together on several cases that required the *Trib*'s cooperation and were friendly.

That sealed the deal, and within a few hours, Jenny and I were transformed into Leonard Glass and Hortense Whitmeyer. Supposedly, anyone trying to gain access to the encryption codes, would be redirected to a couple of phony email addresses.

Barnes also said that he'd start a thorough investigation of the system, to see if he could find out how it had been breached. "If there's some weakness in our systems that's led to a murder, I sure as hell want to know about it."

I thought of something. "We met a systems analyst by the name of Thaddeus Gray up in Pleasanton. He was very interested in the case. Maybe he could be of some help." I wrote down Mom's address and phone number. "He's real busy on some project for the U," I said, "but maybe you could persuade him to lend a hand."

Barnes said he'd try to track him down.

I thought of something else. "It would help to know the identities of all the most egregious of the bloggers."

Harry thought for a while. "I'm afraid I can't help you there. I just can't let you have those names, but I can keep a tracker on all of them. That way, if one turns up dead, we'll know. That would put a whole new light on the matter." He looked at Frank. "One dead blogger is nothing much. Two will give you cops a bloody headache, but you'll get all the help you can from us."

"Isn't that kind of like shutting the barn door after the horses have escaped?" I said.

He shrugged. "Take it up with the congress and the supreme court. See if you can organize a constitutional amendment."

There was no arguing with the law, however stupid it might be.

Anyway, we were ready to begin our careers as bloggers.

"Hortense Whitmeyer?" I said to Jenny later. "How the hell did you come up with that one?"

"She was my fifth grade teacher. I hated her."

❧❧❧

I stopped at Ruby's Snack Shack, just across the street from my place. Ruby was a red-headed bombshell, but her hulk of a husband convinced me to keep my hands to myself. At dinner time, they served more substantial meals than snacks, and I had the Yankee pot roast. It was always delicious. Ruby once told me she got the recipe from her mother.

I asked her if her father was alive.

"I dunno," she said. "He ran out on us when I was just a kid."

"Do you know if your mother wants to get married again?"

Her boobs did great things when she laughed.

❧❧❧

I just sat and stared at my laptop. I had writer's block. I didn't know where to begin. Nothing would come to me, so I just started reading comments at random, hoping one would get my creative juices flowing. It didn't take long. The internet is so crowded with dick-heads that you can't go more than five minutes without one of them setting your blood to boiling. I hate willful stupidity, and there was enough on display to choke a donkey.

An elephant, even.

CHAPTER 26

After a few good, stiff drinks, I sat down around midnight to review our evening's work. We'd picked out an article to comment on at random. It was written by a well-known conservative columnist and was an attempt to pin all the problems in Washington on a dictatorial president who refused to compromise. Pretty much standard right-wing fare.

I scrolled down to the comments.

Refusal to Compromise Typical of Obama's Dictatorial Style
By Mitch Daniels
Syndicated columnist
Posted 7:20 PM CST

Comments:

The Voice of Reason wrote:
7:30 PM CST
Why have we not heard from Philosopher Phil in a while?

I hope you cretins haven't driven him away finally, but intelligent people can only take so much. His is one of the few sane voices in this whole debate. It's a total pleasure to read his comments after wading through acres of the disgusting ooze spread by the rest of you. He's the only reason I'm even here. A voice of sanity and reason deserves some intelligent backup. There are only a courageous few of you doing a decent job against tremendous odds, so I figured I'd better stop being a voyeur and join the fray.

I can't wait to be vilified. I'll take it as a baptism by fire and a mark of honor.

Aristotle responded:
7:45 PM CST
@Voice of Reason
Welcome to Hell. If you've been following the "debates," you know what you're up against. I hope you've got staying power. Waiting for your first comments.

Crazyman responded:
7:50 PM CST
Great. Another leftist asshole heard from. You should all pack up and move to Russia where you belong. We're tired of you elitist motherfuckers trying to tell us real Americans how to live. Are you even sure you're really Americans? I'm not. You sound like a bunch of foreign agitators and Israel-Firsters.
IMPEACH OBAMA '14

Crazyman responded:
7:51 PM CST
Elitist.
Why doesn't the fucking Trib have an edit feature?

LouieLouie responded:
7:55 CST

Why don't you edit your shit before you post, not that it would help any. lol.

Wilson38 responded:
8:01 PM CST
How about staying on topic? Who gives a crap about who shows up? What is this, a social club? Go to Facebook if you're looking for friends.

HenryVIII responded:
9:02 PM EST
OK. So what do you have to say about it troll?

Philadelphia Lad wrote:
9:05 PM EST
It's glaringly obvious that if the Republicans weren't setting about to destroy Obama, as they have been from the start, we'd be having none of these problems. Who's Daniels trying to kid anyway. Why does the Trib keep allowing him to pump out this neocon garbage?
Time for a shakeup on the editorial board.
He won't be missed.

Horatio Alger wrote:
8:10 CST
For the first time in ages, I agree with Daniels. I usually find him too liberal for my taste, but he's right on the money here. For Obummer, it's my way or the hiway. He's doing more to destroy our way of life than anyone in recent history. Look at the shambles. Economy, down. Standard of living, down. Unemployment, up. And now he wants to saddle us with Obamacare. Thank god he's out of there in a couple of years. Worst president since Jimmy Carter.

The Thinker responded:
6:20 PM PST
I'll agree that Carter was a terrible president. But you're full of shit about Obama. All you have to work with is lies. Stupid lies that can be disproved in five minutes with a simple reference to Google.
The economy is on the rise.
The standard of living is about where it's always been. How else can you explain record box office and sporting event takes?
Unemployment is down.
Your hatred of Obama just makes you stupid.

Colleen responded:
8:30 PM CST
Anyone who uses terms like Obummer, is too juvenile to be posting here. Go back to Ranger Rick and let us grownups talk.

Horatio Alger responded:
8:37 PM CST
Up yours, bitch.

Dragon Lady responded:
8:40 PM CST
Take it easy there, sonny boy, or I'll be forced to hang your ass out to dry. You'll keep a civil tongue when you speak to ladies, or you'll answer to me. I eat chauvinist bastards like you for lunch.

Horatio Alger responded:
8:43 PM CST
You can eat me any time you want to, cunt, if your mouth is big enough, and what's with the threats? Are you planning to use this page for toilet paper?

Dragon Lady responded:
8:50 PM CST
I know where you live. Don't answer your door.

Horatio Alger responded:
8:53 PM CST
Oooh, scary. You should really try to get laid. You need to get straightened out.

Dragon Lady responded:
8:55 PM CST
I'll straighten you out—on a marble slab.
Don't think I can't. I've got a black belt in several martial arts.

Dave36 wrote:
9:01 PM CST
@ The Voice of Reason.
Kind of arrogant there, don't you think? You're the only reasonable one? Give me a break. You intellectual type lefty creeps are all the same. Willing to sell us all down the river for AIPAC and the Israel First crowd. How much are they paying you to come here and spread your filthy Zionazi lies?

The Voice of Reason responded:
9:04 PM CST
You wouldn't be an anti-Semite, by any chance, would you?

Dave36 responded:
9:07 PM CST
Just like all you Zionist supremacists. When all else fails, play the anti-Semite card.
Well, buddy, it ain't working anymore. We're onto

your filthy little game. We see your disgusting little country for the threat to the world that it is. We know you got 200 hydrogen bombs aimed at Europe and the US.

People like you should be lined up and shot for the traitors you are.

The Voice of Reason responded:
9:15 PM CST
What the fuck does Israel have to do with anything, you ridiculous moron? The discussion is about Obama and congress.

What the hell do you use for a brain while yours is at the dry-cleaners, sawdust?

Okiefrommuskogee responded:
9:20 PM CST
What does Israel have to do with anything?
PLENTY.
Who do you think runs our government?
THEIR ALL IN AIPAC'S POCKET.
Our ball-less president can't make a move without their OK.

It's just the old tail wagging the dog.

Where I come from, when the dog gets that bad, we shoot him.

WE SHOULD SHOOT YOU TOO, YOU ZIONIST RAT BASTARD.

Dave36 responded:
9: 31 PM CST
Give it to him right between the eyes, Okie. These assholes all think we're a bunch of stupid trailer trash. Well, I got news for them, we're taking over again. We're going to start making America what it's supposed to be.

We're going to kill all their asses or send them back where they came from.

Their choice.

Philosopher Phil and the rest of the traitorous bastards. They're all on the way out. Just read all these comments. They have no support, and it's about time.

Aristotle responded:
9:45 PM CST
That's all you can ever think of. Violence and killing. You're always yelling about the constitution but you're ready to take away everybody else's rights at the drop of a hat. You're all a bunch of ignorant fools. None of you has the brains to run anything more complicated than an electric train set. The idea that any of you would be running the country makes me want to throw up.

If any of you had any brains at all, instead of tossing around your impotent vitriol, you'd be discussing Daniels' column. Not that it's worth a crap. You probably can't read the big words anyway.

If you clowns are indicative of real public opinion, I'll eat my shirt. You're all preaching to the choir.

Dragon Lady responded:
10:01 PM CST
OOO, you let 'em have it baby. Point them out and I'll whip them for you.

Then maybe we could get together later and you could whip me.

The Voice of Reason responded:
10:05 PM CST
Any chance of me getting in on the action?

Dragon Lady responded:

10:07 PM CST
As a whipper or a whippee.

The Voice of Reason responded:
10:09 PM CST
Can I be both?

Dragon Lady responded:
10:10 PM CST
How big is your whip?

Horatio Alger responded:
10:12 PM CST
Why don't you two just get a room?

Dragon Lady responded:
10:14 PM CST
Do you want to watch through the keyhole?

❧❧❧

It took almost two hours, but there were finally a bunch of comments that actually dealt with the subject of the article.

Boring as hell.

I began to understand what Mason had meant about amusement. Yanking stupid dick-heads was kind of fun. But what had we accomplished?

Several posters were obviously comfortable with violence, but I'd seen nothing yet that would arouse anything more than mild suspicion about any of them. In fact, anyone else reading this shit might suspect the Dragon Lady first and foremost, what with her outright statements about knowing where people live. If she'd planned to draw somebody out, it hadn't worked. At least, not yet. I figured that any curiosity about our sudden appearance would dissolve as we became fixtures. Problem was, if there was a crazed killer out there, how much time did we have until he struck again?

How much time did I actually want to spend inhabiting this hazel hatchery? Even the finest amusement pales with repetition, and this stuff was hardly the finest.

Nobody would be paying us for it either, but this was personal. No money required.

My phone rang. It was Jenny.

"Well, what's it to be? Whipper or whippee?"

"You just made a poem?"

She laughed. "So I did. Dragon Lady has many talents. Beware. I know where you live."

"Don't you think you piled it on a bit thick there?"

I could feel her shrug.

"Just establishing my bona fides. Always come out swinging, I say. Besides, that asshole I answered really ticked me off."

I knew what she meant. "Don't they, though?"

"In spades. Do you think maybe they all live in the same nut-house?"

"If it were up to me, they would. With really heavy bars."

"Anyway—"

I could hear the stifled yawn

"—I'm calling it a night. See you in the morning."

"Sounds good to me."

I really had no patience left, so I had a few more drinks and finally went unconscious.

CHAPTER 27

I spent the first part of the morning reading through a bunch of different comments. I even tried a few other papers, but it was pretty much the same crowd wherever I went. Pretty much the same comments too. I paid particular attention to Dave 36 and the Okie guy, but there was nothing at all to raise my eyebrows any higher than they already felt pinned to my forehead.

It really was hard to believe. I hoped that Aristotle had been right, that these assholes were no way indicative of most people's thinking. Not that most people were particularly adept at the process anyway, but this really looked like the bottom of the barrel.

What seemed weird—and wonderful too, in a way—was that these people were free to spill their vitriol, unfettered either by law or common decency. Is this a great country, or what?

I just wished that more people with functioning brains would get in on the act like *The Voice of Reason* said. Then I thought that most people with functioning brains had better things to do with them. This was the kind of platform that pandered to the lowest common denominator.

I could see how it could be addictive, though, particularly when you had a feud that got real personal. I had to laugh at that. How fucking "personal" can a bunch of anonymous strangers get?

You'd be surprised.

I certainly got the impression that some of them had such weak personalities that even an insult from an anonymous stranger, who they claimed to be superior to, and who really knew nothing at all about them, could send them into fits of anger and hatred.

On the flip side, they often called their verbal victims by terms and descriptions that any disinterested reader could clearly see were their own.

I'd called my friend, Gordon Harrison, a psychiatrist at the U, to ask him what he thought about all of this kind of stuff. He gave me a word, "projection," that explained it all pretty well. Sometimes, people with wild opinions that frighten them, pretend to be the opposite and project them onto others. That way they can be bigots pretending to be humanitarians, and call real humanitarians bigots.

I don't really understand it. I'm just saying what *he* said. I think.

He also said they were usually too weak to do anything much but comment anonymously. Physical confrontation was highly unlikely.

Usually.

Jenny came in late. There were dark circles around her eyes, and her face looked pinched.

I looked at her. "Didn't sleep well, huh?"

"Hardly at all. I can't stop thinking that Cousin George is dead, and the crazy sonofabitch who killed him is running around free. I know that's the same with any murder, but this is different."

"That's what I meant about being too close to a case. You lose more sleep than usual and stop thinking straight."

She managed a smile. "So that's why you're taking the lead, right?"

I'd kind of forgotten about that, but I pounced. "And don't you forget it," I said, and wondered if I was projecting. That psychology stuff can drive you batty. It's best just to use plain instinct to decide who are the good guys, and who are the bad guys. Instinct rarely lets you down. Problem is, letting yourself trust it.

Right now, my instinct wasn't giving me anything to trust.

"Is there anything *new* on-line?" She didn't sound like she was expecting what she wanted to hear.

I shrugged. "I guess it's back to the old grind, trading insults with assholes"

"Aw, boss. Do we gotta?" Her smile was weak.

"One good thing," I said, "if we get horny trading barbs with each other, we don't have any farther to go than the next office."

"You should live so long," she said. "Maybe I'll just lock my door."

"Don't trust yourself, huh?"

She finally laughed, but the dark circles were still there.

I went back to my screen, and she went back to her office. I didn't hear the lock turn.

The first thing I saw stopped me cold.

Still No Leads in Mason Murder
Bill Barrett Central City Tribune
Posted 11:00 AM CST

Comments:

Dave36 wrote:
11:10 AM CST

My guess is that he's too clever for the cops I hope they never catch him. He should get a medal for the great favor he did us. Godless, atheist bastards like Mason are ruining this great country of ours. I hope this is the work of an avenging angel, and that he'll take out a few more like him. He's a fucking hero. Some of the disgusting crap he spewed just made me sick. I certainly wouldn't want my kids tainted with exposure to such godless, communist filth. People who think like that should be deported or tried as traitors. They need to be cut down or this country is doomed.

☙❧

That was the only post so far, and my instincts kicked in. I shouted for Jenny to get in here.

"What's up? Why the noise?"

I pointed to my screen. "What do you make of this?"

She read it over. "So he's nuts. What's new?"

I shook my head at her, like she was the slowest student in the class. Why not? She'd done it to *me* often enough.

"Unless this guy was reading scientific journals, how the hell did he know what Mason had been saying?"

That didn't stop her for long. "Well, he could just have been referring to him as a generic scientist, of course, so that anything he ever said would offend fanatic believers in Creationism or whatever."

I thought about that for a minute, but I was shaking my head. "There's just something a lot more personal about it.

"Maybe." She didn't sound enthused.

"Maybe he's slipped up," I said, "admitted that that he knew that Mason was Philosopher Phil and it was *his* 'filth' that offended him."

"Could he be that stupid? He's supposed to be clever, remember?"

"If I'm right, his first line could have been a boast, and he obviously thinks of himself as a hero. Maybe he does consider himself an avenging angel. Maybe this is a veiled dare to the cops. Maybe he figures nobody much is going to be reading this stuff anyway, so he can take a small chance. He's got to be dying to tell." The more I talked, the more convinced I got.

"If you're right."

Boy, could she deflate a balloon. But her point was well taken. Jenny dragged a chair behind my desk, and we watched the screen for about fifteen minutes, but nobody else posted a comment. We'd been trying to figure out what we could post that would egg him on, maybe get him to slip up some more, but neither of us had any good ideas.

"It would have to be subtle," I said.

She thought about that, and then her eyes lit up. "Why subtle? Supposing we offer him a straight out dare?"

I wasn't sure I liked the sound of that. "What have you got in mind?"

"You'll see. Keep your eyes on the screen." She pushed back her chair and got up to leave.

I grabbed her arm. "Hey, I'm supposed to be in charge, remember?"

She just laughed. "That was an hour ago. Times change, you know." She slipped out of my grasp and hot-footed it to her office.

"What are you going to do?" I yelled after her.

"Watch your screen and shut up," she yelled back.

I watched my screen.

Dragon Lady responded:
11:30 AM CST

I agree with you. Scum like that should be eliminated. It would be a good start to begin with some of the creeps who post here. Philosopher Phil, for instance. We could use a little site clean-up.

"This better work," I yelled, "otherwise, you've scared him off for good."

We waited another anxious fifteen minutes.

Dave36 responded:
11:47 AM CST
Maybe somebody already has. Haven't heard from the bastard for several days, have we?

Dragon Lady responded:
11:52 AM CST
We can only hope, but there's really no way to know who any of us are, unless we tell, and I never tell. (cracks whip)

"Hey," I yelled, "nice little touch. Cracks whip. Other than that, I might be tempted to take you over my knee. You're pushing too hard."

"What? I can't hear you. There's a loud noise coming from your office."

"What's going on?" Peggy appeared outside my door. "What's with all the shouting?"

"We're talking," I said.

"Why don't you just use the intercom? You know, those little buttons on the phone?"

"Too much trouble," I said, "this is a lot easier."

"Well, you're freaking out the people in the waiting room?"

"Who are they, and what are they doing here?"

"I don't know, waiting?"

She'd definitely spent too much time around Jenny, but that eternal question mark was driving me nuts.

"Well, tell them to make an appointment for next week and send them home. We're too busy to take on any new cases right now."

"Okay, boss."

"Stop with that 'boss' crap already," Jenny yelled.

"Okay, boss." She laughed, and scampered away to get rid of the waiters.

I was pretty sure that Dragon Lady had really blown it. The screen didn't change for a long time. I nearly jumped when the post finally appeared.

Dave36 responded:
12:10 PM CST
"There are more things in heaven and earth, Horatio, than are dreamt of in your philosophy."

"What the fuck was that?" I shouted.

"Shakespeare. Hamlet." She sounded excited. Did I ever mention that Jenny had gone to acting school?

She looked in at my door, looking better than she had in days.

"I think he just told us he can do it. Didn't he?"

It was my turn to be skeptical. I shrugged my shoulders. "None of this would hold up in court, you know."

She refused to be cowed. "We're not in court."

I was puzzled. "What kind of asshole can quote Shakespeare and still be as crazy as he is?"

Now it was her turn to give *me* that go-sit-in-the-corner look. "You haven't read much Shakespeare, have you?"

I had to admit it.

"It's full of people like that. They all give these beautiful flowery speeches before they kill somebody."

"Not like Batman? 'Take that, kapow?'"

"Can batman make you cry?"

"Only after I've paid fifteen smackers for the movie."

That was only the second time in days that she laughed her real Jenny laugh.

She disappeared back into her office.

Dragon Lady responds:
12:15 PM CST
Cryptic little bastard, aren't you? I may be forced to punish you. Expect me at your door.

We waited a long time, but he never answered.

"Now what?" I said.

She reached for my phone. She had to reach across me, and I had an urge to grab her boob in my mouth. I didn't.

"Harry Barnes, please," she said into the phone. There was a pause "Tell him it's Jenny." She waited for a bit.

"Red? It's Jenny. We might have something for you." She looked surprised. Then she looked at me. "He expected our call. He was watching the comments too."

I grabbed the phone. "What d'you think? Is there something here?"

"Well, a possible lawsuit for sure if you're wrong."

"Why should I care? They'll be suing you."

He laughed. "Come on down, and we can discuss it with our legal team."

❦

Frank was already there. I'd called him as soon as I hung up from Barnes. He looked glum. There were three other guys I hadn't seen before, Miles Gordon, editor-in-chief, and William K. Thatcher III, the publisher, were the big guns. They were in full uniform. Even Barnes wore his coat. The other guy was Mel Shapiro. I recognized his name from a series of articles he'd done about inefficiencies in the housing agency. He was working on an article about the comments sections, and Barnes thought he'd be interested. He was still in his shirtsleeves.

From Frank's appearance, I figured we had our work cut out for us.

We'd eaten lunch at the City Diner, but it had been greasier than usual, and I was worried that I might belch or even fart. I thought Jenny looked a little uncomfortable too. Goddamned cheeseburgers. The curly fries too. I used up five of their crappy waxed-paper napkins.

Too bad it was so good.

Frank started the ball rolling. Just as I'd thought, the DA wouldn't do anything without serious evidence.

"They actually agree that there might be something here, but their hands are tied by the law." He looked at Thatcher. "They won't give you legal cover."

Thatcher's expression never changed. "Well, I'm willing for the paper to take the heat, but I'm going to need a goddamned good reason. From what I've pieced together so far, it sounds like nothing but a lot of vague speculation. Still, if we can prevent murders, I'm willing to stick my neck out." He looked at me. He even smiled. "I'm well aware of your reputation, Mr. Gold and, if you'll remember, the *Trib* was on your side during your trial."

"Yes, you were, and that was one of the few bright spots in the whole affair. I thank you for it."

"So why haven't you bought a subscription?"

The question caught me totally by surprise. I just laughed. "I only subscribe to Jewish-owned papers. I once made a vow to God."

It was his turn to laugh. "There aren't any."

"Sure there are. I get the *Jewish Chronicle* delivered every Friday."

He hesitated just a moment, then he laughed again. "Touché. Anyway, your activities in the Wagner affair and the vampire killings attest to your ability." He lost the smile. "Otherwise, you wouldn't be sitting here now." He thought about that for a second. "Well, *I* wouldn't, but I am, so it's up to you to convince me to stick my head in a legal noose."

I took a deep breath and filled him in on everything I thought. Jenny was right in there with me, and we made the best case we could with the meager evidence we had, if you could even call it that. I guess we anticipated any questions he might have had, because he never interrupted. Neither did anyone else.

When we'd finished, he looked at Gordon and Barnes, in turn. "What do you guys think?"

Barnes was the first. "I say the whole thing is nuts, but so is the comments section, so there's not much sane to latch onto. What do you think, Miles?"

"I think they make a good enough case to warrant taking the chance. Unless we get lucky and catch a killer, maybe nobody will ever even have to know."

Thatcher laughed. "Isn't that what Nixon said?"

Everybody cracked up on that one.

"Okay," he said. "Against all my wiser instincts, we'll get you his identity. The rest is up to you." He picked up the phone. A few seconds later he said, "Okay. Send it in an email to Barnes." He glanced at his watch. "I've got an important meeting in five minutes." He stood. So did the rest of us. No matter who you are, you take care to worship the boss. He shook my hand. "It's been a real pleasure to meet you Mr. Gold. If anyone can solve this, you can." He let go my hand and grabbed Jenny's. "You too, Ms. Martin." He leaned in and whispered something in her ear. She smiled.

Right after he left, the name appeared on Barnes' screen.

"Here it is," he said, "David Addison. I don't have an address or phone number, we don't ask for them, but I can give you his email address." He looked at Frank. "You should be able to trace that."

"Maybe, but I can sure run the name through the system and see if anything shakes out."

We left with Frank promising to get back to me as soon as he had anything.

Shapiro collared us before we left. "If there's anything I can do to help you catch the Nazi bastard, let me know."

I promised I'd keep him informed.

"The idea that any of those screwballs could act out scares the crap out of me," he said.

⁂

I asked Jenny later what Thatcher had whispered to her.

"He said he was only stroking your ego, and he knew perfectly well that I was the brains of the outfit."

"Like hell, he did."

She just smiled and nodded her head.

⁂

The jangling of the phone jerked me awake. I've got one of those old-fashioned dial types. I love it for that ring, but it made my head feel like a cracked melon. I must have been more tired than I'd thought. I'd fallen asleep in my easy chair. I looked at the clock. Seven-thirty. It was dark so I figured it was evening. Then I remembered it was dark at seven-thirty in the morning now, too.

It was Frank.

"What time is it?" I said.

"Seven-thirty."

"Seven thirty a.m. or p.m.?"

"What the fuck is wrong with you? It's nighttime for crissakes."

"Thanks." My head was clearing. "Got something?"

"Good news and bad news. The good news is we managed to get an address."

"Okay. What's the bad news?"

"We've got nothing on him. Not even so much as a parking ticket or a citation for spitting. Mr. Crazy Citizen is squeaky clean, and there's nothing to point to any aliases."

I wrote down the address and telephone numbers, one was his cell.

"Thanks, Frank. I'll keep you informed."

"Sure you will. When hell freezes over."

"Have you been outside lately? If that's not hell, I'll eat my shirt. I slipped and nearly broke my neck getting up my front steps."

"Take it easy." He was laughing, "If anything kills you, I want it to be me."

"Besides," I said, "it's not police business, is it?"

"What difference does that make?"

He hung up.

I called Jenny with the news.

"I don't want to do anything tonight," she said. "I'm just exhausted. Do we know where he works?"

"Frank didn't say. Why don't you just get a good night's sleep? I'll try do some research and call you in the morning."

"Sounds good to me. Night."

I thought that I could use a lot more sleep myself, but I poured a drink, turned on the laptop, and nearly fell asleep waiting for it to go through its miserable, fucking, wake-up routine. What's with those little boxes that pop up saying that something's wrong? They used to bother me until I discovered that X-ing them did not cause the machine to explode, nor did it seem to do anything else. Still, I had visions of having set loose armies of tiny ones and zeroes working their way through the innards, like out-of-control Pac-Men. I expected that, one day, the damned thing would just disintegrate.

It was only recently that I finally lost my fear of it—anyway, never mind that Jenny kept assuring me that I couldn't break it.

"Oh, yeah?" I once said, "find a good medium and ask my dead mother about that. She said I could break anything—and I did."

Just like Frank, I couldn't find David Addison anywhere. Google drew a blank, at least as far as *our* David Addison was concerned. There were at least a dozen others listed, but they were dead ends. None of them lived here anyway.

I had the same lack of luck with Facebook. This guy was keeping a low profile. I knew I was supposed to keep an active Twitter going, for business reasons, but I always found myself laughing too hard to press the keys. By the time I got to "Twit," I just gave up. What grown man would be caught dead on something that sounded like a teenage girls' pajama party? Beside a pedophile.

When Jenny told me that all the politicians were on it, I had my answer.

No one.

And I'd recently put away a couple of pedophile pols.

After about an hour's searching, I gave up and went back to my drinking, but I forced myself to stop after two more. I'd need to get up early to stake out his place. Then I thought that I didn't even know what the sonofabitch looked like.

CHAPTER 28

Ludlow was a small neighborhood near the west edge of the city. It was middle class with two- story townhouses marching up and down both sides of the streets. The original development featured five different designs, so it was not too monotonous. Each house had a garage below. The one at 2543 Orange Lane was Addison's. Luckily, he didn't live in an apartment building, so we could just sit in our rented car, warm and toasty, until he left for work, If he did. There was always the possibility he worked at home. He could be unemployed too. Maybe that was one reason he was so pissed off.

At seven-thirty, the garage door opened and an older model white Corolla pulled out. I know it was a Corolla because it was written across the trunk. Otherwise, all the newer cars look alike to me. A man was driving alone. I waited until the garage door closed again before following. We didn't go far. A mile from his home, Addison drove into the parking lot of the Edison Insurance Building, a ten story glass cube.

I pulled into an empty slot and waited for about a half-hour, just to make sure he wasn't simply dropping in to pay his premium, or something. In the meantime, Jenny was fiddling with her iPad, trying to find the Wi-Fi network. The first time I'd ever seen it, I thought it was a big Etch-a-Sketch."

"It's an iPad, you boob," she said. "It'll do almost anything a laptop can do, and it's a lot more expensive than an Etch-a-Sketch."

She finally managed to connect. She Googled Edison Insurance and got 10,320,000 hits in .002 seconds. She only needed the first one. The rest of it was just plain bragging. She scrolled through the list of agents.

"Here he is," she said, "David Addison, agent. There's a number."

"Great. Now what?" I said.

"I dunno, you're the lead, remember?" She had a broad smile on her face.

I can't remember when I had a greater desire to kiss her. Instead, I said, "Times changed again?"

"Uh-huh."

"This is what, CFT?"

"CFT?"

"Central Female Time."

She laughed. "You got it."

"So it's my call?"

"Right."

I took out my phone and called the number on the screen. It was answered by a receptionist in the auto insurance department. I made an appointment for nine. I told her someone had recommended Addison to me. She seemed surprised by that.

"They did?" is what she said.

Maybe he didn't get too many recommendations.

We hadn't eaten, so we headed to an IHOP across the street until a few minutes before nine. Over breakfast, my headache finally dissolved. I left Jenny in the Edison main lobby playing with her iPad. There was no point in her sitting in the car with the engine running for heat. Not at close to five bucks a gallon.

I took the elevator to the sixth floor. I wasn't sure what I was going to do, but I wanted to see this guy up close, try to get some idea of what he was like. The receptionist directed me to room 617. Addison's name was on the door.

He got up from his chair and shook my hand. His grip was tentative and weak. He was a mousy little guy, maybe five-five. He was balding, about fifty, and his eyes were a watery brown, not the eyes of a killer. Maybe not of a good insurance salesman either. There were a couple of pictures on his desk, but I couldn't see the faces.

He shrank even more when he sat down behind it.

"What can I do for you, Mr. Garfield?" His voice was mousy too, slightly high-pitched and nasal." He looked down at a note on his desk. "You said that someone recommended you?"

"Yes, but for the life of me, I can't remember who. I just remember him mentioning your name. I had a cousin with your name, so I guess it stuck." I was wearing my most pleasant smile, but he seemed ill-at-ease. Was it me or was he always like this? "I'm thinking about buying a car, and I'd like to know what it'll cost me to have it insured."

He was all business, but he still seemed nervous. I told him that I was having trouble deciding between three cars, a Beemer, a Mercedes, and a Lexus, and that the insurance premiums would probably be the deciding factor.

I watched him as he consulted various fee schedules. He never stopped being twitchy. I decided that was his natural state. It turned out that the cost of insuring the cars was roughly the same for each.

"Damn," I said, "now I still have to make a decision.

Well, thanks for your help. I'll call you when I've made my choice." We shook hands and I left.

I'd been hoping for some kind of opening to discuss current events and maybe bring up the Mason killing, you know, shoot the shit, but he wasn't the shit-shooting type, and I never got an opening.

"Well?" Jenny said when we got back to the car.

"He's a dried up little prune," I said, "I'm finding it very hard to see him as a killer, but he also seemed to be naturally nervous as hell. There's something not right with that guy so, who knows?"

"I have some info of my own," she said. "I looked through the Edison website. Under profiles, they have short bios of all their agents. Addison's was short. He has a wife and kid. A girl."

"Maybe you could get friendly with the missus, maybe shake something out of her."

"Bor-ring," she said.

I wished she'd stopped there.

"I've been thinking. What if I just go up to him and tell him I'm the Dragon Lady and I can do it too?"

I gave her a hard look. She was serious.

"You'd probably give him a heart attack."

"Well, I can't think of anything else. It could take days to get anything out of his wife."

"Off hand, neither can I, but hold on for a second, okay? Let me think about it. It could be dangerous."

We kicked the idea around during lunch and finally decided to go ahead, as long as she wore a wire and I could listen in.

She laughed. "I always knew you were a voyeur. Do you get off peeking in windows too?"

"Ha, ha. If you get in trouble, I want to know about it right away."

She batted her long eyelashes at me. "So my hero can

come and rescue poor little old me from the clutches of a maniacal insurance salesman? Maybe you forgot I have black belts in several martial arts."

"Never you mind. I want to know what's going on. I haven't paid your life insurance premium yet. Business is business."

I loved her laugh.

✑✑✑

As soon as we got back to the office, I called Lazy Lazar. His real name was Seymour, but his laconic style earned him the nickname. He'd been a hot-shot lawyer once, but a penchant for larceny and fraud finally got him disbarred. Lucky for him, he only spent a few years in prison. It was like one of those country-club places, and he got "rehabilitated" by enrolling in an electronics class. By the time he got out, Lazy was a whiz at putting together gadgets, and he made a lucrative business out of making and selling surveillance equipment to the cops, private dicks, and anybody else who wanted to spy on somebody.

Until a few months ago, he'd been out of my league pricewise, but since his youngest son, Sammy, and I had been good friends when we were kids, he'd sometimes give me a good deal on used equipment.

He picked up on the fifth ring.

"Shut up already. I'm here."

"How ya doin, Lazy? Joe Gold."

"Hey, Joey. How the hell are you? I've been following your ass in the papers."

"Fine, Lazy, fine. You gonna be around your shop for a while? I need a good body-cam."

"Sure. I've nowhere else to be. Come on over."

Lazy worked out of a phone-booth-sized shop strewn

with bins of wires, cables, connectors, and god-knows-what-else. It was all just a front. The real deal was in the back, where he put together his creations. He said he kept the shop door locked half the time, and the other half, almost nobody ever came in to buy any of that stuff in the bins anyway.

He was a short, squat little guy, with bristly hair that stood out from his head like wires. I had a vision of him getting regular jolts of juice. He wore thick glasses. His eyesight had been failing, and he didn't know how much longer he'd be able to keep working. He was almost eighty. I once asked him why he did keep working.

"Just for fun," he said, "just for fun. And to keep busy, of course. If I didn't have this, I'd be sitting around in my empty fucking apartment feeling sorry for myself. This way, I get to watch the assholes all trying to put one over on each other. Fun. I can't tell you what a kick I get from selling this crap to husbands, wives, and their lovers, brothers and sisters, and all the non-related assholes eating their hearts out over somebody or something that's not worth a shit."

He wore that smile that sometimes made me think of a leprechaun.

I know there's no such thing as a Jewish leprechaun, but that's how I thought of him anyway.

He'd met Jenny once before, and he leered at her the same way he did the first time, Lazy never lost his liking for the ladies. Now he was looking her up and down with an eye to concealing a wire and a camera.

"Wear something with buttons," he said.

He walked over to a standing shelf that reminded me of an auto mechanic's, only instead of the rolling drawers revealing wrenches and such, they were filled with electronic gadgets. He removed something and brought it over. It had a short wire with a long bump on the end. It looked like a snake that swallowed a barrel. The other end was a black button.

"It's a camera with a fisheye lens," he said. "Things will look a little distorted, but you'll have a good view of the room." He went over and opened a drawer in his desk. He held out a plastic bag full of identical black buttons. "If you don't have something with black buttons, sew these on. Nobody'll ever catch it."

"What's that little doohickey on the end?" I said.

He actually beamed. "That, my dick friend, is a marvel of modern technology, and I made it myself. That little 'doohickey' is a powerful receiver/transmitter. Whatever the camera sees, you can see on a monitor up to half-a-mile away. The whole thing is powered by a watch battery. Well, three of them."

I was suitably impressed. "What about audio?"

"It's built-in. Here, look."

I took a close look at the "button." You could just make out where the lens, which was black, was surrounded by a narrow band with a tiny hatchmark design, also black. From an appropriate viewing distance, it looked like any other button.

"The outer ring is a microphone, a pretty damned good one for its size too. It'll pick up a whisper."

I liked what I saw. Jenny nodded her head when I looked at her. But something else was bugging me. "How can I talk to her?"

Lazy nearly danced around. "Wait'll you see this." He went back to his Dr. Caligari's cabinet and returned with a tiny, pink plastic plug, like a small earplug. "This baby is not just a speaker, it can read signals from the 'doohickey.' With this, you've got all the bases covered. It fits comfortably in your ear. Until you hear Joe's ugly voice, you'll never even know it's there." He laughed. "So you'd better practice not jumping when you do."

"How much?"

"For you, Joey, a special price, three grand." He laughed when he saw my face. "Relax. I'll rent it to you for a grand a week."

"I looked at him. "How many of these do you rent out in a year?"

"About fifty."

"How many do you sell?"

"I've only got five. What the hell would I rent if I sold them?"

I laughed. "Ah, Lazy, you're still a *goniff*."

"Yeah, but now I'm legal." He smiled with his whole face.

A Jewish leprechaun I'm telling you.

ↄ৲৵ↄ

We spent the afternoon practicing with the equipment. I had no real idea how any of it worked, but work it did. With a special USB thingy plugged into a computer, I could pick up a clear signal. The fisheye lens took some getting used to, but it did give almost a hundred-and eighty degree view.

Jenny cursed a lot as she replaced the green buttons on the sexy cardigan she picked to wear under her suit jacket. It did great things for her tits. Nobody'd be looking at the buttons.

"Keep your back close to the wall whenever possible," I told her, "I can see if anybody's trying to blindside you, but I can't see behind you."

She did jump the first time I spoke into her ear, but after a few trials, she got used to it. By five o'clock, I was parked in the company lot, and Jenny was waiting to corner Addison as he was leaving his office. The picture on the iPad was bright and clear.

Addison opened his door. His face, though distorted, registered surprise. His mouth and eyes opened wide when Jenny said, "How're you doing there, Dave? Dragon Lady here. We need to talk."

I could see her hands on his chest, pushing him back into his office. He didn't resist.

"Okay, big Dave, what're we gonna do?" She made it sound like she might be offering him a blow-job, or something.

The fisheye was far enough away from him so that I could clearly see the terror that was etched on his face. His eyes kept darting around but they always came to rest at my—at Jenny's boobs. I could tell. The camera nestled between them at about nipple height, his eyes were looking straight at them.

"A—about w—what?"

I didn't hold it against him. Jenny could make better men stutter.

"About all the assholes we have to read every day in the comments. What else?"

I could see he was rolling this around in his head. The fear never left his eyes. "H—how did you find me?"

"How did you find Philosopher Phil?"

I wouldn't have thought that his eyes could get any wider but I would have been wrong. Then I got about a million volts.

"Philosopher Phil?" He was croaking like a stuck frog in a biology class. "What about him?"

"C'mon big Dave, I know you killed him."

"*Killed* him?" The frog was far from dead. "What are you talking about?" The panic in his voice was real. "What makes you think I killed him? What's going on? Who are you?"

I whispered into the mike. "This guy may be for real. I think he really doesn't know."

She wasn't ready to give up, though.

"Who the hell are you trying to kid? I know all about it. As soon as I heard about Mason, I knew it was you."

"Mason? What the hell are you talking about? What's Mason got to do with—" He stopped cold. The terror in his eyes was giving way to understanding. "Mason was Philosopher Phil?"

"As if you didn't know. It's okay, your secret's safe with me. Relax."

"I swear I don't know what you're talking about." The fear was back, "I don't know anything about this. I had no idea that Mason was Philosopher Phil. You have to believe me."

Can a frog whine?

"Get out of there," I said. "He doesn't know shit. He's not our guy." I really hated getting slapped in the face with a red herring, but Jenny wasn't quite finished. She always could think on her feet.

"If I ever see another posting anywhere from Dave thirty-six, I'll plaster your name all over the news. Then I'll come after *you*. Got it?"

The mixture of terror and relief on his face said that he did. He nodded his head so hard I thought it might fly off.

Jenny and I got out of there in a hurry on our way back to square one.

露

"Well, we learned one thing," I said to her on the way to her place. "When you grab a bull by the horns, expect to be gored."

"Jeez," she said, "really. You could have knocked me over with a feather. All that work for nothing."

"What nothing? It cost us a grand, remember?"

"Well, we've got this stuff for a week. Maybe something else will come up."

"I wonder if I could hide it in the secretarial pool powder room at City Hall."

"Why? You can see any of them naked any time you ask."

"Who told you that?"

"I'm a detective, remember?"

"I was thinking I might be able to earn a little extra cash by uploading it to one of the spy-cam porn sites."

"Do they actually pay anyone?"

I shrugged. "Probably not. Maybe I'll research it."

"Maybe you won't," she said, and there was no maybe about it. "Do you think he'll keep his mouth shut?" she said.

"After the terror you put into him, I'd bet on it."

She laughed. "Did you see the look in his eyes?"

"I did."

I figured I must've looked like that when Mr. Magoo raised his knife to cut my throat a few months back. It wasn't really funny, I suppose, but the sonofabitch had it coming.

"I doubt that we'll ever hear from Dave thirty-six again," I said.

ↄ৩ↄ৩

Thinking about hiding the camera in the secretary's john made me think of Wanda, She and I had a kind of arrangement that, if our paths crossed accidentally, we'd have sex. Wanda was a gorgeous blonde, and she wasn't looking for a relationship. Hell, she was only twenty-two. Thinking about her was giving me a hard-on, and I gave her a call. I figured she was probably getting laid right about now, so I was surprised when she answered after the first ring.

"Hello?" Even the way she answered the phone could get you hard. I once told her that she could probably make money in the phone sex business.

She'd laughed. "I did that for a year in college, but there were just too many creeps."

"Hello?" Very breathy.

"Hi, babe. It's Joe."

"Joe? Joe who?"

"The Joe you once said was the best fuck you ever had."

"Oh, that Joe." She couldn't keep it up, though, she was starting to giggle. "What can I do for that Joe?"

"Well, I figured you could start with a blow job. Then I could go down on you. Then we could screw doggie style. Then we could do it missionary. Then we could do it any way *you* want."

By now, she was laughing hard. I was laughing and hard too.

"Whatta you say? I'll pay for a taxi."

"There's a guy I know always sends a limo."

"I'm fresh out at the moment, though I am thinking of buying a car."

"Ooo. What kind?"

"Well, right now, I'm having problems choosing between a BMW, a Mercedes, and a Lexus. Come on over and I'll tell you all about it."

She did.

I laid it all out for her after I'd laid *her*. About an hour later.

"Well," she said, "now that we've gotten *that* out of the way, what's this about cars?"

I told her about the Mason killing and how I thought the killer was somebody in the comments sections. I had to explain it to her too. Like most people, she'd never even heard of the comments section.

We were having our traditional after sex snack of bologna sandwiches and kosher pickles. I loved to watch her eat pickles. I thought that I might be getting hard again. She'd lick them up and down and then slide them in and out of her mouth before taking a wicked bite off the top. That usually did it for my erection. She always laughed. We were sitting at the table naked, so I couldn't hide anything from her.

"The problem now," I said, "is that we'll never get the *Trib* to come up with any of the other identities unless I can show proof. It's a vicious cycle, without the names, I can't get the evidence."

She thought about that for a minute. Then her eyes brightened. "Y'know, I might know somebody who can help."

"Who?"

"Well, he's a hacker, so I can't tell you, but I'll bet I can get him to hack into the *Trib*."

"I'll bet you can too, honey, as the price to hack into you."

She laughed. "Don't be silly, he can hack into me for nothing."

"Nothing? I never thought of you as cheap."

She laughed even harder. "Not cheap, *gratis*. There's a huge difference."

I went down to the street with her to make sure she got a taxi home. She promised to call me by noon.

CHAPTER 29

I told Jenny the next morning.

She cocked her head at me. "You know, for an old man, you're incredibly horny."

I was offended. "Who you calling old?"

She surprised me with a soft tone. "You really like Wanda, don't you?"

"I love Wanda. She's one in a million."

She laughed, but it was gentle. "I think it's you who's one *of* a million."

"I know that. So what?"

"Don't you ever worry about catching something?"

"Not with Wanda. She may be young, but she's not stupid. Besides, if I run out, she's always got condoms in her purse."

"In her pursey?"

"Purse, purse. You heard me."

⌁⌁⌁

Wanda called just before noon. "It took a BJ in the law library when nobody was around, but he'll do it. He wants to meet you."

"I thought he was shy."

"Here's the best part. You're a big hero of his. You buck the system, so he thinks he can trust you"

"That's great. But then why did it take a…" I stopped before I said it. Stupid question.

Wanda was laughing. "Actually, I did it afterward."

"Always leave them happy, huh?"

"*You* should know."

ℰↄℰↄ

Larry X was in his mid-twenties. I didn't know what I was expecting, but it was probably some half-deranged fanatic with a fixation on corporations. I expected a wild look in his eyes, but the only time I saw it was when he got his first look at Jenny. Everybody gets it. Well, those of the straight male persuasion anyway.

Given that, he seemed like a normal person. He had a pleasant, open face, blond hair, and blue eyes. I wondered if he was a surfer, He looked like the all-American boy.

"What's the X stand for?" Jenny said.

"Whatever you want. It's algebra." He was smiling.

She let it drop.

"Wanda clued me in on what you want, but she was a little fuzzy on the details."

"That's Wanda," Jenny broke in, "fuzzy."

Did that sound like a bit of jealousy, or had she seen her naked?

"What exactly am I supposed to hack into at the *Trib?*"

"I need to know the actual identities of some of the people who post anonymous comments on news stories and columns."

"Why? I only ask because I'm careful about who I hack. I don't hack righteous folks."

"Who's not righteous?"

"Politicians, countries, corporations, and anyone else who treats people like shit."

"Hell, that could be almost anybody," Jenny said.

He looked at her. "You have a low opinion of people."

"We've been around longer than you," I said.

A fanatic might have been insulted, but Larry just laughed. "You sound like my dad."

"He sounds like a smart guy."

"He was. He taught me all I know about hacking."

"I assume he's deceased?"

"Nah. He's doing ten to twenty at State for industrial espionage. He was smart until he got caught."

He had us both laughing. I liked this kid. He had a sense of humor. Fanatics never do.

"Why do you need to get those names?"

By now, we had the story down to a pat *spiel* and we rolled it out for him.

He was practically rolling in the aisle by the time Jenny told about her meeting with Addison.

"You guys are righteous," he said when we'd finished, "I'll do it. If I can."

"If you can?" I said, "I thought you guys were infallible."

"That's what we'd *like* you to believe," he said. "Fear makes people stupid and careless. You can ask my dad about that. Still, patsies like the *Trib* are usually a pushover. I doubt I'll have any trouble."

"What do you think?" I asked Jenny after he'd left.

"I think I might like a date with him."

Now, *I* was jealous.

"Did you notice how much time he spent schmoozing with Peggy before he left?"

"Did you notice how he looked at me?"

I couldn't deny it. Then I wondered if she'd be up for

a threesome with her niece. I'm nasty. I admit it. I felt myself getting hard, even it wasn't me in the threesome.

❧❧❧

I'd told him to get the identities of the Okie, Crazyman, and Horatio Alger for starters. He thought that was a good idea, for three names he could be in and out in seconds with none the wiser. He tried to explain how he did it, but I stopped him after about three incomprehensible sentences. Jenny's face was registering a blank too, so I figured I wasn't the only stupid one. Misery does love company.

So does stupidity. Witness the comments sections.

There was really nothing beyond their general disgustingness to lead me to think they were killers, rather than pathetic little creeps like Addison, using the internet as a kind of masturbation arena. But people can always surprise you.

For the rest of the day, we scoured the comments for anything meaningful, but there was nothing anywhere beyond the usual stupid bullshit, lies, and vitriol. I noted down a couple of more possibilities I hadn't seen before, but they too were nothing you could get a court order for. Barnes had been disappointed when I told him about Addison, but he only said that this was the end of the road for him and the *Trib* for the time being.

"When you've got something substantial, you can get a court order," he said.

Lucky for me, I didn't need one.

Just before five, Larry called with the names. I figured that the *Trib* had a real problem. If Larry could do it, so could some other hacker. I wondered if Barnes had gotten in touch with Gray.

OkiefromMuskogee was somebody called Homer

Winslow. Jenny picked up on that one right away.

"It sounds like a *nom de plume*, Winslow Homer was a nineteenth-century American painter."

"What'd he paint?"

"Nothing you've ever seen. He didn't do nudes."

"Well, whoever he is, we've got his address."

Crazyman turned out to be Walter Evers, and Horatio Alger's real name was William Sparks.

We Googled them all, but nothing turned up. All these characters were nonentities. Maybe anonymous posting gave them a sense of existing. None of them was on Facebook either, and everyone knows that if you're not on Facebook, you don't exist.

We went to dinner at Arturos. Arty had finally recuperated and was glad to see me. I had a sneaking hunch that he'd actually sneaked off to Vegas. I hoped he hadn't blown the profits from twenty Thanksgiving turkeys, but he was usually pretty cool about his gambling.

We kicked around some ideas while we chowed down on some delicious mixed seafood scampi. The food was better than the ideas. The problem was, Jenny wasn't willing to get Barnes in trouble, and if any of our targets raised a fuss with the *Trib*, they'd blame him, guilty or not. The trick was to engage them without their ever thinking of the *Trib* at all, and, by now, we were fresh out of ideas.

"Let's call it a night," I said, "maybe we'll get some fresh perspective in the morning."

ℭℭℭ

When I got home, I called Wanda to tell her to thank Larry. She seemed out of breath.

"You can tell him yourself," she said. "He's right here."

I begged off. "That's okay," I said, "go back to what you were doing."

"Okay," she said, and hung up.

She is one with a million, I thought, and laughed out loud.

I poured a drink and turned on the late news. A university professor had been killed in a motor vehicle accident on the campus. Apparently, James Eldridge had been one of the leading lights of the Philosophy Department. I never could warm up to that stuff. Trying to plod through some of their writing sometimes made me want to kill them myself. Lucky for them, most of the ones I knew were already dead. I'd never heard of this guy.

Just before the weather report, my phone rang. It was Barnes.

"Aristotle's dead."

At first, I was confused. Then it hit me like a ton of bricks.

There was nothing to do now but get drunk.

෴

The next morning, I found out it had been a hit-hit-hit-and run. It happened on his quiet street. Neighbors heard the sounds. They were unanimous, the car had knocked him down, backed over him once, and ran over him again as it sped away. Nobody got a license plate number. Another vicious killing, but the killer was being crafty. The MO of this one couldn't be more different from Mason's—except for the naked hatred it bespoke.

As usual, the cops had no leads beyond reports of a black sedan racing at high speed off the campus. Still no license numbers.

I didn't want to think about Aristotle's last moments alive, but I couldn't help it. Now, I was really pissed.

We were in Thatcher's own office this time. Frank had just handed him a court order to divulge the names of anyone we considered necessary. I didn't bother to tell him that I already knew three of them. It was all academic now anyway. Things had been torn out of my hands.

"Got 'em right here." Thatcher said. He pushed a sheaf of papers toward Frank, who was sitting across from him at the conference table. "What's next?"

"We'll have to track them all down, see if they can establish alibis for Thanksgiving and last night. Those who can't will get a closer look. That's all we can do right now."

"What do we tell the public? I mean, do we say we're looking for a crazed killer?"

"The commissioner thinks you should keep it under your hat until our investigation is complete. We don't want to alarm the suspect, whoever it is."

"What about the safety of possible targets?"

"We'll put them under protective surveillance."

"Is that good enough?"

Frank just shrugged. "If we have any hope of keeping it quiet, taking a shitload of people into custody would kiss it goodbye."

"What if one of your suspects decides to go public in the comments—"

I broke in., "None of these guys wants anyone to know who they are." I saw fingers crossed in my mind. "They'll keep their mouths shut. Just make sure you threaten them outright. Some of them are pretty stupid."

"Besides," Barnes said, "sooner or later the shit's gonna hit the fan, so we should try to put that off as long as we can."

"Second the motion." Gordon was in.

Thatcher turned the discussion back to Frank. "How long do you think an investigation will take?"

Frank shrugged again. "Depends on how long the list is."

"It's not really that long," Jenny said, "maybe five or six people who could be considered viable suspects."

He thought for a while. "Maybe two, three days, but I can't promise. Once you start turning over rocks, a lot of ugly bugs crawl out."

"What can *we* do?" I was worried we might get cut out of the action, now that it had become official police business.

"For the time being, stay out of my hair. I'll let you know if there's anything you can do."

I could see that he really meant it. He always did. I didn't see any reason why now should be any exception. I also didn't see any reason to listen to him either. I never usually did. I smiled at him. He didn't miss it.

"Fat chance," he said, "huh?"

"Why, Frank, I wouldn't dream of interfering in an official police probe. You know that."

"I do?"

"Don't worry. I won't step on your toes. Just keep dancing."

He just shook his head. "I've never arrested you, have I?"

"Don't think so. Came close a few times, though. As I recall."

"I'm looking forward to our first time, so watch where you do step."

∽∾∽

"What the hell happened?" Jenny sad after we left. "I feel like I've been yanked into an alternate universe."

I gave her a hard look. "You haven't been dipping into Peggy's sci-fi collection, have you?"

"Don't you?"

"Something like, it I guess. It's like one of those exploding cigars, isn't it? You sit back and enjoy those first few puffs of satisfaction, and then it blows up in your face."

"I don't smoke cigars."

"You know what I mean."

"So, what do we do next?"

"What can we do to avoid stepping on Frank's toes and still get somewhere?"

"I don't know. What?"

I shrugged. "Beats me, but I'll think of something."

∽∾∽

It didn't take Frank as long as he thought it would. Half the force was on it.

"Every one of those suckers has an alibi for both nights. Good ones."

We were gathered back in Barnes's office, Thatcher was out of town for the weekend. It was only a day later, and you could cut the dejection with a butter knife.

Gordon was the next to speak. "Maybe we've just been barking up the wrong tree. Maybe both murders are totally unrelated and have nothing to do with the comments section at all."

"I could buy that easier if we had any other leads, but we don't. Neither man had any serious enemies." Frank heaved one of those famous sighs of his. "I hate to say it, but we're stumped. I really don't know where to go next."

I'd been doing a lot of thinking about where to go next.

"Maybe we should check out the others more carefully. Maybe the bastard is hiding as a reasonable person." I looked at Frank, "Did you check their alibis too?"

"There didn't seem to be any reason to."

"Got anything else to do?"

"Since you put it that way, no." He actually looked a little chagrined, but he didn't have to. There really had been no good reason to ask them for alibis. If it hadn't occurred to me, why should it have to him? He really was no better a cop than I was. He'd taught me well. Still, now it seemed like a glaring mistake. That might have only been because we had absolutely nothing else, but it needed to be fixed.

"I'll get on it and get back to you," he said and left the room. His shoulders slumped more than usual.

Barnes looked at me. "What more can we do to help at this point? Got any ideas? I'm fresh out."

"I suppose we could get some more names," Jenny said, "but we might as well wait until we hear from Frank about these. No point in getting ahead of ourselves."

ᘓᘐᘓ

I wanted a drink, but it wasn't even five yet. I had a solid rule against drinking before seven. I usually broke it at six-thirty. What's half-an-hour?

I'd asked Jenny to take in a movie with me, it was Saturday night after all, but she didn't really feel any more like it than I did, so I actually started drinking at six. Like I said, it was Saturday night.

I'd been depressed ever since Frank's report. I'd never even gotten a chance to avoid stepping on his toes when we'd hit the dead end, and it didn't look any better for the next day either. I hate being sidelined, but I couldn't interview them all anyway. That didn't stop me from feeling shitty. I felt personally responsible for this case. That might have been a little much, but I did. I'd been certain we were on the right track. What had I missed? There had to be something.

I turned on my laptop and navigated to the comments on a story about Eldridge, about his contributions to modern philosophy. There were zero comments. A story about the investigation into his killing, as unenlightening as it was, drew a few more. None of the crazies showed up. I was willing to bet that it would be a while before any of them got up the nerve to post again. Most of the comments were perfectly reasonable about the shortcomings of the police force. There was no need for exaggeration.

The missing crazies turned the comments into the dull crap they really were anyway. Why ordinary people imagined that they have the secrets to solving all the world's problems is a mystery to me. I don't know enough about most things to hazard an opinion about them. Some of these characters knew even less than I, but they could write long paragraphs outlining their wisdom. It was kind of funny, but without the insanity and vitriol, it was like watching a Bugs Bunny cartoon where all the characters lived in an old age home. Sylvester was too decrepit to chase Tweety anymore, Elmer Fudd had arthritis in his trigger finger, and Daffy Duck was up on the fifth floor of the old folk's home with the rest of the vegetables. He'd really gone daffy.

It just depressed me some more, so I Googled some porn. Endless loops of cum slathering girl's faces, and dicks ramming pussies depressed me too. I was in bad shape. I thought about Wanda, but I figured I was too drunk and depressed to get it up, so I didn't bother to call. It was late anyway.

I finally passed out.

⁌⁍⁌⁍

Sunday morning brought a visit from Roscoe. I didn't feel like getting up, but his incessant yowling and the annoying scratching on the window finally drove me out of bed. Just as I'd expected, he had a look on his face that said, "Turkey? What turkey?"

I really didn't feel like playing his game so I just opened whatever can came to hand and nearly threw it at him. I left the window open and climbed back into bed. *Screw the little bastard*, I thought. That's what Mrs. Greenspan always said after he ate her canary and, right now, I was agreeing in spades.

I was just about out when I smelled something bad. I opened my eyes. Roscoe was sitting on the bed, inches from my nose. He had a concerned look on his face. He cocked his head as if to say, "You don't look so good, buddy. Anything I can do?"

I couldn't help but laugh. "Yeah, Roscoe," I said, "you can move away. You stink."

I'd swear he shrugged. Can cats shrug? He rubbed up against me once and took off. I guess he figured I was a hopeless case.

෴

By the time I finally got out of bed for good, the day was almost over and I was facing another night. I was hungry, but I had no energy to cook, so I went across the street to Ruby's. Sunday night was Meat Loaf Night, and the sight of Ruby's bouncing boobs almost gave me an appetite to dig into those hunks of meat. Harrison would have called it displacement behavior, or something. I ate it all anyway. It was delicious. It always was.

I was certain that Ruby was too.

CHAPTER 30

I dragged myself into my office at about ten. "Morning, boss," Peggy said and handed me a sheaf of messages, "I guess these are for you?"

I looked at her. "Well, are they or aren't they?"

She looked blank. I was still too hung over to bother, so I just grabbed them and went to my office. I must have looked pissed, or something, because she let out a long "sheesh" behind me. I slammed my door. I gazed at the messages, thumbed through them, and tossed them. Right now, I didn't give a shit who was screwing who over.

Jenny knocked a few minutes later. "You okay?"

"Yeah, fine, come on in."

She kind of tiptoed in. She'd seen me like this before. Too many times. Frustration brings out the worst in me. It always did. Even when I was a kid, if I couldn't get my way, I'd throw a hissy fit. It never did me any good, though. My mother was not what you would call "a patsy," and she was the only person who could outstare me.

I was plenty frustrated now. Every lead had been a bust, from Avenger 2 on, and I really didn't believe that Frank was going to come up with anything. If we were still working on the assumption that the killer was a commenter, I was willing to bet that he would have been unable to keep from venting his bile, but we'd eliminated all of the crazies.

"You don't look so hot." Jenny actually sounded worried. That made *me* worry.

"That's funny. I've just about reached a boil."

"Well, so have I. Maybe we need to take a cold shower."

"Together?"

She laughed. "When will I learn?"

"Hey, somebody has to be the straight man," I said.

Joking with Jenny always made me feel better, and some of the depression lifted.

Some.

"I know we have to wait on Frank, but I'm not much on waiting, you know. It's driving me batty."

"More than usual?" She wore that wide-eyed innocent look.

Now, *I* laughed.

"Well," she said, "I'm going back to my computer and check over a bunch of comments again. We must have missed something."

"What?"

"I'll know it when I find it."

"If you find it."

"Well, it's better than just moping around."

"Different strokes. I like moping."

"Suit yourself." She laughed and left me alone again. I was feeling better.

My email carrier has a news feed, and I diverted myself with the stories for a while. About ten percent are straight news. The rest of it is mostly dopey stuff about celebrities and other hangers-on in Hollywood. Apparently, all anyone has to do to become famous nowadays is make an amateur sex tape. They're all doing it. I read a story about an entrepreneur movie mogul who'll make one for you with totally professional results. His is one of the hottest new businesses going.

There were also plenty of pictures of all the babes on various red carpets. It always blew me away. When I was a kid, all the movie stars I drooled over were always dressed like royalty. Nowadays, the *schmattes* that half of them wore made them look like the leftovers at a high school mixer. Even worse were the candid shots of them out on the street. You wonder what they could have been thinking.

Schmatte. That's a Yiddish word that can be used for a dishrag, or for what your rival for the presidency of the local *Hadassah* is wearing. It's rarely used in any other ways.

Of course, those that the article writers called the sluttiest were my favorites. A lot of those babes would look good in a dishrag too, a little one. They'd even look better without it.

Fashion.

There were always at least two stories about how a dog went ape shit when his soldier master returned. Most of the dogs I knew always went ape shit when their master returned, even if he'd only gone out for smokes.

I amused myself for a while trying to guess who some cute kid's celebrity mom or dad was. I was never right on those.

Then there were the articles that told you how you didn't know the right way to fry eggs, or something equally as damaging to your ego.

The "what never to tell your spouse" stories were legion, and no two ever gave the same advice. I'd tried a lot of the home remedies for mosquitoes, but they never worked. There were lots of stories about people who were never expected to recover from their illnesses but did, and some about those who were perfectly healthy one minute and dead the next. My favorites were always the cute kittens with funny captions. You can't go wrong with kittens. Even a hard-boiled asshole like me can always say "awww." I wondered if I could submit a picture of Roscoe.

I'd once thought of a commercial. Roscoe sprays all over the fire escape window, and some cute little housewife comes by, cocks her head at it, gives it a long-suffering smile, and proceeds to merrily clean it up with some green stuff she squirts on a sponge. Little sparkles follow it as it wipes a swath through the mess.

Somebody else would have to write the music.

I finally got tired of the news and decided to do what Jenny was doing, but I thought I'd go back farther. Barnes had opened the archive to us for as far as a year back, and I started then. Since Jews seemed to bring out the worst in them, I just scrolled through articles about Israel and the Middle East. There were a lot of the same people but, whenever I came across a new one, I copied it and put it in a new folder marked "comments."

By lunchtime, I'd just about brought myself up-to-date. I checked with Jenny. It turned out that she'd been doing the same thing, so we could compare notes. I sent Peggy out to bring back some lunch, and Jenny and I hunched over our computers, reading through the posts. I told her to write down the two most likely candidates to be our killer. I would do the same, and we could compare our choices. I was getting excited again.

About three, Frank called to tell us he'd drawn a blank, just as I'd figured he would. I told him what we were doing. "There's really no reason to think that he'd be posting at the time of the killings. It's just as likely that he'd keep a low profile. He's smart, he'd be certain to figure that someone just might connect the deaths to the comments, and that they'd concentrate on the present just like we did. If I'm right, I would expect to see him disappear for some period before the killings."

"How long?"

"Hell, I don't know. We're playing this by ear."

"Unless you have something really solid to go on, I doubt that I can get you any more court orders, and the *Trib* won't stick its neck out without them. Barnes made that crystal clear when I called him. Goddammit, we can't even be sure that we haven't been fishing for a red herring. The chief is bugging us to work some other leads."

"What other leads?"

"That's just it. I'll have to make them up. Both of those guys were very well liked, and I haven't been able to hear tell of any serious enemies. Eldridge left behind a wife and two kids, y'know. Somebody'd really have to hate his guts to do that, and Mason too, but there's no hint of any such fuckin'person."

"Well, if we come up with anything substantial, I'll let you know." I didn't bother to tell him that I didn't need a court order.

"Good luck, and you'd goddamn well better."

I'd rarely heard that degree of dejection in his tone. I figured he was just as aware as I was of the fact that we'd have to do this one on our own, and he didn't like it.

Then I thought, *Do what on our own?*

An hour later, I had an answer.

Jenny and I came up with the same two names in the same order. My instincts told me we were on the right track. One of them, Home of the Brave, had stopped posting three days before Thanksgiving, the other, Ahab, two weeks before. Both exhibited the degree of hatred that one would expect of a killer.

I called Larry X and told him what we wanted. He said he'd try to get it for me by morning. "The *Trib*'s increased its firewalls considerably since this went down. It could take a while."

I wondered if Barnes had gotten Thaddeus Gray in on the act. I called him.

"I meant to mention it the other day," he said, "but with all the activity it slipped my mind. The woman who answered the number you gave me said he'd left town, and she had no forwarding address or phone number. I tried to see if the U had any information, but nobody in the engineering department had ever heard of him. Nobody else did either. Are you sure he said he was working on a project there?"

I was certain of it.

After I hung up, I filled Jenny in.

"Something doesn't smell Kosher," she said.

"Damned right," I said, "I smell a pig. Why did he lie to us?"

We thought we knew, and I spent a sleepless night thinking about it. Even the Haig Bros couldn't help.

When Larry called me in the morning to say that Ahab's computer had an address in Pleasanton, all the pieces started to fall into place, and I didn't like the way they were falling.

CHAPTER 31

Unlike our first trip, the drive to Pleasanton was full of conversation. We had a lot to digest, and we were choking on a bone called Gray. Who the hell was he? Now that I had something to latch on to, I wondered about his arrival by plane that morning. We had only his word for it. He could have come in anytime and shown up at Mom's after killing Mason.

"Problem is," Jenny said, "he'd have had to have been there several times before in order to terrorize poor George. He was a stranger to Mom, so where had he stayed?"

"Maybe he actually lives in Pleasanton."

"So why the subterfuge? Why did he stay at Mom's?

"Maybe his place was being fumigated."

"In this kind of weather?"

"Getting a jump on spring?"

"That's ridiculous."

"I've got nothing else, genius. What's your guess?"

For once, she was speechless.

I thought about it some more. "Maybe there was some other reason he couldn't stay home. It really doesn't matter. Does it?"

"Who knows? Maybe it does."

Larry had been unable to get a physical address for the computer. He'd said that if he fiddled around in the system too long, they'd detect him, but he promised to try again. "So far, I've only been able to trace it to Pleasanton. I'll need to do some tricky triangulation of the local Wi-Fi access points to pinpoint a location. If he's only on a wired network, it could take a lot longer, and it doesn't help that the last post is old—"

I stopped him from going on with the technical details. They were all just so much gibberish to me. "Just get me an address as soon as you can," I said and hung up.

"He's got to have a car," Jenny said.

"A black sedan, maybe," I said. "Mason said it was a black sedan that ran him off the road, and Eldridge's neighbors said it was black sedan that killed him. Not much to go on, though, must be a million of 'em. All these damn cars look alike."

I'd called Carson to tell him we were coming and about Ahab's being in Pleasanton. He wasn't pleased.

"Shit," he said, "you mean it's back in my hands again?"

"I'll tell you all about it when we get there."

છજછ

He wasn't wearing a happy face when he greeted us, and I wasn't sure how he'd take it, "This is kind of *sub rosa*, if you know what I mean. We're working on our own lead, the city cops know nothing about this."

"Why the hell not?"

"No need. Until I can get some meaningful evidence, there's nothing they can do. They wouldn't provide me with an address, so we had to go through the back door to get it."

"Hacking? That's a federal offence, you know." He

stopped and gave me a long look, then he smiled. "It's a good thing I'm not a fed. I see how you come by your reputation. Just for the record, you never told me any of this."

"Any of what?"

I asked him about any impressions he had of Gray, but he'd only seen him for a few minutes. "He looked like a wimp to me, not like a killer," he said.

"What does a killer look like?"

"Point taken. Just keep me out of it unless you get in trouble."

He wrote down a number. "This is my home phone, if I don't answer my cell." He smiled. "My wife makes me turn it off when…you know."

We knew.

I'd called ahead to make sure there were rooms available. There was one. The same one we'd had before. I was looking forward to it. Jenny maybe not so much.

"Just keep your gun to yourself," was all she said when I told her.

Mom greeted us like old family, her personality was infectious, and we soon *felt* like old family. After we settled in, we sat her down for a talk.

"What do you know about this Gray fellow?" I said.

She looked surprised. "Mr. Gray? Why, not very much. Why do you ask?"

"We think that he might be our killer," Jenny said.

Her eyebrows shot up her forehead, pulling open her mouth. "A killer, you say? Little Mr. Gray? Why—why—how can it be?"

I filled her in on the details. She became agitated as I went on. She actually turned quite pale when I told her we traced a commenter's computer to Pleasanton.

She seemed shaken. "But where in Pleasanton?"

"That we don't know yet, but we're working on it,"

Jenny said. "Please calm yourself. Try to relax."

Mom seemed shocked and didn't say anything for a few seconds. "Do you mean he could be livin' anywhere here?" Her usual bubbly self was nowhere to be seen. "And you say he may have killed that professor at the U?" She did seem to be calming down. "Imagine that. You never really know who anyone is, do you?' And before you could bat an eye, the bubble machine started up again. "It's a funny, funny world, ain't it, my dears?"

I couldn't argue with that.

She got serious again, but only for a moment. "Do you think that I could be in danger?"

"I wouldn't think so, unless you were one of the rational bloggers out there.

She laughed. "Not very likely. Why, land's sakes, I wouldn't even know where to begin. My main contact with the internet is to download recipes." Then the smile disappeared. "But I can identify him. Wouldn't that make me a target?"

"I doubt it. We could identify him too, and so could Captain Carson. I doubt that he'd try to get all of us."

Mom was back to her old self again. "It's actually pretty excitin', ain't it? Like one of those TV shows."

"It's not a TV show," Jenny said.

"Well, p'shaw, you know what I mean. My life ain't very excitin', until now. You detective folks get to do this all the time. You're used to it."

Not really," I said, "the day you get used to it is the day to quit. Before somebody else makes you. For good."

She stopped laughing then. I thought she understood.

She was no help at all, though. She said Gray had called her that Friday morning, said he was at the airport and the room he'd booked was canceled. Did she have an available room? He paid her in advance for a week.

"He was pretty quiet. All I know about him is what he

told us at dinner that night. I hardly ever saw him the few days he was here. He'd go out in the mornin' before breakfast and come back in the evenin', and he took his dinner in his room. Tuesday mornin', he told me he'd been called away unexpectedly, and he was leavin', No forwardin' address or number. I thought it was strange, but then, he was pretty strange, come to think of it."

"Did he have a car?" I asked.

"A car? No, I called for a taxi."

"Did you hear where he went?"

"No."

It didn't seem like there was much we could do beside wait on Larry to come up with an address, so we opted for an afternoon nap. Jenny'd been eyeing something on one of the shelves. She went over and picked up a slender brass pitcher. She handed it to me.

"Here, I got you a holster for your gun."

I looked at it and shook my head. "Way too narrow. I can think of a better use for it, though." I leered at her.

"Feelthy, feelthy." She laughed. "In your dreams."

"Okay then, but don't be surprised if you wake up and I'm pointing my gun at you."

She laughed again. "Just try not to polish it on my thigh, okay?"

"I could still sleep on the couch, you know."

"Don't be silly. What's a little dick between friends?"

"Little?"

God, I loved her laugh.

I think maybe we both passed out. I came to in the same position in which I'd lain down. So did she. My wood was nowhere near the vicinity of a thigh.

෨෨෨

Dinner was a very different affair than it had been the

last time. School was back in session, and the dining table was full. We'd decided that Leonard Glass and Hortense Whitmeyer had met here as students, and we were now on a kind of second honeymoon. Nobody seemed to give a crap, except for a couple of girls who thought it was "sooo romantic." When people finished eating, they disappeared back into their rooms, except for the two who were on dishwashing duty that night. I guess there were some important exams coming up. Mom prided herself on being able to pick the best candidates for her largess.

"I'm only interested in those who are serious and apply themselves," she said. "This ain't a fraternity house, and I don't let any of them out of their rooms after nine o'clock neither." She smiled. "Except on weekends. Can't be too hard on 'em, you know."

It was okay with us. We played the self-absorbed lovers. It was gruesome.

Eventually, we were alone, and we moved to the sittin' room for an aperitif . Mom brought us a tray with a crystal decanter and crystal glasses. Classy, I thought. The decanter held a ruby liquid.

"It's my own," she said. "There's so many things in it that I just call it my own elderberry wine."

"I hope arsenic isn't one of those things," Jenny said.

Mom's face lit up. "Land's sakes, I do believe you know the reference. Hardly anybody does nowadays. Bunch of ignoramuses.

"I think *Arsenic and Old Lace* is one of the funniest movies I've ever seen," I said.

"Yeah," Jenny said, "too bad you don't look like Cary Grant, though. More like Boris Karloff."

She had me. I just stuck my tongue out at her.

Whatever was in it, the wine was delicious.

Lethal, too.

When we woke up, Thaddeus Gray was seated across

from us. He was holding a gun. Mom was seated next to him, and she wasn't smiling. I couldn't have been more surprised than I'd been when it was Julie at Hooker's Camp holding the gun.

This kind of shit has got to stop, I thought, *it's ripping my ego to shreds. I missed all the signs and fell for the schtick.*

Some fucking instinct.

My cell phone rang. It was lying on the table in front of us. Probably Larry with an address I didn't need any more. Mom reached down and shut it off.

I figured we were in deep shit.

Again.

CHAPTER 32

I couldn't have imagined a stranger scene. The room lights were low and the lights on the Christmas tree in the corner were going nuts, like it wasn't water in the bowl at the bottom but some kind of hooch. A light snow was falling outside, illuminated by the soft glow of the street lights, and Gray and Mom looked like some nice old couple welcoming the kids home for the holidays.

Except for the gun, of course.

Mom got up and went to pull the drapes shut.

"No sense in takin' a chance that some folks walkin' by might peer in now, is there?"

I was wondering about some kid just wandering through for a snack in the kitchen, but the idea didn't seem to bother them much, so I figured it wasn't likely. She had said they weren't allowed out after nine anyway. I remembered that.

I tried to ask what time it was, but my voice wouldn't come out of my throat in anything but a kind of croak. Whatever was in the "elderberry wine," was pretty potent. I was getting *Mickied* way too goddamned often. I figured it couldn't be good for me.

"What's that?" Mom asked and there was a smile on her face. "Don't worry, hon, your voice'll come back in a few minutes. If I heard you right, you want to know what time it is, right?"

I was able to nod my head a little. Whatever it was, it obviously had a paralytic effect too.

"It's a little past ten, though I can't think what difference it makes."

I couldn't either but it seemed important to me to know.

Jenny must have been doing better than I because her voice was clear and strong.

"Why? Why are you doing this?"

"Because we're sick of all the liberals tryin' to destroy this great country of ours. That's why. Somebody has to stop 'em. Why not us? If we wait for the politicians to do it, it'll never get done."

"Murder?"

Mom laughed, a truly evil laugh, and for the first time I saw her as malevolent. Did I say she looked like something from a Hollywood casting agency? Probably the same one Alfred Hitchcock used.

"Murder's in the eye of the beholder, hon. You might call it gettin' rid of the trash, too."

I'd never before heard Jenny howl. It sounded like a wounded animal.

"Trash?" she hollered, and her voice was full of tears and rage. "George Mason was a swell guy. I loved him. You're a goddamned fucking monster."

Mom stood up, took two steps toward us and slapped Jenny hard across the cheek. I couldn't turn to see, but I heard it.

"You've got no call usin' filthy language. I don't hold with it in my house. You'll keep a civil tongue in your head, or I'll slap you even harder. Have you got that, missy?"

Jenny said nothing, and I thought I understood why all

the students in the place seemed subdued. I'd gotten that impression, but it had been fleeting and I hadn't thought much about it—until now.

I wanted to do something, but I still couldn't move. I was also staring down the barrel of Gray's pistol. It looked like a .22, probably the gun that killed Mason. It wasn't much of a weapon for an assassin, but I thought about slugs in the gut. I tore my gaze away and it landed on the tree and all the blinking lights.

Merry Christmas.

I thought I might puke, but I beat it back. It was probably the wine.

My paralysis disappeared just then, and I turned my head to look at Jenny who was seated at the other end of the long sofa, there was a nasty red mark on the side of her face. I could feel rage boiling up, but I'm pretty good in tough jams, and I managed to control it. Still, the look I gave Mom wasn't lost on her. Trouble was, it only made her laugh.

"Too bad for you that we've got the gun, ain't it?" she said when she finished. "If looks could kill, huh?" She laughed some more and there was definitely a tinge of madness in it. There was nothing at all of "good humor."

Mom sat back down. I couldn't bear to look at her anymore, and I didn't want to fixate on the pistol, so I turned my attention to the tree again. That was a mistake. The blinking lights grabbed me, and I could feel the seizure coming on.

Ever since I got hit by a bus when I was a kid, blinking lights could flip me out.

I tried to look away but I was hypnotized. I could feel myself stretching out and slipping down into a hole. The buzzing in my ears was growing to a shriek, and again I thought I would puke. The lights were getting real bright and rays were shooting off of them. I thought this was just the wrong goddamned time for this shit—then everything went black.

My fits usually only last a few seconds, rarely more than a minute.

The next thing I was aware of was Jenny. She was standing and had the pistol pointed at Mom. I could see that her hand was rock steady, and I knew she could hit a fly at twenty feet, even with a piece of shit .22.

I was lying on the floor and actually had a pretty good look up her skirt too, but I was concerned with other things at the moment.

There was a loud moaning. It was coming from Gray. He was hunched over on the floor next to me holding his arms around his guts.

"What the fuck?" I guess I must have said it aloud.

"Are you all right?" Jenny's voice came through a tunnel.

It took me a few seconds to realize she was talking to me.

"What the fuck happened? I think I had a seizure."

"You did. You started to fall off the couch, and I managed to take advantage of his surprise with a little Taekwondo just as he was getting up."

She nodded toward him. "He'll be all right in a few minutes. I didn't have enough time for a really hard kick."

"Too bad," I said. "Where'd you kick him?"

"The solar plexus."

"Why so high up?"

She just chuckled.

☙❧

The seizures go as quickly as they come. In a few seconds, I was able to get up. I grabbed Gray by the back of his jacket and hauled him up too. I tossed him back into his chair. He didn't look very threatening anymore.

Jenny and I both sat down again, but the scene had flipped.

"You want to give me the gun?" I said.

"No. I'm hoping that fat old piece of crap will try something."

Mom wasn't laughing anymore.

Somehow, the coffee table had gotten knocked over. I bent down and searched around until I found my phone. I turned it on and punched in Carson's number. I hoped he wasn't too deep into Mrs. Carson. He answered on the third ring.

When I told him what had happened, he didn't say anything for a long time, like he was trying to figure out if this was a joke. Then he sighed and said he'd be right over.

"Better bring a net," I said.

For a while, we all just sat quietly. I was having a rough time keeping my eyes off the blinking tree lights, so I finally just went over and yanked the plug out of the wall. I could see that Gray was struggling to regain some composure. When I figured he'd about recovered from Jenny's kick, I asked him who he was.

"Who the fuck are you, you little bastard?" were my exact words.

He looked daggers back at me but said nothing.

I turned to Mom. "Where'd you find this creep, the Mafia Yellow Pages?"

She only borrowed some of Gray's daggers.

"How'd you figure that killing a few nobodies was going to change anything?" I said.

Mom's smile made a sudden reappearance. "What do you call a hundred lawyers at the bottom of the ocean?" She actually guffawed. "A good start."

Gray cackled right along with her.

I figured them for a Waldorf Salad. "How did you find out who they were?"

Gray finally spoke up. "I told you that I'm a systems analyst remember? Newspaper encryption is rarely state of the art."

"So, you're a hacker."

He smiled. "I prefer to think of myself as an artist of communication technology."

"And the killings," I said, "were those art too?"

He looked right into my eyes and laughed. "Do you have any hobbies, Mr. Gold?"

The way he said it chilled me to the bone.

Murder as a hobby.

I looked at Mom. "Recipes, huh."

She smiled. "As soon as I sat down at the computer, I'd remember my Wilson, and the words just came out of my head."

"Out of my head." The truest words she'd spoken.

"Why Ahab?"

"My Wilson always called the government Moby Dick, so it kind of came natural."

Poetic too.

I still didn't feel like a hundred percent. I was on the verge of nausea and shaky. I looked over at Jenny, the gun in her hand never wavered, but I was going to be a lot happier when Carson got here. I wasn't sure that one gun was equal to two screwballs, and I figured that, in spite of their laughter, they had to be pretty desperate. They were both facing the needle, and they had to know that. They might be nuts, but they weren't stupid.

And Mom was a big woman, never mind her age.

I heard a car pull up outside. No siren. A few seconds later, I heard the back door open and Carson's voice.

"Joe?"

"In here," I yelled, "the living room." I couldn't remember the last time I'd felt so relieved.

Carson walked in, took a quick look at the scene, came over, and put his police issue .38 up against my temple. He was looking at Jenny.

"Hand the gun to Mom, Ms. Martin. Grip first—Now."

It was like cold water splashed on my face.

I wasn't even nauseous anymore.

Instead, I thought I might crap my pants.

✷✷✷

Sooner or later, every detective knows he's going to be facing the last mistake, the one that'll kill him. I've been there several times myself, but this one looked like the end, for sure. Nobody knew where we were. I doubted that anyone would even suspect we were missing until we'd be missing for good.

How had I misread the signs?

Had I?

My mind was working on overdrive. What had I missed?

No matter how many times I played the scenes back in my head, I couldn't find anything that would have led me to suspect any of this. It all made sense only in hindsight. They'd played us perfectly.

"Why did you bring us here that first night? Why didn't you just let us book a hotel room?" I stared straight into Carson's eyes. I didn't dare let on how scared I really was. I had to play the tough guy. I figured that was my only chance to get out of this pickle with my skin intact—and Jenny's too.

Maybe.

"When I realized who you were, I called Mom. It was

her idea to check you out. To see how sharp you were and maybe figure out how to throw you off. Too bad for you, I guess, you stuck like glue."

"I told you to be careful, Mr. Gold." Gray had recovered himself completely, now that he had the gun back in his hand, "and Miss Martin too. You should have paid more heed. It's truly a shame. I do truly admire your skills. I don't suppose there's any chance at all of persuading you to put your admirable skills at our disposal, is there?"

I finally remembered who he'd reminded me of, an old movie actor named Peter Lorre. "Go fuck yourself," I said—and regretted it immediately.

Mom's slap was plenty hard, only Carson's pistol in my gut stopped me from slugging her back.

"I warned you," she said, "I don't tolerate profanity in my house."

In spite of everything, I couldn't control a laugh. I thought of the Nazis I'd read about who would wash their kids' mouths out with soap for cursing, and then head to the office to sign death warrants for Jews.

"Do you find something funny about that?" Her eyes were narrowed, for some reason they reminded me of a pig.

"Yeah. You're a funny fuck."

I braced for another blow, but Carson grabbed her arm. "That's enough of that, Mom. I told you to keep me out of this, and you blew it. Now go sit down while I figure out what to do about it."

Mom didn't seem any too happy about being spoken to like that, but she shut up and sat down.

Up until now, Jenny hadn't said a word. Now I could tell she was really pissed. "What the hell gives any of you the right to be judge, jury, and executioner? Who the fuck do you think you are?"

Gray just laughed and pointed to his gun. "Any more questions?"

She turned to Carson. "What about you? You're supposed to uphold law and order."

He didn't flinch a bit. "How long do you suppose law and order would last if the liberals ever got real power? Look what happened in Russia. The Commies wrecked the place."

I couldn't believe what I was hearing. Russia? Commies? Had we fallen into a time warp? Carson was as nuts as the others. It was obvious that there was nothing we could say that would make any difference to this bunch of crazies. I figured we were done for this time. I couldn't see a way out that didn't end up with us getting dead.

I looked at Gray. "What about you? You're just a hired gun. Do you go along with this crap, or are you just amusing yourself?"

He smiled a smile that froze my blood. "You may be laboring under a misapprehension. Mr. Gold. I am not, as you said so colorfully, a 'hired gun.' Mom is my mother, and I am an obedient son. We are merely continuing the work begun by my father before he was murdered by the liberals in our government.

Now he had me.

That stopped me cold.

Huh?

"Who the fuck are you people?"

I don't think I'd ever heard Jenny use the word "fuck" more than once in a week, that's how pissed she was.

I figured that Carson had some kind of hero-worship thing going, because he took on the job of introducing us to the great people, as though they were too important to deign to introduce themselves.

"Mom's husband was Wilson Mulrooney."

He said it as though that would make everything clear as a bell. It was more like mud to me.

Silence hung in the air for a while until Jenny remembered. "Mulrooney…Mulrooney. Say, wasn't he the guy killed in a shootout with the feds over some land or something in Montana? Back about twenty five years ago, I think."

"Twenty-two, and that land was the last free state in this whole goddamned country that was still worthy of the name." He started to sound like the narrator of some kind of documentary. You could almost hear the patriotic sounding background music. "The Commies in Washington weren't about to let the people take back their rights. Wilson Mulrooney fought them tooth and nail. When the liberal courts turned him down, he finally realized just how big the conspiracy was and he fought them on their own terms, with bullets. He was the last great American patriot, and they shot him down like a mad dog."

I looked at Mom. There were tears in her eyes.

Gray's were bone dry.

Try as I might, I couldn't even dredge up a part of a memory. Whenever it had gone down, I must have been on a bender. Back in the day, I could disappear into a bottle for weeks at a time.

I looked around at the three of them, and the last shreds of hope dissolved in my mind. I didn't know what had brought Carson into this family melodrama, but he was obviously as insane as the others, and I'd told him we were here on our own. I'd likely sealed our death warrants. About the only chance we had was to try and drag this out as long as possible and hope they'd make a mistake.

It soon became clear that we weren't going to have much time for that.

Carson was nervous. "That's enough talking. Time to

get out of here," he said. "Mom, go get their overcoats and anything else they left in their room. Make sure you leave nothing behind."

It didn't take long, we traveled light.

We left the house through the back door. I spotted a black sedan in the garage windows, but we weren't going to be using it.

"Where's your car parked?" Carson was definitely agitated.

"Down the street." I said.

"Show us?"

With Carson, Mom, and Gray, or whoever he was, walking behind, we led them to our rental car. The snow had stopped, but the streets were deserted, and I saw no one peeking out from any of the windows. Had they, all they'd have really seen were four people out for a walk, and they'd forget all about it as soon as they looked back inside. The only one to be seen was somebody in a car parked near a streetlight about a block away. I couldn't tell if it was a man or a woman, and I'm sure we made as big an impression. We were as good as invisible.

"Get in." Carson gestured us in with his pistol. I slid across to the driver's seat. "Mom, you and Willie get in the back seat and keep them covered," he said. "If they try anything, shoot her." He reached into the pocket of his overcoat and took out a second pistol. It looked like a .45 automatic. He handed it to Mom. "Insurance."

"Where are we taking them?" Gray wanted to know.

"Drive up by the old quarry. I'll be right behind you. Take the old access road off Forty-One."

I couldn't see him, but I heard Gray grunt. There was the hint of a laugh in it. I looked over at Jenny. She was looking at me. Neither of us was smiling.

෴

Most of the time on the drive to the quarry, I was trying to come up with something to do, but I couldn't think of anything that wouldn't likely get us killed, what with me doing the driving and all. The rest of the time, I was looking at the scenery and thinking that I might never see it again.

It was strange how the snow-covered verges, and the rolling fields behind, shone in the nearly full moon that hung above, and reminded me of one of those Currier and Ives pictures my mother had loved. A lump arose in my throat.

Usually, I hated this time of the year.

The bare trees lining the narrow road were outlined now with a blanket of snow and filled me with a vague longing. For what? For the life that I saw slipping away with every mile?

Even then, I couldn't believe it was going to happen. Reality can drive you insane. Maybe that's a mercy.

Carson followed about five car lengths behind. He was driving his own SUV instead of a police cruiser. Anyone who passed us would not remark about it at all.

It would be as though we'd simply disappeared off the face of the earth.

I drove at a turtle's speed. I just gave them the finger when Mom asked me to hurry up. My slow pace obviously didn't bother Carson who just kept a steady distance behind. Maybe he was rethinking the wisdom of dumping us in the quarry and was in no hurry to get there either.

Even I couldn't believe that one. Killing us was the only option open to all of them. I wondered how deep the quarry lake was.

For the last time in my life, I didn't have a chip to bargain with.

I kept looking over at Jenny, but she just sat there, rigid, staring straight ahead, lips locked tight.

I tried to engage them in conversation, hoping to maybe get them riled up to do something stupid, even if they did have two guns.

Mom wasn't in a talking mood.

"Just shut up and stay that way," was all she said.

⁓⁓⁓

I figure it was about a half-hour before Gray told me to turn left onto an unplowed road. Judging from the feel under the tires, it was gravel. At one point, I felt dirt beneath the snow, and the road began a slow upward spiral taking us, I assumed, to the top of the quarry.

What would happen next required no imagination.

My slow speed minimized the possibility of sliding on the snow covered track, but even so, I went into several skids. It didn't help any that my palms were soaking wet. All the while, Carson's headlights were lighting up the way I'd come. I did my best to slow down time, but I couldn't get any better than whatever it took to keep from stalling. All too soon, the road opened onto a flat plain.

My headlights lighted up the snow ahead—until it ended in an ominous blackness. It reminded me of a trip to the Grand Canyon when I was a kid. We'd pulled into a parking lot after dark and the yawning darkness in front of the headlights was pretty scary, even with the chain in front of it.

There was no chain here.

I stopped—until I felt the cold steel on the back of my neck.

"Keep driving."

For a second, I toyed with the idea of doing a Thelma and Louise, and taking the bastards with us.

For a second.

I didn't have the guts and I knew it. Suicide wasn't my style anyway.

I drove on at a snail's pace. Now they knew it too.

"Stop here." He didn't have to say it twice. We couldn't have been more than a few yards from the edge.

The back doors opened,

"Stay where you are. Don't try to get out."

The back doors slammed shut.

Carson's lights illuminated the dashboard, and I could see them coming up in the rear-view.

It seemed like an eternity until I felt our bumpers kiss—and the inexorable push toward the edge began.

It took me a second to shout to Jenny. "Jump! Let's at least make them shoot us."

I opened my door, and I could hear Jenny open hers. I hit the ground rolling, and out of the corner of my eye, I saw the car go over the edge.

I had no idea what to do next but it didn't matter.

The world erupted in a bright, white light.

At the same moment, the sounds of multiple sirens pierced the silence.

It took me a couple of seconds to figure it out, but my mother didn't raise no dummy.

Somehow, in some unknown way, we'd been saved.

I realized that at about the same time the shots rang out.

For what seemed like forever, I just lay there on the ground. All the sounds around me were merging into one extremely loud buzzing. All the flashing lights sucked me into another seizure, and everything went black.

CHAPTER 33

My name was being called from somewhere down a long tunnel.

"Joe…Joe…wake up. Snap out of it. Can you hear me? Joe."

It sounded like Jenny,

I opened my eyes.

It was Jenny.

At first, I couldn't take it in. Then I remembered. "Are we still alive?"

I really wasn't expecting the flood of laughter and tears that poured out of her, but the feel of her boobs on my chest as she hugged me was terrific. I figured we must be alive after all. It felt so damned good that it was a while before I thought to ask how.

"How?" All of a sudden Frank was standing over us, "Because I never fucking trusted you, that's how. Because your girlfriend Wanda was worried about you, that's how. And because I bothered to check the record on your friend Mom. That's how. Any more questions?"

I stared at him for a second. "Well, yeah. How?"

He couldn't keep the smile from his puss for long. "Y'know, I'm getting kind of tired of pulling you out of the jams you get yourself into. Maybe next time I won't bother."

"You'll miss me," I said.

I heard Jenny's great laugh, but it was tinged with hysteria.

ഇ෩෩

We were wrapped in blankets, sitting in the back seat of Frank's car drinking cop coffee from a thermos. It tasted like ambrosia, whatever the hell that is. Anyway, you get the idea.

Gray's body was now decently covered where it lay, and Mom and Carson were sitting quietly in handcuffs in the back seats of two cruisers. I counted four cars in all, three state troopers and Frank.

It seems that he decided to put a tail on us. Trust could be such an overrated virtue sometimes. I'd always thought so, but how did I miss the tail? Maybe I was getting too old for this crap.

Being a cop, he checked out the address the tail gave him. It didn't take long for him to sniff out the Mulrooney connection. "That alone might not have meant too much," he said, "if that Wanda babe from City Hall hadn't called me. She was real worried about you, said you weren't answering your phone. She knew you were onto something dangerous, and she knew the address of Mom's place." He cocked an eye at me. "Does it matter if I know what she had to do with anything?"

I smiled at him. "No."

"Then I won't ask. Anyway, it didn't take me long to put two and two together, and I figured I'd better hightail it out after you. You, I don't care about, one way or the other. But a lady like Miss Martin here deserves better."

Jenny smiled at him. "It was all my idea, you know."

He heaved one of his patented sighs. "I always knew

you were the brains of the outfit, but this was not very smart."

He actually scowled at her, like he was reprimanding his daughter. That made me smile.

"Lucky for you I called a friend in the state troopers and alerted him that something was going down. He was willing to help. He sent an unmarked to stake-out Mom's place. I guess the cop recognized Carson and got suspicious about him driving his own car. When he saw you all come out of the house, and Carson follow your car out of town, he called it in. He figured you might be heading to the quarry. Luckily, he was right. We got here just in time, it seems."

I nodded toward the stiff under the canvas. "How'd that happen?"

"Stupid asshole started shooting at us. The other two gave up quietly." He cocked another eye at me. "Do you have any idea who these people are?"

"I'm beginning to find out. Fill me in. I know about Mulrooney."

"Well, there isn't all that much to tell. He was just one of a bunch of lunatic survivalists who plagued law enforcement at the time, mostly out West. He was trying to establish what he called a Free State, which I guess means he didn't want to pay his taxes. After he got killed in a shootout with the FBI, his wife and kid disappeared. Nobody really cared any more. When I spotted the name on the property rolls for Mom's place in Pleasanton, I checked back and satisfied myself that it was really her. I don't know what happened to the kid."

I pointed at the body. He didn't seem too surprised, though. Frank is a terrific cop. He taught me everything he knew, and then some. Maybe I said that before.

"He killed Mason and Eldridge," I said, "but I don't think they were the only ones. He's—he was—a natural born killer. Mom had to be the brains. I can't really figure Carson, but he seems to idolize Mulrooney. He talked about Russia and Commies for crissakes. Go figure."

"Russia and the Commies?" He laughed, "Jesus, Mary, and Joseph, I'll never get over how pathetic these assholes always are."

"Yeah," I said, "but look at all the fucking damage they can do."

He shrugged. "That's what keeps food on my table." Frank was a cynic. He's a cop. It goes with the territory. "You wanna see where you almost ended up?"

I was game and so was Jenny. Frank led us in slow motion to the edge of the quarry. The cops had placed several portable searchlights there, and they lighted up the abyss. Even hanging onto Carson's SUV, still standing only a couple of feet from the edge, I felt a touch of vertigo when I looked down. About a hundred feet below, there was a large black hole in the ice at the bottom. Our car was nowhere to be seen.

I shivered. "Anyone know how deep it is?"

"I've been told forty feet." He gave me a hard look. "Chances are you'd have been there 'til the world came to an end."

I gave him a smile back. "If not for you," I said. "Thanks. I owe you."

"If you really want to repay the debt, quit the detective business and get a respectable job."

"Me? Respectable?" I laughed.

So did Jenny, and I was glad to see that the hysteria was gone. That girl always did have a solid head on her shoulders.

∽∾∽

Mom got sent to some hazel-hatchery with prison bars and no computer privileges, and Carson got the death sentence, even though he never killed anyone. He was still sitting in the pen waiting for the results of his latest appeal. He'd probably get switched to life.

The cops hated to kill cops, even those who had it coming. They managed to figure about ten killings they could attribute to Gray, but Mom wasn't talking so they ended up with nothing but suspicion.

Jenny and I got another fifteen minutes of fame, which was good for business.

I never looked at another comments section again.

Born in Milwaukee and educated in Boston, Theodore P. Druch went on to augment a Master's Degree in Near Eastern Studies with a "higher" degree at Timothy Leary's LSD commune at Millbrook, NY. After his graduation from the Psychedelic Academy, he went on to become a general contractor in San Francisco, mostly remodeling old Victorians. Their houses anyway.

At the age of fifty-eight, he and his partner, Maria Ruiz, chucked it all and ran away from home to see the world. They spent ten years traveling to fifty-two countries and living in several for extended periods. They spent the next six years in Puerto Vallarta, Mexico, where he rekindled an old love of writing. He was an active member of the Puerto Vallarta Writer's Group, and he and Maria conducted a weekly workshop for serious authors. He was organizer and chairman for the Seventh Annual PVWG International Writers Conference in February, 2012.

While in Puerto Vallarta, Druch wrote and self-published four full-length books. *Footsteps on a Small Planet* is an account of their travels around Mexico and Central America by motorhome. *Timothy Leary and the Mad Men of Millbrook* recounts his experiences living in the notorious psychedelic commune for the last years of its existence. *African Odyssey* details an impromptu trip through central Africa that he and Maria were forced to take before they could legally return to their home in Nairobi, a short weekend jaunt that lasted for a month. *The Reaper's Carol* is a graphic account of his six-month struggle with a life threatening illness that nearly put an end to his writing for good. He also edited *Coast Lines*, three anthologies of the writings of the members of the Puerto Vallarta Writers Group.

He and Maria, also a prolific writer, are currently living in Sacramento, California.

www.ingramcontent.com/pod-product-compliance
Lightning Source LLC
Chambersburg PA
CBHW070758120726
47910CB00001B/218